Book 1 of tŀ

MW01136297

By K D Grace

Blurb:

When Susan Innes comes to visit her friend, Annie Rivers, in Chapel House, the deconsecrated church that Annie is renovating into a home, she discovers her outgoing friend changed, reclusive, secretive, and completely enthralled by a mysterious lover, whose presence is always felt, but never seen, a lover whom she claims is god. As her holiday turns into a nightmare, Susan must come to grips with the fact that her friend's lover is neither imaginary nor is he human, and even worse, he's turned his wandering eye on Susan, and he won't be denied his prize. If Susan is to fight an inhuman stalker intent on having her as his own, she'll need a little inhuman help.

Dedication:

In The Flesh is dedicated to Helen and Melanie, who critiqued it when it was just a short story that needed something more. Thank you both for driving me harder, challenging me more, cheering me on, and making me a better writer.

Table of Contents:

Chapter One

Chapter Two

Chapter Three

Chapter Four

Chapter Five

Chapter Six

Chapter Seven

Chapter Eight

Chapter Nine

Chapter Ten

Chapter Eleven

Chapter Twelve

Chapter Thirteen

Chapter Fourteen

Chapter Fifteen

Chapter Sixteen

Chapter Seventeen

Chapter Eighteen

Chapter Nineteen

Chapter Twenty

Chapter Twenty-one

Chapter Twenty-two

Chapter Twenty-three

Chapter Twenty-four

Chapter Twenty-five

Chapter Twenty-six

Chapter Twenty-seven

Chapter Twenty-eight

Chapter Twenty-nine

Chapter Thirty

Chapter Thirty-one

Chapter Thirty-two

Chapter Thirty-three

Chapter Thirty-four

Chapter Thirty-five

Chapter Thirty-six

Chapter Thirty-seven

Epilogue

Chapter One of Blind-Sided

About the Author

If You Enjoyed In the Flesh

Chapter One

"Susan, this is going to sound completely barking, but I think he might be God."

What the hell do you say to that? 'My boyfriend might be God'? I mean it's not exactly common convo for a girls' night out. Okay, so neither of us was famous for our successful love lives. Mine was basically non-existent, but Annie Rivers was notorious for her bad choices—usually married men or narcissistic twats with a wide range of addictions. But as far as bad choices went, this was a doozy. Aside from the fact that it was totally mad to think Lover Boy was God, even I had to admit it was right up Annie's alley. Let's face it, God—any of the gods for that matter—is not known for being faithful or particularly nice.

Annie hadn't mentioned that she was seeing anyone, but I knew she had a lot on her mind with her heavy load at the estate agency and the renovation of what she was now affectionately calling Chapel House. Under the circumstances, I was surprised when she invited me up to Manchester for a long weekend, but she said she needed some girl-time, and we were long overdue for a good catch-up. Since I had no deadlines pressing and found myself with a bit of free time, I jumped at the chance to escape my claustrophobic flat in Brixton and spend some quality time with my friend. The last time we'd been together, she had just made an offer on the deconsecrated church.

"It happens all the time," Annie told me when I went with her to view the place. "No one's religious any more, so small churches are deconsecrated when they're no longer in use, and they're sold as boutiques, office buildings, houses and even pubs. But this one is about to become my home."

She had chatted away enthusiastically about the lounge that would be where the altar was, how the whole nave would be open-plan living at its best, kitchen with an Aga, study in what had been the small choir loft, and the perfect master suite that she'd always dreamed of. What good was money if you couldn't spend it?

This time, however, when I arrived, she was otherwise occupied.

"You're early." Breathing heavily, Annie peeked from behind the door she had opened only a crack.

I wasn't early, but I wasn't stupid either. Her hair was mussed, and the flush in her cheeks was a testament to my bad timing.

"Shall I come back in an hour? Two?"

She threw a quick glance over her shoulder, and from inside I caught the strong scent of jasmine, Annie's favorite flower. "Thanks, Susan. You're a dear."

"Okay, you lucky cow, but when I come back, I'll expect details." I barely managed a kiss on her cheek before the door slammed in my face.

After what I felt was an appropriate amount of time at a nearby Starbucks, I returned with a nice bottle of chardonnay and my best 'tell me all about him' smile. I knocked; then I knocked again.

I was just beginning to think she was having such an orgy that she'd forgotten about me when the door opened and she squinted out into the fading evening light.

"Susan?"

She was wearing her robe, but the glow was gone, and there were dark circles under her eyes. She forced a smile. "I must have fallen asleep." Her anemic embrace alerted me to sharp angles and jutting bones that had been cushioned by shapely curves when I saw her three months ago.

"Honey, you're thin. Must be too much shagging and not enough chocolate. I can't wait to see what you've done with the—"

She flipped on the switch behind her, and it was evident in the harsh light of a bare bulb that, for all practical purposes, she had done nothing with the place.

She looked around and color rose to her cheeks. "I've been busy."

"Things wild at work?"

"I've taken some time off," came the curt reply.

In spite of all her big plans, Chapel House was still a church, complete with dusty pews and an altar covered in plastic drop cloths.

"I see the previous owner hasn't moved out yet."

She ignored my comment. "I'll show you around."

"No need. You showed me around last time. Just find some glasses and fill me in on all your news." I followed her down a narrow hallway into a more recent addition to the building, added on to a small lady chapel no longer in use. It had become a kitchen and a couple of rooms for classes and meetings, now all divided off by hanging drop cloths, just as they had been when she'd shown me the place three months ago.

"You can sleep there." On the floor behind one partition was a mattress with a duvet thrown over it. There was a dusty wardrobe in one corner and a backless chair for a makeshift night table. "Bathroom's down the hall." She gave a listless nod in that direction.

"Annie?" I took her in my arms. "What's going on? What did you and Shag Boy get up to anyway that left you this exhausted?"

"Don't call him that." She pushed me away with an effort that seemed uncharacteristically fragile for the woman who had been her company's best agent three years running. "I'm just tired, that's all."

I took her hand and led her into the kitchen. "A glass of wine and a nice Chinese will set you right. You should have told me he'd be here. I could have come some other time, or he can stay. I mean I have earplugs, you know. And anyway, when do I get to meet him?"

She offered a shrug and shoved limp blond hair behind her ear. "It's complicated."

Isn't it always?

I ended up drinking most of the bottle of chardonnay, and a lovely takeaway was wasted as Annie picked at her Mongolian beef and practically fell asleep at the table.

"Come on." I took the glass from her hand and pulled her to her feet. "You're exhausted, and I'm not sympathetic, but you can't tell me juicy gossip when you're falling asleep in your rice. Now which of these lovely rooms is the master suite?"

"I sleep there." She shot a glance back down the hall toward the nave. "I like the way the moonlight comes through the big windows in the apse above the altar," she added quickly.

"Are you the sacrifice?" I took her arm, surprised at her

strength as she jerked away.

"I told you, I just like the light." In spite of her protests, I walked her up through the nave, trying to ignore the disquiet clawing at my stomach as she shuffled up the aisle between the pews, past the transept and the chancel, to a pallet of blankets and pillows on the floor at the foot of the altar. The air was redolent with the scent of jasmine, but there were no flowers that I could see. A chill fingered its way up my spine.

"Annie, I've always known you were a little weird, but this is just creepy."

"No really, look." With a feline stretch, she lay back in a pool of moonlight and I caught my breath at the effect. It was as though she were lying under a luminous waterfall. In the monochrome tones of growing night, she appeared startlingly transparent. As the robe that she wore fell open, her nipples peaked, and the woman who had always been a little bit shy about her body tugged and shoved aside the robe until she lay naked atop the blankets, her pale hair spread across the pillow like a reaching halo. The moonlight exaggerated the arch and curve of rib bones way too visible for the woman I knew.

Goose flesh rippled over her rice paper skin, and for a moment, in her writhing and stretching, in the soft moan that filled her throat, if I hadn't been standing there watching, I'd have thought her to be making love with someone. In spite of what my eyes told me, I gave a quick glance around the room to be certain we were alone, and even then, I wasn't sure.

Annie was usually the take-charge chick, but action seemed

better than letting myself be freaked out by what was probably, what was *hopefully*, nothing.

I sat down next to her and pulled the mound of tangled blankets up around her chilled body, tucking her in. Before she could protest, I laid a hand against her forehead. "Annie, tell me what's wrong. Have you seen a doctor? Are you ill?" My insides knotted at all the horrible things loss of weight and constant tiredness might herald.

"No! No, Susan, nothing like that, I promise you." She sat up and threw her arms around me in the most enthusiastic show of affection I'd had since my arrival. "Oh, Susan, I want so much to tell you everything. I can hardly contain myself, but I just get so tired. You'd understand better if you knew him."

"Does he at least have a name?"

She squeezed my hand and lay back on the pile of pillows.

Outside, somewhere close by, someone was burning garden trash. I looked around to close the window, but none of the arched windows in the nave were open. Judging from the way my eyes burned, it must have been quite a bonfire.

Annie coughed and cleared her throat. "Please, Susan, if you're my best friend, don't ask any questions. Just let me tell you in my own time, in my own way."

"All right. I'm listening." A flutter of a breeze curled around the altar and rustled the plastic ever so slightly.

For a long time she didn't speak. Her lips were the only things about her that were still full and shapely, but even they seemed pale and colorless in the moonlight. She smoothed the blanket carefully over her thighs. "I knew he was watching me even while Todd and I were still together."

"Todd? You mean the married bloke?"

She nodded. "So many times I felt like someone was near me, looking out for me. I really didn't realize who was pursuing me until after I broke up with Todd, about the time I moved in here."

She lay silently for a few seconds, still smoothing the blanket unnecessarily. "I realized I no longer wanted to live without him. That was the first time our relationship became... physical."

"Became physical," I chuckled. "Right."

She ignored my sarcasm. The bow of her mouth, the way she curled a lock of hair around her finger, made her seem childlike, innocent. "Oh, Susan, you'd understand if you knew him."

I'd call the police if I knew him, I thought, all the while wishing the neighbors would stop with the damned burning already.

"I know you must be thinking I'm crazy."

"Hon." I squeezed her hand. "I've always thought you were crazy, so what else is new?"

She forced a jagged little laugh and continued, "He was so angry when I invited you."

The disquiet I felt escalated into something a little more tetchy. "Jesus, Annie, he controls who your friends are? That's really sick."

"No, it's not that. He's been wanting to meet you for ages. He was angry that I waited so long to do it. He finally forced the issue. He felt I didn't want you to know about us, that I was ashamed of him. I wasn't," she added quickly, "I could never be. And anyway, it doesn't matter. In the end, he convinced me that you were someone who would understand."

That I had somehow gotten this bloke's attention made me feel slightly queasy. "What else does he know about me?"

"He knows everything, Susan. He knows what we're saying now, what we're thinking, what we're feeling."

"What the fuck is he, a mind reader?"

In the growing gloom, she seemed as insubstantial as the plastic on the altar. She pulled the blanket close around her with tightly fisted hands, knuckles chalk pale. "Susan." Her voice was a thin whisper that I might not have heard in a place less silent. "This is going to sound completely barking, but I think he might be God."

Chapter Two

We sat for a long time, me waiting for the punch line, or for some comment about the size of Shag Boy's cock. When she said nothing, I felt obliged to fill the silence. "Most men want you to think they're God." My voice echoed nervously in the empty transept. "But the first time he forgets to put the toilet seat down, you'll know it ain't so."

I suddenly felt as though someone was breathing softly against the back of my neck. My skin prickled and went cold. The odor of burning garbage was consumed in the scent of jasmine. And just like that, Annie was fast asleep.

I didn't want to wake her. She seemed so exhausted, and as uncomfortable as it made me, I would just have to wait until morning to hear why my best friend thought she was shagging God. Surely she was just having a laugh.

Alone, and with nothing to do on what I thought would be a girls' night out, I opted for a good wallow while I finished the rest of the chardonnay. The last group that had used the church before it was deconsecrated was evangelical and believed in adult baptism by immersion. They had installed a large bathtub in what had been a storage room between the two toilets.

A quick check through the cupboards revealed no bubbles or bath oils. I found it hard to believe that Annie, the spa queen, wasn't taking full advantage of such a tub. But other than washing up liquid and my shampoo, there was nothing, and the dust in the bottom of the tub was proof Annie wasn't using it. Undaunted, I cleaned it and filled it with water up to my chin. Then I lay back, wishing I'd thought to bring my rose bath gel.

The combination of wine and warm water was just beginning to relax muscles that had been clenched tight since my arrival at Chapel House when the room was suddenly awash with the scent of roses. I opened my eyes with a start, certain I'd caught a glimpse of a reflection flashing past the steamy mirror above the sink.

"Annie? Is that you?"

There was no response. I sniffed the air. Perhaps there were roses in bloom somewhere close by. The whole evening had made me jumpy, and though living in a deconsecrated church suited Annie down to the ground, it didn't make me feel great. I'm a writer—my imagination is far too vivid to want to stay in a place with a back garden that had been a churchyard from which who knew how many bodies had been exhumed and reburied. Annie had told me that with the twisted smile of someone who happily watched horror films alone with a big bowl of popcorn and a bar of chocolate and thought nothing of it.

I, on the other hand, felt even the air around me crawl over my skin and threaten to crush the jackhammering of my heart as I saw ghouls and ghosts and serial killers in every corner. That was only while I was awake. When I managed to sleep, *if* I managed to sleep, the real fun began in the dream world.

Creep factor aside, I couldn't keep from wondering if Annie had shagged Lover Boy there on the altar. Annie was just irreverent enough to do such a thing. Maybe she'd even asked him to pretend he was God and she was his sacrifice. I sipped my wine, then closed my eyes again, settling back into the silence.

The scent of roses grew stronger. I arched against the tub, feeling warmth flood my torso. Goose flesh spread down my chest, tightening my nipples and tracking a heavy path low over my belly. With a sigh, I shifted my hips and opened my knees, feeling the warm, liquid caress as I sank lower into the tub, into the heat, rocking slowly, rhythmically against the resulting ebb and flow of the water as the space around me contracted into a tight embrace, pulling me downward and away from myself.

With a little yelp, I jumped and opened my eyes, splashing water onto the tiled floor and barely avoiding a mouthful. I must have drifted off to sleep and dreamed, though I couldn't remember what. I could only recall the rise of goose flesh beneath a feather touch, the exhalation of humid breath whispered against my ear, but if there had been words, I didn't remember them.

I lay there in a rising cloud of steam, holding my breath, listening, trying to hear something other than the hammering of my pulse. The scent of roses receded and with it the urge to linger. Suddenly I felt tired. I dried myself and stumbled to my makeshift bedroom. Barely noticing that there was no sheet on the mattress, I fell into bed and was instantly asleep.

In the morning I awoke to the smell of a fry-up, which was a good thing, because I was ravenous. I dressed quickly and found Annie in the kitchen looking fragile, but better.

She smiled up at me from cooking eggs. "Good morning. Sorry about last night. I forget sometimes how much stamina it takes to…" She blushed and returned her attention to the eggs.

"Quite an animal, is he?"

She chuckled softly as she scooped eggs and bacon onto plates and brought them to the table. "Let's just say he's—"

"Insatiable? I mean, last night you said you thought he was God, so I figured he must be really amazing in bed."

While I shoveled down my breakfast, she only held her tea mug between cupped hands and smiled down into the steam. "I said that?"

"Don't you remember?"

She didn't answer, only clenched her jaw and stared into her cup.

Annie was the hands-down winner of the too-much-information award when it came to her love life, and her reluctance to talk frightened me, so I quickly changed the subject. "What's the plan for today? Retail therapy? I hear there's a handbag sale at Debenhams."

She picked up her plate and scraped her untouched food into the rubbish bin, careful to avoid my gaze. "Susan, I honestly don't feel up to going out today. I just really need to rest. Would you mind going without me? I'll be all right. I'm just tired, that's all."

By the time I finished my food and was ready to go, Annie was once again fast asleep, curled in her nest at the foot of the altar.

Outside, the smell of burning rubbish stung my eyes and the back of my throat.

I had little enthusiasm for the handbag sale, nor for lingering at the make-up counter. Instead I found myself back at the Starbucks, Mac open, researching God's love life, which turned out to be a long history of seducing humans.

Zeus visited Danae in a shower of gold. He seduced Leda in the form of a swan. Eros came to Psyche in the dead of night, forbidding her to look upon his face. Hades dragged Persephone down to the Underworld. The Virgin Mary was impregnated by the god of the Bible. In the New Testament, Christ is the bridegroom, and the church his bride. And the list went on and on. Perhaps even the *indwelling of the Holy Spirit* was just another way for divinity to experience flesh.

I had always loved mythology, and I'd read all these stories before. I'd just never put them together to get the whole picture. And though I was seeing an aspect of divinity that I found rather disturbing, I couldn't help feeling there was still a piece of the puzzle missing.

I suppose I should have felt relieved. Annie wasn't as unusual as I'd thought. God was the ultimate stalker, and he didn't seem to be very faithful to his lovers. Just Annie's type. I tried not to think about the implications of my experience in the bath the previous night. After all, it was just mythology. I'd had a lot of wine, and there's never any accounting for my vivid imagination. After all, I'm a writer. I make my living as a teller of tales.

"What are you reading?"

I jumped at the sound of Annie's voice and quickly minimized the page. "Didn't expect to see you here."

"I'm feeling better."

"How did you know where to find me?"

She leaned down and whispered next to my ear, "My lover's

God, remember? You can't hide from him."

I barely had time to register shock before she reached down and restored the page. "Trying to learn a little bit more about him, are we?" She smiled at the monitor and nodded knowingly. "None of this does him justice. He's the Hound of Heaven. He's always pursuing those he loves, and there's no escaping. Once he's set his eyes on you, he'll do whatever it takes to make you his own."

I suddenly felt cold.

Chapter Three

Back at Chapel House, Annie went straight to bed, meaning I was faced with the prospect of another creepy night alone. "I think I might go home," I said, sitting on the pallet next to her, watching her struggle to stay awake. "You don't feel well, and I'm only disturbing you. If I leave now, I can be home before midnight." Besides, I'd be glad to get away from the rubbish burning, which suddenly smelled particularly foul.

"No! You can't leave." She grabbed my arm in a grip that was surprisingly strong. Her voice was thin, breathless, punctuated by the racing of her pulse. "Please, Susan, I need you here with me. Please don't go. I'll be better tomorrow. I promise."

Once I had agreed to stay, she relaxed back into her pillows. Her eyes fluttered shut, and sleep was so instant that for a second I thought she had fainted, or worse yet, she was dead. There was no denying that, in the pale light, she looked like a corpse.

I brushed my fingertips over her cheek, smoothing her hair behind her ears, where I could see the assurance of a shuddering pulse against the translucent skin of her throat. If I watched closely, I would almost swear I could see the blood coursing through the turquoise veins just beneath the surface. She moaned softly, her eyelids fluttered, and the rise and fall of her chest indicated the deep even breath of sleep. Slowly, so as not to wake her, I stood and made my reluctant way back to my makeshift room.

I pulled up a mindless novel on my iPhone, something light and funny. I didn't want anything with even the slightest bit of creep factor. I just wanted to be well distracted until I could fall asleep, which I was pretty sure wouldn't happen any time soon. I was wrong. Sleep overtook me nearly as quickly and completely as it had poor Annie.

Long toward morning I woke with a start. The room was awash in the scent of roses, and I was certain someone had called my name. "Annie?" I half whispered. There was no reply, no sound other than the anxious breathing that must surely have been my own. Surely.

The pitch black of the room pressed in all around me like another presence, so close that I felt if I switched on the light, I would suddenly come face to face with it. The bile of panic rose in my throat. I threw off the duvet and fumbled for my phone, dropping it on the mattress before I could finally slice the blackness with a sliver of light. The drop cloth curtains trembled on either side of me, no doubt from my own panicked actions, and the smell of roses thickened.

Careful to keep the sliver of light, I slipped into my robe and hurried to check on Annie. Even in the stairwell I could hear her moans. As I neared the transept the air felt charged and heavy, like that moment in a storm just before lightning strikes. The hairs on my neck rose and goose flesh prickled up my spine. I held my breath as I tiptoed closer. The plastic drop cloths had been shoved onto the floor in a heap, and there in the moonlight she lay, thrashing atop the altar, her hair splayed around her head, night shirt pushed up over her hips. She arched her back and cried out, reaching her arms upward to something I couldn't see.

I wanted to run. Instead I stood frozen, bathed in cold sweat, waiting for logic to explain everything away as the moonlight around her seemed to explode and coalesce with her ecstasy. The smell of jasmine cloyed at my throat, making my head ache.

After what seemed like an eternity, the urge to flee finally took control. Heart pounding, I stepped back, hoping to leave unnoticed, when suddenly I felt a rush of wind against my face and breathed the musky odor of sex. I stumbled, unable to hold back a small yelp. My phone slipped through my fingers and bounced under a pew as the scent of jasmine gave way to roses.

In the heavy press of darkness, I half ran, half fell down the hall back toward my room, tripping over the edge of a drop cloth thrown across the floor and coming down hard on both knees with a breathless curse. I pulled myself to my feet, gasping for oxygen, groping at the wall for the switch, desperate for light—any kind of light. Though I was disturbed by what I had seen, I was more disturbed by the fact that it had aroused me even through my fear. As my eyes adjusted, light coming in from the small window in the door of the makeshift kitchen bathed the room in shades of gray.

Another gust of wind blew the door open with a loud crash. I yelped and jumped forward to force it shut. Then I could have sworn I heard my name, called out with such longing that I couldn't stop myself. With hands slippery from nervous sweat, I fumbled the door open again and stepped out onto the patio. The clutter of terracotta pots looked like strange squat specters in the dance of moonlight and shadow.

Making my way past derelict strawberry jars, several bags of ancient compost and a wheel-less wheelbarrow, I emerged into a large garden overgrown with weeds. It was the deconsecrated churchyard, I reminded myself with a shiver. In the bright moonlight, I stood holding my breath. Listening.

Annie had taken twisted pleasure in speculating about the graveyard that had once been the back garden. She had imagined exhumed medieval skeletons taken to museums to be studied and cataloged. She had imagined underground catacombs where ghosts of priests and murderers alike scurried on secret missions, some sinister, some holy.

I shuddered at the thought and pulled the robe tighter around me. I had not found her speculation amusing then, and I found it even less so now. I found nothing about this place amusing.

Fighting my way through a tangle of ivy, I came to a stone bench that looked like it might well have belonged in a graveyard. Not wanting to go back inside Chapel House, I sat down, hoping desperately that if I thought long enough, I'd find a rational explanation for everything that had happened, or I'd wake up and discover it had all been a bad dream. Staying in places with intriguing pasts often brought me unsettling dreams.

I smelled roses again—old roses, not any sort of modern hybrid. Only old roses would smell so strong and so sweet amid the rank growth of weeds. As I breathed in the scent that seemed to be coming from just over my shoulder, I felt a humid breeze on my neck, brushing my nape, like breath exhaled with the settling of a kiss. The leaves rustled around me, and the bench was suddenly in shadow. With a start, I turned to hear the sound of footsteps retreating down the path.

"Annie? Hello?" I clambered to my feet and followed the rustle of leaves, the scent of roses always just ahead of me. "Annie, this isn't funny, all right? This isn't funny!"

I hadn't remembered the garden being so large. It felt as though I wandered the paths for hours. My spine constantly prickled, but a quick glance over my shoulder always revealed no one following me. The paving stones were mossy and slick beneath my bare feet. I stumbled along, ignoring the scratch of bramble and the sting of nettle, shoving my way through leaves damp with dew until I broke through, as though I'd just pushed aside a curtain. With a gasp, I stopped short, nearly losing my footing on the moss.

The smell of roses was overwhelming. The sense of not being alone crawled along my spine on little insect feet. In a small copse set between aging lilac bushes taller than my head and a gnarled hawthorn hedge that might once have been part of a formal garden, he loomed over me. I swallowed back a scream just before it could escape, as I realized he was an angel, or at least a statue of one.

Slightly more than human size, his weathered marble toes barely touched a low plinth, as though he were just alighting. One large hand was extended toward me in invitation. The other rested on his chest, over his heart. He was naked except for a sculpted veil of stone that covered his groin. His perfect form shone silver in the moonlight, muscles tensed in anticipation, empty eyes locked on mine.

With my heart battering my ribs, I stood frozen there next to him as something ancient, something primal, moved over my skin, like the brush of spider webs and dust motes. What might have begun as a caress became an invasion as it thrust its way deeper, into secret places, places in myself where even I never dare go. Whatever it was, it knew me, it understood me, and its longing for me was terrible.

The scream that echoed through the garden must have been mine, though by the time it happened, it was no longer an adequate expression of what was happening to me. I was pushed to the ground—or perhaps I fell. I barely felt the bruise of cold stone against my buttocks and spine, lost as I was in the realization that what I had feared, what I had disbelieved, was now upon me, and I could hide nothing from it because there was nothing left in me that it didn't already know.

It closed around me, blocking out the moon, smelling of roses, hammering into me until I was certain I would break apart. And once I was certain it no longer mattered, I stopped fighting. I stopped pleading. My words became sand in my throat. And when I stopped fighting, the rock solid crushing of my soul became a gentle touch, a brush of full lips against my own, a cupping of breasts and groin. It brought with it an awareness that in the midst of my own darkness, there was need, there was desire, there was lust as dark as whatever it was, whoever it was that held me.

I stopped struggling and gave into it. The night convulsed like leaves in a storm, and I was falling through the bottom of the world, falling forever with nothing to stop me, nothing to slow my descent, and no knowledge of what lay beneath. And that too no longer mattered.

Chapter Four

I woke up with a jerk that made my neck pop. I was lying naked, curled around the pillow in the middle of the mattress in the makeshift guest room. The tight space that had been heavy and humid last night was now freezing cold and I was shivering. I gulped oxygen as though I hadn't breathed all night.

Then a wave of relief washed over me. I sobbed out loud. "It was only a dream! It wasn't real. Dear God, it wasn't real!" My throat felt like I'd been eating ground glass and my head ached. Everything ached. Only a dream! Thank God! Thank heaven! Thank fuck! Thank everything!

In the gray morning light that bathed the windowless excuse for a room, I crawled off the mattress and shoved my way into yesterday's clothes, thrown carelessly across my travel bag when I'd come to bed last night. Then I frantically began to pack. Dream or not, I was out of here as soon as I could extricate myself—politely or otherwise—from Annie. I wasn't her keeper. I couldn't make her do what she didn't want to. I'd call her mother. That's what I'd do! I had her mother's number somewhere. I'd call her to take charge, then I'd hope for the best. From a safe distance.

I'd just finished washing my face and running a toothbrush over my teeth when I heard a commotion down the hall.

"I told you to stay away! I told you I didn't want you here. Do I have to call the police?"

I threw open the bathroom door and raced down the hall to the kitchen where the noise was coming from. Annie stood at the door, robe wrapped carelessly around her, holding a butcher knife in one hand and her phone in the other, shaking both at a dark-haired man in faded jeans and an *Elvis Lives* T-shirt. For some reason the man looked familiar, but then again, how many of Annie's lovers had pined for her and tried to get back in her good graces after she dissed them? More than a few of them had come to me for advice on how to win Annie's heart. Jesus! The woman couldn't be happy with a made-up stalker, she had to have a real one, too!

"What the hell's going on here?" I roared, the pent-up helplessness from last night giving way to anger. "You heard her. Get out!" I yelled at the man. But to my surprise, instead of coming to my side, instead of standing shoulder to shoulder with me like she always had, Annie turned the knife on me.

"And you! You little whore! I was afraid this would happen, Susan, I tried to tell him. I begged him not to bring you here, but he said to trust him, to trust you. But how could I trust you? How could I trust anyone with him?"

"He brought me here? Who brought me here? What the fuck are you talking about?" But even as I asked I was terrified that I already knew.

She gave me a hard shove, and I found myself stumbling over the threshold, shoved up against the man at the door, who caught me to keep me from falling. "Get out! Get the hell out, both of you. And don't come back." Then she slammed the door in our faces.

"Annie! Annie, wait! We need to—" The smell of burning garbage was suddenly so overwhelming that I gagged and choked for breath.

The dark-haired man grabbed me by the arm and pulled me away from the door and out into the courtyard. With both of us coughing and choking, eyes streaming from smoke we couldn't see, he half marched, half dragged me through the wrought iron gate and out into the alley behind Chapel House. There, he pulled open the door of a small lorry and tried to shove me inside.

"Let go of me! Let go!" I squirmed free and nearly fell on my arse as he released his grip and another wave of the burning rubbish reek nearly overwhelmed me. "Who the bloody hell are you?"

"I'm the fucking builder! Or at least I was. Now get into the damn truck and let's get out of here before we both suffocate."

I did as he said, barely getting the door closed before he revved the engine, shoved the truck into gear and pulled out onto the street, the horrible smell receding in our wake.

Neither of us said anything until he pulled into a Little Chef off the motorway. He was around the truck and opening the door for me before I could engage with what had happened in the—what was it—just twenty minutes I'd been awake this morning?

He offered me his hand, and I blinked, horrified to discover that I was blinking back tears. "I don't have any money. I don't have anything," I managed. "It's all back in Chapel House. Even my phone."

"I know." He settled me onto my feet then reached behind the seat and pulled out a battered leather jacket, spreading it around my shoulders, bathing me in the comforting scent of wood smoke, ozone and clean male sweat. It was only then that I realized I was shivering. "It's on the house."

He shut the door and I noticed for the first time the logo printed in bold white against the dark green of the truck. *Weller Building.*

"Are you Weller?" I asked, as he placed a hand under my elbow and steered me toward the café.

"Michael Weller," he said, opening the door and nodding to a booth in the corner. "And I take it you're Susan."

"That would be me." Once we were seated, he handed me a menu, but I slid it back across the table to him. "I just want coffee."

He grabbed my outstretched wrist and held tight. "Listen to me, Susan." He glanced around to make sure we were alone. There was only one other couple in the café this early on a Sunday morning and they were clear across the room. "You have to eat."

He leaned over the table, and for the first time I noticed the bright blue of his eyes—how they contrasted with his dark hair and sun-bronzed skin, and the dark stubble on his chin and square jaw that made him look edgy, just up out of bed. His eyes were startling in their intensity, like some artist had created a face that was more intriguing than it was handsome, but had added, as an afterthought, a stroke of something hypnotic, something beautiful and raw, almost frightening. And yet, the man had been my savior. From what? From a bad dream? From a friend who was slowly going off her rocker?

"Listen to me," he said again, dragging my attention back to his words with a tight squeeze of my wrist. "He starves his lovers. As he grows stronger, they grow weaker, and the more attention he pays to them, the less interested they are in food or drink or…" He looked out the window at the sparrows flitting in a sorry looking berberis that had probably been a lackluster attempt at landscaping when the place was built. "The less interest they have in anything, really."

Then he looked back at me and I was startled all over again by his eyes. "He becomes their world, and once he's drained them dry and moved on to someone else, they... they have no reason for living."

With a shiver I remembered the knife in Annie's hand.

"Are you ready to order, Michael?" I jumped at the sound of the waitress' bird-like voice.

He glanced up and offered a smile to the chunky middle-aged woman with newly manicured nails, then he returned his gaze to me. "Two full English, Izzy, and keep the coffee coming."

For a second, I feared I'd throw up, as I watched the woman's blood red nails grip the pen, take the order on the pad. I closed my eyes and grabbed onto the table, trying to make sense of everything.

When the waitress left and I was sure I wasn't going to disgrace myself in the Little Chef, I spoke between my teeth. "You make it sound like he's real."

The waitress brought coffee and water. Michael asked after her kids, both now off at uni, and I wondered how he could make pleasant conversation under the circumstances.

When she left again, he waited until I'd had a sip of coffee, all the while holding me in his startling blue gaze. "Oh, he's real all right, and you know it as well as I do. How long have you been at Chapel House?" he asked, looking me over like he was a doctor and

I was a patient with some unspecified ailment.

"I got there Friday evening. I'm on holiday. I was surprised that Annie invited me. She's always so busy, but she said she had some time off, and wouldn't it be great to catch up. And then, when I got there—"

"Strange things started happening."

"An understatement," I grunted. "She says he's God." My face burned with embarrassment at saying such a ridiculous thing, but Michael didn't laugh. "He's not a ghost, is he?" I asked as an afterthought, only then letting the weight of the statement sink in, the fact that I was talking about my friend's imaginary lover as though he were real. And what was worse, my opinion was being validated by a man who seemed completely lucid and of more than average intelligence.

"He's no ghost, but he's not a god either."

I took a gulp of my coffee and burnt my tongue, aware of Michael's blue gaze.

"Susan." He took my hand and gave it a reassuring squeeze that really didn't reassure me at all. "Susan, have you… have you dreamed since you've been at Chapel House?"

Michael nodded to my right bicep, where the jacket, way too big for me, had slid off my shoulder to reveal four oval bruises the color of overly ripe plums. I slid out of the jacket and shifted in the seat for a better look. They could have almost passed for the inked fingerprints the police take when they book someone.

Bile rose to my throat. I swallowed hard and turned to examine the other arm, finding similar marks. "It was a dream. It was just a dream. It had to be." I hadn't noticed when I woke up in the gloomy gray of the windowless room, wouldn't have thought to look, when all I wanted to do was get the hell out of Chapel House as quickly as possible.

But there was the experience in the bath, the smell of roses, the constant feeling of being watched, being touched; there was what I'd seen last night with Annie splayed on the altar. And then… what had happened after. It couldn't be real. None of it could be real. And yet the bruises were there, and it was no mystery what had caused them.

The waitress appeared with the food, but I don't remember much after that. My brain chose that moment to rebel, because none of this could be real. It was all a bad dream, and I was in my own bed in my own flat, having the worst nightmare ever. Had to be! Absolutely couldn't be anything else!

I remember shoving my way out of the booth and running for the door, desperate for air, desperate for the return of sanity, desperate to get away… far, far away. Mostly I remember being desperate to wake up.

Chapter Five

It was the trickle of sweat under my arms and along my ribs that brought me back to myself. My arse ached from sitting on the hard cement. The sun baked down on my back and a large hand gently stroked between my shoulder blades. At some point, Michael had joined me. I couldn't say when.

"You're all right. You'll be fine. It'll be okay." His voice was barely more than a whisper, but his touch was solid and comforting. "I know it's a lot to take in, but better you know. If you don't know, you can't fight." He stood and offered me his hand. "Come on back inside. I've had Izzy keep the food warm. You need to eat."

Back in the Little Chef, Izzy delivered the reheated plates, offering me a look of sympathy. Then she gave Michael a smile and a nod, refreshed our coffee cups and left. He gestured to my plate. Grudgingly, I forced the first bite of eggs past my gag reflex only to discover that they tasted pretty damn good.

Michael watched as I gulped two more bites, stuffed half a piece of toast in my gob and washed it down with coffee. He raised his own cup and held my gaze. "When was the last time you ate?"

"I don't know." I thought about it while I polished off a rasher of bacon. "I guess the last real meal I had was the takeaway I ordered my first night at Chapel House."

His gaze was beginning to make me squirm. "That's a long time between meals."

"I've had a lot on my mind, what with Annie behaving so strangely and all." But even as I said it, I felt the skin on my arms prickle. I wasn't known for my lack of appetite. I, who never missed a meal augmented by several snacks in between. The only time I wasn't hungry was when I was asleep, and even then sometimes I dreamed of food.

His own meal barely touched, he sipped his coffee, then leaned across the table, still holding me in blue scrutiny. "Susan, tell me about the dream."

I'd eaten my breakfast and half of his and sat shivering in his jacket by the time I'd finished telling him about last night, struggling to keep the details to a minimum and the whole experience at a safe distance.

We waited for Izzy to fill the cups again, then I plucked up my courage, rubbing my arms, now tender where the bruises bloomed and darkened. "It wasn't a dream, then."

"Some of it was, fortunately." He nodded to where I still chafed my arms. "Those are evidence that it wasn't all a dream, but the fact that you woke up in your own bed… Well, something interrupted his efforts, I'd say."

"But how could that be?" I remembered the feel of being battered, being invaded, falling through the bottom of the world; I remembered the empty eyes of the angel, his hand extended to me in invitation.

He leaned closer across the table until his forehead nearly touched mine. I was struck by how large he really was. I'm tall and well muscled, but he made me feel petite, delicate. Why hadn't I noticed that before? His big hand came to rest on mine, and his voice was a soft rumble I felt deep between my hipbones, almost like the first intimations of a storm. And fuck, if he didn't quote John Donne!

"Batter my heart, three-person'd God, for you
As yet but knock, breathe, shine, and seek to mend;
That I may rise and stand, o'erthrow me, and bend
Your force to break, blow, burn, and make me new.
*****

Take me to you, imprison me, for I,
Except you enthrall me, never shall be free,
Nor ever chaste, except you ravish me."

By the time he was finished, I was shivering uncontrollably, and I would have laughed if I hadn't been so frightened. "So *he's* not God, this imaginary lover who seduced my friend and nearly raped me, but the rape part was a dream because *God* rescued me from this devil or demon or whatever the fuck he is before he could do the deed? Is that what you're trying to tell me?"

He downed the last of his coffee and pushed his plate aside. "I'm only trying to tell you that nothing that's happening to Annie or to you is straightforward. Things are always way more complicated than the stories in the mythology books, or even in the Christian Bible, make them out to be."

We sat in silence for a long moment as a young couple tried to settle two small children and a toddler into a booth nearby.

"It was a seduction, not a rape," he said, absently watching the man maneuver the squirming toddler into a high chair. "He doesn't want to take you by force. He wants you to come to him willingly. He's not above hurting you if you don't, but it's your free will he wants most. He wants you to want him like you've never wanted anything in your life. Your lust, your desire for him, that's the thing that empowers him most, you see?"

Even the thought of my experience in the bathtub made my nipples tense, and the fact that the sensation low in my belly wasn't entirely fear made me flush with anger. "No. No, I don't see. I don't see at all. Is he a demon?" I spoke the word through my teeth, the shape of it the bitter pip at the center of sweet, ripe fruit. "Or... maybe an incubus? I mean he did come to me in a dream, didn't he?"

"He's neither, but he has characteristics of both. He's what he needs to be. He has no definition, not really, and he's attached to the place, you see? That place, the place where Chapel House was built, was a site of power long before Christianity came to Britain, long before there was even a name for the ancient powers, the forces that command the changing of the seasons and the ebb and flow of the tides. That was back when people lived in fear of the dark, and offered sacrifices to drive back the forces they didn't understand, the forces that led to famine, starvation, death. He was always there. That place, it's his place, and he's happy to share it, needs to share it, actually, but his hunger is as bottomless now as it was when the blood of virgins and young warriors stained the altar stone."

"How the hell does a builder know all this stuff?" I asked, tugging his leather jacket tighter around me.

He shrugged. "I make my living doing renovations of listed buildings mostly. I do a lot of old barn conversions as well, and church and chapel conversions, of course. I specialized in that area because I find the history of the places I renovate fascinating. I know just enough about archeology to understand that old buildings often have a history older than the building itself, and that history often connects them with the space where they're built. When your friend hired me to renovate Chapel House, I jumped at the chance. I got more than I bargained for," he added as an afterthought.

There was another long silence while the little family discussed the menu and the toddler fussed and wriggled. "I have to get my stuff," I said.

"He won't let you go easily," Michael replied, slapping down money for the bill. "Especially if what Annie said is true, and he had her send for you. You're the one he wants. You're the one he's chosen."

"You said he wanted me willing. Well I'm not."

He held my gaze. "You weren't even tempted?"

I felt color rush to my face, and the bruises on my arms tingled as though they had just been caressed tenderly. He didn't wait for my reply. It was obvious, I guess.

"Susan, you have no idea just how persuasive he can be. If you wanted him, if you were tempted even a little bit, he's already found a way in. The only way to keep him from getting what he wants is to get as far away from him as possible, and even then he won't make it easy."

"Jesus," I murmured, closing my eyes.

Michael said nothing, but I could feel him watching me.

"And Annie?" I asked, at last.

He looked down at his hands, now folded on the table as though he were about to say a prayer.

"What about Annie?" I asked again, feeling my chest tighten

and my throat constrict.

"I don't know." His voice was barely audible. "If he's had her call you. If he's already grooming you."

"He's not grooming me," I said, a little louder than I intended. "I'm not his for the taking, and I want my friend out of there."

He said nothing, just sat there, still looking at his hands.

"I have to get my stuff," I said again. "My phone, my car keys, my computer. All my stuff is there. I want it back."

This time he did look up at me and smiled. "Yes, she told me you were a writer." Then he added quickly, "In the beginning, when she first hired me, she told me, and I know enough about writers to know that the tools of their trade are their treasure. Especially in this day and age." Then, before I could respond, he stood and offered me his hand. "Come on. Let's get your stuff back."

Twenty minutes later we stood together at the front door of Chapel House, our knocks going unanswered. My calling through the door that I just wanted my stuff drew some suspicious looks from passersby, but no response from inside.

"She's in there," Michael said. "She's just not responding."

"So what should we do? Call the police?"

"I don't think so." He took me gently by the elbow and turned me about. "I know another way in. You were staying in the guest room, right? I'll get your stuff. You wait in the truck."

We walked in silence back to the alley where he'd parked, and he helped me up into the cab. "Wait here. I'll be right back."

"Hold it." I grabbed his arm. "My phone. I dropped it in the transept last night when I… when she was with him… when he came after me."

He placed a hand on my shoulder and squeezed gently. "Don't worry. I'll get it."

"Be careful, Michael," I called after him as he headed through the wrought iron gate.

It felt like I waited ages for him to come back. I was just about to get out of the truck and see if I could find him, when I noticed a splash of color under a bramble thicket on the alley side of the fence. I slid from the seat, leaving the door open in case I wanted to return in a hurry. Reminded of the bruises on my arms, I wondered just what good I thought that would do.

There under the brambles were my things, as though someone had tossed them in a heap over the fence. Ignoring the prick of the brambles and the sting of nettles, I tugged and pulled both my travel bag and my shoulder bag free. Holding my breath, heart pounding, goose flesh climbing my spine, I dragged everything back into the truck then slammed and locked the door behind me.

My computer was safe in its sheath inside the shoulder bag, right where I always carried it. Down in the little side pouch next to my car keys, I found my cell phone and my wallet. Everything was in place. The clothes in the travel bag, my toiletries; everything had been neatly packed before it had been tossed over the fence.

The relief of having my stuff back was short-lived, though. My thoughts returned to Michael. What the hell was taking him so long? Was he still looking for my stuff? He didn't know Annie had thrown it out, after all.

Once again I slid out of the truck and closed the door carefully behind me. The alley was deserted. I smelled neither roses nor burning garbage. Perhaps Annie was occupied with her lover and neither of them noticed me. Or perhaps they were occupied with Michael and he was in trouble. As an afterthought, I opened the door again and pawed through the space behind the seat until I found a screwdriver, not a big one, but big enough to do some damage if I needed to. But then, what was I going to do? Use it on my friend? Clearly it would do no good on this lover of hers. Nevertheless, I gripped it tightly, shut the door behind me and headed through the wrought iron gate.

Almost immediately I found myself engulfed in the overgrown garden. With heart pounding, I stood for a moment, trying to get my bearings. It had seemed like a straight shot from the back door to the gate this morning when Annie had kicked me out. Surely I would have remembered the way. Surely it wasn't so complicated.

I squared my shoulders and moved forward into the garden, convincing myself that all I had to do was follow the main path.

Ten minutes later, I realized the folly of my decision as I pushed and shoved through ivy and overgrown hawthorn, adding new scrapes and scratches to those already stinging from recovering my bags. I smelled neither roses nor garbage, only the thick, rank scent of summer vegetation.

Surely I'd be okay. Surely I'd not drawn any unwanted attention. But where the hell was Michael? What was taking him so long? Christ! What if something had happened to him? Annie clearly wasn't herself. What if she'd taken the butcher knife to him? What if he was somewhere inside Chapel House, wounded and bleeding, while I was out here wandering around in the garden, unable to get to him?

Once again I wished desperately to wake up from the bad dream and find myself safe and secure in my own flat in my own bed. Instead I was brought up short, coming face to face once again with the stone angel, its empty eyes locked on me, outstretched hand beckoning me, as though he might lead me to safety. But it was the sculpted face so full of concern, so focused on me, that held my attention—the face, suddenly familiar, suddenly recognizable. Though the eyes were empty, aged marble and not stunning blue, there was no mistaking the strong lines of high cheekbones, the square jaw. Even the broad shoulders, the posture of strength and determination, all familiar to me.

"Michael?" My strangled whisper sounded like a shout in the deep silence. But then again, I might have yelped. I might have even screamed just before I turned to run.

Chapter Six

If I had been lost in the garden trying to get to the kitchen door of Chapel House, I was even more so trying to get away. In my panic, there was no being quiet and, with each snapping of twig and rustling of undergrowth, I was certain someone was following me, certain I could hear footsteps right behind me. I had been attacked under the sculpture of the angel. Christ, had it been Michael after me all along?

Though my own breathing sounded like a rush of wind, and the hammer of my pulse thrummed like thunder, still I was certain I heard the breath of another just behind me. Frantically I glanced over my shoulder, seeing nothing but the sway of the brambles and overgrown lilacs I'd just shoved my way through. Too late, I turned my attention back to the path. My foot caught on the upturned edge of a paving stone disturbed by an ancient hawthorn root that resembled a thick serpent shoving its way up from the depths. I did a belly flop, an outstretched bramble scratching my cheek as I went down.

For an instant the world went black, flashes of color exploded behind my eyelids, and then my vision returned. I would have screamed as the sudden scent of roses overwhelmed me, but there was no breath left for it and, stunned as I was, I couldn't quite remember how to move. It was that same sense of paralysis I'd experienced in nightmares when I needed desperately to run away, to flee some horrible danger, and yet I couldn't move.

Though my body refused to respond to the need to run, parts of it responded perfectly to the touch down my spine, the kneading caress of my bottom, the heat of muscle and sinew and heavy maleness stretched out alongside me, an insinuating knee between my legs making room for further exploration of fingers I could feel on bare skin in spite of knowing full well that I was still completely clothed.

Another hand curled in my hair, pushing the tangle aside to expose my nape and the back of my neck, to clear a path for lips and teeth and tongue. I think I might have said "please don't," but then I might have simply said "please." Though my mind wasn't fully engaged, my body most definitely was. My nipples ached, my hips shifted. Oblivious to the hard rock of the path bruising ribs and belly, I responded only to the invisible fingers that had found me embarrassingly wet and needy.

A little voice somewhere so far off that I could barely hear it kept whispering that I should fight back, that I should run away. It was hard to listen to that voice when I felt like my whole body would burst into flame with longing for more of whatever it was, whoever it was teasing me so exquisitely. It was hard to listen to that small voice inside myself when something outside me whispered louder, whispered words I didn't understand at first, all the while nibbling my earlobe and trailing kisses down along my shoulder, now somehow exposed.

I must have gotten lost in the voice. I don't know how long. It could have been a second, it could have been an eternity, but my next conscious thought was that I had been maneuvered onto my hands and knees, bottom raised, legs open, that my jeans and panties were down around my thighs and a body much larger than my own mantled me, warm, naked, smelling of male lust, dark and heavy and primordial-thick as the fecund vegetation around me. No matter how good my imagination, I was certain the weight of an erection rubbing low against my spine was real, becoming more real with each passing moment as it slid up the cleft of my buttocks, seeking me out like a stag in rut.

"No one can give you what I can, Susan."

This time I understood every word, felt the shape of warm lips against my ear. "I can show you such ecstasy, such beauty. I can show you the meaning of the universe and everything in it. I know your longings, your dreams, the depth of your heart, and I want you. To be wanted, to be possessed by a god, is that not everyone's deepest desire? And yet you, my beauty, you want more than that, don't you? You want to possess God. Just like Lucifer before you, you want what God has. You want me to open myself to you, to pour my wisdom into you, my creative force as surely as I pour my lust into you."

The hands had become insistent, groping breasts and belly, fingering me open, touching every part of me in ways even I didn't know I wanted to be touched. The voice, the whisper, became so intimate that I could feel it inside my head, inside the blood pounding at my temples.

"And then you want to take the mind of God and translate it, write it down with your gift of words and share it with the rest of humanity. Oh, I know you, my darling, and I know your deepest longing. You are the object of my lust, Susan, and the object of my love. I want no other. I desire only to make you my lover, and in doing so I will give you the mind of God."

"But you're not God." The words erupted from my parched throat, as though I had vomited them from the depths, just as the scent of roses gave way to burning garbage, and I gasped for air, shoving and clawing at the pavement against the weight on top of me.

A gust of wind whipped my hair around my face as I managed to pull myself into a sitting position. Suddenly free from the heaviness of the masculine body that had not really been there, at least not in the flesh, I fumbled my jeans up over my arse, embarrassed, angry and frustrated, but mostly just really, really scared.

The flash of a knife was my only warning before Annie was on top of me, shoving me back down onto the jagged paving stones.

"I told you to get out!" she screamed, jamming a knee in my ribs. I caught her wrist and rolled just in time to keep her from plunging the knife into my stomach. "Your stuff, I threw it over the fence. You should have taken it and left. I don't want you here. I never wanted you here. Now you've ruined it all. I'll kill you! I will. I need him, and he needs me. He'll understand that once you're dead."

She tried again to bring the knife down, but this time a large hand grabbed hold of her arm and yanked her off, tossing her into a bed of overgrown geraniums as though she weighed nothing, all the while she screamed and raged and cursed me.

The next thing I knew, Michael jerked me to my feet and flung me over his shoulder like I was a sack of grain. I screamed and did my best to squirm free, making useless attempts to knee him in the stomach. "You lied to me! It's you! It was you all along, you sonovabitch! It was you all along!"

The air reeked of burning rubbish and my lungs burned like fire. The wind had risen to near gale force and I could do nothing but close my streaming eyes and hang on as Michael shoved through the rank vegetation, jerked open the wrought iron gate and manhandled me into the passenger seat of the lorry.

"Let me out," I managed around a hacking cough. "You lied to me! Let me out now!" But instead, he belted me in the seat and locked the door.

"It wasn't me, goddamnit! Now shut up and sit still until I can get us out of here or it'll all be over."

I didn't argue further. I knew he was right. We needed to leave now. The wind rattled the truck as though it would turn it over, and for a terrifying moment I thought it might. The air, even inside the cab, was foul enough to make breathing secondary to not asphyxiating. Michael had pulled the collar of his T-shirt up over his mouth and nose, and I did the same with his jacket, stiff-legging the floorboard and bracing against the dash with the flat of my palm as Michael revved the engine and downshifted, shoving his way through a brutal headwind. He cursed, stomped hard on the gas pedal, and we sped toward the street.

With a screech of tires on pavement and a quick swerve into traffic, the wind died completely away, and the air cleared as though nothing out of the ordinary had happened. To everyone around us it was just a normal summer day.

"What about Annie? We can't just leave her. He'll kill her," I said when I could speak again.

"He won't kill her." I didn't miss Michael's frequent glances in the rear-view mirror. "He'll punish her by fucking her until she's too weak to move, all the while telling her that she's his only love, that his heart's broken that she could be jealous, that she could think he'd want anyone else."

I fought down panic at the thought. "She's already weak. She's just skin and bones, and she can hardly function now."

"It won't matter," he replied. "He knows just how close to the edge to take her. He'll never kill her, and he'll never let her die while she's with him. Even when he replaces her with someone else, he won't hurt her. He never kills his lovers once he's through with them. He doesn't have to. He's become their reason for living. Without his attentions, they're all more than willing to sacrifice themselves to him. Look," he said, glancing at me, then back at the mirror, "right now there really is nothing you can do, and by going back you put yourself in danger. Don't let her weakened condition fool you. She'd kill you in a heartbeat, and you'd be surprised just how strong her jealousy, her lust for him, will make her."

"There has to be something we can do."

"Not right now there isn't. Not after what you've just been through, and not when both his attention and hers is fully on you. Now get some rest. You're exhausted."

Rest wasn't my intention. Forcing him to turn the truck around so I could go get my car and get the hell out of Dodge until I could figure out what to do was my intention. I sure as hell had no reason to trust him now.

But I did rest. I slept the sleep of exhaustion, blissful and dreamless, with no room for thoughts of what might have happened if things had played out uninterrupted by a crazy friend with a sharp knife and a man who might be an angel, or could possibly be even worse than what he'd rescued me from. Christ, sleep was the safest place for me. None of those thoughts needed to be visited, especially not when everything in me felt like an open wound too tender to even touch.

When I woke up, I was in a large bed, settled between midnight blue sheets that smelled slightly woody. From the angle of the sun it was clear most of the day had passed without my knowledge, which suited me just fine under the circumstances. I was still in that state of blurred consciousness I often had when waking. I was no longer in the oblivion of the unconscious, but not fully aware of the goings on in the waking world either. There's something to be said for not being fully aware.

My unconscious struggled to pull me back down into the dark cushioning layers of sleep, and the part of myself that was conscious made a heroic effort to comply. Not wanting to wake up became an imperative, one that my body would have been completely willing to obey had I not noticed Michael standing on the balcony beyond open French doors, silhouetted in the mauve and melon tones of the setting sun.

"You're awake," he said, turning to face me. I could tell he was fresh from the shower. He was naked to the waist, dark hair curling around his ears. The white gauze curtains billowed on a breeze around his body, obscuring and revealing and obscuring again.

Beyond him I could just make out the hunched backs and rocky outcroppings of the fells thrust up against the horizon. I thought we were in the Lake District, but I wasn't sure. What was it, an hour by car, forty-five minutes? How long had I slept? I had no memory of him bringing me into the house or putting me into bed. That I was still fully clothed eased my fears a little bit. I figured if whatever it was that had attacked me in the gardens at Chapel House was anywhere near, it would have removed my clothing to take his jollies and made sure I was awake for the ride. I shivered in spite of the thick duvet spread over me, keeping my eyes on Michael, whom I still didn't trust, whether he had undressed me or not.

For an instant, with the curtains concealing his legs and groin, with his hand outreached to push them aside, revealing the curve of bicep and the straight broad expanse of chest and shoulders, he could have passed for the statue in the ruined garden.

Suddenly I was wide awake. Panic rose up my spine. I bolted from the bed and was halfway to the door before he caught me by the arm and gently steered me back into the room, settling me into a large wingback chair in front of a stone fireplace with no more effort than if I'd been an errant child. "It's all right. You're safe."

"Safe, am I? Safe?" In spite of my best efforts to calm down, my voice rose with each word.

"You didn't dream, did you?" he asked, pushing a strand of hair away from my face with the curl of a finger.

I shook my head. "How did you know?"

He shrugged one well-muscled shoulder and offered me a self-deprecating smile. "You were exhausted, and I knew if I could get you to sleep, I could keep you from dreaming."

"You? You got me to sleep? Jesus," I whispered. "How?"

"Just the power of suggestion. Nothing magical or anything." He looked away, suddenly unable to meet my gaze. "Not really, anyway."

With a flash of memory, I recalled my first encounter with the angel in the overgrown garden, the inviting hand, the look of longing. The encroaching evening went silent around me, or maybe the thought, the impossible thought forcing its way front and center in my mind had simply blocked out everything else, everything not relevant to the situation. It was a thought I really would have preferred not to have, but there it was, filling my brain, refusing to go away.

I braced my feet hard against the floor to keep my legs from shaking, took a deep breath and gave that thought substance. "You're an angel, aren't you?"

And, just like that, I slid deeper into the rabbit hole.

Chapter Seven

"You're an angel. The sculpture in the garden at Chapel House. It's you, isn't it?" The fact that the question sounded totally insane seemed irrelevant considering the way the weekend had gone so far.

He shrugged and I watched as a blush climbed his throat, spread across the tightening of his jaw and up his cheeks. "I'm retired," he replied without looking at me. "The sculpture's old. A friend of mine did it a long time ago, taking the piss really—especially by putting it there in that particular garden." He ran a large hand through the fall of damp hair. "It's her way of reminding me that I'm grounded now, tied to the earth just like every other mortal. No matter what I was, at the end of the day, I'm dust, and I'll return to dust, if I'm lucky."

"Wait a minute, angels can retire?"

He shot me a quick glance. "Well, it's all a matter of semantics, isn't it?"

"Then you're not a builder?"

"Oh, I'm a builder all right, and a damn good one. After all, Jesus was a carpenter," he reminded me.

I squinted hard in the fading light, studying the lines of his face, the plane and slope of his strong upper body, the slow, deep rise and fall of his chest as he took in and released each breath. But I could find no distinction, nothing that would give away the fact that he was an angel and not an ordinary man. Oh, he was nice to look at, he was interesting to look at, but he wasn't beautiful, as I thought an angel would be. Obviously the nose had been broken since the sculpture was made, and he seemed thicker through the shoulders and chest. Perhaps that was all down to hard physical labor in lieu of playing a harp and mooching his way around the pearly gates.

There were several white puckered scars just below his ribs. Two looked to be puncture wounds of some kind. The other was an angry gash that surely must have all but eviscerated him. Without thinking, I reached out and traced the long pale arc of scar tissue that followed the shape of his lower left rib and disappeared in the shadow under his arm.

He tensed beneath my touch and the skin along the path of my finger goose fleshed. "I had to force the issue of my retirement." His words were barely more than a whisper, and his gaze was locked on the logs in the fireplace, laid, yet unlit.

"Christ," I whispered. "Why? I mean why the hell would you give up immortality to be one of us?"

He covered my hand with his and held it against his side. At last he raised his gaze to meet mine. "I would have done anything to get away, and at that point, I didn't care if I lived or died. It felt like it was all the same."

"Are you a fallen angel then?"

This time he laughed out loud. "Stupid term, fallen angel. Truth be told, gods are bastards—all of them, any religion, any mythology, they're all arrogant, megalomaniacal bastards. They want control, and when they don't get it, well, they're even worse bastards. The woman who made the sculpture, she knows that at least as well as I do."

"Is she an angel too?"

He shook his head and looked away again, the smile slipping slightly from his face. "No angel; a pawn really. At least she started out that way." His eyes flashed bright in the fading light and the smile returned. "But sometimes even the pawns thumb their noses at the gods and get away with it. It cost her. It cost her dearly, but no one controls her now."

"So what, she was a sculptor, and the gods didn't like her work, was that it?"

He released my hand and knelt to light the fire. With the sun setting, the chill of evening came on fast. "Oh, she's not actually a sculptor. That's just a part of her cover. She's a thief, stealing back things the gods have taken that don't belong to them."

Every question he answered raised a dozen more. That what we were discussing sounded totally nuts wasn't lost on me, and yet neither was the fact that it was all either very real or I was still asleep dreaming in my bed, a cherished possibility diminishing with each passing moment.

We both watched as the logs caught fire from the kindling. Flame blossomed, turning shadows of ordinary things into ghouls and ghosts that writhed and danced on the walls. Once he was sure of the flame, he stood to close the balcony doors. "I work for her sometimes. When she needs me. She uses me when what I do as a builder dovetails with whatever job she's on at the moment."

I shifted in my seat to look up at him as he returned to settle back on the chair arm. "So you're trying to steal something from Chapel House? What is it, a flaming sword?"

He laughed. "Not anything that obvious. Chapel House and I

have a long history, as you might have guessed from the sculpture."

"Annie really did hire you to do the renovations at Chapel House?"

He nodded. "All part of the plan."

"It must have thrown a monkey wrench into your scheming when she fell in love with a demon, or whatever he is, and told you to bugger off."

"Doesn't matter. I seldom let something like that stop me." He pulled a shirt from a peg next to the door and slipped into it. "I've brought your things in, and I would imagine you'd like a shower. Then we'll see what we can scrounge for dinner. If that's all right."

The shower was more of a wet room really, big and luxurious, clearly designed to fit the man who used it. I wondered if he'd built the house himself, planned it all exactly like he wanted it. The bed was big, the rooms I'd seen high-ceilinged and spacious, all with views of the fells.

The walls of the shower were built of large sandstone tiles that made me feel more like I was standing under a waterfall on a wild river in some hidden desert canyon. Ghosted fossils of fern leaves made lacy patterns on the rough dun slabs. He must have selected each slab of sandstone carefully. The shower, with its stony artwork and its multiple heads, even its ledged seat that looked as though it were only a rocky outcropping in a cave, were all well thought out, beautifully designed by someone who loved and appreciated the out of doors.

Yes, Jesus was a carpenter. Perhaps building and creating was a part of the psyche of divine beings. Was Michael still a divine being, or had it been necessary for him to learn his craft by practice and training, like ordinary mortals did? He'd said the sculpture of him in the garden was very old. Perhaps he'd had a long, long time to perfect his craft.

I shivered at the thought and reached for the soap. It was slightly rough, like the sandstone surface and felt good against my skin, reminding me of the gentle *scritch, scritch* of a lover's fingernails over bare flesh. It had that same woody scent I woke up to in his bed, down between his sheets, though it lacked the base notes of clean perspiration and sleeping, dreaming male.

I wondered if angels—retired angels, that is—*did* dream. And were those dreams ever the kind that brought the pungent earth and ozone scent of male lust to the forefront in that masculine olfactory cocktail? I breathed in the smell, fresh and woodsy, and moaned at the soft rough *scritching* against my naked skin, wondering if Michael's hands would feel such. He was a builder, after all. Surely those calloused hands were rough enough to make delicious shivers up my spine, and any place else he touched me.

I imagined the feel of Michael against my flesh, the feel of his large hands moving over me, cupping and exploring, the feel of his mouth tasting mine. That he had created such a sensual space, and I was now certain that he had, made my imagination wild with images of the two of us beneath the waterfall, and the smell of my own lust peaked.

At some point in my ruminations about Michael, my fertile

imagination sent me seeking pleasure with my own hand, fingers moving of their own volition while I lathered my breasts, with the rough *scritch, scritch* of the soap pebbling my nipples and making my tender heaviness tingle and ache. The realization of just how needy I was came as a surprise after the experiences of the last twenty-four hours, but then it shouldn't have, should it? I'd practically lived the whole weekend in a state of arousal—at least when I wasn't terrified out of my mind. And really, almost every horror film I'd ever seen coupled sex and terror, even orgasm and death, so closely that the two bled into each other. One always expected the couple's sexy encounter in a horror film to end in gruesome bloodshed or worse. In the garden this afternoon, even as terrified as I was, I was just seconds away from orgasm.

I shivered in spite of the cloud of steam rising around me. I had researched stories of the gods seducing mortals and taking them as lovers. That was certainly an archetype, but what I had failed to consider was that the monsters also sought out mortal lovers. Hadn't Frankenstein's monster wanted a bride? Didn't King Kong steal away Fay Wray's character? Didn't Dracula seek out his Mina? Beauty came to love the Beast. Even Psyche herself was taken to the domain of the monster she was told never to look upon for fear of certain death. The revelation that the monster was the god of love himself cost her dearly. But it was a price she was willing to pay.

At the end of the day, maybe there really wasn't that much difference between the gods and the monsters. Even in the horror films, more often than not, terror gave way to a different kind of lust, a much more deeply rooted lust, a lust as closely connected to death as it is to procreation and pleasure, a lust lost in time and well connected to monsters and demons and blood and the fear of childbirth, at the same time, all bound up with the desperate need to form the beast with two backs. Christ! The lust for the monster was as much a part of our psyche as was our terror of him.

I wondered, would I have been able to hold off, would I have been able to resist the monster's advances, if Annie hadn't chosen that moment to use me for knife practice, if Michael hadn't shown up when he did and whisked me away? And would I have cared if they hadn't? Would I have been perfectly happy if I'd been left to rut against the paving stones with such a powerful being, who was maybe both monster and god? He had promised me the mind of God, the ultimate creative force that was the absolute Holy Grail for every writer. He knew exactly who I was, what I needed.

I was reminded in a rush of heat that he could take me to places sexually I couldn't even imagine. Monsters could do that, and their lovers were willing to pay any cost for the experience.

I rinsed off quickly and stepped out of the shower, unsteady on my feet and still unsatisfied. As I picked up the towel to dry myself, a wave of anguished lust clawed its way up from my center and spread like fire over my chest and all the way to the crown of my head. In an instant it burned everything away but raw aching hunger, leaving an abyss that surely could never be filled. How the hell would I survive this? Surely Annie would not, *could* not, and I hated her for having him, even as he used her up and tossed her aside. I hated her for having what should be mine, what was mine. No one could appreciate what his affections could offer like I could;

no one could translate his lust, his power like I could. He knew it, and I knew it.

For a terrifying moment, I pictured myself with the butcher knife. I pictured myself sneaking into Chapel House while Annie was in a post-coital stupor. It would be easy to do, and I knew he wouldn't stop me. In fact, he would welcome me, help me do away with the body, help me escape the suspicions of the police and the investigations that would follow.

I caught my breath in a gasp, only just remembering my need for oxygen, and I relaxed the white-knuckled fist clenched painfully around the hilt of the imaginary knife I dreamed of using. I came back to myself standing in front of the mirror. The towel had fallen to the floor at my feet; water still pearled on my hot skin. My reflection was obscured by the steam. The image on the other side of that thin film of condensation could be anyone. I could be looking at *his* face, not mine, the face I'd never seen and yet, like Psyche, suddenly, desperately longed to see.

I should have stayed. I shouldn't have questioned it when he wanted me. I should have taken his gift. I could have taken the knife from Annie, as weak as she was, and Michael had said himself he was just dust. The scars proved he bled just like anyone else. I could have finished it right there, and if I had, if I'd had the courage, it would be me in *his* arms now, me lying beneath him, letting him fill me with the wisdom of the ages, with the creative power I hungered for. I ached to know what it felt like. I longed to know who he was.

I staggered, and nearly fell against the sink, and then I was myself again. With a curse that felt gut deep and a quick swipe of my hand, I cleared the mist from the mirror and yelped and nearly jumped out of my skin at the reflection of Michael standing behind me.

"You were crying," he said. "I called out. I pounded on the door, but you didn't answer."

"I… I couldn't hear you." The room tilted slightly, then righted itself. "Oh, Christ, Michael, he was here. How can he be here? I wanted to be with him. I wanted to do things, horrible things."

"He wasn't here." He bent and picked up the towel, swaddled me in it and lifted me into his arms. Which was just as well—I'd completely lost the will to move, or even to stand. With me clinging to his neck, sobbing against his shoulder, he carried me to the wingback chair, settling in it himself, holding me on his lap like a child. "He wasn't here, Susan. Trust me, he wasn't." He pushed the damp tendrils of hair away from my cheek and wiped tears with a large, rough thumb. "But you were with him, he's touched you, been inside your head. You're now connected to him, and you feel the pull of his lust."

I sat for a long time, nestled against Michael's broad chest, listening to his heartbeat, like an anchor keeping me in my body, keeping me in my right mind. I wondered how an angel's heart differed from my own. I wondered how his struggles and his desires differed from those I lived with.

At last I found my voice. "I feel… so empty." I felt tears sliding down my cheeks again, tears that I'd barely been aware of while I was in the bathroom, as though they were such a small representation of the way I felt his absence that they were barely worth my attention.

"I know. That's exactly what he wants you to feel."

"He said that he'd show me the mind of God, that he'd share all he knows, that he'd be my inspiration and help me write it all down."

"He knows your deepest desire. That's the first thing he ever finds out about those he seduces. He learns their darkest secrets, their most private longings, and their deepest fears. Anything he promised you, he'll deliver, Susan. But what he doesn't tell you is that once he's had you, once you've been with him, everything that mattered to you before will seem meaningless. You live for him, and you burn with emptiness when you're not with him, as though you'll die if you don't have him."

I wiped viciously at my eyes. "Oh God, Michael, what am I going to do? What the hell am I going to do?"

"You're going to fight him, that's what you're going to do. And I'm going to help you." His lips brushed my ear as he spoke, and involuntarily I squirmed to get closer to him, realizing with a start that I was still horny as hell. But I couldn't take advantage this way. I couldn't. It was lust of such magnitude as I'd never felt before, and it was dark and horrible and terrifying and, fucking hell, I wanted to be consumed by it. But that wasn't Michael's problem. To drag him into it was not an option. Besides, I barely knew the man.

"I… I should get dressed." My voice sounded breathless and distant. I tried to push my way off his lap, but he held me there, hands gentle but firm. It was then that I felt him, hard with his own lust. He sat very still. I held my breath.

At last he spoke, still careful not to move. Even his lips barely formed the words. "Susan, I know what you're feeling right now. I understand it, believe me, I do." His gaze met mine in the firelight. "I know what you need, and unless you're completely daft, you have to know my response."

This time he shifted slightly. I caught my breath in a tight little gasp, and with it inhaled the scent of his lust, lightning and ozone, dark, damp earth. He slid the flat of his palm down to rest on the small of my back and the towel fell away.

"If you let me," his breath came heavy and quick against my cheek, "I can make it easier for you." He moved a splayed, calloused hand up over my ribs, and we both groaned. "If you let me, I can help."

Chapter Eight

I stretched up just enough to brush his lips with mine. My nipples grazed his chest, warm and still bare from his own shower. The tingle of flesh against flesh coursed through me. Michael wasn't in my head, wasn't in my imagination. I could see firelight dancing over the rise and fall of a masculine landscape. I could smell him, the clean shower scent mingling with the tang of body heat. I could smell the ozone and musk of his arousal, could almost taste the yeasty humid spiking of his desire at the back of my tongue. I nearly wept with the solid muscle and bone feel of him—the bulging of a bicep as he lifted his hand to curl fingers in my wet hair, the tensing of his thighs as he shifted beneath me, the straining against the soft denim of his jeans—the very solid promise that his need was at least as great as my own.

His mouth was both hard and soft, yielding to mine, intuiting my every move, tongue and lips, teeth and jaw. Was it because he was an angel, I wondered? My insides knotted at the thought, ice blooming next to fire. Did he also have some way of manipulating my needs, kindling my lust until I felt like I would burn if I didn't get relief? Did he also have some sinister purpose hidden from me? Had I not looked up at the cold stone of his image just before I was attacked?

As though he read my thoughts, he tightened his fist in my hair and bit my lip, making me shudder with as much pleasure as pain. Then he raked his teeth down over my jaw to kiss and nuzzle my nape. There, against the hammering of my pulse, he whispered, "there's nothing supernatural happening here, Susan. I'm flesh and bone, just like you."

He trapped my palm low on his belly, and his gaze locked on mine as he guided my hand down inside his waistband, sucking a harsh breath as I wriggled and twisted my fingers until I found him, deliciously commando. He was heavy and warm and smooth against my touch, like steel sheathed in silk.

Impatient as I was, I tore open his fly with an awkwardness worthy of a teenager, causing him to flinch and grind and lift his hips toward me, as though that might ease my clumsiness, as though that might end his denim imprisonment more quickly. And when he was free in my hand, he bucked upward, nearly landing me on the floor in his efforts to get his jeans down over his arse and kick them aside. Then, one hand still fisted in my hair as though he feared I might try to stop his mouth from gorging on mine, he tossed the forgotten towel across the room, cupped my buttocks and stood.

I gave a little yelp of surprise and wrapped my arms and legs around his body, now as naked as my own. It was only a couple of steps to the bed, and he lowered me onto it with incredible control, still strategically positioned between my thighs with me grinding and shifting in a battle to get him where I needed him most. But he resisted, holding me completely and totally at his mercy. He nibbled the hollow of my throat as though there was no hurry, as though he could take all of eternity to explore my body, and he absolutely would if he decided to. He cupped and kneaded each of my breasts in turn, stroking and tweaking until my nipples peaked and ached and tingled.

Ignoring my squirming, what little I could manage from

beneath him, embraced and held captive as I was, he slid a splayed hand down my belly and in between us, opening me with thick, calloused fingers, finding my need, stoking the flames, teasing me. In desperation, I reached for his erection, but he slapped my hand away and nipped my throat. "Be patient, Susan. I'm not about to mount you like an animal in rut. I understand flesh and blood, the drive of its life force. And," he dropped a kiss onto my sternum, "I understand the deceit of divinity to which we're all vulnerable."

"I don't care. I don't care, goddamnit." My voice was rough and barely audible, my throat was dry and achy as my mouth formed the words, breathing them almost soundlessly into his mouth. "I've been waiting, needing, wanting since I got to Chapel House. Please don't make me wait any longer."

And just when I was certain I'd go insane if I couldn't get him inside me, just when I'd all but clawed a raw strip down his back and buttocks in an effort to get him where I needed him, he pulled away, rose up on his knees and looked down at me, breathing like he'd been running hard. "I don't have to control your mind to pleasure your flesh. Say you want me, Susan, and I'll know if you're lying. I won't take you until it's me that you want, and not him."

"Bloody hell," I gasped, writhing beneath him like a python over a flame. "I want you, Michael, you fucking know that I want you. Please, don't make me wait."

And he didn't.

I swallowed back the last word in a gasp with the bruising force of his first thrust, somewhere between pain and pleasure. It had been a long time since I'd had sex, and Michael was substantial. I felt myself stretched and full beyond full, aching and raw. He would have held himself there, moving carefully, giving me time to adjust, but I kicked him hard in the kidneys, eliciting a soft grunt. Then I grabbed his butt in a grip that involved plenty of fingernail, feeling the hiss of his breath against my face as I forced him deeper into me, as I rose up to meet him.

He got the message. Any gentleness he might have shown me evaporated in another hard thrust that threatened to tear me apart, and I cried out with the exquisite pain of it, almost too much, and yet not enough. After all that had happened, could there *ever* be enough? The edge of that pain drove me to the anger, to the frustration I hadn't known I'd been holding back ever since Annie and her lover had begun to toy with me Friday evening. I growled, I raged, I screamed.

Michael fucked me, bruised me, ravaged me, and I welcomed the solid, battering ram humanity of him, sweating and grunting and thrusting, hand fisted tight in my hair, mouth leaving bite marks on my breasts and shoulders, stubbled cheek abrading the soft skin along my throat and above my nipples.

Each time he drove me to the edge, each time I held my breath ready and needing and teetering on the brink, he pulled back. Then he watched me writhe, listened to me curse him and beg him, then curse him again. He watched me with hooded eyes, eyes full of hunger, but more than that, eyes full of something I was too desperate, too angry, too needy to interpret. And just when I was on the verge of tears, he'd mount me again, take me a little deeper, a little closer, sharpen the focus of my lust a little tighter, and pull back once more until I hated him, I loved him, I needed him, I threatened to kill him before he took me yet again.

When, after an eternity, he allowed me to come, it wasn't the release I'd been expecting; it wasn't something I fell over the edge into as my orgasms usually were. It was a tidal wave driven by a storm, battering me, shaking me, breaking me apart in its aftermath. And while I convulsed, helpless and weak beneath him, he took his own release in wrenching, sobbing grunts.

As he collapsed on top of me, he gasped against my ear, "There, you see. I've marked you." He slid now gentle fingers across the bite mark already darkening above my left nipple. "You can't belong to both of us, but you have to belong to one of us if you're ever to be safe from the other."

"What the fuck? Belong to you? What the hell is that supposed to mean?"

I tried to shove my way from under him but he held me tight, letting me struggle as though he barely noticed it. "I told you we'll fight him together, Susan. It's the only way I know to win. He can't take you if you're tied to someone else," he shrugged, "oh, he'll still try, but at least it'll be much more difficult for him."

"So that's what all of this was about. You fucked me to mark me for battle." I tried again to shove him off, but he kissed me as though we were simply having a quiet post-coital cuddle.

"I said I could help you, Susan, and there's a lot more to helping you than just making you come."

It was ridiculous that I should feel used by his revelation. I had been the one to use him, after all. Hadn't I just wanted him to make me come? I mean, sex with Michael was way better than masturbating, when I knew full well I couldn't have masturbated without giving *Him* more space inside my head.

"Of course." I avoided his gaze, which was no easy task since he was still on top of me, inside me. "I forgot, you were at Chapel House on business. Tell me, am I a part of your plan for stealing whatever it is you're trying to steal?"

"Your help will make it easier," he said, shifting his hips just enough to make me aware that he wasn't getting any softer. He was an angel, after all. Maybe that meant he was insatiable. Like it or not, my body responded to his shifting, but I forced myself to hold still. I would not be distracted.

"You said you marked me. Well, so did He. What about His marks?" I nodded to the fingerprint-shaped bruises on my biceps. "He left his marks before you did."

"True, but His mark was given without your permission; fortunately I got you away before you gave in." He placed a soft kiss on each bicep in turn and this time I did squirm.

Then his words sank in and I shivered in spite of the heat of his body still on top of me. "What do you mean, you got to me before I gave in?"

The muscles along his jaw tensed and relaxed and he looked away. "You woke up in your own bed, didn't you?"

I suddenly felt as though little insects were crawling up the back of my neck. "Christ, Michael, you were there last night? In the garden? You—"

"I took you back to your room and watched over you until

the dream dissipated. If I hadn't, it would have been more than a dream." He met my gaze again. "If I hadn't been there, then more than likely either you or Annie would be dead by now and someone would be looking for a place to bury a body. I took you to your room and watched over you until morning. Then everything else that happened, me showing up at the door and Annie throwing you out… well, it was just a matter of timing." He slid a warm finger along the blooming bite mark. "But this will make it easier for you."

"Maybe so, but I still don't belong to you," I said, shoving him with the flat of my hand. "I don't belong to anyone."

He rolled enough to the side so that he was no longer crushing me beneath his weight, but he stayed inside me, still refusing to release me. "Gods never see it that way."

"But He's not a god, you told me that."

"He thinks He is, and He shares a lot of common traits with the gods I've known. I suppose it's possible He might be a bastard child of some lesser deity. But even if He's not, entities connected with the earth, especially consecrated ground, have enough power to be pretty damn formidable, god or not. Whatever He is, He's staked you as his territory, and you don't have much of a chance for fighting back, unless you team up with someone who knows how to fight dirty."

"And you know how to fight dirty because you're an angel?" I asked.

This time he rolled completely off me and sat up on the edge of the bed, the long muscles of his back and shoulders gone stiff.

"Michael?"

For a moment he said nothing. I could hear his breathing suddenly fast and shallow above the crackle of the fire. At last he took a deep breath and replied, "I know how to fight dirty because I was once his lover."

Chapter Nine

For a long moment I couldn't breathe. I couldn't speak. I felt cold to my core, and there was a strange ringing in my ears, but worst of all I felt jealous. "You were his lover? How's that possible?" I managed, forcing the words up through my throat, which threatened to close. "How the hell is that even possible?"

"What do you mean, how's that possible? You and I just made love. Same general principles."

"Same general principles, my arse." I pushed up off the bed, grabbed the towel and wrapped it around me, feeling suddenly very naked indeed. I paced at the foot of the bed, jealousy just at the edge of my consciousness like the irritating buzz of a mosquito seeking a place to bite.

"What? Do you think an angel can't be vulnerable, can't want the same things you want?" The smile that curved his lips was almost a grimace. "I was a lot more beautiful then than I am now. But beauty's a fleeting thing." He waved his hand absently, still not looking at me. "I knew that was a part of the price, and I didn't care. I would have done anything."

"Well, if it's beauty He's after, He sure as hell doesn't want me. Annie's the one with the looks. Not me."

Suddenly he stood and pulled me to him, the look on his face shifting from confusion to complete understanding. "You're jealous."

I said nothing. There was no point denying what had to be written all over my face. That Michael had been with Him, that Annie was with Him, and that I still wanted to be, in spite of everything, messed with my mind.

"I understand your jealousy," Michael said. "Once He's touched you in some way, in any way, you can't help but want Him. You can't help but want Him to want you, and only you. That's His power."

I didn't reply. What could I say? Instead I turned my back on him, trying to focus, trying to be logical. I didn't want to be jealous, and I didn't want to want Him. I knew what the result of wanting Him, of giving into that want, would be, and yet, I still wanted.

Michael grabbed my arm again in a grip that was none too gentle and pulled me back to him. "Susan, it has nothing to do with beauty, what He wants. Beauty is far more fleeting than… other things." He lifted my chin with a thick curled finger, forcing me to meet his gaze. "That He wants you, I can completely understand." He pulled me close against his still naked body, making sure I was fully aware of his desire for me, then he took my mouth in a kiss distracting enough that I would have been perfectly happy to linger in a lip-lock with him for twenty years or so. But then he released me, guided me back to sit on the bed, and pulled his jeans up over his hips.

"Tell me," I said, watching in fascination as he zipped his substantial self into the tight fit of denim. "Tell me what happened."

He shoved another log onto the fire, then plopped down into the wingback chair. For a long time he stared into the flames, so long that I thought maybe he'd chosen not to answer; maybe it wasn't something he could talk about. But at last he took a deep breath and spoke. "I thought it would be easier being human." He lifted a shoulder in a lop-sided shrug. "I suppose we all romanticize the things we wish for before we actually have them. We don't know the pitfalls and the difficulties until we're faced with them, and then they're such a shock, sometimes it's too late." He forced a laugh. "You'd think someone who had spent eons as a being only slightly less than divinity would have been aware of the threat of demons and spirits and such things that do a whole lot more than go bump in the night. I'd even met demons and incubi and spirits of the land. They never seemed all that threatening to me, but then I wasn't human, was I? I know it's insane to think that I could forget, after all, it was a part of my job to protect humans, to ease their suffering from such beings."

He grabbed the poker and gave the log he'd just put on the fire a hard shove that resulted in a shower of popping and crackling sparks. After another long moment of gazing into the flames as though he sought wisdom there, he continued. "They were never any threat to me as an angelic being. I just assumed that would be true when I became human. I knew how things were. I understood, and I was still me, at the end of the day. Surely I was safe from such things. But I wasn't, was I?"

"How did it happen?" I asked. A part of me didn't really want to know. A part of me couldn't bear the thought of anyone else being with Him. But He was a monster, I reminded myself. He was bad news, very bad news. Even as I thought it I couldn't keep from thinking about how it felt when He touched me, how it felt when He spoke to me, almost like His voice was inside my heart.

"A part of my job was to be the Guardian of sacred spaces."

He smiled and shook his head. "Sorry to disappoint, but I wasn't *that* Michael, not the archangel. I was just *a* Michael, and I was one of many whose job was to safeguard sacred spaces and the people who worship therein." He chuckled softly. "I suppose you could say I was the divine version of a security guard. Not very glamorous, is it?"

"And you were sent to protect people from… Him?"

"Sort of," he replied. "There are lots of beings attracted to sacred spaces because they are sacred. They shine like beacons to supernatural eyes. And because mortals come to those spaces open and more vulnerable than they are in more mundane spaces, they can be the perfect places for these divine parasites, for lack of a better term, to attach themselves."

"Are you saying He's a parasite?" The idea made me squirm. I liked the idea of some divine monster, some misbehaving godling wanting to seduce me, but I wasn't so keen on the idea of a parasite attaching itself to me.

"More than likely he was the original guardian spirit sent to protect the place and its worshipers. Stability isn't any more a given with protective and guardian spirits," he shrugged, "with any kind of divinity at all, actually, than it is with mortals. And the truth is no one really knows what will drive them over the edge and when."

"And is the same true of angels?" I asked.

"If you're asking me how stable I am, well, I'm probably not the one to ask, but I think it's pretty safe to say I'm a lot more stable than I was back in the day."

"Back in the day?"

Now it was his turn to pace, staring straight ahead as though he could see into the distant past, as though he could see what had been as easily as what was. Maybe he could.

"In the beginning, I was sent to help him, sent because the powers that be observed a growing instability in him. They thought he was just overly tired. Some guardian spirits attached to places are content to serve and protect their place in total anonymity, and pretty much for all eternity, without so much as ever wavering. They're so connected with the place, they seldom have need for contact with the mortals who hold that place sacred.

"But He," a shiver ran up his spine, "He became fascinated with the mortals who worshiped in His space, and since that space had been a Christian place of worship for several hundred years, it fell to those who served the Christian god to set things right. It should have been easy for an angel. It should have been a walk in the park."

The silence stretched between us, broken only by distant thunder. It took a second for me to realize I'd been holding my breath.

He moved to slip the throw from the back of the chair over my shoulders and I realized not only was I was still clad in just the towel, but I was shivering. I inhaled with a shudder and found my voice. "But it wasn't."

"It wasn't." He returned to pacing in front of the fire. "You see, the thing was, that I didn't realize that something was amiss. I didn't realize anything at all. In fact, it seemed almost the opposite to me. It seemed like everything was exactly as it should be and that He was…"

"He was what?"

Michael stopped mid-stride and stared into the flames, as though seeking answers there. "It seemed as though He was the only sane thing about the place, and even more than that, it seemed like He was a kindred spirit. He loved humanity. He was fascinated by their tenacity, their ability to be both strong and vulnerable. And He was particularly fascinated by their ability to live in the physical world. Oh, that was a weakness, of course it was. Mortality always is and always has been a weakness, the ultimate weakness. And yet to live in the flesh, to feel pain and suffering and joy and love and lust and tenderness, to experience the five senses—how could any non-corporeal being not crave that? How could any god think that to exist without flesh was superior to blood and bone and all the passion and trauma and chaos that went along with it?"

"And clearly you shared His opinion," I observed, nodding to his body.

"I did." He came to sit beside me on the bed and took my hand, chafing my cold fingers. "Though had I had any idea the cost back before I made the decision, back before I chose the path of no return, I might have been too terrified to do what had to be done."

"You mean that once you became human, you succumbed to Him and became His lover?"

Michael shook his head slowly, and the chafing of my hand became a death grip. "Oh no, it wasn't that at all. I became His lover long before I became mortal. In fact, I became mortal because I loved Him."

Chapter Ten

"Wait a minute." I jerked my hand away from his. "Let me get this straight. You gave up being an angel not because you were angry at God, or the gods, or whoever the hell it was you worked for. You gave up being an angel because you loved Him?"

"Oh, I stand completely by what I said earlier; all gods are bastards, and to serve them is folly. They have no loyalty but to their own pride." He reached to push a strand of hair behind my ear and I shoved his hand away. He simply shrugged and continued. "I felt that way when I was sent off to babysit Him. Well, that's how I saw it at the time—me being sent off to serve a lesser being. I was a bit of an arrogant prick back then." He offered a twitch of a smile. "Guess I learned a thing or two about who was the lesser being, didn't I?"

"But you said you became human because you loved Him. Care to explain that?"

"Fuck, Susan, you make it sound like I'm a cheating husband or something. Yes, I became human because I loved Him, but if I hadn't believed that I was giving Him a gift, if I hadn't believed that it was what He wanted more than anything, I don't know if I would have done it, okay? I... I just don't know."

For a moment we sat in silence, him twisting the edge of the duvet between his fingers. At last he spoke, avoiding my gaze. "I'm not sorry now. But for a long time... Well, let's just say it was a high price I paid." Then he added, as though I needed further explanation, which I suppose I did, "He was so genuine, so unassuming with me. I was completely taken in, completely unaware of His deception until it was too late."

I felt like I was invading his privacy. I felt like I was asking questions that were none of my business, and yet, my life was in this man's hands, this ex-angel's hands. So I asked anyway. "Why did He want you to become human? I would have thought as an angel you'd be able to… you know… a whole lot longer and you'd not… I don't know… you'd not get tired. As an angel you'd have the stamina to keep up with Him."

This time the laugh was bitter enough to make goose bumps rise on my arms. "He wanted the feel of humanity. He wanted the touch of flesh and blood, even though He could only have it vicariously. No matter how often He took me, no matter that I was as insatiable as He was, I still wasn't flesh and blood. I didn't know it at the time, but He'd already developed a dangerous lust for mortals. Later, much later, after the woman I work for had freed me from Him, I came to realize that He fed off the humanity of his lovers." The straight line of his jaw hardened like iron and his fists clenched. "He… He got off on using them up. It was only really good for Him if He knew that in the end they would sacrifice themselves for Him. A god complex, I suppose, but then who could argue with Him?"

He glanced up at me, then looked away. "I guess He finds human mortality more arousing than any other part of being corporeal. Probably because the bastard never has to experience it."

"Jesus, this just keeps getting more and more convoluted," I said. "Did you just say the woman you work for, the one you steal for, she saved you from Him?"

Michael shoved to his feet and pulled me up off the bed too.

"Look, can we continue this conversation later? I'm starving. For now, why don't you get dressed?" He nodded to my bag sitting next to the bathroom door. "You need to eat. We both do. When you're ready, join me in the kitchen and I'll tell you whatever you want to know. As much as I can anyway." He turned and left without another word.

In the kitchen, I found him dumping spaghetti into a pot of boiling water. He looked up and offered a smile that belied the serious situation in which we found ourselves. "Hope you like carbonara. I'm not a chef, but I don't do bad with pasta." He poured a glass of pinot grigio and handed it to me. Then he put me to work on a salad while he sautéed the pancetta. We worked in companionable silence, maybe both of us trying to pretend that we were just ordinary lovers with the munchies after hot sex.

And the sex had been hot. My stomach bottomed out at the thought of the mark he'd left above my breast, and then just as quickly I felt an overwhelming chill at the sight of the bruises on my biceps. I grabbed up the blue hoodie he had left carelessly draped over the back of a kitchen chair and wriggled into it. He smiled again. He liked the idea of me wearing his clothes. I liked it too, but it was way less satisfying to know I wore them to cover bruises left by another would-be lover.

I didn't want to talk about it. I wished we could both just forget it. I liked Michael. I liked the way he shot me admiring glances when he thought I wasn't looking. I liked the way he brushed by me to get the strainer, casually resting a hand low on my back. A hand that lingered slightly longer than absolutely necessary, just long enough to become a fleeting caress, just long enough to make my pulse race and my nipples tighten. I liked the outdoorsy woodsy scent of him. I liked the heat of him, the solid feel of muscle and bone. I liked the presence of him close by, and I liked that we could be silent together without having to clutter the atmosphere with mindless drivel. But then again, when the time came to talk, as it most definitely would, I might actually have preferred that it should be mindless drivel instead of the topic that hung in the air like a dark cloud.

We made it through dinner with talk of his work and mine, with laughter and a few shy smiles and passing glances, with a brush of knees and ankles beneath the table. By the time he pulled the chocolate chip ice cream out of the freezer, I was already hoping for round two between the sheets.

Then I opened my mouth and blew it. "If you fuck me enough, will it make me forget about Him?" I hadn't intended to say anything, but there it was, what I wanted and what I didn't want, all rolled into one ill-timed question.

He spoke around a large mouthful of ice cream. "Wouldn't that be great? That's a cure I could happily live with."

I laid down my spoon, suddenly no longer hungry. "Are you talking about a cure for me or a cure for you?"

He held my gaze in a look that was anything but angelic, and for a second I could believe that there really wasn't that much difference between angels and demons. Of course he was human now, Michael was. Wasn't he? "I want you very much, Susan. I'm sure you haven't missed the signs. But just like you, I want Him more. Damn Him to hell, but I do."

I fought down the lump in my throat, surprised to find myself feeling hurt by such an admission. Surprised to find myself dangerously close to tears. But how could it really come as any surprise? "Then you're not… over Him?" It was a stupid question, and yet, I hoped I'd simply missed the cues.

He moved his chair closer to mine, the legs scraping across the slate floor, and very gently he chafed my arm. "I told you, Susan, no one gets over Him. If I had been only human, if I'd not had… help, I wouldn't have survived. But surviving, living without Him is not the same thing as getting over Him."

I pulled my arm away a bit more brusquely than I'd intended and forced a laugh I didn't feel. "So we're rivals then, are we?"

"I'd rather not think of us that way."

I gulped the rest of my wine for courage and poured another glass. "I find it really strange that your… partner in crime would send you into the mouth of the dragon to steal whatever it is you're supposed to steal. How does she expect you to survive it and walk away with her prize? You did tell her, didn't you? I mean, you did say she helped you get away from Him."

He cleared his throat and sat back in his chair. "Oh, she knows, and yes, I'd be dead if she hadn't helped me, but to be honest, I don't think she cares all that much if I survive it or not."

"Fuck," I said under my breath. "Well then maybe you should let *her* go in after the plunder instead; maybe you should let her go up against Him, see how she likes it."

This time he chuckled, and it was genuine. "As interesting as that might be to see, I don't think there's even the slightest spark of attraction between the two of them. Haven't you ever met someone that everyone else fancied like crazy, but you just couldn't see why? Well, I'm pretty sure it's like that between them. Remember, she's the one who got me away from Him."

I shrugged. "Then it seems to me she'd be the perfect one for the job."

"Trust me, she chose wisely in sending me." He stood and took my hand. "But it doesn't matter if we're both hot for him or not. Right now, Susan, what matters is that I'm hot for you, and if I'm not mistaken, the feeling is mutual. Though it won't make either of us forget Him, it'll make us both stronger, and the bond between us stronger, and we both need all the strength we can get. Besides," he ran a large hand through his hair and left it standing in soft spiky peaks I couldn't resist reaching out to smooth, "I don't want to think about Him, or her." He pulled my hand to his lips and kissed my palm. "I've already had my ice cream." He raked me with hungry eyes. "Now I want my dessert."

Without another word, he led me back upstairs, pausing at the bedroom door to kiss me thoroughly while ridding me of the hoodie and all items of clothing beneath, a favor I returned in kind. Then, kissing and groping and giggling, we stumbled to the bed. In the leisurely explorations that followed, it was a long time before either of us spoke, and besides, our mouths were well occupied with tasks much more pleasant.

When at last my brain engaged through the thick fog of arousal, I remembered how to speak again. "This must be what sex before going to battle feels like," I managed between efforts to breathe.

Michael didn't answer. His tongue was well occupied between my legs. This time there would be no forcing the issue. This time I knew that he would make me beg for it before he took me, and he'd make it well worth the wait. This time I could be patient too and revel in the feel of him exploring me, pleasuring me, driving me to the point of no return. I tried to push the idea that it might just be a revenge fuck out of my head, but some thoughts push back harder than others. Did I really want to make Him jealous, I wondered? What would He do to me if I did? Was Michael thinking the same thing? "Am I your revenge fuck?" Damn it, why couldn't I keep my mouth shut?

He bit the inside of my upper thigh and I yelped as he came up, face shining with my wetness. "Possibly." He wiped a forearm across his mouth, then gave each of my nipples a hard suck, wriggling in between my thighs with his knees before he thrust up into me and rose above me on his elbows to look down into my eyes. "But that shouldn't worry you much. If we're each other's revenge fucks, then won't we both go out of our way to make it so damn good that He'll truly have something to be jealous over?"

I laughed in spite of myself and his kiss muffled the sound to a giggle that ended in a soft moan twinned by his own deep-chested sounds of pleasure as he began to move inside me. And suddenly I wasn't laughing, suddenly I was moving with him, thrusting up to meet his body, hands fisted against his hard shoulders, thighs straining to grip him tighter. Muscle. We were one giant muscle tensing and pumping and pushing with one goal—release.

And as I convulsed against him, as he growled out his own orgasm, I realized that at the end of the day, the mutual release we sought was not from each other but from Him. The real question was whether or not we wanted that release bad enough to let go of what we both felt for Him and do what had to be done. Was that even possible? As I lay there in his arms struggling to catch my breath, I suddenly realized that what neither of us could do alone, we just might be able to accomplish working together. But that thought was for after, after we both had some much-needed sleep.

Chapter Eleven

In that space between sleep and wakefulness, in that place where you're never really sure what's real and what's a dream, I became conscious of someone fondling my breasts. Someone with large hands, someone with very warm, expressive lips, someone who was both deliciously sloppy and yet surgically precise in eliciting desire far removed from both mouth and breasts. The love bite above my left nipple ached and tingled with the stimulation, and I arched and groaned and reached out in the darkness for Michael, in whose arms I'd fallen asleep after way more ravishing than I would have thought either of us could survive considering the day we'd just had.

Then the buzzing of my phone dragged me into the waking world. I rolled over and fell out onto the floor, biting my tongue and cursing under my breath, trying not to wake Michael and, at the same time, surprised that he was still sound asleep. I grabbed my handbag from where it sat on the floor next to the nightstand and fumbled for the phone, slipping into the bathroom to answer.

"Susan! Thank God I got you. I'm so sorry, I'm so, so sorry, Susan. I don't know what happened, I can't explain it. I was asleep by the altar one minute and then the next thing I knew I had a knife and I…" Annie's voice on the other end of the device dissolved into wracking sobs, with me stupidly trying to calm her, trying to convince her that it was nothing, that it was no big deal that my best friend had come at me with a butcher knife.

At last there was silence except for her breathing and snuffling. I sat naked on the commode, shaking as though I'd been out in the cold. It was nerves, I told myself, just nerves. She couldn't get to me on the phone. *He* couldn't get to me on the phone. And then Annie dropped the bomb.

"Susan, I need you to come get me. I need your help. I'm a mess, I know that now, and I need to leave. I need to get out of Chapel House for good before it's too late."

"All right." My voice sounded breathless, unsteady, like it belonged to someone else. Christ, what was I saying? What was I agreeing to? Was I nuts? "Just let me wake up Michael and we'll be there as soon as we can."

There was silence on the other end of the phone, and for a second, I thought she had disconnected. "No, please don't bring that man. You mustn't. He's dangerous, Susan. I know he's charming and sexy, but he's dangerous." Her voice was wet with tears again, rising in desperation as she spoke. "He'll hurt you. He'll hurt us both. He isn't who he says he is. Please, you have to come alone. It's the only way I can get away from here."

"Annie," I drew a deep breath, as much to calm the shakes as anything, "my car's still at Chapel House. When you chased us away I had to leave it there. I can't come for you without Michael's help."

"Yes you can! Take his lorry. I know you can drive it, at least as well as he can. Please! He's got another car. He can come later and get it. Please, Susan, please! There's no one else I can turn to."

There was another long silence in which I could hear her crying in helpless gasps. I never could stand to hear her cry. "Look, I don't even know where I am. I slept the whole way to Michael's after we left Chapel House. My phone has a good GPS. I'll set it and then let you know how soon I can be there. There shouldn't be any traffic at this hour. Oh, and Annie, you meet me outside. I'm not going into that place again, do you understand? You meet me around by my car ready to go, or I'm not waiting. I'll text you as soon as I'm close. Okay?"

"Yes! I'll be there, I promise. Oh, Susan, thank you so much. And Susan, please hurry." The line went dead.

I should have realized something was wrong when Michael slept through even that much of a disturbance, but I wasn't at my best. And when I rifled through the basket on his nightstand where he kept his keys, then stumbled into my clothes and he still didn't wake up, I should have suspected something wasn't right. I should have. But how the hell did I know how soundly the man slept? Though I half hoped my less than quiet efforts would wake him and force the issue, when they didn't I found myself in his lorry alone driving south on the M40 toward Manchester, Chapel House programmed into the GPS on his dashboard. I remembered when I got in that I'd seen him stash it under the passenger seat when we went to the Little Chef. Annie was right. I could drive a small lorry with no problems. I'd driven a delivery van to help put myself through uni. I stopped long enough to get a large coffee at an all-night petrol station and then it was a straight shot in the wee hours to Chapel House.

I tried not to think about that fact too much. I planned to park the lorry a few blocks away so Michael wouldn't be at risk when he came for it. Then I would meet Annie at my car, shove her in, rev the engine and get the hell out of Dodge. There was no contingency plan. I could barely get my head around the idea that I was going back to that horrid place at all. But I was not, under any circumstances, going back inside, or into that damn maze of a garden either. I didn't dare. Even thinking about it made the bite above my breast tingle and my nipples harden inside my bra. Michael's mark. Would *He* find Michael's mark offensive? Would it make any difference to Him? I had no intention of finding out.

I gulped coffee, burnt my tongue and drove on with the radio cranked to keep me awake and to keep me from thinking about Him, about what I would do if He came for me, about what I would do if Annie showed up with a knife. Fuck, I didn't even have Michael's mobile number. But he would know. He would know where I'd gone, and I would come back as soon as I'd scooped up Annie, whether she liked it or not. I could get his address from his website. It was listed on the door of his lorry. I wasn't sure how much I trusted Michael, knowing that he was an ex-angel and a thief, knowing his connection to Him, but at the moment, whether Annie liked it or not, he was my only ally.

I found a quiet place two blocks from Chapel House and parked the lorry just as intimations of dawn were graying the night sky. I left the keys in the truck bed, just beneath the edge of a toolbox under a tarp.

It wasn't a good sign when I called Annie and she didn't answer. I left a message and a text that I would be at my car in two minutes. I would wait for her in the car no longer than five minutes, and then I was out of there. Best live to fight another day, I thought, shoving the phone into the pocket of my jeans and knuckling my car keys at the ready.

Chapel House was dark and silent, at least what little I could make out from beyond the overgrown garden where I'd parked my car what seemed like a hundred years ago now. I had already pulled up Annie's number again by the time the car came into view, with her nowhere in sight. "You've got five minutes to get your arse out here. Do you hear me? Five, starting now!" I disconnected and punched in a text with the same message.

When I got to the car, she still wasn't there, and I wasn't surprised. It took every ounce of self-control to keep from checking over my shoulder toward the garden gate. I felt certain I was being watched. I felt like my skin would crawl off of me as I got into the car and locked all the doors. Fat lot of good that would do, I was sure, but it still made me feel like I was doing something. Then I waited. Five minutes came and went, then ten. Chapel House remained dark and there was no sign of my friend. I called again and texted. I had just started the engine to make my getaway and regroup when the phone rang. I yelped and jerked so hard that my neck popped like gunshot. I answered without greeting. "Annie, for fuck's sake, where are you? I'm waiting. You have to come now."

At first there was just sobbing, and I broke into goose flesh, suspecting the worst. "Annie?"

She sniffled and I could hear her heavy breathing. "Susan, I'm sorry, I hurt my ankle. I can't walk. I need you to come, please. I just want to get out of here. Please come get me. I'm so, so sorry."

"Sonovabitch," I mumbled beneath my breath. "What the hell did you do?"

"I was in a hurry to meet you and I missed a step, came down wrong. I think I broke it."

"All right. All right! Tell me where you are and I'll come get you." If I were a praying woman, I would have been saying every prayer I knew. I was anyway, and making up a fair few as I shoved out of the car and headed into the lion's den. She said she had left the front door unlocked. She said she was just inside. But she wasn't. Fortunately the ambient light of the coming dawn and the fact that I'd had time to let my night vision adjust to the dark interior meant I could see all the way up the nave to the transept. There, the pale glow of the setting moon shone off Annie's hair, her frail body barely visible beneath the blankets of her pallet next to the altar.

I held my breath and moved on tiptoes up the aisle, all the while feeling as though I were being watched from just beyond my peripheral vision. I sniffed quietly. There was no smell of burning garbage, no scent of jasmine or roses, just the smell of dust on aging stone, both overpowered by the smell of sleep and sex as I drew nearer to where Annie lay.

For a horrifying moment, I thought she was dead. It was only as I knelt next to her and touched her cheek, which was unusually cold, that I saw the rise and fall of her chest beneath the duvet. Annie was sound asleep, her mobile phone clutched in one hand. I carefully pried it from her fingers and checked her calls. Sure enough, mine was the last number she'd called less than five minutes ago, I would guess, and yet she now slept like the dead, tracks of tears on her cheeks still visible in the anemic light of her mobile.

With goose bumps rippling over my arms and up my spine, I leaned forward and shook her none too gently. "Annie! Annie, wake up," I whispered. "We have to go, now." But she only moaned, rolled over and pulled the duvet tight around her. For a moment I knelt next to her, wondering what the hell to do. I couldn't just leave her. I'd come all this way, and she was within my grasp. There didn't seem to be any threat at the moment. Maybe there were times when He wasn't paying attention, times when one could sneak in beneath His radar, so to speak, and if this were one of those times, I couldn't afford not to take advantage.

"Annie!" I shook her again, harder. Still nothing. As an afterthought, I lifted the duvet and looked at her ankles beneath the light of my own mobile. Her feet were bare and dirty, ankles stick thin, but there was no bruising, no swelling, no trauma at all that I could see. I threw off the duvet entirely and saw that she wore a summer dress that fell below her knees. On the floor, she lay sprawled on a wrinkled sheet. Maybe I could drag her. She couldn't weigh much now, and I was strong and well-muscled.

I glanced behind me down the length of the nave. Surely I could make it, and then there was just pavement to the car. I could do it if I had to, and it certainly looked like I would have to.

I was just smoothing the sheet beneath her to ease my efforts when she grabbed my wrist in a vice grip. I yelped, the sound of my voice echoing across the transept.

"What the hell are you doing here?" she asked. Her eyes were wide and black in the low light, as though they were empty.

"Jesus, Annie," I tried to pull away but she held me tightly. "You know what I'm doing here. You fucking called me to come get you."

Even in the dim light, I could see the confusion clouding her expressive face. "Why would I do that?" she asked, still clenching my wrist with a hold I was certain would leave bruises. Then her lips curved into a beatific smile and she chuckled softly. "Oh yes, now I remember. He asked me to call you. He said when you got here, I could rest and He would punish you for your interference, and then He promised that when I woke up, when He'd finished with you, everything would be okay again."

Without another word, she released her hold on me, rolled over and was instantly sound asleep. I was left kneeling next to her, not knowing whether to try and complete my task or to run like hell. A cool breeze ruffled the plastic sheeting over the altar, catching the frail moonlight like a ghost rising from the grave. The space around me was suddenly awash in the scent of roses, and I realized I was too late to do either.

Chapter Twelve

The fight or flight instinct had been short circuited. I could do nothing but kneel over Annie's sleeping form while the scent of roses grew stronger and stronger and the impotent terror inside me remained trapped like ice just beneath my sternum. I don't know how long I stayed that way. Time never ran the same when He took control, but it was the feel of His hand tightening against my throat that brought everything back into sharp focus, along with the shocking awareness that I could no longer breathe. Panic rose up my spine as the pressure increased around my neck, a caress just tight enough to constrict the flow of oxygen. The world around me shimmered and effervesced as I struggled not to lose consciousness.

"If you relax it won't hurt, and you might actually enjoy it." I couldn't tell if His voice was coming from in the room next to me or if it were in my head, but the cascade of goose bumps over my body left me in no doubt that it was His voice, and His hand at my throat. "You strike me as a woman who might just enjoy a little pain with her pleasure, Susan." His chuckle was like soft fur against naked flesh. "Oh, don't worry, my darling. You're safe with me now, and I protect my own."

It was a total surprise to find I had unbuttoned my blouse and reached behind to unhook my bra, my hands moving of their own volition, my whole body desperate to be exposed to Him, desperate to feel His touch, even as the danger I was in spiked my pulse and flooded my body with adrenaline with which I could do nothing, trapped as I was.

"I promise I'll keep you safe from harm," came the velvety

purr next to my ear. "I do not, however, promise that I won't make you pay for running away from me." Then He brushed my left nipple with invisible fingers. Suddenly Michael's love bite, just above the areola, burned like a branding iron fresh from the flames, and I screamed.

I must have lost consciousness, because when I came back to myself, my breast still stinging like fire, I was stumbling through the brambles and ivy of the garden, as though someone were pushing and shoving and herding me against my will. But then that was exactly what was happening, wasn't it? I was moving in jerky, shambling steps like a marionette with an amateur puppeteer at the strings. To my horror, I had no control of any part of my body, least of all the arousal that should have been the last thing I felt at that moment.

The small part of me that was still me, hiding in some tiny place in my brain, pushed and cursed and shoved her way to the forefront, reminding me that I was still there, that I couldn't afford for one minute to lose control. I couldn't afford to let fear, or worse yet, lust, take over. In spite of the shit situation in which I'd found myself, it was still a shock when I became aware of the heat of His body—the body that wasn't real, I struggled to remind myself— pressed tightly against my back, pushing me forward.

He spoke next to my ear. "Surely you didn't think Michael's mark could protect you." The soft breeze of his voice lifted a wispy strand of my hair, and I shuddered. "He can't even protect himself without the help of that bitch who owns him now." As His words turned bitter, I tasted them like bile at the back of my throat, along with cold terror from the realization that what I both most feared and most longed for was as much inside me as it was out.

Frantically I sought the tiny part of me I could still access, and found it there, holding strong. That should have come as no surprise. After all, what would be the point? Where would His victory be if He drove me from myself, drove me from my own sanity before I gave Him what He wanted?

The next moment, I was being shoved at the foot of Michael's statue. As He released His puppeteer-like control, I lost my footing and banged my cheekbone hard against the edge of the plinth before catching my balance. The world around me erupted in an explosion of stars and pain that seemed somehow both closer than my own flesh, and yet distant, as though it didn't matter, as though it no longer truly belonged to me.

"Oh, he'll come for you, of course he will." He spoke as though we were having a light conversation at the local pub over drinks and nibbles. "He's very heroic, our Michael." He mantled me now from behind, undoing my jeans with nimble fingers and sliding his hand inside. In my peripheral vision, I was certain I could now make out the shape of bicep and shoulder in the gray dawn, the shadow of muscular thighs pressed on either side of me, but then perhaps that was just in my head too.

"The dear boy is also very delusional, my darling." His kiss was warm against my ear, his words humid. "In his heart of hearts, he knows he's coming for me as much as he's coming for you. Yes, delusional like you are, Susan. You came at my calling, no matter what you tried to convince yourself about poor dear Annie, who's now sleeping peacefully while I punish you." He clicked his tongue. "The darling girl needs a lot of sleep these days. Insatiable though, my Annie, just as Michael is. Just as I'm sure you will be too."

He pushed my hair aside and possessively kissed and nibbled the back of my neck until I quivered beneath Him, my hands fisted against the marble of Michael's feet, nails digging into my palms to keep focus on the part of me still present enough not to want to rut like a beast.

"And when Michael has come for you." My attention was drawn back to the sound of his voice, to the fact that I was grunting and moaning like some animal desperate for relief, desperate for His touch. "When Michael realizes he can no more take you from me than you can take Annie, oh, I think that we shall have a delightful time together, the three of us. We'll have to make it quick, of course." I felt His erection pressing up against the back of my jeans, and I struggled in a sudden wave of panic that He barely noticed, so complete was His control of the situation. "That bitch will come for him, and take him from me, but she won't be pleased, she won't be pleased at all about his... relapse."

There was another bitter chuckle and I caught a slight whiff of burning rubbish. He cupped my left breast and this time I cursed loudly and profusely as He hurt me, the feel of Michael's mark like an abraded blister against my skin. And still I wanted Him. No matter what He did to me, no matter how He hurt me, I wanted Him, I needed Him to fuck me, I needed Him never, never to stop fucking me until I was weak and used up and there was nothing left, until I ended up just like Annie. The less-than-subtle reminder of my no-win situation really pissed me off.

"So you're going to rape me then, instead of being a real man about it? Oh, I forgot, you're not a real man at all, are you? A real man would…"

I don't know what I said after that. I don't know what He did after that. All I know is that it hurt. It hurt a helluva lot, and He made it hurt long enough to feel like an eternity. Just before I passed out He spoke against my ear. "I take no one by force, Susan, but I promise you, when I do take you, you'll beg me to give you the release you need. You'll beg me as you've never begged before. And in time, in good time, I'll give you what you need."

Then I lost consciousness, wanting Him more than I ever wanted anything in my life and hating myself for it.

"Oh, my poor little naïve scribe. Such a terrible way to learn the truth, but at least now you know. It is possible to want the very thing that'll destroy you, and to want it so badly that your own destruction means nothing to you."

It was a woman's voice I heard in my dreams, through a haze of pain and lust so tightly linked that I wasn't sure which might kill me, and I didn't care as long as I got relief from my suffering. A cool feminine hand came to rest on my forehead, and I tried to open my eyes, but that hand slid down like a blindfold.

"Best you don't do that right now. You might not like what you see. Keep your eyes shut for me, darling, and let me check how badly that bastard has damaged you." The accent was strange, nothing I could place, and just barely there, just enough to make me hang on to her every word. Though I wasn't entirely sure that had anything to do with the accent.

"I'm not dreaming?" I managed, before she placed a bottle of water to my parched lips and tilted it until I choked, sputtered and then drank.

"Hardly, hon." Her laugh was like warm honey, but when I attempted to open my eyes for a peek, she shoved the hand back over them. "I said, keep your eyes closed. Now if I have to tell you again, I'll blindfold you and you won't like that one bit."

"Who the hell are you?" I asked, shoving the bottle away and clenching my eyes shut tightly as she removed her hand.

Another disembodied laugh. "I would have thought you bright enough to figure that one out. I'm the bitch."

"You're the thief?"

There was a girlish giggle. "Is that what Michael's calling me these days? Well, it's better than some of the other things I've been called, and some of those even by him. People can be so hurtful at times, can't they? Never mind, sticks and stones and all that, but yes, I am the thief."

"Where's Michael?" I tried to force myself to a sitting position, but she pushed me back with decidedly more strength than I was expecting.

"Michael's still at home, fast asleep, which is exactly where I want him, where we both need him, at the moment." As she spoke, I felt her gentle examination, not in the way I'd felt His touch, but in the way I'd felt the water against my lips. As she moved her hands over me, I could also feel her buttoning buttons and snapping snaps, effectively making me decent, for all the good it would do.

"Oh, don't worry, he'll come for you when he can do some good. I'm not about to risk him and lose both of you. These things have to be timed just right, darling."

"He's asleep because of you?"

She shoved the bottle back to my lips, and I was surprised at just how thirsty I was. "Well, actually, he's asleep because of you. If he'd awakened when you left, he'd not have let you come alone. The boy has some strange sense of honor that's not always very practical."

"Then you came to rescue me?" I asked, pushing the water bottle aside.

"No, of course not." With her thumb, she wiped a dribble of water from my chin as though I were a sloppy child. "I came to make sure you weren't damaged too badly, to make sure that rat bastard doesn't hurt you beyond repair before it's time to do what we have to."

I felt the chill just behind my sternum deepen. "I'm the bait then, to distract Him while you and Michael get whatever it is that you're trying to steal."

This time the laugh was damn near a belly laugh. "Oh no, sweetie! You're not the bait at all. He is."

"What do you mean, he is? Who is?"

"The asshole who terrorizes this place. Who else?"

"What? Jesus! Are you serious? How the hell can He be the bait?"

"Shhh!" She placed a cool finger to my lips. "Afraid you'll

have to trust me on this one, sweetie. Now I have to go before he gets back. If he finds me here, that would spoil everything." She grabbed the bottle away from me, leaned in and kissed me on the cheek and I felt a waterfall of silky soft hair fall around my face as she did so. "Oh, and sweetie, best you don't tell the bastard I was here. Though I do enjoy watching a good temper tantrum, it's not in my best interest at the moment, and certainly not in yours."

As she turned to go, I heard the sound of soft footfalls and the whisper and swish of fabric against skin. I risked a peek. The shape of her in the darkness was golden and nearly blinding. I blinked hard and my light-starved eyes teared. I saw only her back as she opened the door to leave. Her hair was long and bright like living flames. She was light on her feet, like Michael's statue, just touching down from a heavenly flight, but I was as sure as I was of my own name that whoever she was, she was no angel.

It was only as she shut a heavy door behind her, only at the sound of stone scraping stone, at the sudden plunge into total darkness, that I realized where I was. I was in the crypt beneath Chapel House. I could panic. I could scream. I could thrash all I wanted, but no one would ever hear me. No one would ever know I was there.

Chapter Thirteen

Once the panic passed and I was sure I wasn't going to hyperventilate, pass out, or lapse into hysterics; once I'd stopped calling the bitch Michael worked for every name I could think of for not getting me the hell out of there, I crawled forward, as carefully as I could, one hand outstretched in front of me until I found the wall. Then I slowly followed it around, making my way toward where I hoped the door would be.

I don't know why I bothered. It wasn't like I could get out, and even if I could, it wasn't like I could just give Him the slip, was it? That was assuming I'd even have the willpower to try. In spite of feeling like I'd had one helluva beating, in spite of being scared witless, my whole body still buzzed with a desire for Him that hurt almost as badly as the burn above my breast.

Still, finding the door gave me something to do, something to think about other than the fact that I was trapped in a place created to inter the dead. Of course the estate agent had assured us that all of the sarcophagi had been removed along with any human remains, ages ago. All that had been left when Annie took possession was an empty space perfect for a wine cellar.

"Wine cellar, my arse." The sound of my disembodied voice in the thick dark was startlingly loud, so I kept the rest of my ruminations to myself as I felt my way along the bare rock, banging elbows and scraping knuckles.

I was exhausted by the time I found the even-edged crack between the wall of the crypt and the stone that had served as a door for who knew how many generations. I could have cried with relief as I inserted my fingers along the vertical axis and slid them up until I was certain what I'd found was indeed the door and not just some ancient crack in the stone wall. It was such a small victory, but any victory that was something to hang on to, that was something to keep the panic at bay, was a good one.

I tried to recall what I remembered about the crypt when Annie had taken me on the grand tour right after she bought Chapel House. We'd been so excited about her future home that while she speculated about the place's gruesome past, or at least the way she imagined it, I hadn't paid a huge amount of attention to detail, being, I'm ashamed to admit, more than a little creeped out by the place.

In truth, there hadn't been many details to pay attention to. There were no carvings, no sculptures, no grave goods of any kind, not even a stone vase for flowers. The walls were smooth stone without so much as catacomb-like niches for shrouded bodies. It wasn't all that interesting as far as inspiration for good horror stories went. That was probably a good thing, considering my present circumstances. But still, it was a crypt. There had been corpses, lots of corpses, over a long period of time. Best not think about that at the moment. Ghosts and ghouls I could do nothing about, but then again, I could do nothing about Him either, and what was He but a ghoul, albeit an outrageously sexy one.

As I recalled, the crypt was long and rectangular, narrowing at the back to a tunnel that was barely high enough for me to stand in hunched over. It was closed off at the narrowest end by a rusted iron gate that was heavily padlocked. Beyond the bars, I had no idea where the tunnel led, and neither did Annie. If there were any existing maps or drawings of the crypt, she'd not been able to find them in her research of the place. Perhaps it was some kind of sinister escape route, leading to a rendezvous point far beyond the churchyard walls, she speculated—possibly for pirates, thieves, murderers or even clandestine lovers.

That night over way too much wine and double chocolate fudge ice cream, safe in her flat, safe away from the creepiness of the crypt of Chapel House, I'd done some speculation of my own, my imagination running wild with a story about monks and nuns and scholars and bishops, frantic, not to escape through the tunnel in the crypt, but instead, desperate to keep something out. But just exactly what they were trying to keep out, my inebriated brain couldn't quite sort. Still, Annie listened wide-eyed and squealed with delight, goose bumps rising on her arms, as I told her how the most powerful bishops and brightest scholars alike all tried to block the entrance to the tunnel to keep out the evil beyond, and all died horrible deaths for their efforts, along with the poor monks and nuns who served Chapel House, and a fair few parishioners as well. All of this information, of course, was stricken from the records and kept secret, considered knowledge too dangerous for public consumption.

She asked me if it was the tunnel to hell. But by that time I was way too drunk and had way too much of a chocolate buzz to imagine just where that tunnel led, or why it had been closed off. I had all sorts of ideas swirling in my head, though, like I always did when I was inspired, and Chapel House had inspired me as much as it had creeped me out. In fact it probably inspired me exactly because it had creeped me out. And while I was interested in all of

Annie's plans for renovation, I admitted to her, as we laughed and giggled that night, that I kind of liked the place just the way it was. Though, I quickly added, I wouldn't want to live there.

As we both stumbled off to bed, I promised myself I'd write down all those intriguing ideas in the morning when I sobered up a bit, but I never did.

As I sat with my head pressed to the door of the crypt, my mind was suddenly flooded with memories of that night after Annie first brought me there. The place had been officially deconsecrated. Chapel House and its surrounds were no longer holy ground, and yet who can really say what that means?

That day while exploring the crypt, we had no sense of sacred or profane, no sense that we might be desecrating something, or that we might have treated anything with disrespect. In the evening we'd celebrated her closing on Chapel House and we made up stories. Mad, insane stories. It was the first time we'd ever done that, but it meant nothing really. We were drunk and we simply followed our imaginations into the dark and let them run wild while we hung out in the safety of her very posh flat.

But that night I had disturbing dreams. I didn't remember the details, but I woke shivering as though from a nightmare, body slick with sweat, expensive sheets tangled around me. And yet somewhere in the midst of my dreaming, I'd slid my fingers between my thighs, and I woke as desperate with need as I was desperate to escape the nightmare. I had lain there writhing, breathing hard, aching all over as though a lover had brought me to the brink and left me unfulfilled. All I could remember was that in the dream, I opened the door, and once I'd opened the door, I couldn't close it again, no matter how hard I tried.

But then the alarm went off and I was dragged, hung-over, dry mouthed and head pounding, into the waking world. The dream had faded by the time I'd propped myself against the shower wall until the hot water was all gone. When we'd poured enough coffee down our throats and popped enough paracetamol to take the edge off so we could hit the shops, I had totally forgotten it happened.

Honestly, the dream never entered my mind again until this moment. That wasn't like me at all. I kept a dream journal. I sometimes spent hours writing down every minute detail of the most troublesome and the most powerful dreams because I believed that they helped me understand myself. But on a more mercenary level, I also did it because my dreams were quite often the inspiration for my stories. Like so many writers, I found dreams and their wild array of symbols and improper behaviors to be a treasure trove of creativity. Occasionally I even borrowed other people's dreams if they were willing to share.

Before I knew what I was doing, I was bent over nearly double, one hand resting on the stone wall, the other stretched in front of me to guard against obstacles I couldn't see. I made my way into the tight space at the back of the crypt, heart pounding, stomach knotted, and cold sweat stinging my sightless eyes. What? Was I out of my mind? Christ, why couldn't I just leave well enough alone? But there was no goddamn *well enough*, was there? I was screwed and so was Annie if I couldn't figure out how to get us out of here and away from Him.

The space tightened still further. My thighs cramped. My knees ached, and I might have been more claustrophobic than I already was if I could have actually seen just how tight-fitting the tunnel was. I didn't remember it being so far to the end. But then we hadn't actually gone into the crawl space. Annie had just shone her Maglite down the narrow passage and the beam had glinted off the metal bars dissipating in the darkness beyond.

I was just contemplating whether to drop to a crawl and continue on, or to admit defeat and turn back when I suddenly felt the air change. The musty thickness of the crypt gave way to a metallic chill that reminded me of high altitudes where it never got warm, where the wind always blew. The thought had barely entered my mind before an icy breeze hit me in the face and, had the shock of it not given me pause, I would have surely fallen.

Cautiously I extended my foot and found nothing beneath it but emptiness. I yelped and jumped back, falling on my arse as the wind quite literally howled over me.

Once I'd stopped shaking and got the bounce of my pulse in my throat back under control, I lay down on my belly and extended my hands, blinking hard, light-starved eyes desperate to see something; anything. I inched my way forward until my arms and then my head and shoulders leaned out into emptiness. My skin prickled, and I fought back thoughts of demons or corpses reaching up from the pit to grab me and pull me down. There were times when a good imagination was not a plus. The wind stole my breath and whipped my hair like a flag around my face.

I was just about to crawl away and move back into the crypt, when the cold iron smell of altitude was overwhelmed by the scent of roses. This time, I felt strangely calm at His approach. I would hardly say that I was glad for His presence, but then it beat the hell out of the alternatives at the moment.

"What do you want?" I asked, my voice sounding unusually steady under the circumstances.

Chapter Fourteen

"What do you want?" I asked again, realizing that I didn't actually know for sure what he wanted from me—at least not other than the fact He wanted to fuck me. But there had to be more to the story than that, didn't there? Surely.

"I want you to come away from there before you hurt yourself, Susan. Please." The word "please" sounded like perhaps He wasn't used to using it, wasn't used to making polite requests. I felt a warm hand on my back. "You need to eat. Then you can have a bath, and we'll talk. I apologize for locking you up in this horrible place. I was angry. You were right. I behaved very poorly. Come. Please."

As I turned to make my way back I could see anemic daylight from the now open door of the crypt. "Don't try to escape." He spoke as though he'd read my mind. "You can't. And I don't want to hurt you again. I don't like doing that to you, darling, really I don't."

"I don't like it much either," I said, standing and stretching when the crypt opened out into a space high enough to do so.

I walked stiffly through the tangle of vine and ivy into the garden, somehow sensing that I was being guided, though not being forced. This time, He didn't take me past the sculpture of Michael. He took me round close to the aging brick of Chapel House and right to the open kitchen door. Inside, the smell of grilled meats and spices nearly overwhelmed me, and my mouth watered. I didn't know how long it had been since I'd eaten. I didn't know how long I'd been in Chapel House, but I was starving. There was doner kebab and pita bread and a pot of freshly brewed tea.

"Annie tells me you like kebab, and that you like your tea brewed strong. I hope it's all right."

"You did this?" I asked, stuffing a huge chunk of pita into my mouth and swallowing almost without chewing.

"I had her do it. She made the tea and ordered the kebab from the local shop, which delivers. A very useful service when sustenance is required, or so she tells me." He chuckled softly. "Obviously I'm not very adept in a world designed for the enfleshed."

"The enfleshed." I smiled in spite of myself. "That's what we are?"

"It is, yes. Awkward, but not without its elegance, flesh."

"And its shortcomings," I said, rubbing the knot on my elbow, which I had banged heartily on the wall flailing to keep from falling into the abyss in the crypt. "You said Annie prepared this." I looked around the room anxiously. "Where is she? There's plenty here for both of us."

"Oh, she's not hungry," came the reply. "She needs her rest." Then He added quickly, "Please don't worry about her, Susan. I'll keep her safe. I told you I take care of my own."

"Besides, she wants to kill me," I said, suddenly not so hungry.

"She's just very confused. She doesn't understand how it is with us," He said. "But she will with time."

In spite of the sudden loss of appetite, I made an effort to eat. I knew that I'd need all my strength if I were to have any chance of surviving this mess, and what was happening to Annie, her slow starvation, I'd be damned if I'd let that happen to me. "Do you have a name?" I asked around a mouthful of kebab.

"If you wish for me to have a name, then I shall have a name."

I took the teacup into my hand and sipped at the contents, holding it as much for warmth as anything else. "Are you saying that your name is mine to give?"

"I've observed that names matter a great deal to the enfleshed, and that they matter a great deal more to one such as you, my darling scribe. They've long made no difference to me. But even as you sit there I can see your struggle to define me, and I must admit, I find it very exciting, this… being defined by the woman I desire."

The muscles low in my belly tightened at His words, then relaxed, like butterflies taking flight. I squinted into the space across the breakfast bar from me, the space where I perceived Him to be. "Didn't Annie want to know your name? I mean, don't all lovers struggle to define each other, to understand the uniqueness of the person they desire?"

He chuckled softly. "You would think so, would you not? But most people are too self-absorbed to consider the name of another or how the other defines himself, except in how it pertains to them and their need to control that which they love."

"And Annie?"

"Oh, my darling Annie was not so interested in defining me as she was in my definition of her, in my ability to… make her feel more herself."

"By that you mean in your ability to make her come? I would think that would also have a great deal to do with her making you feel more yourself? Surely you can't tell me that was of no interest to you?"

"I am what I am," He replied. This time, I felt Him standing next to me. "I am no less driven by my nature than you are yours. Now come." I felt His hands on my shoulders, and in my mind's eye, I could almost make out the shape of His long graceful fingers, but surely it was only my imagination. "Come and have a bath," He said. "Oh, don't worry, I won't... attack you." There was bitterness in His voice that I felt in my own mouth as though it were my own. I shivered and quickly downed the rest of my tea in an effort to wash it away.

True to His word, not only did He not attack me, but He left me completely alone to bathe. In spite of the stress of the situation, I felt my shoulders relax in the warm waters of the bath as I lay back with my eyes closed. I gave up trying to plan my escape, at least for the moment, and my thoughts returned to the tunnel beyond the crypt, then to the dreams that I'd had the night after Annie first showed me Chapel House.

I was surprised to find that a great deal of that time was sketchy in my memory, and with a sudden flash of insight, I realized I'd never written anything about that day, not in my journal, not in my notebook, not anyplace. I hadn't spoken of it, dreamed of it or even thought of it until just now in the tunnel. A crypt, a deconsecrated church with a sketchy past, a great deal of drunken speculation on the story behind Chapel House, and yet I, a well established writer, who never let anything go unobserved or undocumented, had neither written about it nor thought about it, as though it had never even happened.

But I remembered now, as I sifted through my memories, that the tunnel had most definitely been barred shut and padlocked, and right about where I nearly fell into the abyss. I remembered it clearly now. I remember both of us making jokes about what was beyond the bars. I remember we did it until we scared ourselves, then we turned and left the crypt—not really running, but definitely not lingering, as though we feared perhaps those bars weren't quite as strong as they looked, and perhaps the padlock wasn't really locked.

I remember the feeling of my own flesh creeping as we laughed and joked about the release of demons from the pit of hell and about souls hungering for what He had called enfleshment, but Christ! It was just my imagination. That's what I did! I wrote stories. I spent at least as much time in my imagination as I did in the real world—maybe more.

It was Annie who had no imagination. But then she really didn't need it. Her life already was a story. All of the things she wanted, all of the things that happened to her could have been the plot for a cheap romance novel or an episode of *Eastenders* on steroids. She was the practical one, the one who made bags of money, which she spent on a luxurious lifestyle. She was the one who had no time for love; not real love anyway. Oh, she had lovers, all right. Men queued to be with Annie. But for her it was never more than a dalliance followed by a minor drama of a break-up. There'd be a few tears shed, followed by some laughs with her girlfriends over too much wine, and then on to the next one.

I was the one who would have happily lived in a cardboard box as long as I had something to write on. As for love, well, my passion, the love of my heart, had always been the telling of stories. That kept me way too tunnel-visioned and in love with my own creations to notice even if a bloke did pay attention to me.

And why the hell was I thinking about all this now? Was it fear of losing my friend? Fear of facing my own mortality? I was surprised to find that the lust, which had not left me since my first night in Chapel House, had eased back to a gentle buzz low between my hipbones, and my mind was suddenly clear.

I stepped out of the tub and dried myself, still thinking about the events of that night, which seemed like an eternity ago now. It was then I realized that He had left me unsupervised. I could have left. My car was just outside. My bag was on the floor by the sink. I suppose He'd had Annie get it. Christ, He used her like a zombie. But then at the moment she wasn't much more, was she? With a shiver, I recalled how He had moved me to where He wanted me to go as though I were a puppet on a string. Still, He would have let me walk away just now. I knew He would have. I don't know how I knew, but I did. He'd left me alone on purpose—to see what I would do. So why was I standing stone still and naked, staring at myself in the mirror? Why wasn't I already long gone?

I moved closer to my own reflection, studying Michael's bite on my breast, darkened now to shades of midnight blue and purple.

There was no evidence of the burn from His touch, no evidence of anything other than a healing love bite. Why was I still here? Did I still think I could save Annie? Oh, I wouldn't leave without her, I knew that. I also knew that it was entirely possible neither of us would leave at all. I knew as well that sometimes you just needed to run away, to fight another day, and yet I hadn't, had I?

This time when He approached me, there was no scent of roses, but the scent of a man, a man aroused, but in control. A man who had not come with only sex in mind, a man who had come to court me. An obsolete term, perhaps, but it seemed to fit under the circumstances. My nostrils flared to breathe Him in, and my flesh tingled at the thought of all a person could learn from the smell of a man in his prime. And yet, this was not a man standing next to me. I dared not forget that, no matter what my senses told me.

"You stayed," He said, and I felt his fingers caress my shoulder. I didn't flinch, but closed my eyes and leaned back against warm flesh, flesh that was not really there. My senses traced the rise and fall and shape of Him, and I liked what I felt. It took me a moment to catch my breath, and even though I expected Him to, He made no attempt to do more than touch my shoulder.

"I have… questions," I said, my mind unable to ignore the fact of Him, the fact that He was as naked as I was, and it was not difficult to tell, He was well and truly ready to make love to me if I asked. And if I asked, He would show me what the gods kept secret from all humanity except for their human lovers, and I would never be the same again. Quite possibly, I wouldn't even survive it. All I had to do was ask. He wouldn't deny me.

But He made no further move at seduction. He stood still while I leaned against him, supporting my weight, but little more. "Of course." His voice was warm and humid against my neck. "Anything I am able to tell you I will."

"In the crypt, in the back, the tunnel?"

"Yes?"

"There were bars and there was a padlock, a big one."

"There were, yes. But they're gone now." He cupped my breast, and this time His touch didn't burn when He stroked my nipple with His thumb.

"What happened to them?" I arched against him, like a cat being stroked. "Did Annie have them removed?"

"Why no, my darling little scribe. Don't you remember? You took them out. You removed them in order to set me free."

Chapter Fifteen

"Susan? Are you all right? You're shivering and I don't want you to catch a chill."

When I came back to myself I still stood naked in front of the mirror. But He was right, I was shivering.

"Darling, you're frightening me. Please, go to the bed Annie has made up for you. Get beneath the duvet and make yourself warm."

I did as He asked without thinking, though it was fully of my own volition. He wasn't compelling me in any way I could tell, but the next thing I knew, I was curled in a fetal position on the mattress on the floor, the duvet pulled up to my chin, and still I shivered, as I struggled to get my mind round what He'd just said.

He sat next to me. I could feel the weight of Him on the mattress, and I knew He watched me. "Shall I rouse Annie to make you more tea? Perhaps that would help."

"No. Let her rest." I couldn't bear the thought of seeing her the way she was now, and I really wasn't up to another knife confrontation with my friend. Until I had some plan of action to help her, to get her out of there, it was best to let her sleep.

He made no reply, but lay down next to me and in a moment, I felt His body naked against mine. "Please don't," I whispered.

"I only wish to warm you, my darling. I promise I won't take you until you are ready for me."

How there could be body heat when there was no flesh to generate it, I didn't know. But there was, and I couldn't help snuggling back against Him, doing my best to ignore that He was ready for me, whether I was ready for Him or not. It hit me then, that He was exerting control over Himself by not trying to control me. Whatever lust I had for Him was no more than I would have felt for any well-endowed man who lay next to me when I was under such stress. I knew He could easily change that. I knew He could make me want Him to the detriment of anything else that could possibly matter.

I reminded myself that He hadn't said *if* I was ready for Him, but *when*. I needed, above all else, to remember that. His strategy was to replace Annie with me, and He didn't necessarily have to force the issue to make that happen. All of those things were in my mind, but the fact that I might have been the one to release a monster into the world just happened to take center stage in my brain, at least for the moment.

"What you said. That can't possibly be," I managed between chattering teeth. "How could I have removed the gate and the padlock? I mean I couldn't have. It isn't possible. I had no key. I couldn't have even found my way back to the crypt through that tangle of a garden without Annie's help, and besides, I… I didn't know you were there. How could I have known you were there?"

He smoothed the hair away from my temple and kissed me in the spot where my pulse thundered. "Of course you solicited Annie's help, my darling. She helped you find your way back, but only you could open the gate. Only you could set me free."

"I didn't know you were there," I repeated, my words sounding more like a plea.

"Of course you did, my little scribe. You sensed me there in the darkness, waiting for you, longing for you, and your words breathed hope into me. Don't you remember your dreams?"

"I… vaguely. But I was drunk and I was only telling stories. Often what I'm writing about or thinking about invades my dream world. I don't remember you, though, and I don't remember releasing you."

"Don't you?" His hand moved down then to cup my breast, and the press of His penis became more urgent against my bottom. "You convinced Annie to help us. Ultimately I could see that your plan was for her to get us together in the end, you and me."

"No! That was not my plan! There was no plan. It was only a dream, and I would never use my friend that way. Ever!"

He only kissed my shoulder and spoke quietly, as though He were telling me a story. "Of course it was your plan. Annie would be mine. She would stay with me, satisfy me until you could come to me, until you could be mine. That was always our plan, my darling. I always knew that in my heart of hearts." I felt him shrug. "A figure of speech, of course. I have no actual heart."

"Oh Christ," I whispered, fighting back panic. Had I not awakened in both terror and arousal? Hadn't my last thoughts in the dream world and my first in the waking been that I had opened a door I could not close again?

"This is insane! It was just a dream." With all the force I could muster, I shoved my way up off the mattress and fled to the bathroom, snatching up my clothes on the way, still on the floor where I'd dropped them. "It was just a fucking dream!" I shouted, sensing His presence behind me as I scrambled into my jeans. "I'm not crazy. I know a dream when I have one."

"The dreams of a scribe carry more weight than those of an ordinary mortal, Susan. Do you not know this? Has no one told you? I would have certainly thought Michael would have said something. After all, that's what the bitch who owns him wants."

"What the hell's that supposed to mean? Why would Michael care? He has nothing to do with it. I write stories! People pay me for them," I said, buttoning my shirt over my braless breasts before shoving the bra into my bag. "That's what I do. I don't live out my dreams! I don't open doors into strange abysses, and I didn't release a—"

Before I knew what was happening, He was on me, forcing me back against the sink. The mark on my breast suddenly burned like fire that spread down my torso, and I screamed at the press of Him, still naked, still aroused and all hard invisible muscle that bore down on me like a suffocating weight.

"What, Susan? You didn't release a monster, is that what you were about to say? Do you think that you wouldn't? Do you think that you couldn't? Are you so naïve as to believe that what's inside your head, what you put on the written page is any less monstrous, any less dangerous?"

"What else are you but a monster?" I shouted. "Hurting me like this, hurting poor Annie who did nothing to deserve it! Nothing! If I'm the one to blame, leave her alone, let her go and—"

I swallowed back my words in a yelp as the floor tilted beneath my feet and the air around me crackled with static and ozone, and my head felt full and tight as though I were suddenly on a train passing through a tunnel at high speed. In my confusion, it took me a second to realize the roar that I thought was a sudden clap of thunder was the sound of His anger, followed by my scream as I found myself flying through the air and landing with a thud on the stone floor.

A sharp shockwave raced down my spine and pinwheels of color exploded behind my eyes. For a split second I thought He'd broken my neck, but that was secondary to getting the breath back that He'd knocked out of me. Then, in an instant, the room righted itself and He was gone.

I heard Annie scream as he vanished.

I stumbled to my feet, still barely dressed, lost my footing in a wave of dizziness, and came down hard on one knee, yelling my friend's name as I shoved through the door and down the hall. "Annie! Hold on, I'm coming. Hold—"

Then the kitchen door burst open, and the breath that I'd only just recovered was knocked out of me again as Michael scooped me up, threw me over his shoulder and was nearly to the gate before I could do more than gasp. "Annie! Annie! I can't leave her!" I cried as he shoved me into the passenger seat of my own car.

"Maggie's got her! It's all right! Maggie's got her and they're headed for—"

I accidentally elbowed him in the chest. "Who the hell is Maggie?"

He sputtered and gulped air. "Fuck! How many goddamn times are we gonna have to do the great escape routine? Maggie's the woman I work for, damn it!" Then he slammed the door shut,

cursing as he hopped into the driver's seat and shoved the key home.
I don't know how the hell he got it, and I didn't ask as we pulled
away from Chapel House like we were being chased by all the
demons from Hell, and God knew one of them was fucking bad
enough!

I stiff-legged the floorboard and shoved both hands against
the dashboard with a sense of déjà vu I neither wanted nor
appreciated. Then, when we'd put a good few blocks between us and
that horrible place, I turned on Michael. "He said I set Him free! He
said I'm the one who let Him loose on the world, let Him loose to do
this to Annie. He fucking said you knew!"

Michael cursed under his breath, the tension in his body
evident in his suicide grip on the steering wheel. "I'm sorry, Susan. I
was going to tell you. I said all the time we should tell you right up
front so there'd be no surprises, so you'd know what you were up
against, but Maggie said not to, Maggie said to wait. She said she
had a plan. Some fucking plan!" He ranted, cursing the firstborn this
Maggie would supposedly never have and wishing every plague and
pestilence he could think of upon her—some I'd never heard of.

I didn't hear anything after that except for the beating of
wings against my ears and the desperate draw of breath into my
lungs. It was true. I released Him. How the hell could it be true?

"Susan?" It was the sound of my own name that made me
realize the rant was over and Michael was addressing me. "Did you
hear me? I'll explain everything once we've reached the rendezvous
point. Well, Maggie can explain better than I can, but we need to
make sure you're safe first."

I forced a laugh that was decidedly on the hysterical side, and I really didn't give a fuck. "Safe? How the hell can you even use that word when He's out there? And why the hell do you think I'll actually believe you when you lied to me? You fucking lied to me!" I punched him hard in the arm.

He responded by trapping my hand against his body, driving with one hand on the wheel and the other holding my wrist away from him, but at such an angle that my arm twisted, making any movement uncomfortable. That done, he let me have my rant, the fucker barely breathing hard as I called him every name I could think of, and then threatened him with some seriously creative bodily damage, none of which he seemed concerned about even for one second.

At last he spoke. "Are you finished? Because I need my arm back. A safe driver keeps both hands on the wheel."

"Safe driving is the least of my concerns at the moment, Michael, and believe me," I growled, "we're not anywhere near finished, and I have no intention of dying before I kick you seriously in the balls a few times."

"Fair enough," he said, then released me.

"Where are we going?" I asked once my temper had cooled enough to remind me that I was scared shitless, exhausted and physically damaged, and if I were going to survive whatever happened next, I would need Michael's help, whether I liked the plan of action or not.

"There's a place in Cumbria, up in the fells. Friend of Maggie owns it. No one will find us there."

"And Annie? She's in really bad shape, and she… she's not in her right mind." I swallowed hard, thinking that my friend had tried to kill me, then delivered me right into the mouth of the dragon. But that was forgivable under the circumstances. What was unforgivable was the fact that it seemed to have been my actions that put her at risk in the first place.

"She's in good hands, I promise." He patted my arm gently. "Maggie will know what to do, and at the moment, we need her safe and out of the equation so he can't use her against you."

We turned off the M6 onto the A66 heading toward Keswick with Michael questioning me about what had happened. When I told him of his boss' visit to the crypt, he unleashed some seriously colorful language and slammed his hand against the steering wheel hard enough to rattle the whole car. "Damn her! We had you safe. We had you away from him, away from Chapel House. If I'd been awake, I would have known you were walking into a trap. I would have stopped you. We'd have all been safely away by now."

I gave him a sideways glance. "And what about Annie?"

The muscles along his jaw clenched tight and his shoulders stiffened. "We got her out, didn't we?"

"But that wasn't part of the plan, was it?"

"I don't know what the hell the plan is," he snapped. "Clearly Maggie's keeping me as much in the dark as she is you. We'll have… words, when I see her."

Before I could respond with some things I'd rather have with this Maggie bitch that were much more physical than words, Michael continued. "You need to sleep now. Alonso… well, Alonso is a bit neurotic, though I understand that's pretty typical of his kind. He doesn't like people to know where he lives. Took a page from Maggie's book where that's concerned. Anyway, I'll put you to sleep, and when you wake up, we'll be there."

"Magic? You'll magic me to sleep?"

He shrugged, and I thought I saw a blush crawling up his neck. "I suppose you could call it that. Don't worry, it's harmless, but useful at times."

God! Only three days ago, I didn't believe in magic or angels or monsters. Shows what the hell I knew. I was about to ask who Alonso was, but I was already asleep.

When I woke up, the car had stopped. It was dark outside and some unknown man was carrying me like a child.

"I'm not keen on Magda using High View for her little capers," the man was saying, his voice a purr of a vibration deep in his chest. I shivered and snuggled close for warmth, but felt none.

"I'm not too keen on it either, Alonso. I'd much rather be in my own place where I can pull up the drawbridge, but looks like you drew the short straw this time around."

I was about to ask what was going on—not that I expected anyone to give me a straight answer—but I fell back to sleep in this Alonso's arms before I could manage more than a moan.

Chapter Sixteen

It was deep night when I woke up with my heart hammering in my chest. I was groggy, disoriented and completely naked. It took me a few seconds to convince myself that I was no longer in the crypt at Chapel House. Then I recalled the events of the past—what was it anyway, twelve hours? Twenty-four? Maybe more.

I remembered Michael quite literally carrying me away from Chapel House. I remembered Annie's screams, and I remembered waking up in the arms of some man named Alonso, who clearly wasn't happy at having unexpected guests in the middle of the night… or at least I thought it had been night. Nothing was very clear to me at the moment. The past few days were an insane blur that I still hoped against hope to wake up from and find it had all been just a bad dream.

Once my eyes had adjusted to the ambient light, the room was far from dark. The heavily carved wooden bed I was in looked ancient and battered. Next to the bed a trunk, no less battered, served as a bedside table, with a bare-bulbed lamp on top, cord disappearing over the edge into the dark. The other furnishings in the room looked to be a double-doored wardrobe and more trunks, lots more trunks, and wooden crates. Clearly the room had been thrown together in a hurry to accommodate me, though as I turned onto my side it was easy to feel that the sheets and bedding were not only clean, but of the highest quality, possibly even brand new. The bed faced a large curtain-less window, which opened to the night, to the light coming from the waning moon and the star-filled sky.

Without turning on the lamp, I stood and moved to the

window, nearly tripping over my bag, which I had no memory of Michael grabbing before sweeping me away, but then I had not much memory of anything but fear and lust and anger. There was quite a bit of anger thrown into the pot when I found out Michael had kept the truth from me. The thing was, I had no memory of the truth myself. Could everyone be lying to me? None of it made sense.

How could I have ever released a demon spirit from His prison beneath the crypt of Chapel House and set Him loose on my friend with the plan of returning to claim Him as my lover? I was a lot of things—and like most writers, I had a fair-sized streak of self-absorption—but I wasn't vicious or cruel, and I considered myself a fairly decent human being in spite of all my neuroses and foibles. Of the two of us, Annie had always been far more self-absorbed, and I figured that was a part of her gift, a part of what made her as successful as she was. Not that I wasn't successful, but my idea of success was quite different from hers.

As I moved toward the window, I had an overwhelming need to breathe fresh air and was surprised to find that though the glass in the window itself seemed ancient, it opened with very little effort on my part. The air was that of high places, bracing and sweet, cold enough to raise chill bumps across my bare arms, and delicious enough that I was reluctant to shut out the freshness.

After inhaling several lungfuls of the intoxicating fell air and gazing up at more stars than I had any idea could be in a night sky, I made a more coherent effort to take in my surroundings. The slate floors were covered with a path of what looked to be very old Turkish carpets that ran from the bed to the window, in front of the wardrobe, and then to a door across the room, behind which I discovered a well-equipped bathroom—far more modern and luxurious than the rest of the room.

I splashed my face with cold water, ignoring the urge to have a wallow in a very large claw-footed tub. From somewhere in the house, I heard the sound of voices, or thought I did anyway. I found my clothes neatly folded on a large trunk at the foot of the bed and slipped into them, now shivering from the cold breeze coming in the window I was not yet willing to shut. If someone was up in the house, perhaps they could answer some of my questions. Would Michael be here? What about this Maggie woman? Oh, I had a thing or two I wanted to say to her all right, don't think I didn't!

I pushed open the door that looked new and unvarnished and, on tiptoes, made my way down a long hall, my feet silent on the slate floor. The place was not unlike the crypt at Chapel House; the walls were bare stone and the windows along one side were deep, as though they belonged in some medieval castle, and certainly the view out the window in my bedroom had done little to diminish that notion.

I half expected the staircase to be narrow and winding down the inside of a tower, but I didn't make it to the stairs, wherever they were. Just down the hall next to my room, a set of open French doors led into a darkened study. There was an open set of identical doors across the room, which led out onto a balcony. It was from there I heard voices carrying on the night air from down below. I couldn't make out the conversation, but I did make out my name, so I eased my way across the room and out onto the balcony. Below, I could see a narrowly terraced garden above a beck running steeply down the hunched back of the fell.

In the garden on a stone bench sat two men in quiet conversation. Neither of them was Michael, but I recognized the darker of the two as Alonso. He sat with his arm around the shoulder of the other. The tone of their speech was soft and conversational, and I leaned forward over the stone railing, holding my breath to hear something, anything that might give me a clue as to what was going on and where I was.

Alonso was speaking to his companion, who offered a soft laugh at whatever the man had said. It was as Alonso slid his hand down the man's back to rest low on his hip and drew him close that I realized what I was watching, what I was listening to, had become intimate and no longer had anything to do with me. Just as I was about to retreat into the study and go back to my room, Alonso pivoted on the bench and looked up at me.

I swallowed back a yelp and stumbled away from the railing. Not terribly subtle, but it was dark, and I'd managed neither to fall nor cry out. I certainly had done nothing wrong. The doors to the study had been open and inviting. If Alonso had not wanted me there, all he would have had to do was close the door. But then again, supposedly I was notorious for opening doors not meant to be opened.

I was halfway across the study when Alonso's large form suddenly blocked the door in front of me. This time I did yelp.

His full lips twisted in a wicked smile, then he offered me a very formal bow. "Alonso Darlington at your service, Madame." The man was not quite as big as Michael—nearly as tall, but of a more slender build. Still, he gave the illusion that he was much larger than even the angel. "I'm sorry for startling you, Ms. Innes. I forget sometimes to make noise when I approach. I have startled Reese terribly more times than I care to admit. Though the other members of my staff and my colleagues are used to my… unusual ways, for Reese's sake, I truly am trying."

It wasn't so much his silence as it was his speed that startled me. No human could have moved from the garden below so quickly. "Reese is the one you were with?" I asked, steadying myself on the edge of a large antique desk that dominated the room, willing my pulse to slow to a gallop. If this Alonso wasn't human, the last thing I wanted was to anger him by saying the wrong thing.

"The one you saw me with." His face lit up with a smile that I knew full well was reserved for thoughts of one's lover. "Yes, that's Reese."

"I… I'm sorry. I didn't mean to intrude."

"Your intrusion, my dear, is hardly your fault. And I do apologize for the state of the room you have been forced to endure. High View is being renovated at the moment, after a very long period of being uninhabited, and we are in a shambles. And of course, I'm deeply sorry for my less than cordial welcome."

"You don't like Maggie, whoever the hell she is. I got that. Frankly, I don't like her very much either, so no need to apologize."

"It isn't so much that I don't like her. I have a great deal of respect for the woman, and in truth, I owe her much." He moved to stand next to me, and I sensed him studying me, but looking into his eyes made me feel ever so slightly off balance, so I looked away, taking in the surroundings of what was not a study at all, but a lovely library that would have fit right into any stately home I'd ever toured. The kind of library within which I could have happily taken up residence in and never left. "It's just that whenever Magda Gardener shows up, things get more complicated than I'd like them to be, and I try very hard to keep things simple and to not draw attention to myself. It was she, by the way, who suggested I leave the library open for you to explore. She seemed to think you would take pleasure in it."

Then, as if he anticipated my next question, he added, "Your friend is sleeping peacefully. Magda and your angel are with her at the moment."

"He's not my angel," I snapped.

Alonso offered a low, throaty chuckle. "Oh, I think that he is, my dear." Before I could protest, he pulled an iPhone from the pocket of his black jeans, punched in a number and waited for a second, then I heard a woman answer.

He offered me a quick, reassuring smile that was nearly as hypnotic as my first glance into his eyes. "Talia, darling, if you're finished, our guest is awake and we have need of you in the library." He returned the phone to his pocket and motioned me to the leather sofa in front of his desk.

I happily obliged, my legs still feeling none too steady.

"You must be hungry. I've had Cook prepare something for you, figuring that the monstrosity who held you prisoner would have had little forethought for your creature comforts." Then he added,

"No doubt your angel has encouraged you to eat. Food is always essential in the presence of magic or one can find oneself in serious trouble."

I didn't tell Alonso that the monstrosity he referred to had, indeed, seen to my creature comforts, though I had no idea how long ago it had been. It bothered me that I found myself wanting to defend Him.

Alonso sat on the edge of the desk and crossed his legs at the ankles. I noticed he wore scuffed hiking boots, but then that was to be expected in the fells. "You say you have no memory of releasing this… entity into the world?"

"I have… sketchy recollections of dreams I had that night, the night it must have happened, but honestly, I don't know how I could have done such a thing. I couldn't even find my way around the shambles of a garden at Chapel House, and I had no idea where the key was to the place where He was apparently kept prisoner. I seriously doubt if Annie did either."

"He… yes, well, it would have been easy enough for Him to guide you and for Him to give you the location of the key if a physical key were necessary. I'm inclined, however, to believe that the key was magical, and you, being a scribe, would indeed have the imagination to figure out what was needed to release… Him."

"But why would I do that? Why?" I asked.

Almost before I knew he had moved, Alonso sat next to me and took my hand into his, which was large, slightly calloused and cold. My first urge at the rush of current up through my arm and straight to my heart was to pull away, but his grip was firm, and I was afraid to move, feeling like a rabbit in the headlights. Then he spoke, and I found myself relaxing into the hypnotic lilt of his voice, with its slightly strange accent and its deep-chested baritone. "For the love of your craft, Ms. Innes, for the love of your craft. That certainly is reason enough. Surely you know that by now."

He stroked the back of my hand with his thumb, and I found myself calming still further. "Were you not inspired by the crypt at Chapel House, by the tangle of the garden, by the fact that it was once holy ground? I'm certainly no writer, and yet such places stimulate my imagination. Do you not think that such an entity as the one you've released would have recognized your urge to tell a story, your imagination so stimulated, and taken advantage if it were at all possible?"

Then he leaned close, holding my gaze, and I felt as though I were falling. "Does not the Bible itself say that *the word became flesh and dwelt among us, that the word is living and active and sharper than any double-edged sword*? Words hold power, my dear woman, power that nothing else in the history of human culture, nothing else in the history of our human nature, holds. The storytellers of old were revered. They sat in the presence of kings and queens as their equals."

With a sweeping gesture, he took in the bookshelves that rose from floor to ceiling all around us. "Some of the words in this room were written thousands of years ago. Those who penned them have long ago turned to dust, and yet we read their words, their stories, and we're transported, at times transformed, by the minds of men and women long dead. Surely you don't think that an entity who has existed as long as the one connected to Chapel House would not know this, would not seize the opportunity to take advantage of the magic of the mind of a scribe and the stories she can create?"

"But it was never my intention. I didn't mean to. I only… We were drunk, excited about Annie's new home. We were celebrating, telling stories. I… I always tell stories."

Alonso smoothed the hair away from my face and held my gaze. "You underestimate the power of your magic. I understand, my darling. You're not the first scribe to have done so, nor are you the first to have paid a high price for such a mistake. You're among the greats in that."

He glanced around the room at the myriad books, and then offered me a reassuring smile. "Never mind. First you must eat, and then we shall see what we can do to aid your memory."

Almost as if by magic, a man dressed in full livery arrived with a silver tray and sat it on a table near the window. Alonso took my hand and guided me to sit in front of eggs, toast and porridge, all washed down by rich, dark, French roast coffee. He watched me eat silently, making no effort to join me. But then it was the middle of the night.

I had just finished the last of the toast with homemade raspberry jam when a tall woman in a form-fitting turquoise dress knocked softly on the open door and let herself in. I couldn't take my eyes off of her. She was—well, for lack of a better word, she was stunning. She had dark, thick hair, startling blue eyes, and she had that way about her that made more ordinary people, myself included, want to be close to her so that they could look at her, just constantly look at her, because surely this kind of strange beauty couldn't be real. Then I was reminded of Alonso's sudden movement, of his all but admitting he wasn't human, and I suddenly wasn't so sure about the woman either.

Alonso stood and embraced her, kissing her on the cheek. The two mumbled softly for a few seconds, glancing occasionally over their shoulders at me. Then he took her hand and led her forward. "Ms. Innes, I'd like you to meet Talia. She's a colleague and a dear friend of mine. She knows your problem, and recovering lost memories and understanding people's dreams is her specialty." He shrugged. "Well, one of them, anyway."

The woman studied me for a second, then smiled and nodded her greeting. I seemed incapable of doing anything more than smiling and nodding back.

"Now that introductions have been made," I forced my gaze away from her and back to Alonso, "if you've had enough to eat, my dear Ms. Innes, and you're ready, Talia is going to sleep with you."

Chapter Seventeen

"What?" I came out of the chair, nearly upsetting my coffee cup onto the white linen tablecloth the servant had spread. "Talia's going to sleep with me? Are you crazy?" I could imagine Annie getting a good laugh out of this, elbowing me in the ribs, saying if I wasn't up for the task she'd be happy to oblige.

"Oh, it's nothing sexual," Alonso reassured me, gently patting my arm.

"Well," the woman said with a modest shrug and a dip of her blue eyes that said she was checking me out. "It could be, if you want it to be."

Before I could totally panic, Alonso slipped an arm around my shoulder and glared at this Talia person. "You'll have to forgive my colleague, Ms. Innes. She has a very strange sense of humor. I promise, she'll do nothing you don't invite."

I didn't miss the threat in his voice, clearly aimed at the woman. Then he turned his full attention on me. "And I would suggest that what you do invite be nothing more than the sharing of dreams, considering that your... love life, as it were, is already somewhat complicated. You don't need to add another complication to the menu."

"To the menu." The woman chuckled wickedly. "Oh, I like that turn of phrase, darling. Perhaps you should have been a scribe yourself." She spoke to Alonso, but her gaze was locked on me. "She does look practically edible, don't you think? Though I'm guessing you're probably well-sated after feasting on Reese."

Alonso growled at her. He actually growled and, I think—

yes, I'm certain, he bared his teeth! My skin prickled and the fine hairs on the back of my neck rose. For a moment, I swear the man seemed more animal than human and, between him and the woman, who eyed me like I was dinner, I felt like I had been set loose in the primordial woods with the wild beasts.

"What's going on here?"

I started at the sound of another woman's voice, one I'd heard in the dark of the crypt, and turned to see Maggie, with Michael right behind her.

If I hadn't been wrong-footed and frightened already, I certainly was now. Alonso and Talia might have been scary beasts in the woods, but Maggie was the huntress everyone feared, myself included. Even Talia was instantly subdued by her presence. In the midst of raised hackles, Michael came to my side and slipped a possessive arm around me, literally pulling me away from Alonso, just as a ginger-haired man in jeans and a plaid shirt entered the room.

"Is everything all right?" he asked.

Talia offered half a smile. "Of course it's not, Reese. Come on in. You might as well join the fun." She gave Maggie a sideways glance and stepped up to flank Alonso on one side while Reese came to his other.

For a moment the room was deathly silent. Only Maggie stood alone, nearly blinding in her golden brilliance, and I couldn't keep from wondering how someone so stunning could be so terrifying, and why. Even Talia paled in comparison—especially on my fright-meter.

The minute her gaze turned on me, even from behind the strange dark glasses she wore, I felt a tingle bone-deep, as though I had just passed beneath a high-tension wire and a million volts was just a heartbeat away.

"How's Annie?" Christ in heaven, I don't know how I found my voice in front of her. Maybe because I was still pissed off that she'd left me in the crypt at Chapel House. But she had rescued my friend, something I'd made a thorough cock-up of. I owed her hugely for that.

"I've done what I can for her." Her voice was like honey dripping over hot flame. "She's resting comfortably." She moved forward, gaze still locked on me, until she stood close enough I could feel her breath on my face, cool and sweet like the fell air. I was sure she could see how my pulse raced in my throat at her nearness. "Right now I need to know what you did to release the Chapel House Guardian, so I can learn how to return him to his prison. He was there for a reason, you know. Though I imagine you've figured that out by now."

She gave me no time to defend myself and, if what everyone said was true, I had no defense anyway. "Since you have no memory of the momentous occasion, I need you to sleep with the succubus."

"Succubus? She's a succubus?" I nodded to Talia, who only shrugged modestly. "You've got to be kidding me! I have a demon trying to seduce me, an angel who's marked me, and by the way, Michael, that mark—it hurts like a sonovabitch when the demon gets mad, and now you want me to sleep with a succubus? Honestly, I don't see how the hell—"

"Oh for fuck's sake," Talia broke in, "stop being such a drama queen. Do you really think I want to incur Magda's wrath?" She gave the woman a quick nod of her head. "If you want sex, you won't get it from me. I'll just tiptoe through your little dreamscape all nice and polite-like, and prod a memory here and there as needed. You won't even know I'm there. Your loss," she added with a wicked grin.

"I'll stay with you," Michael said, giving Talia the look he might reserve for a rabid wolf.

She cursed under her breath. "Anyone else want to join in? Why don't we just make an orgy of it? Oh, I forgot—no sex."

"Shut up, Talia," Alonso said. "We've already discussed this."

Embarrassed by Talia's bluntness and by my ridiculous whining when my friend's life was in danger, I squared my shoulders and found my voice, cowardly though it was. "What do I have to do?" I asked, hoping my trembling wasn't as obvious as it felt to me. I was pretty sure it was only Michael's support that was holding me upright at that moment.

"You just have to go to sleep and dream," Talia said.

"The juice," Alonso spoke, nodding to the empty orange juice glass on the breakfast table. "It contained some herbs that will make you drowsy very shortly. You'll sleep in Talia's arms." He nodded toward the door. "You should probably return to your room shortly, unless you want Michael to carry you."

"When were you going to tell me about this juice, about being drugged?"

"I just did," Alonso replied. "Besides, as Magda has said, we really have little choice if we want to put this monster back where he belongs and save your friend's life."

Magda lifted my chin on the curl of her fingers and, I swear, if Michael hadn't been holding me, I would have fallen through the floor. Even through her glasses, there was something about being the center of her attention that made me feel like I was being unraveled one molecule at a time. But when she spoke, the situation became very tightly focused indeed. "Susan, if I can't sever Annie's link with the Guardian, she will die. She's been under his thrall too long. You're the key, like it or not, and if you're not willing to do whatever it takes, then it's best you put a bullet in your friend's brain right now, because her death will neither be easy nor quick. Do you understand me?"

There were no more jokes, no more snipes. The room was silent as a grave as I stepped away from Michael. "All right." I glanced at Talia, who nodded in return and stepped forward. "If it's all the same to everyone, I'd like to make it back to my room under my own power." I was beginning to feel like my tongue belonged to someone else, and the floor seemed a long way from my feet. With Michael on one side and the succubus on the other, I carefully maneuvered my way back down the hall. It was only as Michael kissed me possessively and tucked me beneath the duvet that I noticed Magda perched on the edge of a sailor's trunk in the corner near the bathroom.

"Are you the audience?" I slurred.

"Afraid so, darling. Traditionally the dreamer and her dream walker are witnessed by a third party who doesn't sleep and remains uninvolved in events so she can awaken the dreamers if… there are problems."

"Are you expecting problems?" I looked from Talia to Magda and back again, to find Talia was stripping out of her clothes. For a second that thought disturbed me, but I was way past holding a thought in my head for very long.

"Possibly," came the reply that disturbed me way more than the naked succubus now sliding down under the duvet by my side. Whoever this Magda was, she pulled no punches and made no effort to soften the blows. Clearly the woman didn't have to make nicey-nice.

Michael leaned down and kissed me again. "I'd wish you pleasant dreams, but under the circumstances…" He shot Talia a warning glance, then settled near the foot of the bed on a battered captain's chair that creaked under his weight.

My last memory of the waking world was Talia pulling me into her arms and kissing me as though she were pulling the breath from me, pulling me under, into the world of sleep. Just before I lost consciousness, I wanted nothing more than for Talia to keep on kissing me.

It was a cry of terror that awakened me from a mundane dream of sitting at the big desk in the study of Annie's old flat, tapping away on the keyboard of my Mac. After all the dreams I'd had, or thought I'd had recently, after the way dreams had bled so convincingly into reality, I was totally prepared to be the one screaming like a banshee and making a fool of myself. I was completely unprepared to find that it was Talia doing the screaming.

I shoved my way from under the duvet and fell on my arse in the middle of the floor amid blinding light, confusion, shattering glass and screams. Michael helped me to my feet, and eased me back onto the bed. By the time my eyes adjusted to the light, I discovered Alonso sitting in the middle of the floor with Talia in his arms. She was wrapped in a blanket, sobbing and trembling against his shoulder. Magda knelt next to her and Reese stood behind them, shoving aside pieces of the shattered mirror from one of the wardrobe doors with the toe of his hiking boot.

When Magda saw that I was awake, she moved to my side, motioning Michael away from me. "Are you all right?" She lifted both of my eyelids in turn, staring into each like she was an optometrist.

I shrugged her away. "I'm fine. What happened?" I nodded to Talia.

"The succubus claims the Guardian's inside you, that he confronted her in your dreams. Was he there?"

"Christ, Maggie, you're as subtle as a heart attack," Michael spat. "Do you even know what tact is?"

She shot him a warning glance, and he shut up. "Clearly you weren't seeing the same things she saw. Were you dreaming?"

Suddenly all eyes were on me.

"I was, yes. But it was nothing important, certainly nothing about Him." I shuddered at the thought of the dream visits I'd had from Him. No, if he'd been there I'd have known.

"I know what I saw," Talia said, looking at me as though I had two heads.

"Susan, perhaps you should tell us what you remember," Magda suggested.

I told them, a little embarrassed that I'd had such a mundane dream and poor Talia had clearly had a nightmare. "There's no way He could be inside me," I added. "I'd know. I mean, surely I'd know."

No one nodded agreement. Instead they all gave me the doubtful stare. That did nothing to make me feel better. For a moment, no one said anything at all. Then I remembered my friend, who supposedly was resting comfortably somewhere in the bowels of High View and an icy prickle crawled up my spine. "What about Annie? If He's here, won't He go straight for her? Isn't she an easy target?"

Michael shot Magda an accusing glance, which she ignored. "Trust me, Susan, she's safe from Him."

"Instead he was drawn to the succubus?" I said.

"Everyone is drawn to a succubus," Talia replied with a convulsive shiver. "That was the whole point."

Unnoticed, Reese had gone into the bathroom and returned with a glass of water, which Talia took from him with a nod of thanks.

"I was the bait."

"Jesus!" I suddenly felt queasy. "You mean you went into my dreams knowing you might encounter Him there?"

Talia gave no answer, only sipped at her water.

"Just because it's a dream, doesn't mean it's not real," Magda said. "The only one who would have half a chance against the Guardian if he were to choose the dream route, which I'm guessing is how he got to you, was Talia. She feeds on dreams, especially sexual dreams."

Talia forced a laugh. "That didn't work out so well, did it?"

"So it was you He was waiting for then, not me," I said, standing to pace by the bed. "All I had was a dream about writing—something I do every day."

"Oh, he wasn't trying to seduce me," Talia said. "He was trying to chase me out, and that's exactly what he did." She forced her way to her feet with a little help from Alonso and Reese, then came to pace next to me. "Tell me about your dream in as much detail as you can remember."

I shook my head. "All right. It was a writing dream. I have them all the time. I have them more often when I'm close to a deadline. Usually those involve my laptop breaking down or my entire manuscript being deleted, that sort of thing."

"Look, what might seem completely mundane to you could be critical," Alonso said. I noticed his arm was now draped protectively around Reese's shoulder and the two had crowded into the shadowy space next to the wardrobe, away from the window.

"It is strange," I said, sifting through the jumble of events of the past few days. "Every other dream I've had up until this one has been either sexy or nightmarish or some bizarre combination of the two. Even if I just doze. I've dreamed a lot," I added.

Talia studied me for a second, brow drawn, then she huffed

out a sharp breath. "May I try something?"

"Of course." The words were barely out of my mouth before she pulled me into her arms and kissed me. She kissed me hard and deep, and I returned the favor with more gusto than I would have thought possible. Somewhere far off, I heard Michael protest. Magda cut him off. In the back of my mind, I heard Katy Perry singing *I Kissed a Girl,* and then the world went blank, as though someone had just pushed the reset button.

I sit in front of my Mac, the *tap, tap* of the keys filling the silence like the rhythm of my pulse. The moon hangs heavy, framed by the open window in Annie's study. I'm tipsy, but not drunk, at least not too drunk, but I can't sleep. My whole body buzzes, but it isn't an alcohol buzz, it's like being in the zone when all the words flow onto the page, and the story I have inside me explodes like magic, like an orgasm. I'm breathless and trembling and pushing, pushing, always pushing against it, rubbing against it, feeling it penetrate me, fill me, ride me in the darkness until every last breath, every last word, every full stop burst onto the page, and I'm left weak and trembling and wrung out.

Then I'm no longer in Annie's comfy flat. I'm in the crypt at Chapel House, the darkness awash in the scent of roses—sweet, sweet roses. I'm writing away with insane focus—something that has to be said, something that has to be freed onto the page. And, fucking hell, I'm horny. I'm always horny when the words are flowing. When the story's coming fast and furious, it makes me want to come too. I'm writing. I'm writing. I'm writing!

The silver light bleeding through the bars in the tunnel touches me like the words do, touches me exactly where they do, in places so private no one has ever touched me there before. And I'm shy, and I'm embarrassed, even ashamed, and I'm overwhelmed with desire that burns me and flashes across my synapses like sheet lightning. And I need! Oh God, how I need! I'm writing. I'm writing… but what I'm writing is more powerful than any story I've ever written, and I want more, good Christ, I want so much more! I want it all and I need it with an ache that will surely destroy me if I can't have it.

And the door's not locked, and I'm terrified and aroused, and intrigued, and I can almost see the words flowing onto the page as, with trembling fingers, I open the barred door that creaks with ancient disuse. And He's there like light itself splitting the darkness. And I write Him onto the page, feeling His lust, His need, His passion in every word. And when I'm finished, trembling and spent and replete, He's there, fully present, fully mine to possess.

Then I hear Annie in the bathroom. The toilet flushes, and I hold my breath, hold my secret tight so she won't hear. And when I'm sure she's gone back to her bed, with fingers cold against the keys, I copy everything, all of it, every word, every nuance, every stuttering heartbeat onto a memory stick. Then I hide it away. But before I do, I delete the words from my Mac so no one else will see, no one else will share in my ecstasy, in my passion, in the shame that so arouses me.

It's only then, when I feel His breath against my neck, and the scent of roses fills the night air, that I realize I can't close the door.

Chapter Eighteen

I came back to myself sitting on the floor in Talia's arms, she whispering softly to me, words I didn't recognize from some language that sounded Eastern European. She didn't try to stop me as I pushed myself to my feet. No one did. In fact no one moved. They all just watched as I sleepwalked my way to my bag, unzipped it and pulled out my computer case.

"I bought this the next day," I said, emptying out its contents onto the sailor's trunk at the foot of the bed. "After it all happened."

Around me no one spoke. I had the very distinct feeling they were all holding their breath. "I needed a place. Someplace secure." I reached down into the side pouch of the neoprene lining, fumbling and fingering until I found the tiny flap of soft cloth Velcroed tightly to a pocket that was nearly impossible to detect unless you knew where to look. I'd found it by accident while we were shopping for belts and bags in the local Saturday market. The case was black with bright red roses strewn across it as though the wind had just blown a bouquet through an open door.

"Looks like an old lady's handbag," Talia remarked.

"That's exactly what Annie said." There was a sharp ripping of Velcro in the otherwise silent room, and I felt my way into the pocket, felt my way to the cool, smooth plastic of the flash drive still there, still secret, even from me, until a few minutes ago.

There was a collective inhaling of breath when I pulled it free from its hiding place and flipped open my computer. As the screen flashed and the soft light competed with the bedside lamp in the receding night, everyone drew around me in a tight circle as though I were about to impart a secret. In truth, that's exactly what I was about to do, and more than a little bit of it was still a secret to me as well.

"You don't have to do this," came a voice next to my ear, and I found myself embraced, caressed, tenderly fondled. I breathed deeply, breathed in the scent of roses, and suddenly Michael's love bite on my breast burned like fire.

I yelped and jumped back, fumbling with the flash drive, which Magda caught deftly then shoved into the USB port. As it clicked into place, all the air went out of my lungs as though someone had suddenly punched me in the gut. The room swam before my eyes.

"What is it? What's wrong?" Michael said, sliding his arms around me to keep me on my feet. The others stepped back as though they half expected me to burst into flame. For a second I wasn't so sure myself. "I think Talia might be right," I managed. "Does anyone else smell roses?"

"There are no roses growing in High View," Reese said. "The soil's too rocky and it's too cold."

"What do you mean, I might be right?" Talia pushed her way in close, her blue eyes wide, looking at me once again as though I had two heads.

"I mean…" I turned to Magda. "This Guardian, does he do possessions, you know like demons, that kind of possession." Even as I said it, a sense of disappointment tightened my chest as though I had let Him down, as though I had deeply wounded Him by my act of betrayal.

"In a way, yes." It was Michael who answered. "When I was with Him, He was desperate to know what it was like to have flesh. As a non-corporeal entity, His interactions with the physical world are limited. Oh, He can affect mortals in devastating ways." He shrugged. "Angels, too, I found out. But the physical aspect of Him that corporeal beings think they experienced is only His fabrication to elicit the response in them He can't have Himself. He wants to know what it feels like to walk, to eat, to sleep, to… make love. The thing is, the more He affects a mortal, the less desire they have to interact with the physical world, and the more they desire to remain in His presence only. That leaves Him constantly in need of new lovers, for lack of a better word."

"Bloody hell," Talia whispered.

I saw that the succubus now shivered nearly as hard as I did, even still wrapped in the blanket as she was.

"I…" Michael swallowed hard, and his chest rose and fell as though he'd just been out for a morning run. "I let Him inside me a few times when we were… making love, when He wanted to know what it felt like, what I felt. He would then… use my body as His own. At first it was such an incredible rush of power. I'd never known my body was capable of feeling such things." He closed his eyes in a struggle for control, or perhaps only because it made sharing such an intimate detail of his life in such a public way a little easier. When he continued, he kept them closed. "In the end, the Guardian stopped asking for my permission. He… He came into me whenever He wanted, and when He was there… well, sometimes I didn't even know He'd entered. Then He started taking lovers, other lovers, using me with them." His fist clenched and opened and I could see the half moon depressions where his nails had bitten into his palm. He gave a quick glance around the room, and color rose to his cheeks. "You see, being an angel, I was strong enough to be His vessel, where no human would be."

As he spoke, I felt a tightening in my chest, an aching sensation just below the breastbone. "But I am human," I managed the words as calmly as my near-state of panic would allow. "Surely He knows I'm not a suitable vessel."

"He's not actually possessing you," Magda said. "Not the way He did Michael anyway. He's attached himself to you like... well, for lack of a better word, like a parasite."

"Christ! That makes me feel a whole lot better." The tightness in my chest made it difficult to breathe, and seeing Michael struggling with his memories of having the Guardian inside him only made it worse. I could do nothing more than stand there stupidly, shaking my head and rubbing my chest, which hurt like it had in my childhood back when asthma was a regular part of my daily life. But I had outgrown that a long time ago and hadn't had so much as a sniffle until recently.

Magda patted Michael's shoulder gently, then perched on the sailor's chest next to my computer. "You're a writer, Susan. I'm assuming that also means that you read a lot."

"Of course I do."

"And romance? Do you ever read romance?"

"Read it and write it as well," I answered. "What's your point?"

"Don't tell me you've never had the hero of a story so possess you that you couldn't stop thinking about him, even dreaming about him long after you'd finished the novel?"

Before I could do more than nod, she continued. "And in your own writings, aren't there times when your own stories so possess you that they become more real than the world you live in?"

"Jesus," I whispered. The pressure on my chest now felt like an elephant was doing a tap dance across my sternum with my heart providing a rapid staccato drumbeat. "That's exactly what I was doing that night, the night I wrote that." I nodded to the words on the screen. "I remember now. It was just a story idea, something that came into my mind down in the crypt when I saw the rusty bars over the tunnel entrance at the back. I mean, what writer wouldn't find something like that intriguing fodder for a story?"

I looked around the room, seeking understanding.

Michael took my hand and gave it a squeeze, encouraging me to continue. "I was in the middle of a major project at the time, so what I wrote that night was fast and furious, just to get the ideas down so I wouldn't lose them. I do that all the time. I planned to come back to it later. I thought it would be a great story. But then it all suddenly felt so real. While I was writing it, I mean. I could swear it all actually happened, and for a writer that's an exciting thing, because of course it's all just my imagination, isn't it? At least that's what I told myself, and why would I believe anything else? It's always been true before. But then…"

"Then what?" Magda asked.

"Then I totally forgot all about it. Even when I bought the

computer bag, even when I tucked the memory stick away, I forgot it almost as it was happening. How could I forget it? I never forget a story idea, no matter how lame it might be. How could I have forgotten something like this?" I shivered, and Michael slipped his arm around me.

"You forgot because the Guardian didn't want you to remember. That's how you forgot," Magda said.

"I never meant to hurt anyone." I glanced around the room. All eyes were locked on me. "What am I going to do?"

"You're going to do exactly as I say, just like Michael did. And if you do that, I'll get you and your friend through this, and it'll be okay. I promise."

Before I could ask how she could make such a promise, before I could ask who the hell she was that she could even be so presumptuous, Magda took me into her arms, and for a second the pressure in my chest constricted like a fist. I think I might have passed out, maybe from the shock of her embrace, maybe from His unwanted presence. I don't know. Whatever happened, the scent of roses dissipated and when she released me, I could breathe easily again.

She noted my surprise and her full lips quirked in a smile. "The Guardian doesn't like me. He won't hang around for my embrace." Before I could question what she meant by that, she nodded to the computer screen, and I turned to see the words I'd written about my first encounter with Him.

I wasn't alone in the dark.

To my surprise and embarrassment, Magda began to read

them out loud.

"Wait!" I reached for the flash drive, but in a move that was so fast I missed it completely, she grabbed my hand and shoved it away. I gasped and stepped back, the feel of her touch prickling like static electricity over my skin. "Please don't. Please don't read that in front of everyone," I said, rubbing my hand where she had touched me. "It's…"

"It's personal. Yes, I know."

"What do you want her to do?" Talia spoke up. "Print out copies so we can all read it and have a little private wank session?"

Alonso shot her a look that would have stripped paint. She only shrugged, but with me only managing to blush with the mortification I felt, it was Magda who responded.

"If you want to have a wank, Talia, don't let me stop you, but you'll do it in front of all of us. Alonso and I might be immune to an attack from the Guardian, but no one else in this room is, including you. That means I read it out loud in Alonso's house with both of us present in the room."

Talia said nothing more. In the charged space, there was a shuffling of feet and a lowering of eyes, as though no one was really comfortable with this little arrangement, but then no one was about to argue either. It seemed that everyone would defer to Magda. I gathered she was the only one who had a plan, or at least I hoped she did.

Michael gave my hand another reassuring squeeze. I pulled in a deep breath and braced myself.

Magda began to read.

Chapter Nineteen

I wasn't alone in the dark. I knew that the first time I entered the crypt at Chapel House. I could feel a presence there, almost as though someone stood just behind me, about to reach out and touch me. The shiver over my skin was not so much from fear, though certainly there was an element of fear, as it was from longing, bone-deep longing. I could barely breathe for it, I could barely stand under the weight of it, and I couldn't imagine how such an ache, such a hunger could exist inside my flesh and not tear me apart. I was astonished that Annie seemed completely unaware of anything out of the ordinary, and to be quite honest, I wasn't anxious to share it with her.

She continued to chatter on about her plans to make Chapel House over with a state of the art kitchen—she who didn't cook, and a master suite that would rival the finest hotels in London. Strange that I could listen with one part of my brain and comment on her ideas for an open plan living space, for a library in the choir loft, for a wet room in the sacristy, while with another part of my brain I felt like every cell of my body was responding to whatever it was, whoever it was that I was certain waited there in the darkness, just beyond the beam of Annie's Maglite.

I must have groaned, or made some disparaging sound, or maybe she just sensed my utter mortification as I recalled what I'd written next, but Magda paused and looked up at me. "I'm not trying to embarrass you, Susan, but words have power. They're your words. If you read them, they have more power. At the moment we don't want to do anything that might empower the Guardian further. My reading them, being who I am, will significantly diminish that power so that, hopefully, we might all understand what has happened and learn what to do."

I nodded, face still burning from hearing words read out loud that I'd never meant to be shared with anyone. "I told Annie this story. I remember now. I told her over dinner," I said, feeling as though I owed everyone an explanation, feeling on some level as though I had betrayed them all. "Only when I told her, I changed us around so that it was her discovery, the Guardian in the crypt, her experiencing Him in the darkness rather than me."

I recalled how it rankled, even then, even for the sake of keeping my secret, the thought of Annie feeling what I'd felt, the thought of Annie being so caressed in the crypt. I added quickly. "Annie likes… well, she likes a good nasty story."

I fought back the urge to say that Annie liked being the center of attention, that Annie wanted everything to be about her. None of that was actually true, all of that was simply my own jealousy. Christ, I hated that it was so, but it was.

As though Magda understood, she laid a hand on my arm, and the jealousy dissipated.

Before she could continue reading, a sharp hiss of breath erupted into the tight energy of the room, followed by a whispered curse. I turned to see Alonso clasping his hand to his chest as Talia made a mad dash for the window, slamming the shutters tight against the anemic rays of first light, leaving only the backlit screen of my computer and the lamp on the bedside table to keep the room from total darkness.

"You bloody fool!" she snapped at Alonso. "How useful do you expect to be if you end up toast? Pay attention!" By the time she returned to his side, Reese was already examining Alonso's hand, which looked to be badly burned.

"Jesus! What happened?" I said. "Is there a first aid kit in the bathroom?"

"No need," Alonso looked up at me with a blush. "I heal fast." Sure enough, even as he spoke, the blisters that had looked to be second-degree burns, easily, were healing and disappearing in front of my eyes.

"He's a vampire," Talia said before I could do more than gasp at the sight. Alonso shot her an acid glance. "Well you are, you overly-sensitive bastard."

She nodded to me. "Hell, she's got a demonic parasite, you think she gives a fuck if you're the goddamned undead?"

"A vampire? Right." It said something about the incredible depth of the rabbit hole I'd tumbled down that I was barely fazed by this delightful new tidbit of information.

"Oh, don't worry," Talia continued just in case I might— worry. "You're safe. Alonso's well fed at the moment." She gave Reese a playful glance. "Besides, he never bites his guests. Unless they ask him to."

Reese sniggered. Alonso growled. Then he took in the room around us with a quick glance. "As you've all just witnessed, this is not the most comfortable suite for our little… undertaking. Certainly not for one such as me." He nodded to his hand, which was now completely healed. "Perhaps I may exercise my prerogative as host of this little soirée and invite everyone to adjourn to my study, which, though very well lit, has far fewer windows. For those present for whom neither Reese nor Talia can provide nourishment, I'll have Cook bring breakfast. Second breakfast for you, Ms. Innes," he said, smiling at me. "And we can continue once I am not the only one who is well fed."

When breakfast was over, we all arranged ourselves comfortably in Alonso's high-tech basement study, complete with huge monitors disguised nicely as windows, which Reese informed me, were linked to cameras that gave Alonso the same gorgeous view of the high fells he would see from the windows in some of the brighter rooms on the upper floors.

I perched on a sofa between Magda, who sat with my Mac in her lap, and Michael, who held my hand nearly tight enough to crush bone.

Magda downed the last of her coffee from a delicate china cup and continued the story out loud, me following along as she read.

The departmentalizing of Annie's plans and the feel of the presence in the darkness became much more difficult when I felt the closeness of a warm, hard body against my back and the humid nip of a kiss on the nape of my neck. I explained away my little gasp of surprise to Annie by saying I'd almost lost my footing. I should have been frightened. I should have been terrified, and believe me, I was. But by the time I felt a large hand splayed low against my belly, by the time I was certain of the maleness pressed hard and low just above my butt, I was far more intrigued than I was frightened. Even if terror had won out, I don't think I could have forced myself to move as the hand in the darkness migrated to cup my breasts and thumb my nipples, first one, then the other, and the slow grind and undulation from behind became more demanding.

"The roses, they smell lovely." I managed a breathless response to Annie's ramblings about plans for the overgrown mess of a garden. "You might want to consider a scent garden."

She laughed. "I can't smell anything, but then you were always the one with the sensitive nose. Of course I'll make sure there are lots of roses." She knew they were my favorite, but I couldn't imagine her not smelling them; the scent was nearly overwhelming in the tight space of the crypt. To my surprise, as she rambled on about a patio with a Jacuzzi, the smell of roses was subsumed in my own scent and the humid, piquant scent of a man well aroused. The hand on my breast began a slow, torturous descent, and I wanted nothing more than for Annie to keep talking, keep planning, anything to keep her from dragging me away from this place, at least for a few more minutes.

I asked about the Jacuzzi, hoping that would give me another minute. By the time she got started about the sites she'd looked up online and the builders she'd talked to, I was rocking back against the hardness, craning my neck to yield as much bare skin as possible to teeth and tongue and lips all soft and warm and wet and sharp and hard and demanding. Oh, I tried to be as unobtrusive as possible, but looking back, I wonder how the hell Annie couldn't see? How could she have missed it? But she rattled on and on about some builder just up the road near Keswick who was supposed to be really good, some guy named Michael. Like I gave a fuck.

The study suddenly felt stuffy and overheated, and Michael's grip on my hand convulsed. His jaw tightened, but he didn't look at me.

Magda paid little attention to either my discomfort or Michael's. She just kept on reading.

He was cute, Annie said. That led to observations about this Michael's broad shoulders and nice arse and speculation as to whether or not he would be any good in bed, and was it wise to seduce him before he put in her Jacuzzi or wait till after and seduce him in it. All the while I nodded and pretended to be interested.

I was thankful for the extra time, but Christ, how could she not notice me standing there, legs apart, rocking back and forth and shifting from foot to foot like I had ants in my knickers? In truth, what I wanted in my knickers surely couldn't actually be there, and yet I felt it, fucking hell, how I felt it! I swear, I could feel muscle and sinew. Hell, I could feel the actual shape of an erection as though we were both naked, as though all he need do, this dark being who surely was just my imagination, was bend me over and open me, me struggling to keep my breathing quiet, me struggling to focus enough attention on my friend that she wouldn't suspect I was about to come. Oh yes, I was terrified. I would have, should have, run, if I hadn't been so intrigued, so turned on. I just wanted one more second, and then another and another.

In desperation that shocks me even now as I write this in the dark silence of Annie's flat, I grabbed onto a wrist that I swear was as solid and warm as my own and guided the caress, the tease, the fondling of fingers and palm down my belly toward where I really needed it to be.

Annie yammered on about this Michael, all the things she'd heard about him, all the things she wanted to do to him—at least I think she did. My God, my whole body felt alive, every cell, every molecule. I could damn near feel the coursing of my own blood through my veins. You have no idea what an exhilarating combination fear and arousal make. I lost track of what Annie was saying, and the air was filled with the scent of sex. I could smell him, actually smell this phantom man, who was as near release as I was, and I was sure, as my knees gave beneath me, I felt the warm wet of his orgasm against my lower back. And then for an instant everything around me was silk and darkness, so perfect, so ecstatic. But just beyond that warm tight space, I knew. I knew as well as I know my own breath, I was terrified, and what I felt was like no terror I'd ever known before and, holy God in heaven, I want to feel it again.

And then I was shivering on my knees against the stone floor in the crypt at Chapel House.

"Susan? Susan, you're scaring me." Annie's worried face invaded my field of vision before she half-blinded me with her Maglite. "Are you all right? What the hell happened?"

"Sorry, I got a little lightheaded there. Probably just blood sugar. I missed lunch," I lied, stumbling quickly to my feet, making a quick swipe at the back of my skirt, surprised to find it was dry.

Glancing over my shoulder into the narrow beam of the Maglite, I saw only the empty darkness of the crypt and the tunnel that led back to the rusted barred door. But I was certain someone was there, someone I hungered for way more than I hungered for food. And I was equally certain that I would have Him.

I don't know what happened. I was too lost in the words Magda read to notice anything else in the room until suddenly there was a groan, little more than a heavy breath released in desperation, and Michael came to his feet with all the dignity I suppose one could expect from an angel. He tugged at the collar of his T-shirt as though it were choking him, then he turned on his heel and walked quickly out of the study, shutting the door behind him.

Before I could go after him, Magda grabbed my wrist and settled me back onto the sofa. "Let him go. This is no easier for him to take than it is for you and, I'm sorry to say, it'll get harder before it gets better."

Chapter Twenty

"I think we all could use a little break." Magda set aside the computer. "The last thing we need is to tackle the rest of what Susan has written in a less than calm state."

Everyone was strung out and on edge, especially at the idea that somehow the Guardian had managed to breach the defenses of a paranoid vampire and his dangerous entourage. It didn't help that, thanks to the reading, they were all clearly laying the blame at my feet. Seriously, though, did Magda really think any of us were going to be calm again until this situation was resolved? I certainly wasn't likely to find a few minutes respite anywhere near enough of a distraction to calm my frayed nerves. But then, other than Michael, I was the only one who really understood just what we were up against and how badly He could make us want Him before we even realized He had touched us.

It seemed to me that a little break was the perfect time for me to check in on Annie, whom I had not seen since our strange arrival at High View. But when I asked again to see her, Magda insisted that I wait. "Seeing her like she is now will only make matters more difficult," she explained. "You're connected to her. She's another way the Guardian can get to you, can get to both of you, and through you everyone else here at High View. In fact, it's not even wise to keep the two of you under the same roof, but it was the only choice I had at the time. I've taken every precaution I can, but that means the only way I can keep the Guardian away from her and keep her unaware of your presence or that she's no longer with Him, is to keep her… asleep."

Before I could ask how she could manage that, she made a dismissive gesture. "It's very old magic."

Though how could that surprise me, when I was in the home of a vampire who had a succubus for a confidante, and I was in said vampire's ruined palatial estate with an angel who was out of sorts because of what I'd written while under the influence of some entity similar to a demon? Before I could argue with her about seeing Annie, Magda spoke. "It's not wise to forget that your best friend came at you with a butcher knife, Susan."

She didn't wait for my response. I was quite clearly dismissed. She left the room only minutes after Michael.

For a moment we all sat staring at each other, then Alonso once again assumed his role as gracious host and sent for fresh coffee and pastries while everyone took a short breather.

I was no more able to sit still and make pleasant conversation than Michael or Magda had been, so I excused myself, hoping to take a quick shower. I was wandering down a half-restored passageway, trying to find my way back to my room, when Cook saw me and assumed I was looking for Annie. It turned out her room was at the opposite end of the corridor and Cook had only just been there.

Once Cook disappeared down the hallway with an untouched tray from Annie's room and, after checking both directions to make sure no one was watching, I knocked softly and let myself in.

It took my eyes a few seconds to adjust to the darkened space and, at my first sight of her lying there in the bed, frail and unmoving, I was sure she was dead. I rushed to her side and snatched up her icy hand, fisted around one of the rungs on the brass headboard. But the moment I touched her, she grabbed onto me with reflexes surprisingly fast and a grip terrifyingly strong. I half expected her to pull a butcher knife from under the duvet and come after me again. But then she moaned softly, completely undisturbed by my startled yelp, and her hand went limp in mine. Within a heartbeat she had relaxed and settled back into the thick bedding as though nothing at all had happened, the rise and fall of her chest returning to the slow, even breathing of deep sleep.

Her skin was waxen and gray; her face, even in repose, ravaged with the exhaustion the Guardian's heavy demands had wrought upon her. In spite of the shock of seeing her so, I fought back my jealousy of the attention He had lavished on her, unable to keep my thoughts from straying to what He must have done to her, what they must have done together, how He must have pleasured her. Even as the unwelcome thoughts filled my head, I hated myself for them, but I hated her more for having Him all this time while I didn't.

I recalled my dream with the succubus, if that's what it was; my secret planning with the Guardian for Him to take Annie as His lover until I could return and take my place next to Him. He had promised me that by His side was where I belonged, and I had believed Him without even the tiniest doubt. And then He had taken the memory of that night from me to keep our secret, He said. He promised all of what we shared that night would come back to me once we were together, but for now, it was best I didn't remember. That would make it easier for me to function without Him until I could join Him forever.

That was what He told me, and I believed Him without question. Dear God, could I have really betrayed my friend to such a fate? But even as I recalled that night, that experience, our scheming, I burned with jealousy at the plan He instigated, the plan He said would ultimately be best for the two of us, would ultimately guarantee we would be together.

Annie meant nothing to Him, He had promised me, but He would do what He had to, whatever it took, for us to be together. Perhaps He took those memories from me because He knew I couldn't have endured the jealousy. I would have driven myself insane thinking about her taking my place with Him, her naked on her mattress next to the altar, inviting Him in again and again, and Him taking her over and over, instead of me. It should have been me. I should have stayed. I remember thinking that just before He took my memories.

And when He took them, in the taking, He had touched me, and His touch had been like a promise, one so sweet and so ecstatic that the very anticipation of its fulfillment was only a step away from orgasm, only a heartbeat away from pleasure I could barely imagine.

Then shame rushed back on me like a tidal wave followed in short order by denial. How could I have done this—any of this—to my best friend? Surely it couldn't have been me. Surely it had only been a bad dream, just as I had been hoping all this time. She was the one with the demon lover after all, not me. She was the one who had come after me with a butcher knife. She was the one who caused all this pain and horror… surely she was.

Carefully, as though I feared waking her, or perhaps that my touch would hurt her, I settled onto the edge of the bed next to her, still holding her hand, lightly stroking the back of it with my thumb. "Annie, I don't know what to do," I whispered. "I'm so, so sorry that I dragged you into this mess. I… You have to believe me, I'd never hurt you deliberately. I didn't know. I swear to you, didn't *know*. Perhaps I should go back to Chapel House."

The words were out of my mouth almost of their own volition and, to my horror, I found myself rationalizing my need to return to the place, and to Him. After all, it was the only way I could save Annie, right? I could convince Him to let her go, to guarantee her safety in exchange for me. "If I go back, Annie, and you stay here with Magda and Michael and… well, there's just so much magic in this house. I think if anyone can make you better, Magda can. There's something about her. I don't know what it is, but she can make you better. I know she can."

It seemed the most logical thing in the world to me, as I spoke. I would go back. I would be the sacrifice to save Annie. And Michael too, right? He still had a hold on Michael, but it was me He wanted. I knew that it was. I had always known that, hadn't I? I was the only one who could be to Him what He needed. All the others He'd ever been with down through the ages, all the lovers He had ever taken, all of them had only been His deep longing, His timeless search to find me.

The more I thought about it, the more certain I was of the truth of it. The excitement at the thought of returning to Him grew tight and full beneath my breastbone, and in the dark places at the back of my mind, I was already planning my escape from High View. It wouldn't be easy sneaking away at night, not from a vampire's lair, but I felt certain in myself that He would help me, whether I fled to Him in broad daylight or in the darkness of night. He would protect me from them and aid my escape. And then once I was safely away, safely back with Him, I would send word of my sacrifice and all would be well. I knew it would. He would free Annie and Michael and we would be together, just like He'd always wanted, like we'd both always wanted.

"Oh, Annie," I said, squeezing her hand. "It's the right thing to do. It just has to be. I mean, what else can I do?" I raised her hand to my lips and kissed it fervently. "I just… I just want you to be okay, Annie. That's all I ever wanted."

"It's not all you want."

I nearly jumped out of my skin as I turned to find Michael leaning against the doorframe, hair sparkling with droplets of the light rain that had started outside during the reading of the account of my little encounter. I had no idea how long he'd been standing there, but as I shook myself back to reality, I knew it had probably been long enough for him to understand exactly what was going on. Long enough to realize the dangerous precipice upon which I now teetered.

Chapter Twenty-one

"It's not all you want, just for Annie to be okay. You're bargaining, Susan. In your head, you're bargaining." As Michael came and settled beside me on the bed, I smelled the cold fell air on his skin, and the hard muscles of his forearm were cool as he brushed against me.

He took Annie's hand and gently tucked it back under the duvet, then he took mine in his own. "You want to go back to be with Him. You think if you go back to Him, He'll make everything all better because you're certain that you're the one He's been waiting for all these centuries."

When I tried to pull away, tried to be offended, he held me tight. "I know that's what you want, Susan, because it's what I want, too. It's what anyone who's ever been the center of His attention would want. But they're all dead."

His words were like an ice bath, waking me from a deep sleep with a cold that went clear to the core of me.

He continued. "They're all dead because of Him. It's just the three of us now. And Annie, well, no matter what happens, just like you and me, she'll want that same thing. She'll want with all of her being to go to Him. Until her dying day, that's what she'll want, and that day won't be long in coming if we can't figure out what to do to imprison the Guardian again."

I bit my lip and looked down at his large hand folded over mine, his thumb stroking my knuckles in much the way I had Annie's. "Is that why you left the study while Magda was reading? Because you wanted to go to Him?"

He took a deep breath and looked up at me from beneath thick lashes. "Partly. Your… account of what happened to you in the crypt, your first encounter with Him, made me think of my first time being in His presence, made me think about what it had cost to be free of Him." He suddenly seemed to have trouble breathing. "And it made me realize once again that I'm not free of Him. I want to go to Him so badly that it feels like fire burning me up inside, and I'm not likely to ever be free of Him unless Magda can figure something out."

For a moment we sat in silence.

"I'm sorry," I said at last. "I didn't know when I wrote those things." I bit back a sob. "I didn't even remember writing them until Magda started reading, and even then it's sketchy in places. But I never meant to hurt you. I didn't even know you."

"I didn't think that you meant to hurt me," he said. "I wasn't offended, believe me, I wasn't. It was just, well, I remembered all over again His way… His way of never letting go of anyone He's ever touched, and I felt it more strongly in your words than I had since I was the object of His affection, that's all. Well, that and I was jealous. I'm always jealous when someone else has His attention. Just like you are. Just like Annie is."

"Christ, I've made such a mess of things!" I shoved my way off the bed and paced the perimeter of the room, which was small, almost dungeon-like in comparison to my own. "I can't just sit here and do nothing."

"You're not doing nothing," he said, watching me pace. "You're working with people who can help. Magda has a plan and you have to trust her."

"How can I trust her when she left me in the crypt? And what kind of magic is she working on Annie? How do I know that her solution is not to just kill Annie and be done with it?"

Michael's jaw tightened beneath the stubble that had grown enough to make him look even more dangerous than he usually did. "If she wanted your friend dead, she'd already be dead, not lying here in a clean bed in a safe house."

"A safe house? With a vampire and a succubus, and who knows what else? A werewolf or two? Maybe an army of zombies? Fuck, I'm open to anything these days. Good thing the beasties and ghouls are all on our side, isn't it, Michael?"

"It is, actually," he said in a voice so calm that you'd think I'd just made some benign comment about the weather. Then he added, "They all work for Magda. Well, Alonso does, the others work for him. Talia and Reese are his familiars."

"Jesus, I'm living a Bram-fucking-Stoker novel!"

The unexpected chuckle of a response was laced with a hint of bitterness. "Oh, nothing so simple as that." Then, before I could question further, he said, "Look, Magda does what's necessary, and she seems to be able to see and understand just what that may be without all the squeamish gray areas of conscience most of the world has."

"That doesn't make me feel any better, Michael. What? We're all just collateral damage if she decides it's best to throw the baby out with the bath water? Is that it? Who the hell is she, anyway, and why does she always wear those *Men In Black* glasses?"

His lips thinned to a tight, straight line, as though they were suddenly sealed. "Her story's not mine to tell. You'll have to ask her yourself."

"I bloody well will," I said, turning toward the door.

"Wait!" He grabbed my hand and guided me out into the silent corridor, pulling the door shut behind him. "She's not here at the moment. You can talk to her when she gets back."

"Where is she?"

"On business that's none of mine, or yours," he said, tightening his grip on my hand. "She keeps her own counsel, and for the most part, the less I know about it, the happier I am. I wager Alonso feels the same."

"She's a scary bitch, that's what she is," I said, wishing the instant I'd said it that I hadn't, wondering if maybe she was listening, just waiting to catch me out, to catch me saying or doing something I shouldn't, so she could lock me back down in the crypt. Maybe I was the bait; maybe I was the collateral damage necessary to imprison the Guardian again.

"No one who knows her would argue that point," Michael said. "But she's the only one here who has a clue how to deal with the Guardian, the only one I know to ever imprison Him. And He was there, safely out of commission for a long time, a very long time, thanks to her."

"Until I released Him."

"I have no doubt He deceived you into it. No one was supposed to be able to hear him or be aware of him in any way, and no one has been before you. Magda says it's to do with you being a scribe. I don't understand it all. She'll have to explain."

"I'll add that to my list of topics for conversation at our next girls' night out."

"Despite the woman being a scary bitch, or possibly because she's a scary bitch, she's our best chance of locking Him away again," Michael said.

"You believe that?"

He nodded. "If we do as she says, I think she'll get us out of this situation without that collateral damage you mentioned. If we do as she says." At the passage that led down into the basement to Alonso's study, he turned aside and led me up a winding set of stone steps, circling what had to be the inside of a tower.

"Where are we going? What's going on?" I asked, struggling on the uneven steps.

The words were barely out of my mouth when halfway up the stairs, he pulled me through an arched doorway we both had to stoop to enter, and into a round stone room not much bigger than a janitor's closet. It contained nothing but a twin bed and a nightstand; the only light coming from a small slit of a window at the back of the curved wall.

Nothing else caught my attention as he slammed a heavy wooden door shut behind us and took my mouth in a scorching kiss, pressing me up tight against the wall until I could feel the hard geography of his body shifting and undulating against mine which, before I knew what was happening, was returning the favor.

"Where are we? What the fuck are you doing?"

I honestly didn't care what the answer to the first question was, and the second was just plain stupid, really. I knew the answer, and I knew what I was doing too, as I tugged at his belt. There might have been a small part of me wondering how I could jump from the rollercoaster of concern for my friend and plotting to get back to the Guardian to wanting to shag Michael's brains out, but I shoved the thought aside as he went to work on the buttons of my shirt.

"The mark, *my* mark," he emphasized. "It burns because it's not been reinforced properly. I had intended to take care of it. Believe me, I was looking forward to it, but between the Guardian and Magda, I didn't get the chance. It needs to be made stronger if it's going to help protect you. Or me." He shoved the shirt off my shoulders and all but ripped the hooks of my bra open before he scooped my breast free, bent and began a delicious, tetchy suckle and bite, suckle and bite of the mark he'd left just above my nipple during our earlier lovemaking.

If the Guardian's touch had brought me excruciating pain through that mark, the feel of Michael's tongue, his teeth, his lips brought me exquisite pleasure—far more pleasure than even his skilled fondling of my breasts should have been able to manage.

As I ripped at his fly, he returned the favor, shoving my jeans and knickers down over my arse with a sleight of hand that felt like magic… probably was magic, come to think of it. I wriggled and squirmed them down around my ankles and kicked one leg free, sending a shoe skittering across the stone floor. All the while he sucked and nipped, cupped and explored, and the mark sent heat waves of pleasure through every nerve ending in my body.

"Get 'em off!" I gasped. "Get 'em off, get 'em off!" It had

suddenly become my mindless mantra. I was much less graceful in my efforts than Michael was in his, my hands made awkward, fingers unsteady by my own need. He responded to my uncomfortable tugging and shoving with a harsh, humid grunt against my breast. While wriggling and shifting as best he could in order to aid my efforts, he brought a jean-clad knee in between my thighs to open my legs, then teased me by bringing it up to rub and stroke until I was all but squatting onto it, rocking against it. Then he lost patience, gave a guttural curse, and shoved my hands away to deal with his uncooperative jeans himself. All the while his mouth remained hard at work on my breast, on his mark.

　　　With that same sleight of hand movement that had freed me from my clothing, he managed his jeans—commando beneath, I noticed—though I barely had time to notice anything before he cupped my buttocks in large, calloused hands and lifted me. In one effortless thrusting of his hips, he pushed up inside me, gasping as though someone had knocked the breath out of him.

　　　I arched my back against the wall to get closer to his efforts, my legs circling his waist, one foot still trailing jeans and knickers, frantic to get a grip, frantic to have him where I needed him.

　　　He bit my breast, and this time I did feel pain, delicious ecstatic pain that radiated in waves down over my belly to throb like a heartbeat deep in my core each time he thrust. Then he raised his head, taking my mouth savagely before pulling away, bathing me in the hot coffee scent of his breath and the hotter, darker, scent of his lust. "I won't share you with Him, Susan. You belong to me now, and I might have been forgettable in your little account that Magda so kindly read, but I'm not now, nor will I ever be again."

I grabbed him by the hair with a white-knuckled fist and forced his mouth back to my breast. "Then you bloody well better make sure I don't forget, Michael; do you understand me?"

In response he bit again. I cried out, but this time in orgasm, my head *thump-thumping* against the wall with each convulsive tremor as Michael clamped down hard and suckled as though he were a vampire and I was the main course. In all honesty, I wasn't sure that he hadn't drawn blood. Whether he had or not, the delicious result of the act was his own release, with each brutal pounding of his hips filling me with his fire, burning me, biting me, suckling me until the world disappeared, until I couldn't recall my own name if my life depended upon it; until I could recall only one name, the only name on my lips over and over again, "Michael! Michael! Michael!"

Chapter Twenty-two

"I really need to go." Michael kissed my ear and cupped my breast, thumbing the nipple that was just peeking from the cloud of geranium scented bubbles. After we'd made love, we slipped down the stone staircase to my room, which, I discovered to my delight, was just below his. He'd requested it that way. For my protection, he said, so he could get to me quickly if the need arose. And since High View was in the process of renovations, this was the best Alonso could do.

Once we were back in my room, Michael had filled up the big bathtub and undressed me at his leisure, pausing to kiss and caress as necessary. Then he guided me down into the warm sudsy water and crawled in with me, to bathe me, he said—an act that was accomplished after another, less frantic, reinforcement of his mark. Warm, clean and sated, I leaned back against the humid rise and fall of his chest, half dozing, trying hard to pretend that we were simply two lovers enjoying a little wet afternoon delight.

"I may be borrowing trouble," he said, "but something doesn't feel right. It shouldn't have taken Magda so long to reconvene our little… reading group." I felt his shrug against my back. "Though she's not the kind who thinks to inform anyone of a change of plans. Still. I don't like it. I suppose a delay could be a good sign, but I'm not an optimist when it comes to working with Magda, and certainly not where the Guardian is concerned."

Over my mild protests he stood, causing a mini tsunami of scented water, and offered me his hand.

When we were both dried and dressed, I reeled him in for a

lingering kiss. "You don't have to sleep all alone up there in that cold little tower, you know."

He caught my hand and pulled it to his lips. "Are you inviting me to share your bed, Ms. Innes?"

"Well, I was just thinking that the mark could probably use a bit more reinforcing. Just to be sure. And, just in case you might need to get to me in a hurry or something. You understand."

"You have a good point." He nodded in mock seriousness.

"You have a better one." I rubbed against him.

He groaned into my mouth in a deep lazy kiss. "As much as I'd love to discuss my point with you and give you another demonstration, I really need to find out what's going on." He kissed me again, giving my arse a good kneading as he shifted up tight against me, then he nipped my lower lip. "I promise we'll continue this discussion later."

He turned to leave, then turned back to me. "I need you to stay put in your room until I come back for you. After everything that's happened, the protective spells around this space have been reinforced to keep you safe when you're alone. I'll be back for you, or someone else will, shortly." He waited until I nodded a reluctant agreement, then he left me leaning breathlessly against the edge of the door as I watched him disappear down the corridor.

As soon as he was gone, the world came rushing back. There was no more pretending that we were just ordinary lovers. There was no way to pretend anything was ordinary anymore. Fighting off the rising panic, my first thought was to boot up my laptop and document the events of the past twenty-four hours. Writing things down always helped me focus and see things more clearly—often things that had completely escaped me in the midst of the action, and I very much needed to see things more clearly right now.

Then I remembered that the laptop was still in the study, where we'd all been titillated by my encounter with the Guardian. My stomach knotted at the memory. Well, I fucking needed it! I couldn't just sit around and fret. I needed to do something, anything to keep from going nuts, to keep from convincing myself that the Guardian was the love of my life and I needed to hurry back to Him.

Ignoring Michael's request, I took a deep breath, flung open the door and headed for the study. After all, the study was surely safe from the Guardian, deep in Alonso's vampire-friendly basement. I was sure I'd be fine there. The problem was I'd only been there once, and that was following Alonso's lead. High View was a complicated maze of ruins and renovations one could easily get lost in and never be heard from again. It was the perfect hangout for a vampire and his pet succubus. Not so great for a confused writer, though.

After two wrong turns, one that led to a fairly creepy tunnel, I was just beginning to get seriously concerned that I might really be lost when I turned a blind corner and nearly ran into Talia. I gave a little yelp, and she responded with an amused chuckle. She was dressed in faded jeans, riding boots and a black leather jacket that hugged her perfect curves. Even in the dim light of the passage she looked terrifyingly beautiful—but not like an angel. I knew very well what an angel looked like, felt like. Talia wasn't like that at all, with her waves of dark hair and red lips, with her blue eyes that looked right through you. Talia was like everything beautiful, everything desirable, everything dangerous and forbidden rolled into one breathtaking package. Christ, whatever happened to just normal everyday, sexual attraction between two ordinary human beings? I was out of my depth at every turn, and this was the safe place!

I was about to apologize for being so jumpy and ask directions when she brought me up short. "Are you looking for Magda?"

"As a matter of fact, I am." At least I was now, now that perhaps I had someone to help me hunt her down. I asked innocently, "Do you know where I can find her?" I had a few things to say to the woman and if Michael was overly protective of her, perhaps someone else could point me in the right direction.

"It just so happens I do," she said, folding her arm over mine and turning me down the hall toward the dodgy-looking tunnel.

As she grabbed a Maglite from a shelf near the entrance, I felt a tingle at the base of my spine, but I wasn't sure if it was from the idea of entering the maw of the tunnel with a succubus I didn't totally trust, or just the fact that her hand against my bare forearm made me slightly giddy.

"I would imagine you have a lot of questions for her," she called over her shoulder as the tunnel began to narrow and she took the lead. "Not that I would expect too many answers if I were you. The bitch isn't exactly known for her open door policy."

"You don't like her," I said, scurrying to keep up with the pace of someone who was clearly familiar with the tunnel.

"I like her just fine. In fact, I admire the hell out of her. But I don't expect straight answers from her, and when she does get around to straight answers, usually I wish the hell she would have lied, but then that's just Magda Gardener for you. Can't say that I really blame her for trusting no one and using every resource at her disposal, and believe me, she's got 'em. Resources, I mean."

"She certainly seems to have Michael by the short hairs," I said, stooping slightly as the tunnel narrowed still further and my heart rate accelerated accordingly.

"Hon, she has everyone by the short hairs, even if they don't know it."

"Are you sure you know where she's at?" I asked, shivering as a gossamer strand of spider web raked across my cheek.

Her chuckle was low and throaty. "Don't worry, I'm not going to seduce you in some dark musty corner, if that's what you're afraid of. And, as I said earlier, Alonso doesn't feed on his guests, even uninvited ones."

"Very happy to hear that, on both counts," I said, accidentally scraping my elbow on a rough outcropping of rock I hadn't noticed in the wavering illumination of the Maglite. Then I added quickly, "Michael tells me you're his familiar—Alonso's, I mean."

The chuckle came again. "Oh, indeed. I'm very familiar with Alonso. I offer him blood and he reciprocates, when my energies are drained in his service. I'm his eyes in the daylight, and his flesh when he needs me to be. I add that… feminine touch to his household. I'm not his lover, though. Not now, anyway. He's head over heels for Reese, and that's fine with me. I prefer human lovers.

Their dreams are really quite… twisted, surprisingly. I know, right? Wouldn't you think the dreams of a vampire, certainly a vampire who has been through what Alonso has, would be far more exciting? But," she turned and I suddenly found myself nose to nose with her, breathing in her cinnamon and peaches breath, "vampires and succubi and things that go bump in the night are born of the human psyche, you know. The veil between the dream world and the real world is so much thinner than anyone who hasn't walked both could easily imagine."

She reached out and brushed a spider web from my hair. "I would think a scribe would know that." Then she turned and continued on.

Born of the human psyche? I wondered how that could be when Talia, Alonso, even Michael, were as real and as physical as I was, but I'd save that question for later. There were more pressing ones at the moment. "So let me get this straight, you gain strength from his blood when you've done stuff for him, and he... feeds on you?"

She laughed out loud. "Oh honey, it's way more than strength I gain from his blood. Taking a vampire's blood is better than the best drug or alcohol high you can imagine. There's nothing else like it, unless it's to reciprocate and offer your own blood to one of their kind. Me," she shrugged. "Well, I get my kicks mostly in other ways, and though I enjoy the exchange of blood, even need it from time to time when I'm weakened, I feed on an entirely different kind of energy." Her gaze raked me like a physical touch and I felt my nipples harden. I caught my breath and stepped back. She just winked, then turned and continued.

For a long time we walked in silence, then I had to ask, "You can't feed on the Guardian?"

"No. I have to have flesh, just as Alonso does, though for him the flesh and blood are a very physical need—different from my own. There's a biochemical reaction that takes place in the body, in the brain when I feed, when a person dreams, when a person is aroused, when a person eats or fucks, or gets excited, or nervous, or frightened, or is satisfied in some other way. That's just biology. I feed on that energy. Whatever it is that the Guardian may be, it's not physical. There's no biology where he is concerned. That's the one thing denied him and the one thing he desires most, that physical experience, that biochemical reaction that happens when flesh meets flesh. That's why everyone here but Alonso and Magda are vulnerable to him. Alonso is technically dead and Magda, well who the hell knows with Magda?"

"So, you can't feed on Magda?"

The tunnel suddenly opened into a small amphitheater-like cave, and we picked our way across the rock-strewn floor, slick with dripping water and moss. At the entrance, which was well hidden from the outside by a thicket of heather and hawthorn, we looked out onto the rainy fells. "I've never tried to feed on Magda. Though I have to admit, she's sexy enough; the thought of entering that woman's dreams scares the hell out of me. Now your angel, well he's another matter. He gave up his angelhood ages ago. Technically he's as human as you are now, though he's… well, I suppose you could say he's enhanced. But, as I'm sure you know, the biochemistry is all there in spades. Him I could feast on quite happily, and the two of you together, oh well, that thought positively makes me wet with anticipation. If ever you're open for a little ménage, hon, I promise I'll make it well worth your while."

"I'll keep that in mind." I hated to admit it, but after my experience with the succubus, the thought made me wet too. I quickly changed the subject. "So, Magda is flesh and blood, then, and the… biochemistry is all there, but for whatever reason, you're scared of her and the Guardian wants nothing to do with her?"

"That's pretty much it, yes. Not sure why the Guardian doesn't like her, but I have a feeling that one taste of her energy would fry my circuits permanently. Might well be worth the risk, but I'm not that fucking brave. As for the whys of it all, well I'm not sure even she fully understands, and if you're brave enough to ask, well go for it, chick, that's all I can say."

I would be brave enough to ask, I thought. I needed to understand who the hell this woman was if my life and the life of my best friend and my lover were in her hands. I needed to know if I could trust her. But even if I couldn't, it really didn't matter at this point. She was all we had. "Is she really a thief?" I asked.

"A thief?" The resulting belly laugh surprised me, and I waited impatiently while Talia regained control, wiping tears from the corner of her eyes, still chuckling when she was finally able to respond. "I suppose now that you mention it, that's exactly what she is, but on a scale that would take your breath away, little scribe." She nodded to what looked like a ramshackle shepherd's bothy, half hidden in a wooded copse. "She's in there." She slipped out of her jacket and handed it to me. "Trust me. You're gonna need this. Magda isn't big on creature comforts when she's practicing her magic."

I shivered from something other than cold as I shoved my way into the black leather jacket, warm from the succubus' body and redolent with her musky, peachy, cinnamon scent. "So what did she send Michael to Chapel House to steal? I mean, seriously, wasn't she afraid something like this might happen with the Guardian if they started mucking about?"

I suddenly found myself in the woman's hard blue gaze. She looked at me as though I were some new life form she was only seeing for the first time. "The Guardian was already released when she sent Michael to play cat burglar. Didn't you know?"

"Me? How the hell would I know? I knew nothing about any of this until Michael rescued me from my butcher knife wielding best friend."

"Sweetie." She stepped closer and pushed the hair back behind my ears in a gesture that sent tingles down my spine, her gaze suddenly softened to something that resembled sympathy. "Didn't you know?"

"Know what?" The tingle became an icy chill. "Know what?"

Talia gave a quick glance out at the bothy and then squared her shoulders as though she had just made a major decision. "Magda commissioned Michael to… to steal you."

"What?" I suddenly felt as insubstantial as the spider webs clinging to the ceiling. "What the fuck's that supposed to mean, she hired Michael to steal me? I'm a person, not an object. She can't steal me. And neither can he," I added, trying to keep the hurt from my voice.

"Oh, she can, and she will. She has stolen more people than you can easily imagine, hon. Michael's one of them. And Michael, well, he'll happily aid her because he wants you almost as badly as she does. Maybe more so, considering the power of his mark on your body. I can feel it from anywhere in High View. Shouldn't doubt that I could still feel it all the way to Penrith."

"Why?" The word came out sounding entirely too much like a sob.

"What do you mean why? You're a scribe. Do you have any idea how rare that is? No one else could have released the Guardian but a scribe, and very few scribes could have done what you did. That's the only explanation for His return to the world of the living. It didn't take Magda and Michael long to put two and two together. They knew your friend wasn't a scribe, and they knew that the Guardian was already feasting on her. Remember Magda rescued Michael from the Guardian, and together they imprisoned Him. They both understand the way it is with Him. You're what He's after. Your friend is just a little snack. He knows what you are as well as they do. You hold His future in your hands, and He knows it. That makes you far too valuable for them not to steal you away."

Chapter Twenty-three

"This is where I leave you, hon." Talia laid a gentle hand on mine, and there was a tingle that felt a great deal like sympathy. "She won't welcome a spectator, and I'm not all that keen on being one." She squeezed my hand and turned back toward the tunnel.

I stood for a second, gathering my courage. The rain had stopped, but the forest was shrouded in mist and though there were bright bursts of light coming from inside the bothy, the surrounding fell side was sunk in false twilight.

I could smell heat, almost like a forge before I approached the bothy, but the place was icy cold. There was no smoke rising from the roof. In fact, the place felt deserted, in spite of the trail in the high grass which, to my surprise, was littered on each side with a menagerie of stone garden sculptures—woodland creatures of all sorts; from mice and voles, to rabbits, rats, even a fallow deer. Many were nearly lost in the high grass, and all were so realistic that the deer and the fox both startled me before I realized the gray in which they slunk was not shadow, but the stone from which they were carved. Walking softly through the wet, recently flattened grass, perhaps on some unconscious level fearing I'd startle the stone creatures, but more than likely because, no matter how much I wanted to clear the air with Magda Gardener, I really wasn't looking forward to the woman's company—especially after my conversation with Talia.

The closer I got to the door of the bothy, the colder I got. Though the ice I felt in the pit of my stomach had nothing to do with the temperature, which was rather mild under the circumstances, the temperature around the bothy, however, appeared to be its own little microclimate, for which I knew the Lake District was famous. But this was no valley, no dale; this was a place of magic. Though my breath came in icy clouds as I drew nearer, the scent of heat permeated the air. Flashes of pale light from within played havoc with my vision. The grass and the stone creatures nearest the entrance were coated in hoarfrost, hoarfrost that I felt coating my lungs as I breathed, chilling me in places that had never known cold before.

In spite of the chill, the bothy door was wide open. In fact there was no door at all and yet I had the very distinct feeling if I were not invited to enter, the lack of a door would not have mattered. I would have been forced to wait outside for eternity.

"Come in, Susan." As though she had read my thoughts, I heard Magda's voice before I actually saw her. But as I stepped across the threshold, I shivered as though I'd just walked through a very large spider web and, though the room was icy cold, the smell of hot metal grew stronger, as did the dance and glare of bright light.

Magda Gardener stood with her back to me in the company of dozens more stone carvings so realistic it was as though she had somehow frozen the toad in mid-leap, the wood pigeon in mid-preen, the hare in mid-hop. There were birds, mice, even several butterflies with stone wings so thin, I wondered at the skill of the artist. They all looked as though the stone from which they were carved would suddenly warm to flesh, and they would all go on about their business, oblivious to their recent stone prisons.

"These are amazing," I said, reaching out to touch a badger

that looked as though he would startle at my movement and scurry away.

"They're just stone," she said, her voice nearly as cold as the room. For a moment, I thought the woman was welding. She stood with her back to me, bathed in bright flashes of light from which I raised a shielding hand to my eyes. But there was no hiss of acetylene, no sparks from the torch, and she wore no welding mask. She was hunched over a wooden workbench strewn with stone chips and sculpting tools. I could hear the chink, chink of metal against stone, and the smell of heat was acrid enough to make my eyes water, in spite of the cold. I pulled the succubus' jacket tighter around me, surprised that Magda worked in a loose-fitting shift that appeared to be made of unbleached cotton. It hung mid-calf, moving and flowing with her efforts. As I stepped closer I saw she was barefoot.

"I had forgotten you're a sculptor." With a chill, I remembered the lifelike sculpture of Michael in the tangled garden at Chapel House.

"It's an interest of mine," she replied without turning around. "Something I fell into quite by accident a very long time ago. These days, I use it most often for sympathetic magic, sculpting what I wish to manifest."

"And these," I opened my arms to include the stone menagerie on the dirt floor of the bothy, "what kind of magic are they?"

"Those are magic uncontrolled," came her reply. "Mistakes with which I now have to live."

"Mistakes? They're perfect, so realistic. I half expected them all to scurry away the minute they saw me."

"Would that they could," she said, and the light around her flashed so bright, I closed my eyes and looked away. "Stop," she commanded, as I stepped toward her. "Stay where you are. Let me finish this first."

I did as she said. It was hard to imagine anyone not doing as Magda Gardener said in that voice of authority that you could feel right where all the blood flows in and out of your heart and right where the hips shelter your center of gravity.

"Magic?" I asked, standing on my tiptoes in an effort to see what she was doing.

"It is." The smell of molten metal intensified, and the dance and arc of light reminded me again of an acetylene torch. "It's to help your friend rest and to guard her dreams. I said stay put," she commanded again as I pressed forward, "unless you want to end up like the animals on the floor."

"What the hell's that supposed to mean?" I snapped.

"It means I'm working with powerful magic and unless you want me to make a mistake and lose control, you will shut up and stay still until I'm finished." The tone of her voice hadn't altered. There was no anger, no frustration. In fact, she could have been giving me her grocery list, but the light over the worktable flared, and the air was virtually toxic with the smell of burning.

For a second I felt as though my skin was freezing solid on my flesh and my lungs were solidifying in my chest. But before I could choke or gag, certainly before I could make a move for the door, the light dissipated, the air cleared to the point that I could smell nothing but the fresh fell breeze, and the room was suddenly warmer.

I only noticed her dark glasses lying on the end of the workbench because she reached for them. When she turned to face me, she was wearing them again. "Here, put this on."

She slipped a black cord around my neck on which hung a heart carved from what looked to be the local stone. I drew it up into my hand and ran a thumb over the perfectly detailed feather etched on its surface.

"It's a protection spell," she said, not waiting for me to ask. "No one is to touch it but you. Well, your angel can touch it, of course. But only because the two of you have been physically joined anyway, and he's given you his own protection spell. The heart represents your heart. The quill is a symbol of your craft. A scribe's magic lives through symbol; therefore it's you, not I, who will empower it with what's needed when the time comes. You may not know it yet, but your craft is the most powerful magic you have with which to fight the Guardian."

I settled the heart between my breasts. "And that's why you wanted to steal me?" I hadn't meant to be so abrupt, nor to sound so ungrateful, but I didn't like having choices taken out of my hands.

If she were upset by my lack of gratitude, she didn't show it. "You undid my efforts, Susan, and now the Guardian is free once again to wreak havoc. Anyone who can do what you did, I want as an ally."

"An ally is not a possession," I said.

"On the contrary, I've found that it's usually best when your allies are your possessions."

I barely heard her words as my gaze came to rest on the object she'd been working on. When I reached for it, she slapped my hand away. "I told you the magic is for your friend. Don't touch magic that belongs to someone else."

I was cold again, cold to the core as I studied the tiny image on the table resting among stone chips and dust. It could have been Annie asleep in miniature, just as I'd left her a few hours ago—the body too thin beneath the duvet, the face racked with exhaustion. Even the details of the bedding and her tiny hand gripping the headboard were identical.

Once again I was certain the piece was carved from local stone, but it was polished, and it shone as though it were somehow lit from within. "Jesus," I whispered, bending to look closer. "It could be her, living and breathing in miniature."

"In truth, it does contain a tiny bit of her essence—a strand of hair, a clipping of a fingernail, but it's only stone, Susan. Taken from that cave, in fact." She nodded to the cave I'd just come out of. "After your little visit, I was forced to redo the magic," she said, picking up the piece, which was no bigger than a small chess pawn and turning it over in her hand. "Your unauthorized contact with her raised unconscious longings, made her restless. I've had to strengthen the magic to protect her, and to protect all of us."

I recalled the butcher knife incident with a shudder. "I'm sorry, but she's my friend, and—"

"And you don't trust me with her. I understand that. But not trusting me is exactly what the Guardian is counting on. He'll make you doubt everything you know to be true. Knowing that to be the case, knowing that the moment will come when you'll want desperately, need with every fiber of your being to believe Him, I will tell you the truth now. Susan, listen to me now, in this place of magic, and know I speak truth. I rescued you, with Michael's help, when no one else knew you even needed rescuing. I took a ridiculous risk and rescued your friend as well, though I'm still not sure what I can do for her. I am the only one who has ever fought the Guardian and won, and even though your fantasies of him are sweeter than any romance you've ever written or read, the truth is that in a few months you'd have ended up just like your friend, and the Guardian would be seeking yet another to devour. This would have been your fate had I not rescued you. You know this to be true. And you must also know that Michael fights the same battle, the same desires, but he is already allied with me. He won't fight his battle alone, and neither shall you."

Her gaze locked on me from beneath the glasses, and she slipped the image of the sleeping Annie into a small leather pouch that hung around her neck and tucked it back inside her shift. Then she turned for the door and motioned me to follow her back to the cave.

"Rescue is not the same as stealing," I said, scrambling to keep up.

"I believe the Guardian would beg to differ."

"That doesn't mean I'll belong to you. If we all live through this," I added.

She stopped in the middle of the cave, deep enough that the natural light had dissipated to dusk, and still she wore the glasses. As she held me in her gaze, no—it was more than that, for a moment I was certain she held me in her thrall—but as she held me there, I was suddenly, irrationally, very glad for the barrier the glasses provided. "No one belongs to anyone, my darling girl, but what you will come to understand if, as you say, we survive this little adventure, is that some debts can never be repaid. Therefore the loyalty we feel, the sense of gratitude, goes much deeper than simply belonging to someone. I have stolen you from the Guardian, but at the end of the day, it will be you who will steal yourself for my purposes and give yourself over willingly."

"Your purposes? What the hell are your purposes?" I asked.

"Why, to write, of course. You are a scribe, after all. Come now." She found a Maglite at the entrance to the tunnel and nodded me to follow. "The others will be waiting. It's time we return to Alonso's drawing room to finish your little story."

Chapter Twenty-four

Back in Alonso's basement drawing room, Cook had delivered still more coffee and tea, along with little finger sandwiches that reminded me of high tea at the Ritz, rather than a quick snack in a vampire's lair before I exposed myself again. I took nothing. I didn't think I could force anything past the tightness in my throat, but Alonso handed me a cup of Kenyan tea and a plate laden with treats.

"You need to eat," he said softly.

Michael sat me down and, before I could protest further, offered me up a miniature chicken salad wrap as though I were a child not capable of feeding myself. He'd *stolen* me! He'd fucking *stolen* me, I reminded myself and resisted the urge to, quite literally, bite the hand that fed me. With the first mouthful, however, I realized just how hungry I was. As I opened my mouth for another bite, I decided we'd table the Chapel House robbery discussion until after I'd eaten. With the second bite I remembered poor Annie wasting away in the bed upstairs. The next sandwich I fed myself, then gulped the tea and braced for impact as Magda, once again, began to read the words I didn't remember writing.

"Come to me, my darling. I need you to release me so that we can be together. You, my beautiful scribe, are the only one who can set me free." That's what He kept saying to me, and I swear it felt as though He were whispering it in my ear.

Annie had gone to bed hours ago, and I should have. I should have been fast asleep, but I couldn't settle, couldn't calm myself, couldn't focus on anything but what I'd experienced in the crypt at Chapel House and the sweet whisper of His longing against my ear. I wanted desperately to go back. I could sneak out of the flat and drive over there easily enough, but the garden was a jungle, and it was huge. After all, it had been a graveyard once. I would never find my way back to the crypt, not without Annie's help, and I most definitely didn't want her help. I didn't want her to know my secret.

But the constant nag and niggle, the need to go to Him gnawed at my insides like a hungry beast. And His voice, I could hear His voice calling to me again and again, inviting me to come to Him.

"Release me, my love. Release me and we can be together. I've waited for you for an eternity, and now I can scarce breathe in my longing for you, in my need for you. Please, set me free so we can be together at last."

Each time I heard His voice, it was as clearly as if He had been standing in the room next to me. And my response, well, I'm not sure if my response was out loud, in my head, or in the open document on which I had poured the details of my earlier encounter in the crypt. "I can't release you. I don't know how to get back to the crypt and I don't know where the key is," I said, bracing myself, half fearing that He might say that He could guide me back to that dark, overgrown place, and half fearing that He would change his mind and get someone else—maybe Annie—to help Him. I couldn't bear that. I couldn't bear the thought of anyone else being with Him. I was just about to tell Him I'd do anything, anything He asked, when He told me a secret.

"You need not return to Chapel House, my darling," came the reply I hadn't expected. "There is no key, and the door to my prison, it means nothing. It's only a symbol. One could tear it out from the very rock and rip open the earth above and I would still be a prisoner. You! You are the key, my darling. You've already begun the process of setting me free. Only a little more remains for you to do, and then we'll be together. I'll give you what you want, what we both so desperately need."

"Tell me! Please, tell me!" I did speak out loud then, feeling a longing for Him that I feared would tear me apart if He didn't tell me what to do.

And then He was so close that I could almost feel the physicality of Him, so close that for a moment, I believed He had somehow managed His own escape. I swear, He kissed my nape and spoke against my ear in a whisper that was barely more than a breath. "All you need do, my lovely, is use your magic. I have read what you've written of our first encounter—each word of it like a caress driving me to lust and longing I can scarcely contain, and my heart races with anticipation. Each word is so carefully chosen, each nuance so evocative of our coming together. Your magic, my love, is our story set down for us to share later in our long nights together, when we are sated and reveling in the pleasure of each other. All you need do, my darling scribe, is write my release, and I shall be free, indeed."

There have, so often, been times when the worlds I create as I write bleed through to the real world and both become equally real to me. I think nothing of it. It's a part of what I do, a part of what I *love about my craft. But this! This was different. The words I wrote returned me instantly to the crypt.*

I could almost touch the thick darkness as I entered. I don't know how I could see, and yet I could. I could smell the dust on the ancient stone; I could feel the rusted bars as I curled my fingers around them. And then I felt His warm breath on my face from just beyond the bars. He cupped large hands over mine and His voice was that of a man just awakened from a deep, dream-laced sleep and into the arms of His lover. "You've come for me, my darling, just as I knew you would. Now set me free. All you need do is open the door."

So I wrote me in the darkness of the crypt, me with hands so anxious, but so certain in their task, me exerting all the force I could manage in my effort to pull the gate open on hinges frozen with age. I wrote the sound of rusty metal giving way. I wrote the smell of age and decay yielding. I wrote the anticipation of lovers who have waited an eternity. I wrote the scent of His desire, of His longing, mingling with mine; dark, fecund, primordial. And then the door was wrenched from me with astounding strength, and He shoved it aside and pulled me to Him and for a moment it was as though I had suddenly been reunited with the other half of me. I knew Him and I knew His heart, and I knew the depth of His desire. And I was overwhelmed with longing.

But before that... just before that... only for a moment, the moment He burst from the earth, the moment He shoved the gate from between us, I felt something else. I felt my body turning to ash on my bones in the heat of fire I knew I would not survive and, in the depths of the inferno I willingly plunged myself into, there was neither escape nor relief. My doom was sealed and I went to meet it rejoicing. But that was all forgotten in His embrace. He was free and it was me that He wanted. Nothing else mattered.

If there were words, I don't remember them. If I could have found the words, the right words to express what it was like to be touched by Him, to be embraced by Him, to be loved by Him, they aren't words that human ears could hear or understand, nor that human voices could utter; and if I had written them down, they were somehow lost between the moment of my desire and the moment of His sating me, for honestly, how could it have been more than a moment?

In the next second I was back in Annie's flat, lying on the floor in a beam of moonlight, curled around myself as though I could hold on to the moment just a little longer, the fast fading memory of Him taking me. And He did take me. He made love to me. Surely He did. Or at least I think He did.

And then He stood over me, all silver and translucent like the moonlight. I couldn't see Him, but He filled the whole room with His presence, as He coaxed me to my feet and back to the open document, glowing pale in the dark study.

"And now, my beloved," He said. "Write me as your secret, a secret that even you won't remember until the time comes for us to be together. Write me a place of safety, a place where I may sustain myself, a way in which I may control my longing until the two of us can be together again."

Then He saw the story I had told Annie, and His laugh was

like the purr of a large cat. "*Why, my darling little scribe, you have already written my place of safety, and you have given me this friend of yours to sustain me until you return to me. It won't be long, my darling. I promise you it won't be.*"

For a long moment, the room was silent. All eyes were on me, and not all of them were without accusation. I couldn't blame them. If I could look at myself, my eyes would be full of accusation. And contempt. I swallowed the rawness in my throat and spoke. "It was then that I heard Annie in the bathroom and I realized that I had to keep the memory stick safe. The next morning I didn't remember any of it. Like I said."

"Did he fuck you?" Of course it was Talia who asked.

"I honestly don't remember. Surely I would have. Don't you think?" I looked from Magda to Michael and back again.

"Oh, you would have if the choice had been yours to make. I'm certain of it," Michael said. "But I doubt that He took you. If He had, you'd have never been able to stay away from Him. And for whatever reason, He wanted you to stay away until he had Annie call you back."

"But why?" I asked.

"Because you, He wants to savor. In His mind's eye, He'll not use you up, but He'll keep you. You're the one he's waited for," Magda said. "You're the one who could release Him. You're the one who could write Him and His story. You're the one He wants as His consort."

There was a murmur of surprise around the room and an

uncomfortable shifting about. But that all receded to background noise at the thought of being His consort. I was right. I had been right all along. I was special. It was me He wanted above all others. It was me He had waited for, me He loved.

It was the tingle of Michael's mark that brought me, grudgingly, back to myself, back to the reality of the situation. I gulped down the last of my tea, now cold, in an effort to clear my head. "But you said, you both said, He'd use me up as He has the others before," I finally managed.

"No doubt He will," Magda replied. "You are human, after all. But using you up won't be His intention. It seldom is."

Still, she was wrong, a little voice in the back of my mind told me. I was different. Me, He would never hurt. Michael's mark stung and burned and I bit my lip until I tasted blood, knowing that my logic was flawed, knowing the danger I was in and the danger I'd put everyone else in. Focusing, even with the burn of the mark, was an effort I could just barely manage. "If I set Him free by writing His freedom, then why can't I write His recapture too?" I asked.

It was Michael who answered. "Because you really, desperately wanted Him free. But no one," he laid his hand against my breast, next to the mark and the pain eased. "No one who has been with Him could ever want to put Him back in his prison with that same intense longing."

Once again we all sat in silence. I knew Michael was right. I might have freed the Guardian, but I could never put Him back in His prison because there was just too much of me that didn't want Him there.

As though Michael understood what I felt and, no doubt he did, he slipped an arm around me and pulled me close. An act which made the buzz of the bite above my breast once again pleasurable rather than painful.

"So then, Magda, what do we do?" Alonso asked.

Before she could answer, Cook shoved his way through the door, bleeding heavily over one eye. "Ms. Annie—she's gone."

Chapter Twenty-five

"What the hell do you mean, Annie's gone?" I said, practically catapulting from the sofa. "She can't be gone."

"I'm sorry," Cook addressed Alonso rather than me. "I brought her tea, and I was surprised to see she wasn't in her bed. I had hoped perhaps she was improving. But she must have hidden behind the door. She hit me with the candlestick." He touched his bleeding head once more as though he couldn't quite believe it had happened. "When I came back to myself, she was gone. I can't have been out for more than a few seconds."

I turned on Magda. "You said your rock magic would keep her asleep, out of harm's way, you said."

"Clearly I was mistaken." She didn't seem to be the least bit rattled by the fact my crazy, half-starved friend was wandering around somewhere at High View.

Alonso was on his feet and through the door almost before I realized he'd moved. He called over his shoulder as he headed down the hall, "I've got the whole place monitored with cameras so I can enjoy the property in the daytime and protect my perimeters. The control room is just down the hall. If she's outside, we should be able to find her."

We all scrambled to follow.

I fell into step beside Magda. "I'll never forgive you if something happens to her."

She raised an eyebrow from behind the dark glasses. "The responsibility for your friend's desperate situation does not lie at my feet, little girl, in case you've forgotten."

If she had gut-punched me, I would have felt the impact no more.

Michael moved next to me, clearly overhearing the exchange, and slid an arm around my shoulder.

I jerked away. "The blame may lie at my feet, but it was rather convenient for the little act of thievery you two were planning at Chapel House, wasn't it?"

Now it was Michael who had the freshly gut-punched look.

I shoved past both of them and fell into step next to Talia, who offered me a sympathetic nod. "Alonso once told me that when comrades are reduced to placing blame, then the enemy has already won." Seemed it was the day for gut-punches.

We all crowded into a room not much bigger than a closet, which was crammed with monitors and keyboards. Alonso sat down in a captain's chair and began systematically pulling up the cameras around the property, all of which had the capability of zoom. In some places, the places where the property was most vulnerable, there were multiple cameras for multiple angles.

"Nothing so far," he said. "The mist is making it difficult to see anything. I've checked the vehicles in the drive and those in the garages, but none are missing. I would assume it's her plan to go back to Chapel House. In her weakened condition, if she tries to go on foot or hitchhike, it would have to be almost entirely under the Guardian's power. The woman is little more than a skeleton."

"He could do that," I said. "When she attacked me, I couldn't believe how strong she was."

"But that was more fear of losing Him than it was any aid of

His," Magda said. "The ability to get back to Him from here, I would think, would depend entirely on His strength."

"And on Him wanting her back," Michael added, eyes locked on me rather than on the monitors, which so far had revealed nothing but a very soggy red squirrel, hunkering down in a fir tree to avoid the rain. Otherwise the place was deserted.

Alonso had sent the builders away when we had arrived, not wanting to put them in any danger or raise any suspicions.

It was then that it hit me with such import that I grabbed onto the back of Alonso's chair to keep my knees from buckling. "He doesn't want her back. He's deserted her totally, and she has to know that by now. And if she knows it…"

As the implications hit home like an exploding bomb, I raced for the door in a burst of adrenaline, yelling back at Michael, "The tower, where your room is, does it lead to the roof?"

"Fuck!"

That was all the answer I needed. I took the stairs out of the basement two at a time, with him right behind me. He passed me as we sprinted through the hall on the main floor, but then ran into one of the maids with a tray full of dirty dishes from our tea. He spun her around and barely managed to right her before both tray and maid could do a swan dive on the hard stone floor as I sped past the little *pas de deux*, barely missing being clotheslined by a flailing arm.

The steps up the tower were narrow and winding, and I reached the ancient wooden door to the parapet a split second before he did. It stood wide open, and the view beyond stopped me in my tracks, stopped my breath, stopped my heart.

Michael had done the same, coming to a screeching halt right behind me.

The tower of High View was shrouded in a light mist. The roof of it was barely big enough in diameter for a tall man to stretch out across. It was surrounded by a stone battlement clearly built for decoration, high enough to lean against, but not high enough to be defensive. There, on the far side, Annie was just stepping up onto the top of it. The rain, which had become a downpour, plastered her borrowed nightdress to her body and rendered it transparent. She truly did look skeletal beneath it. Her foot slipped, and I screamed, but the wind and rain carried my voice away from her and she thankfully didn't hear me as she righted herself.

Before I could run to her, Michael threw an arm around my waist and pulled me tight against his body. "Let her go. It'll be so much easier for us if you do."

I was suddenly overwhelmed by the smell of roses, and yet when I turned, there was no one behind me but Michael. Fingers of ice climbed my spine and I felt as if the world were tilting beneath my feet as he offered me an unnatural grimace of a smile and a jerk of his shoulders. "After all, that is what we planned from the very beginning, isn't it, my darling? She was only ever a substitute, a stop-gap, as it were, until we could be together."

"Michael?" I stumbled out onto the parapet and fell backward on the wet stone. Before I could scramble to my feet, He grabbed me by the arm and jerked me upright with bruising strength and uncharacteristic awkwardness, the smile on His face stretched too far, His eyes opened too wide. His breath came in labored, syncopated rasps.

"Yes, of course Michael is here, just as you see, my darling. But as you can also see," He gave a spastic laugh, "he's not in control right now."

The smell of roses was suddenly so strong that I felt as though I were drowning in them. "How?" I managed, the wind blowing my breath back into my mouth. I tried to pull away, but His hand circled my wrist like a manacle that was too tight.

If it were possible, He smiled even wider. With His free hand, He groped my left breast so tightly that I gasped. But it wasn't until His thumb slid over Michael's mark that I screamed in pain, more pain than I had ever felt in my life. The smell of roses was subsumed in the stench of burning garbage. I would have fallen if He hadn't held me there, hand around my wrist, stretching me upward as though I were weightless, until my toes barely touched the ground. Almost before it began the pain passed, and with it the stink, leaving me dazed and wondering if it had happened at all.

"Remember, Michael allowed me use of this flesh, this lovely angel flesh of his. A very long time ago, it was, but time is of little relevance to one such as myself, and *his* mark on *your* flesh is my way back into *his*." The spastic laugh came hot and heavy against my face. "Oh, the poor lad was wrong in his assumption that by fucking what is mine, by marring it so, he could keep it from me. Even more importantly, my darling, he was wrong in assuming that I didn't pleasure your body that night when you returned to release me from the crypt, that I would not reward you for your gift to me by making love to you when we both wanted it—needed it so desperately. Oh yes indeed, he was very wrong. I had you that night, my darling. I had you over and over again, with you begging me for more each time. You wore *my* mark deep in your very soul long before Michael's feeble attempt to take what isn't his."

He leaned in and kissed me with the awkwardness of an adolescent boy. "Then I took the memory from you because I needed you able to function, able to do what had to be done until I sent for you. Michael's marking you as he did was an extra gift. The lad didn't realize, but in doing so, he gave me the gift of enfleshment." He chuckled softly, more naturally, and I smelled roses again. "I think perhaps now it is time for me to give you those memories back, my darling, so you'll stop fighting me, so you'll understand your place is by my side, and now, so is Michael's."

Before He could bestow upon me memories I knew I was better off without, He was interrupted by a cry that sounded like an excited child. We both turned to find that Annie no longer stood on the battlement, but was next to us, eyes fever bright, the broad smile she wore belying her ill condition. "You came for me, my darling. I knew you would." She took in the way He held my wrist and the way I struggled and her smile broadened still further. She practically buzzed with excitement. "And you'll give her what she deserves, just like you promised?"

"Oh, I will indeed give her what I've promised, Annie, but sadly that promise doesn't involve you."

She looked from Him to me and back again. The smile slipped from her face. She shifted from foot to foot. "I… don't understand."

"Annie! Annie, He's going to hurt you. You have to get out of here before—" I caught my breath in a cry of pain as He pressed His thumb against Michael's mark.

Annie's response was to laugh and clap her hands like a delighted child.

"Stop laughing, stupid woman!" Both Annie and I jumped, startled by the power of His voice even above the rage of the storm. "She is my beloved; I have sent for her. Do you not know? It's not your place to laugh at my chosen."

And just like that Annie was trembling all over, once again feeling the effects of the weather, the cold and the last few months of her ordeal. "But what about me?" Her lower lip trembled and she wrung her hands.

I glanced desperately back at the stairs. Where the fuck was everyone? What was taking them so long to get to us? They had to know where we were. They had to!

"My darling, you already know the answer to that question." He nodded back to the battlement. "You've served me well with your flesh, my dear Annie, and for that I shall never forget you, but your job has always been to prepare the way. How could you have ever doubted that? Surely you understood this when I had you send for the scribe."

She studied me for a long moment, as though seeing me for the first time. Then the anguish on her face disappeared and she came forward, pulled His hand away from my breast and kissed it, which He allowed her to do like some beneficent king.

The moment He removed his hand from Michael's mark, I

could breathe again. I could think clearly again.

"Run along now, Annie darling," He said, giving a little shooing motion He might have given a favorite pet who was making a nuisance of itself. "Now your job is finished. Time for you to rest. Leave us to our lives together and free my beloved from her concerns for you."

The wind howled around us and the mist thinned enough that I could see the battlement and the woods beyond. Perhaps He was right. It was inevitable. Even Magda said so. And at the end of the day, if Magda's magic couldn't heal Annie, then really, what could? What was left to her but to be sent away to some asylum where she would be drugged and tied to a bed to drool and piss herself until she wasted away, pining for the lover who would never return for her. It was a kindness, really. It was best to remember her the way she was, the way she had been when she was whole, when she was my best friend. Though really, what did any of those memories matter now?

I watched as, on trembling legs, she fumbled her way onto the battlement.

All the while He spoke softly to me, reassuring me, telling me that it was for the best, teasing me with little flashes of memory, of moments in the crypt, of the instant He first entered me, when I suddenly felt the entire world, every molecule of it, every breath of it. He tempted me with little glimpses of Him nursing at my breasts with the innocent discovery of a child, and yet at the same time, with the passion of a lover powerful enough to set the tangled garden on fire and the whole city along with it.

In an instant I saw the eternity we'd spent together that night.

The heat of the body He'd not then possessed took me to heights of ecstasy I could never have imagined. I, not unlike Annie, had come to those heights of my own free will, only to throw myself off into the abyss that would have terrified me had He not been there to catch me, had He not been there to kiss me everywhere, to enter me again and again, spilling the ocean of Himself into the tiny space that was my flesh, and spreading me over its surface until there was nothing left of me but a thin, transparent skin, permeable only to Him. I hadn't known I could come like that. I hadn't known I could be so opened, that I could contain so much and still long for more.

Dear God, how could I ever, ever walk away from Him? What difference did the death of one person mean in comparison to being with Him? What difference did the death of everyone who lived in High View, in Penrith, in Manchester, in all of Britain, matter in comparison to being the one He chose to love?

"Michael will stay with us too, my love," He was saying, as I watched Annie trembling and struggling and pushing her way up to stand on the very edge of the battlement, toes curled over rain-slicked stone. "His flesh, his angel flesh, will be mine, will be yours, and we will be together, united as I've always wanted."

A gust of wind whirled around us and something cold and wet thumped me in the chest. With a startled gasp, I reached up and felt Magda's heart-shaped stone warming to my touch. Without thinking, I curled my icy fingers around it for warmth.

There was a gasp, a curse, the sharp smell of burning garbage. Suddenly I was free, running toward the battlement, screaming Annie's name at the top of my lungs.

Chapter Twenty-six

"Annie, no! Annie, don't do it! Annie, please! Annie!" I screamed her name to be heard above the howl of the wind. The fine hairs on the back of my neck prickled with terror that Michael's invaded body would reach out and grab me and pull me back, or worse yet, race ahead of me and take the decision completely out of Annie's fragile hands.

It was only a few steps to get to her. I should have been able to reach her in three quick strides, but it might as well have been a million miles. I swear the distance between us stretched and elongated to an impossible space.

It was Him. He was doing it! I knew He was. Even as it was happening, I knew it wasn't real, but no matter how hard I struggled to reach her, it was like being caught in a nightmare, one of those in which the harder you run, the slower you move, and the farther you have to go. It was as though everything had switched into slow motion, my begging and screaming being blown back in my face, a mindless cacophony of desperate sound. The agonizing moment she stood in the wind teetering on the edge of the battlement stretched and elongated with my tortured efforts to reach her. Then, for the briefest of seconds, the wind died down just a tiny bit, and she turned and looked at me. In her eyes, for a moment, I saw my friend still there, still inside the ravaged body. I saw recognition in her eyes. "Annie! Dear God, Annie, hang on!"

But then the wind rose again, swirling around us like an evil thing intent on tormenting us, which was a very real possibility.

"Susan?" I heard nothing, but saw her lips mouth my name as

she reached out her hand toward me. It was the very effort to save herself that off-balanced her. She screamed and teetered on the edge.

We both screamed and I dived toward her with both arms flung outward, reaching, stretching as far as I could and beyond, her fingertips just brushing mine, with me raging into the wind, "No! You bring her back! She's not yours! You fucking bring her back!"

But I wasn't fast enough. How could I not have been fast enough? For a thousand years, no—for a million years I watched her topple slowly, endlessly off the battlement as though that instant of my own helplessness, of my own horrible guilt, lived and breathed in a suspension of eternity in which I had nothing to do but dwell on what might have been if I could have gotten to her just a fraction of a moment faster.

Suddenly the breath was knocked out of my lungs by a force like a freight train that hit me from behind, and I was pushed hard toward the open door as a blur flew past me and disappeared over the battlement. I tumbled backward and hit my head against the stones hard enough to rattle my teeth and jar my brain.

For a second I lay stunned, pinpoints of light flashing behind my eyes, hearing nothing but a loud ringing in my ears, and then I heard people scrambling up the stairs. Magda was at my side one minute, then at the battlement the next. Reese moved with her.

At first I could make no sense of what was happening. Then a large hand reached over the stones and caught hold of Reese's wrist and suddenly both Reese and Magda were pulling and straining and leaning so far over the battlement that I feared they'd go over too.

Still half-stunned, I looked around for Michael, who was nowhere to be found. It was Talia who offered me a hand and helped me to my feet, but her attention was on what was happening at the battlement.

"Did you get her?" she called into the wind.

My heart stopped as I watched. Then it started again, it started to race like a wild thing the instant I realized it was Michael who Reese heaved up onto the battlement. Michael, holding on for dear life with one arm, while with the other he handed the sobbing, trembling Annie into Reese's care.

"Take her, and get her out of here," Michael's voice carried on the wind. "I'm not safe."

Reese hefted my friend into his arms and gave me a reassuring smile before he hurried toward the open door.

Michael collapsed on the wet stone, drenched and shaking and gasping for air.

"Jesus, Michael, what did you do?" I said, rushing to his side. "When I didn't see you, I thought you'd jumped, too."

Before I could throw my arms around him, he stopped me with a raised palm. "I should have. I would have if it hadn't been for Annie. Stay back. I told you, I'm not safe." Then he turned to Magda. "Get her away from me. Now."

"Michael, what are you doing? We'll figure this out. It'll be okay. He's not in you now. I can feel He's not." I tried to fight Magda, but her grip on my arms was like iron as she turned me toward the door. "Michael," I called over my shoulder, straining against her hold. "Don't push me away. Michael, I can help."

He pulled himself to his feet with an effort that looked as though it hurt him and, for a moment that was all too brief, his gaze locked on me. "I'm sorry, Susan. I'm so, so sorry." Then he turned his back and hunched against the battlement, shoulders rising and falling as though each breath were a desperate effort.

"What's he going to do? What the hell is he going to do?" I fought for all I was worth, but Talia flanked me on the other side and the two women maneuvered me to the stairs.

"It'll be all right," Talia said, but there was very little conviction in her voice. Inside, she slammed the stair door behind us, effectively shutting Michael on the roof.

Alonso waited for us just beyond the daylight. He took me in his arms and bodily carried me, kicking and screaming, down the stairs as Magda turned back to the roof.

At the bottom of the stairs, Alonso pushed me up against the wall, pressing one forearm across my shoulders, just above my breasts so I couldn't move. With the other he took my chin in his hands and forced me to meet his gaze. "Susan, he's not going to jump. Magda would never let him do that, and it's hardly his way. Calm down."

The sheer force of him prickled over my skin like electricity, and I relaxed.

When he was sure I was calm enough to hear what he had to say, he smoothed the rain-soaked hair out of my face and spoke. "Michael's right. He's not safe, as you just saw, as we all just saw. It isn't safe for you to be with him right now, not until Magda figures out what to do." He gave the succubus a nod and she disappeared down the hall. "Talia will bring you some dry clothes, and then she'll stay with you until Magda can sort things out."

"I'm not any safer than he is," I said, fighting back a sob.

He wiped an escaped tear with the tip of a cool thumb. "Then I shall stay with you. Not that I'm exactly safe, either, but I'm probably your best bet at the moment."

Once I had changed into a dry, if rather oversized, tracksuit, Talia informed me that Annie was safely back in her bed, this time with stronger magic to protect her.

Though I had little confidence in any form of magic after all that had happened, I still held the stone heart that Magda had made for me in a suicide grip every second that I was alone.

Alonso dismissed the succubus and led me back to his study. There, he pointed me to a roll-top desk in one corner where my Mac sat. "My good sister was a writer, and a fine one, indeed." He chuckled softly. "Of course that was long before the days of computers, but I know a writer's mind. I know that sometimes the only way to make sense out of the chaos is to write it down, and if you are a scribe, as Magda says, then it's even more true for you."

"Thank you," I managed as he pulled out the chair for me and settled me at the desk.

"Not at all, my darling girl. We all work out our demons in different ways."

Right on time, Cook delivered tea and homemade shortbread.

"Allow me," Alonso said, pouring the tea into a porcelain cup from a matching tea service that I suspected would have brought a fortune on *Antiques Roadshow*. As he did so, he inhaled deeply.

"Though I can no longer enjoy a good cup of freshly brewed tea myself, I may still take pleasure in the scent, in the warmth, and in the sharing of the experience with those who can enjoy it." He offered me a steaming cup.

I sipped and felt the heat curl down deep in my belly, where everything had turned to ice from the incident on the battlement.

"What about your demons, Alonso?" I asked, as he settled onto the sofa with a battered copy of Marcus Aralias's *Meditations*. "I'm sorry, I know it's none of my business. I guess I just needed to know that I'm not the only one doing battle, though clearly you haven't failed so miserably in you efforts as I have."

"Oh, I've had more than my share of failing miserably, darling girl." He laid down the book and stroked his chin. "In the old days, anything that stood between me and what I wanted—I simply drank its blood, then killed it." He offered a little chuckle when I shuddered. "That obviously didn't work too well in the end, and I had to find a way to live with who I am, what I've done, and what I must do to survive. Talia has been a friend and companion to me for a very long time, and her help in sorting my dreams, in offering me solace, has been invaluable. Of course now Reese is the delight of my heart, and wise far beyond his years. But in truth," he shifted on the sofa and held me in a dark gaze, "it was Magda Gardener who saved me from my worst demon, and that was none other than me and my own self-loathing."

"But not without a price," I said, tasting the bitterness of my words.

He shrugged. "Everything has a price, my darling girl. It's up to each of us to decide if it's a price worth paying and, in my case, it's not a price that I have ever regretted." His chuckle was almost a purr. "Of course the woman can be a bloody nuisance at times, but I can overlook that. If she needs me, I'll be there, and she knows it and is quick to return the favor."

We sat in silence for a moment, both lost in our thoughts. I wondered how it was that, though everyone feared Magda Gardener, and no one was ever particularly happy when she showed up on their doorstep, everyone always willingly did for her whatever she asked of them, and they seemed to do it out of respect for her, rather than fear. "May I ask you a question?" My voice sounded overly loud in the quiet room.

"Of course."

"Magda says it's because you're a vampire that the Guardian can't get to you?"

He nodded. "He must feed on the living just as I must, so I am of no use to Him."

"And what about Reese? Why haven't you turned him into a vampire? Aren't you afraid the Guardian might take him?"

"Oh, I'll bring Reese over if he wishes it one day. But only if I'm certain that he wishes it. There's no undoing the deed once it's done, and the price is a very high one, indeed. Never to see the light of day, never to taste the pleasure of a good cup of tea, always to feel the insatiable hunger for blood. Always to live in fear that you might be found out, and worst of all, the fear that you might hurt or even destroy the ones you love. It isn't a decision to be taken lightly, and Reese knows this well. But you see, Reese sups regularly from my

heart's blood, and he is the lover of a vampire, my familiar. He is…
polluted, if you will. Oh, the Guardian could still take him, but only
as a last resort."

"And Talia? She drinks from you."

"She's also less vulnerable because she's under my
protection. Everyone who works in my household is… I suppose you
could say… tainted by my blood. The Guardian would find that very
distasteful, and of no interest as long as He has His mind set on you.
Nonetheless, Magda is wise to do all she can to protect what's mine.
You see, what's mine is also hers."

"So in a way you're her familiar."

At this, he laughed out loud. "I suppose you could say that.
Though I've never quite thought of it that way, and I'm sure she
would no more approve of that parallel than would your angel."

The mention of Michael made my throat tighten and the
room blurred as my eyes misted. "Michael! Dear God, what he's
been through." I laid my hand against his mark, which still stung as
though I had abraded the skin somehow. "How can this be
happening to him again?"

Alonso was instantly at my side, offering a pristine
handkerchief from his pocket. "I don't know, my darling girl, but I
do know that Magda defeated the Guardian before and brought
Michael safely away from Him."

"And I released the bastard to torture him again."

He knelt in front of me and lifted my chin so I was forced to
look into his bright eyes, which instantly made the world seem
slightly askew before it righted itself again. "Do not think for one

moment that this is your fault. You were deceived. You were deceived!" He took my face in his hand so I couldn't look away. "You know your heart, Susan. You must trust what you know. You're a scribe, for God's sake! You know your own soul better than any other mortal can, and I've been around long enough to be a very good judge of character. It's in the nature of the Guardian to deceive. It's what He does, and it's in the nature of a scribe to reveal the hidden and release it into the world, to unlock secrets. He knew that as you never could, and He took advantage. The laying of blame is always easier than facing the truth, my darling girl, and there are times when one needs an unbiased eye to lay the blame where it properly belongs. I shall be that for you, Susan Innes, if you'll allow me the honor. I shall tell you without bias that you are not to blame for the release of the Guardian into the world. The blame for all that He's done, all that He has ever done, lies squarely at His miserable feet, and no one else's. You must believe me in this if you, or any of those you love, are to survive, and if there is to be any chance of returning this monster to His prison."

Before I could respond, the door to the study swung open. Talia came in, followed by Reese, and not far behind him Magda. Michael brought up the rear.

"Michael! Thank God! Are you all right?" When I tried to go to him, he glanced at Alonso and shook his head.

Alonso nodded his understanding and gently but firmly settled me back at the desk.

For a second Michael stood, as though he wasn't certain what to do next. Whatever it was that crossed his face in the split second before he regained control of his emotions both terrified me and broke my heart. Feeling me tense, the vampire's grip tightened gently around my wrist. For a second longer, Michael stood at the door. Then he squared his shoulders, took a deep breath and pulled it shut behind him, moving to take a chair on the far side of the room, carefully avoiding my gaze.

"We need to talk." Magda settled in the big wingback chair near the fireplace. "Clearly the Guardian has forced our hand, and it's time to end this before more damage can be done."

Chapter Twenty-seven

It was the first time I'd seen Magda Gardener looking anything but calm and relaxed and only just slightly this side of laughing at a good joke. She looked tired. She didn't just look tired, she looked downright worried, and that scared me. Clearly it scared everyone in the room, although after what had happened on the battlement, Magda Gardener's countenance was probably just the icing on the shit-storm cake we were all facing. That sucked, but it was Michael sitting across the room, doing his best to avoid my gaze that shredded me.

Alonso offered me his hand and gently guided me to the loveseat to sit next to him, the battered copy of Marcus Aralias falling to the floor with a muted *thump*.

Everyone settled, then waited expectantly, all eyes on Magda Gardener—all eyes but Michael's. He only stared at the floor, looking pale and drawn. There were dark circles under his eyes that hadn't been there before we'd all made our mad race to save Annie.

With an icy shiver I realized he was showing the same symptoms Annie showed, the result of the Guardian's attentions.

But before I could dwell on Michael's situation, Magda spoke. "I've done what I can to protect Michael from another invasion, but with magic there are never any guarantees, especially not in dealing with the Guardian."

"I don't see that you have much choice but to return me to Chapel House," I said, and I was surprised to find that I had no ulterior motive this time, other than wanting Michael and Annie free from this horror and everyone else safe.

"You're right. There is no other choice." It was Michael who replied. He lifted his gaze to me. "You'll be returned to Chapel House and me along with you."

Magda cut in. "He wants you both. Having you both is His way of proving He can do whatever He wants, and we can't stop him." She ran a hand through her windblown hair, which settled around her like a writhing halo. "It's a good bet that once you've both been returned to Him He'll see to the death of your friend, then begin working away on Alonso's people as well. It's His way to punish us for thinking we can best Him, to punish me for having done so before."

"Jesus! You can't let that happe—"

"Shut up, Susan. The time for negotiation is over. I'm telling you exactly what He'll do because He doesn't negotiate. He has no feeling of human emotion, no understanding of compassion or empathy."

"I won't give up people under my protection, Magda. You know this," Alonso said.

"I know you're a fool, Alonso, driven by your heart to the bitter end. That's why you'll do exactly as I say. That's why you'll all do exactly as I say, because your humanity is your strength. It's the one thing He doesn't understand. We can use that against Him."

"You have a plan then," Talia said.

"I do." Magda bit her lip and squared her shoulders, taking in everyone in the room with a gaze that was made all the more impressive by the dark glasses she always wore. "And if you all do exactly as I say, *exactly as I say*," she emphasized the words as though our lives depended upon them, which was more than likely the truth, "then I'll have the Guardian safely back in His stone prison by this time tomorrow."

She raised a hand when Alonso started to speak. "There will be no negotiation, no second guessing, no questioning. Is that clear? Susan?"

I felt as though her gaze beneath the glasses was turning me to ice. I nodded mechanically.

"I mean it. I'm the only one who knows how to deal with this bastard and I'll tolerate no interference."

"So what's your plan then?" Reese asked, moving to sit on the arm of the loveseat next to Alonso.

"Tonight, Michael and Susan will steal a vehicle and slip away, back to Chapel House, where they'll fervently negotiate with the Guardian to release Annie and everyone else in exchange for them."

"Why a night escape? In case you've forgotten, this is a vampire lair," Talia said. "The place will be far less vulnerable when the vampire is able to move about freely."

"I've forgotten nothing," Magda replied. "Didn't you just hear Alonso say that he would do whatever it took to protect his own?" She nodded to Michael and me. "They're not his own. They bring danger into his house. The Guardian will have no trouble believing that Alonso will turn a blind eye, even possibly leave the keys in the getaway car. Remember, He has no concept of loyalty or compassion. He'll believe it, trust me."

"And then what?" I asked. I didn't realize I was trembling

until Alonso slipped a comforting arm around me, and the look that crossed Michael's face as he watched was raw anguish.

"And then I invite Him in," Michael said. "That's what He wants more than anything, to experience the sensations of being in the flesh. That's what I can give Him. He wants to experience taking you with my body." The muscles along his jaw twitched, his lips thinned to a grim line and I could see the pulse in his temple hammering a rapid staccato. For a second he struggled, as though the power of speech had suddenly left him. Then he drew himself up to his full height and his eyes locked on mine. "I… I have to let Him if we're ever to end this."

I nodded, for a second losing my own ability to speak as my throat constricted and I felt as though the room were tilting around me. "I understand," I said. I didn't. I never would, but I certainly had no idea how to fight this bastard, especially not when most of the time what I wanted on a visceral level was for Him to fuck my brains out. "And then what?" I finally managed.

"Once He's inside Michael, He's vulnerable," Magda said. "It'll be your job to hold His attention, which shouldn't be too difficult since you're the object of His lust and He'll be enjoying you physically, something He won't be able to resist. You just need to hold His attention until I give the word."

The room was deadly silent. I would wager everyone was holding their breath. I certainly was.

"And this is very important, Susan." She turned her full attention on me again. "When I give the word, you close your eyes, you close them as tightly as you can, and you don't open them for anything. Not for anything, until I say it's okay."

"I don't understand. How's that supposed to help me or Michael? If I'm lying there helpless with my eyes closed and—"

"Michael knows what to do. And everything hinges on you keeping your eyes closed. I don't care if you understand or not. That doesn't matter. What matters is that you do exactly as I say, that you close your eyes and keep them closed until it's over."

"Susan." Alonso gently squeezed my hand. "Please don't argue. Do as she says. Magda knows what she's doing, and if you do as she says, you'll come back to us safely."

Michael, who still held me in his laser gaze, nodded his agreement with Alonso and Magda. "The plan will work, Susan. It's the only plan that will work, and you have to trust Magda. You have to trust me."

I nodded. But I didn't trust either of them, not really. I didn't trust anyone against the Guardian. He didn't think like a person would, and while He might not understand human emotions, He was incredibly intuitive, and He did understand human actions.

It wasn't just that, though, it was the way Magda and Michael were behaving—the furtive glances, the stiff upper lips. Something wasn't right. I wasn't being told what would actually happen. I was being told to trust in a place where I had not seen any reason to trust—not because people didn't have my best interests at heart, but because we were all dealing with insurmountable odds and I was being asked to go in blind. But still I nodded my agreement; I nodded my consent and the trust I didn't feel. There was nothing else I could do at that moment.

That seemed to be enough for Magda, though. She gave a decisive nod and stood. "Good, then I suggest you get some rest. Michael will stay with me for safety's sake and Alonso, if you would see to Susan's safety, I'd appreciate it. When the time comes, when it's fully dark, you'll escort Susan and Michael out in what will be seen as your effort to keep your own people safe. I'll find my own way to Chapel House, and by the time they arrive I'll be waiting there. Oh, don't worry," she waved a dismissive hand at me, "I promise the Guardian will have no clue that I'm there. I'm good at hiding, and I've hidden from way scarier bastards than Him."

As everyone stood to leave, Michael strode out without so much as a backward glance, and I felt the lack of him as though someone had ripped my heart out.

It was Alonso who supported me, whispering softly against my ear. "Let him go, my darling girl. Let him do what he must for Annie, for you."

Everyone filed out of the room except Talia, who came to Alonso's side. "Cook's waiting in your room. It's his turn, and you need to feed." Before he could protest, she said, "Now's not a good time for you to be weakened, Alonso, now go and feed. I'll take care of this one," she offered me half a smile, "and when you're done, we'll be in her room."

Alonso dropped a cool kiss on my forehead and left the room with a quick backward glance.

Feeling like I'd been gutted with a spoon, I followed Talia up the stairs to my room. Neither of us spoke, and though I was completely strung out, I knew I wouldn't sleep.

As she opened the door and stepped aside for me, I was just about to ask if we could go back for my computer when she shut the door and locked it. Before I knew what was happening, she pulled me into her arms, taking my mouth with a deep, probing kiss.

I gasped and tried to push her away as her power overwhelmed me. My knees gave, and we half settled, half fell onto the Aubusson carpet.

"Listen to me, Susan Innes," she spoke against my mouth in between urgent kisses. "We don't have much time. Michael asked me to give something to you after everything was all over." She covered my mouth with her hand when I tried to question. "But I made an executive decision not to wait. I don't believe in subterfuge, and I don't believe in keeping vital information from people. It causes more damage than it does good, and you're the scribe, not some silly helpless little girl. Now hold still, be quiet and let me give you what he wants you to have."

She kissed me again, and this time I wrapped my arms around her neck and kissed her back. The floor gave way beneath me. The whole world gave way. I knew that Talia was more than just a succubus—though that was frightening enough—but her powers were far more formidable. Michael had called her a living flash drive, and I understood why as she took my mouth in what was so much more than just a kiss, and suddenly it was Michael I was kissing.

We stood together in the hallway by the stairs, him pressing me tightly against the wall, him caressing me, him holding me. But he slapped my hands away when I tried to undo his jeans. "There's no time for that now," he said, "I need you to listen to me, Susan, just listen. I love you. I've loved you since long before I ever met you. Angels have eternity stretched out before them. They can see all time as it plays out; no beginning, no end. It's a terrifying thing to face time with no end. In order to stay sane, we choose a moment, an experience, a person, and we focus on them. They are our true north. You were mine long before my fall from grace. You were my reason for holding on and my reason for fighting my way back from the Guardian.

"Perhaps this is the reason for my whole existence, and now that I'm human, now that I am mortal, I can give it all up and let it go knowing that you're safe, knowing that you'll go on to become the scribe you were intended to be. Listen to Magda. She'll teach you. She'll guide you, and she'll comfort you when you feel you can't go on. Only listen to her, and never forget that I love you. If anything of a person lives on, then let it be that, let it be my love for you."

And once again I was lying on the floor wrapped in Talia's arms, struggling hard to get away. "He's going to sacrifice himself. I can't let that happen! Let me up, damn it! Get off me, Talia."

But she didn't. Instead she straddled me and pushed me down hard to the floor, trapping my wrists in her hands. "What I gave you," she managed, breathing hard, "that was from Michael. What I give you now is from me, what I've discovered, because you need to know. You need to know what's happening."

This time the kiss was little more than a breath at first, and then it was as though I were standing on the battlement in the storm, and I was the one falling, endlessly falling from the tower. But all that disappeared with a jerk and a tremor, and I found myself standing in front of Magda Gardener's little bothy, safely hidden behind a hawthorn thicket. Oh, it wasn't me, of course. It was Talia, but I saw it all through her eyes. I knew I shouldn't be there, but I had to know what was going on. Someone needed to know what Magda was up to, so I hid and watched and listened as she spoke with Michael.

"You know there's no other choice now," Michael said. "If you turn me while the Guardian's inside me, then He won't be able to escape. He'll be trapped." His laugh was tinged with bitterness. "The bastard has inadvertently given us a way to trap Him, and what churchyard doesn't benefit from one more stone angel?"

"I can't do that, Michael. You can't ask that of me. You can't." The anguish in the woman's voice vibrated through the whole room, even through the rocks of the foundation and the menagerie of sculptures around it.

"Magda, Magda, listen to me." He knelt in front her and took her face in his hands, careful not to disturb the glasses. "You have no choice and you know it as well as I do. He's gotten into me. He won't go away, and He won't stop until He has Susan, and Annie is dead. Then, you've already said it, He'll come after all of Alonso's people, starting with Reese, just for revenge's sake. And once that happens, there'll be no one standing in His way. Magda, you know I speak the truth."

"Not you, Michael. Not you! You don't deserve this." The woman was actually crying. "No one deserves this."

"That's right, no one does. But that's not important, that doesn't matter. Annie and Susan, keep them safe. That's what matters. Susan, she is a scribe, a true scribe. She writes the truth of what happens, she writes the possibilities. You have to keep her safe. And besides," he said, settling back onto a rough wooden bench, "I love her. You know I love her."

I heard the soft patter of something hard and tiny, like seed pearls hitting stone, but ignored the sound as Michael continued. "Don't you see, once He's inside me, He's vulnerable. We can trap Him forever and it'll all be over. Finally it'll all be over."

Magda Gardener laid her glasses aside and buried her face in her hands.

For a long moment Michael sat silently next to her. Then he reached out and took her into his arms. When she straightened, he turned and looked away while she reached for her glasses. And then she wiped her eyes with her fingers and the sound of seed pearls broke the silence.

It was then that I saw it—the tears on Magda's cheeks were wet only for a moment. I blinked and blinked again. Surely I was imagining it, but the tears were transformed to tiny stones, not much bigger than grains of sand as they slid off her cheeks and into her lap and fell onto the floor.

"Do you understand?" The voice came from a long way off. "Do you understand now, Susan?"

I glanced around me at the stone menagerie of every animal, no matter how small, perfectly carved in incredible, impossible detail. Another stone angel, Michael had said. When you change me, he had said. It couldn't be. When I give the word, Magda had said, you close your eyes, you close them as tightly as you can, and you don't open them for anything. Not for anything, until I say it's okay. That's what she'd said. That's what she'd repeated. That's what she'd stressed. She always wore the dark glasses. She wouldn't let me look at her when she came to me in the crypt. It all made sense now, and yet it was impossible, so totally impossible.

"It can't be. It just can't be. It can't." I came back to myself sitting on the floor leaning against the bed, my head resting on Talia's shoulders, repeating over and over again, "It can't be. It's impossible. It can't be." But I knew the truth at last, in my gut I knew the truth. "Magda Gardener—she's… she's Medusa."

Talia held me in her bright blue gaze. "Now you understand. And you needed to understand because you're the scribe and you write the story."

Chapter Twenty-eight

"She's going to turn him to stone. She's going to trap the Guardian inside him. Isn't she? Isn't that what she's going to do?"

No answer was necessary, I knew the truth of the plan, and Talia didn't bother to respond.

"I have to stop her! I have to stop her from murdering Michael!"

I didn't make it to my feet. She pulled me down hard enough to jar the breath out of me and held my arm in a vice grip I was sure would leave bruises. "Sit down, stupid woman! Didn't you hear anything she said? She doesn't want to do this. Do you think she would ever, ever consider such a thing if there were another alternative?"

"But she's Medusa! She's fucking Medusa!"

"I fucking know who she is," Talia said. "And so does everyone else in this household. She's the woman who saved us all from our worst nightmares. She's the woman who does what she has to in order to protect her own, and sometimes that calls for sacrifice."

"But it's not her sacrifice, is it?" I said. "It's Michael's sacrifice."

"Don't you think she would gladly give herself in his place if she could? She'd do anything for Michael. They've been together for a long time, longer than either of us has been alive, but the Guardian has left her no choice. Even if she were to refuse it, Michael won't. For your sake, Michael won't."

"Then let it be me! Let me be the sacrifice. Surely a stupid scribe can't possibly be worth the value of an angel, and it's my fault. This is all my fault!"

"It can't be you, little girl." She released my arm and let me get up this time. "You can't hold Him long enough to let Magda do what she has to. You can't hold Him long enough to distract Him."

"How do you know?" I paced the carpet, eyeing the door, wondering if I could make a break for it, though not at all sure how to get to Magda's bothy if I did.

"I don't know," Talia said. "But as for your value, yes, a scribe is worth more than an angel. Much more. Haven't you read there are myriad angels? They're three for a pound at Sainsbury's."

When I glared at her she backpedalled. "All right, the ones who leave heaven are few and far between, but that still doesn't matter. A scribe is rarer by far, and a real one, one that could do what you did, is a precious thing. None of us has ever met one before, and neither has Magda." She raised a hand before I could interrupt. "But even that wouldn't matter to her if there was another way. Michael has been her friend and companion for a very long time. She does this for two reasons. Michael will have it no other way, first of all. And secondly, there is no other way, and your Annie's life is not the only life at stake."

"I don't care! I won't accept it! I can't. If I'm a scribe then maybe I can hold Him just like Michael can. Maybe I can distract Him."

Talia folded her arms across her chest and looked me up and down. "Possibly, but Michael would never allow you to make that sacrifice. Besides, such a thing is a waste of a scribe's powers."

"I don't understand."

She stood and moved in front of me, blocking my path and, for a second, I thought she was going to kiss me again. Instead she held me in a hard blue gaze. "You're a scribe. You wrote Him free. You wrote the Guardian free. Oh, it's true that He deceived you into doing it, but at the end of the day you were the one who wrote the script, Susan. The proof is downstairs on your computer." She nodded toward the door.

I stepped back and nearly fell onto the bed. Suddenly there didn't seem to be enough oxygen in the room. My heart felt as though it had gone into freefall. "Wait a minute." My words came out thin and raspy. "Are you trying to tell me that I really could… write Him back into His prison?"

Before she could answer, there was a soft knock on the door, and we both jumped.

Alonso stuck his head in looking like someone had just run over his dog. We stepped apart and turned to face him, but vampires don't miss much, or at least this one didn't. He glanced at me and then at Talia and simply said, "You told her."

"She needed to know," Talia replied, holding his gaze defiantly.

"Yes, she did," came the unexpected response. "I was coming to tell her myself, and then…" His voice drifted off and his gaze moved toward the window behind me, where the shutters were still tightly drawn from his last little run-in with daylight. He forced his gaze back to his familiar. "It's just as well you did."

"You're going to Magda," Talia said, as though she were

already certain of what Alonso would do. But then, she was his familiar and his friend and they'd been together long enough that they probably both read each other pretty well.

"I am, yes. I'll try and present an alternative plan."

"Do you have one?" I could see by his expression that he didn't.

"I am known for, what is the saying, pulling things out of my arse at the last minute. We shall hope that my arse will provide. Otherwise…" His voice drifted off for a second time, and then he forced a smile. "Otherwise I shall petition for a little more time, then perhaps we can find another solution, though I'm not hopeful."

"Does anyone ever call her Medusa anymore?" I asked, fighting a rise of bitterness in my throat at the thought of what was about to happen.

"Not in a very long time," Alonso replied, "and such a pity that the stories and lies about her have tainted such a noble name. Her name means to protect, to rule over. Did you know that, my darling girl?"

"I… didn't. No."

"And she is truly worthy of that name." He stepped in so close to me that I could feel the breath he didn't need against my cheek. "She paid a terrible price to be free of that past, and it's no hardship for those of us who know her story to honor her with whatever name she chooses for herself. In truth, our parents give us names they choose, names that suit them, but only we can know our real identities."

For a moment, we all stood in silence. Then he squared his

shoulders to the task at hand. "I'll leave you in charge of our little scribe, Talia. I have asked that her laptop be brought up for her in case she should choose to chronicle the events." He leaned in and kissed me on the cheek. "Don't borrow trouble, my darling girl. The day is not yet lost and we must stay in the moment allotted to us." He brushed my hair away from my cheek, then turned and left just as the maid arrived with my Mac.

Talia took it from her and placed it on the makeshift desk, then she settled in the middle of the bed cross-legged, almost as though she were about to meditate. For a long moment, we both looked at the laptop as though it were about to explode, then I moved cautiously and sat down in front of it. Then I stood up and paced. "I don't know how to do this, Talia. I don't know what I'm supposed to do."

"Well I sure as hell don't know," came the reply that was only just this side of indifferent, though I'd learned never to take Talia at face value. "Shall I have Cook bring some coffee? Tea? Whisky?"

I shook my head and kept pacing, and she kept watching from the bed. "What you did to me." I nodded to the carpet on which she had pulled me down. "I was there. It was me, at first with Michael and then watching him and Magda together after. I was there. It was so real I could reach out and touch what was around me."

"It's my little specialty," she said, looking down at her nails, which I noticed were short, but well manicured. "One of my specialties."

"It was real. Completely real."

"Of course it was real. You were seeing what I wanted you to see, exactly what I wanted you to see." She shrugged. "Michael, I like. I respect the angel, I always have. What he asked of me, I wouldn't have done for most people. It's…" A blush crawled up her cheeks. "Well, for me and for the person I'm with it's very sexual, but if he had been someone I hated, or simply someone I wished to feed upon, I could have just as easily turned it all back on him. I could have just as easily given him night terrors, made him think that he had actually killed Annie on the roof, or even made him think that he wasn't even on the premises when it happened, that he was in Manchester with a chick he'd picked up at a club, fucking her brains out."

I shivered and reached for the hoodie Michael had given me. "And you get off on that kind of thing."

She shrugged. "I'm a succubus. I don't expect you to understand what drives me any more than I understand what draws you to that laptop to play with words for hours at a time. But there are some things that exhaust me, some things that drain me rather than energize me, and being a messenger for someone else is one of those things. That's why I try to avoid it if possible."

"So you were exhausted after giving me Michael's message."

"Not so much. His was a message of love. Those are easier, and the other… what I saw, well, it was mine to give."

I paced a little more and like clockwork, one of Cook's assistants—I figure Cook was taking a little break after feeding Alonso—brought a tray with sandwiches and fruit and a pot of tea.

The succubus poured, I sipped, had a bite of a smoked salmon and cucumber sandwich, then settled into the chair in front of the laptop.

I was barely aware that I'd been writing, that there were words appearing in the open document until Talia leaned over my shoulder.

"Bloody hell," she whispered. "You do know what you just wrote?"

I nodded and waved her away. I knew exactly what I wrote. The goose bumps riding up my spine were evidence. She paced and I wrote.

By the time she came back to read over my shoulder the third time, I had begun to notice a strange buzzing in my head, not unpleasant, like the sounds insects make on a hot summer day. A little more unpleasant was the feeling that I had slipped slightly out of sync with the world around me, that wherever I was, no one else could go.

With a little start, I realized that I'd had that same feeling the night I'd written about the Guardian in the study at Annie's flat.

"You're insane," Talia said. She had stopped pacing and I had no idea how long she'd stood behind me, reading over my shoulder as I wrote.

"Takes one to know one," I said and kept writing as fast as I could, breathing as though the speed of my writing was such that I had gone into oxygen deficit, while my heart raced with each word.

She didn't bother replying, but now she was reading out loud.

"Shut up," I said. "I need quiet."

She did for a few minutes, then she cursed loud enough in

my ear that I glared at her through the reflection of the computer.

"You're out of your bloody mind," she said. Her voice was almost as breathless as mine. "He won't. He wouldn't. Would he?" Then she nodded. "That might work, but fucking hell, scribe, are you sure?"

"That's about the stupidest question ever," I replied and kept writing.

"She would never let you, Magda, and certainly Michael wouldn't."

"In case you haven't figured it out, I'm not asking their permission." I kept writing, still faster, and she leaned over me so closely that I had to elbow her away to keep her from fogging the monitor with her breath.

Still I wrote on. I wrote on to the end. I couldn't stop. The words kept coming from some wellspring I didn't know existed and yet I knew it had always been there. I wrote until I forgot to breathe. I wrote until I believe my heart forgot how to beat. I wrote until my mind saw pictures of what I wrote, and not words, as though it were already happening this very second right in front of me, and I felt it all unfold in the space just behind my breastbone, even as it terrified me, even as it refused to be unwritten.

By the time I was finished, the buzzing in my head sounded like a swarm of angry hornets, and everything beyond the words on the monitor had become nothing more than an unfocused blur of light and color. My whole body ached as though the feat had been a physical one, as though I had endured a beating for every word I wrote.

Even Talia's voice had become nothing more than a series of disjointed sounds with no meaning. "You need to stop. You need to stop now. Susan, you have to stop!"

It was Alonso's hand on my shoulder, firm and solid, the reflection of his face in the monitor that brought me back with a gasp. My hands fell away from the keyboard, and I would have toppled off the chair if Alonso hadn't caught me and carried me to the bed. He held a water glass to my lips and forced a few bites of chicken salad sandwich between my lips before the world around me came fully back into focus.

I was surprised to find both the vampire and his succubus leaning over me, her hand resting on his shoulder.

"Are you all right, my darling girl?" His eyes were dark, his pupils dilated.

I ignored the question. "They wouldn't listen, would they?"

He shook his head. "Sadly there was nothing to listen to, and the truth is the longer they put off the inevitable, the more we risk the Guardian invading again. And who knows what havoc He might wreak the second time around. I am truly sorry, my dear little scribe."

"Thank you for trying." I squeezed his hand. I was about to tell him that I thought there might be an alternative when Talia said it for me.

"You need to see this," she spoke quietly next to his ear and nodded at the Mac still open to the document I'd been working on. "The scribe's been busy."

Alonso leaned in and kissed my forehead. "I shall look,

Talia, but you must see that she eats and has something to drink. Whatever she has done has clearly been taxing upon her person."

Alonso settled in at the computer and scrolled back up to the beginning of the document. I was halfway through my second sandwich when I heard him catch his breath, and he shot a glance around at me and then at Talia. She only gave him a raised eyebrow and handed me a cup of tepid tea, which I took gratefully.

For the next few moments I had little time to spare as Talia all but force-fed me everything that was left on the tray Cook's assistant had delivered and I ravenously did my best to accommodate, like she was a mother bird and I her nestling. But I couldn't keep from noticing the way Alonso sat on the edge of the chair, the way he leaned forward, the way his shoulders had tensed.

When I could stand it no longer, and there was nothing left for Talia to shove in my gob, I pushed up off the bed and moved to his side. "Well?" Clearly he was done reading, but he only sat now staring at the monitor, at the words, and I knew exactly what he was looking at. "It can work, Alonso. Don't you think it can work?"

For a long moment, he didn't speak. Then he took a deep breath and looked up at me. "There'll be… consequences, consequences you can't possibly foresee."

"I know that. I'm willing to take that chance."

He looked at Talia, and whatever it was that passed between them was way more than a conversation, though I could neither see nor hear it. She only gave him a slight nod of her head. Then he stood so quickly that the chair went over backward. I yelped, for a brief moment reminded again that the man I had come to respect, the man who had given me shelter was, after all, a vampire.

Once again my skin was pocked with goose bumps, and my heart raced as though it were being chased by something deadly. In truth, it was being held by something deadly, or I was, at least, as he grabbed me to keep me from falling, and settled me on the trunk at the foot of the bed, where he knelt in front of me, looking up into my eyes, my hands, now nearly as cold as his, held tightly next to his chest.

"It can work, this plan of yours, my darling girl, as you know very well it can. Though there are always variables one can't know until the moment of execution, but it can work."

"Then you'll help me, both of you?" I already knew that Talia would. In spite of her constant attestations to my lack of sanity, I could feel her excitement as she lingered over me and read.

"If I help you," he said, holding my hands against the place where his heart would have beat if he lived, "if we do this, then you must know, there'll be no turning back."

"I know." I braced my feet hard against the floor to keep my knees from shaking. Christ, I really would like at least a little bit of dignity at moments like this, but I found myself fighting back tears as he pulled me into his arms and held me to stop the shaking. There had been no turning back for a very long time now, I thought, as I buried my face in his shoulder, clenching my eyes shut so tightly that I saw sparks of light. It had just taken me this damn long to figure it out.

Chapter Twenty-nine

It took an eternity for us to get to Chapel House and, at the same time, we arrived far too soon. I wasn't ready, but then I knew there was no being ready, not really. How could I ever be ready for what was to come? But now that my mind was made up, more than anything I just wanted to get on with it.

For a moment, I hated Michael for taking the choice from me. I hated Magda for agreeing to his demands, and I hated them both for keeping it all from me. Beyond that, I felt Michael's withdrawal from me, his absence with a pain that nearly brought me to my knees. But there was nothing for it. I squared my shoulders and took a deep breath. Focusing on the task at hand was the only way to deal with the pain right now. Michael would live. That's what mattered most.

I left the Land Rover without giving myself time to think. There was no comfort to be had by lingering, nothing that could be done to make what I had to do any less a solitary act and, while both Alonso and Talia assured me that the plan would work, I was very well aware that there were variables none of us could foresee. I knew only too well how crucial timing was.

From the back of Chapel House, I entered the garden through the wrought-iron gate, concentrating on the *thump, thump* of Magda's stone heart talisman against my breastbone, the weight of it heavier and heavier with each step I took. It was the feel of it against my skin that centered me, kept me focused, in spite of my anger at the woman. Very soon, none of that would matter.

The tangle of overgrown garden that had been an

impenetrable maze when I was last here now was only a slight distraction. I wasn't trying to escape. I wasn't trying to steal anyone away. The Guardian would not hinder me from my return to Him.

I was only halfway to the kitchen door when I was all but overwhelmed by the heavy scent of roses. I was really beginning to hate the fucking scent of roses. My stomach clenched fist tight, and for a moment I thought I would vomit. But I knew things now, things that even the Guardian didn't. They might not make a difference in the end, but they did to me.

I closed my eyes and thought of Michael sleeping in his bed in his lovely home with the sun coming up over the fells. I thought of crawling into bed next to him and breathing his clean, outdoorsy scent, rather than the cloying, funerary scent of roses. I thought of being folded in his arms, next to the strong, steady beat of his heart. Which would continue to beat when I was finished here. I thought of Michael alive and sleeping peacefully, and I found my voice. "I'm here. I've come back. Just like you knew I would."

Instantly I was embraced from behind, with such force and bodily presence that I had to glance over my shoulder to be certain there was no physical flesh.

"I knew you would return to me, my little scribe."

The voice was summer heat against my ear, and I was reminded with the sudden tightening of my nipples beneath an invisible caress and the catch of my breath as my heart began to race, that no matter what magic Magda Gardener had woven around me, no matter what I had schemed and written on my Mac before I left High View, I was still horribly vulnerable, and I still wanted Him more than I ever wanted anything in my life. When He touched me I could barely remember my own name, let alone what I was supposed to do when the time came.

I found myself wondering if maybe Magda and Michael were right to give me no more of a task than to lie down and spread my legs. That I could just about manage. More than likely I would have no choice anyway, at the end of the day.

I took another deep, steadying breath as invisible lips kissed my ear and the nape of my neck, as a splayed hand rested low against my belly, pulling me back against an erection that felt flesh and blood real.

"I had to," I whispered. "I had to come back to plead for Annie's safety, for that of my friends. Surely you knew that I would."

"Of course I knew that, my darling."

Somewhere in the back of my mind I was aware that my jeans were open, and I leaned heavily against the broad chest at my back, shifting my hips to ease the path of His hand as He wriggled warm fingers down inside the waistband of my panties.

"If you love me, as you say you do, then surely you can give me that. I've returned to you of my own free will, as you asked. Surely you can grant me that one simple request, the safety of those I love. Consider it a gift for your beloved. They're nothing to you, after all. It's only a little thing I ask."

The air moved around me in a sudden rush of wind, hot and rancid with the smell of burning garbage.

"You understand, of course," He said, "that you would have

saved those you love a lot of suffering if you had stayed with me to begin with." The shrug of His body felt almost like a thrust. "Oh, I realize that you had no choice in the matter when you were abducted by that bitch, Magda Gardener, and the angel, but even that doesn't fool me, my darling. I know well that you left willingly.

"That you came back willingly is also a lie. You came back because of my threats to those you love."

"But I came back," I said. "The vampire didn't want me there any more than you did."

"The vampire, yes. He may be long dead, but his familiars all live and draw breath. He was wise to return you to me. Still," there was another shrug of a thrust, and I realized to my horror that I was all but riding His hand as He slid it deep into my panties, "all I would have had to do, dear little scribe, was wait. In time you would have returned to me in desperation, just as all those who love me do. In time there would have been nothing Magda Gardener, the angel, nor the vampire and all his minions could have done to thwart your efforts to get back to me. In time there would have been nothing short of your death that would have kept you from me. And that I would have never allowed. So you see, you have nothing to bargain with."

A simple twitch of His fingers and I orgasmed, the heat of shame rising up my neck and burning my face even as I waited breathlessly for Him to bring me off again.

"That I was impatient to have you back in my arms, that I was impatient to pleasure your body and have you pleasure mine—now that through my angel, I may have a body for you to pleasure—

well, that is all that kept me from waiting for you until you came back to me of your own accord and threw yourself at my feet."

I don't know how He managed it or how I missed it, but I found myself on the mattress in the windowless space Annie had prepared for me as a guestroom.

"I would have you on the altar to celebrate your return, my love, as is fitting for my consort, but it is tainted with your friend's lust for me. I would have it cleansed and purified before I have you there. For now, I shall ravish you here. I shall punish you and hurt you for playing the whore with the angel, who belongs to me as surely as you do. I shall make you suffer even as I love you, even as you beg me for more." Invisible hands eased me down on the bed, and I braced myself, concentrating with what little of my wits was left to me on the weight of the stone between my breasts. "This shall be the place of your punishment, the place of your purification, and only when you are repentant and once again pure, shall I enter you on the high altar."

He pulled away suddenly and, for a second, I thought He had left me. "Where is the angel?" He asked.

"Oh, he'll be here soon enough," I said, lying back on the pillow, cupping my breasts and thumbing my nipples, knowing if He were anything like most men, that would focus His attention quickly enough. "I wanted some time alone with you before he got here." I ran my hand down to stroke myself between my legs, absently stroking. The scent in the air was suddenly spicy, like Christmas evergreen laced with sandalwood and cloves. "You've been inside him. You've possessed him, used his body."

"And I shall again. Do not try to deceive me, little one. He will come to me, and when he does, I promise once I've been inside him, possessed his body, there will be nothing you can do to persuade him to help your pathetic friends."

"Oh, I know he'll come," I said, nibbling on my lip and catching my breath as I played with myself. Even scared shitless as I was, it wasn't hard to masturbate, even to bring myself to orgasm, when just being in His presence kept me only a hair's breadth away. "It's just that I want to know what it feels like too. You've never inhabited a woman's flesh, have you? Or perhaps you can't. Perhaps you can only inhabit men, maybe only angels. Have you ever possessed anyone other than Michael?"

The scent of him became more strongly cloves and nutmeg. "Of course I may possess who I will, though most vessels are not strong enough to contain me for very long, and I am loath to use up a good lover too quickly."

"I'm not just any vessel. I'm a scribe, and you promised me when I freed you, you promised me what every scribe desires. Don't you remember? You said you could give me the mind of God." My breath hitched and I made a show of nibbling my lip, of moaning softly. Though in truth, it was hardly a show. It was just doing what I had to do to keep from begging Him to fuck me.

"As you so rudely reminded me, I am not a god." There was just a tiny whiff of garbage among the fragrance of holiday spices.

"You're right. I was rude. I apologize." Then I drifted off for a few seconds, caught up in my own lust. I think it might have been the *thump* of the stone heart against my breastbone that brought me back to myself with my thighs spread wide, knees bent, feet flat on the mattress. The air was rank with the scent of male heat, and I had the sense of Him on the bed with me, face between my thighs, watching with deep fascination, the dance and dart of my fingers.

"It feels good." The cloves and nutmeg scent peaked.

"You have no idea," I gasped, swallowing back the words in a little whimper and writhing against the mattress.

"I hear that for women it is different. For women there are no limits to the number of times they may take their release… well, for women who are with mortal men, that is."

I nodded with another little whimper. In truth, if it weren't for the *thump, thump* of Magda's talisman constantly reminding me why I was there, I would have been lost in my own lust, groveling for Him to take me.

"Please," I begged. "I know you can do whatever you want, but you told me, that very first night when I released you from your prison, that you could show me the mind of God. Surely that had to mean you would possess me, take my body as your own, fill me with you, with your mind. Let me know what it is you feel, what you think, how you see the world, even if it's just for a few minutes, even if it's the last thing that will ever matter to me as myself before you take me over completely and I stop caring about anything but you. I'm not stupid. I know that's what awaits me, no matter what you say. And, after all, I did release you."

"It is true, my little scribe, you did set me free—truly a feat no one else in a thousand years could accomplish. Therefore, what I have promised, I will perform."

I felt His palms move to the insides of my thighs and the intimate muscles of my body convulsed with anticipation.

"It is but a small thing for me," He said, running a tongue I couldn't see over my flesh and parting me with slow wet kisses. "And I am most curious. Therefore, I shall do as you ask, and I shall give you the mind of God."

I think I might have screamed as His presence moved into me, as my body stretched and spread and expanded outward like the beginning of the universe. Then, just when I was certain I would fly apart into nothingness, the world righted itself, and my body was filled completely with Him. Before I could adjust to the sensation, He spoke.

"I shall enjoy wearing the flesh of a woman." As though it were no longer mine, my hand caressed my breasts with the awkwardness of a teenage boy, while He slowed my efforts between my legs so that He could explore the flesh He now possessed.

I felt split in two, and at the same time, for the first time in my life, I felt whole, feeling the rhythm of my heart *beat, beat, beat,* against the solid stone of Magda's talisman.

"Oh yes, it shall be a pleasure for both of us, my little scribe, but only until the angel gets here," He added quickly. "For without the angel's body, I will never be to you more than a touch you cannot see, a caress you cannot return. I will have his flesh, possess it as my own, and then, my lovely, I may service you as you deserve."

Chapter Thirty

Michael eased open the kitchen door of Chapel House, still miffed at Susan, who had shoved her way out of the Land Rover before he could find a parking place. The woman had no sense of self-preservation.

As he shut the door behind him, he was instantly drawn by the sounds and scent of sex, amplified by the Guardian, like a homing beacon pulling Michael to Him as surely as if He had thrown a rope around his neck and tugged him down the hall toward the makeshift guestroom where Susan had slept.

In spite of himself, in spite of the promise he had made not to feel anything, the sight of her naked and writhing on the mattress, the knowing exactly what was happening to her, how the Guardian was making her feel, stiffened Michael. The more ashamed he was that he could respond so inappropriately under such dire circumstances, the more aroused he became.

But there was little time for thoughts of his shame. It was as though a very large dog, wild with pleasure at the sight of him, suddenly overwhelmed him, nearly knocking him off his feet before wriggling and shifting and twisting until it had worked its way up inside him, right into the very centre of his heart. And then, just when he felt as though his chest would burst, just when breathing became impossible and he was on the verge of panic, the feeling spread throughout his body like a wave washing up on a beach. He was taken aback by how pleasant the experience was, though he had once known that sensation well. In fact, he had once anticipated his joinings with the Guardian more than he did his next breath.

"Michael, my darling angel, welcome home! I knew in time you would come back to me, and indeed, the timing could not be more perfect," came the voice inside his head. "If one of us can pleasure our lovely little scribe well, how much better can we two together please her? Oh, the thought of the three of us together so delights me, my darling! I am filled with such anticipation."

Yes, Michael thought. Yes, it delighted him too. And it made so much sense now that he thought about it, now that he could see the logic of it. How much better could they pleasure Susan together?

His cock jerked against the fly of his jeans in anticipation. Almost before he knew what he was doing, his hands were on his zipper, then awkwardly groping his cock with delight. The fact that his hand seldom left his cock when the Guardian was in residence had been one of the ways Michael could tell He was present when their relationship had gone tits-up and the Guardian had resorted to sneaking inside him while Michael slept.

Though Michael could not imagine now how their relationship could have been anything but exquisite. Surely the fault must have all been his. Or perhaps it had all been Magda Gardener's fault. Perhaps she had lied to him about the Guardian, planted seeds of doubt in his mind about the Guardian's love for him.

"Oh, how I have missed the feel of your manhood, lovely boy, and the many fine uses we put it to together. But back then, we had not our lovely little scribe. I can hardly contain myself with thoughts of the heights of ecstasy we three shall reach together."

Michael shared his anticipation with a pounding pulse and a weight in his balls that was almost unbearable. It was Susan they both wanted, Susan they both loved, Susan they would pleasure together. He smiled at the thought of just how she would come, just how she would writhe and moan as they serviced her.

"I want you inside me, I want you inside me, I want you inside me," came Susan's breathless mantra from the mattress, and he was only too willing. Perhaps this decision was the wise one, after all. Perhaps the three of them could be happy together.

He found himself wondering how he ever could have doubted. Perhaps he would just tell the Guardian about Magda's plan. Though the Guardian couldn't defeat her, surely he could thwart her. Surely he could find a way to keep them safe from her so that they could be together as the Guardian had always intended.

This was his chance to make Susan happy again. Certainly she had not been happy when they'd left High View, and neither had he. After the interminable ride together from the vampire's lair, with her too angry to even speak to him, ripping his heart out every mile of the journey, after she had shoved open the door and pushed on ahead of him as soon as they'd arrived at Chapel House, it was balm to his soul to see her writhing for him, aching for him, as he was for her.

"How shall we take her, my angel?" the Guardian asked, still fondling his cock with Michael's hand. "What shall we do to her? Shall we pleasure her first, or punish her for leaving us, for making us suffer, for leaving us alone? She must be punished, you know."

With borrowed eyes, He glanced down at the hand on Michael's cock, then pulled it away and wriggled his fingers as though needing to understand how they worked. "I have never had flesh with which to punish my lovers before, with which to cause harm for betrayal. How delightful this shall be. I think that before we give her what she so longs for, before we pleasure her into unconsciousness, we should punish her the same."

To his surprise Michael found himself dragging his belt from its loops with spastic jerks. When it was at last free in his hand, almost before he knew what he was doing, he had lit a candle that sat in a saucer on the chair which served as a makeshift nightstand. Then he held the oblong buckle of the belt over the flame until the room smelled of hot metal, while on the bed, Susan only mewled and writhed, gasping over and over for him to put it in her.

"I have never marred human flesh," the Guardian said inside Michael's head. "My lovers have always been only too happy to inflict the punishments on themselves at my demand. Oh, what a treat this shall be! Besides, if she wears our mark, then she won't soon forget what happens to those who disobey us, will she, Michael?"

Even as it disturbed him, he couldn't stop himself from kneeling on the bed next to Susan, leaning forward to press the hot metal of the buckle into her bare breast. Even as he drew nearer, she ignored the danger, as though the pain of the burn meant nothing compared to the desperation of her need as she begged him again and again to mount her. To his horror, he found that the hand not holding hot metal opened her legs for just that purpose, as if the pain of one would in no way diminish the other. Even as he cried out and tried to pull away, his body did the Guardian's bidding, just as it had always done, even as he screamed and begged for Him to stop.

"Oh, God! Oh, Christ! No! Please no! Please, Magda! Do it now! Please do it now, only don't let me hurt her. Dear God, please don't let me hurt her."

He fought his way up from under a wool blanket, in the back of a stripped-out van drenched in icy sweat, still yelling, "Magda, do it now! Please, don't let me hurt her!" at the top of his lungs before a hard hand clamped over his mouth and he found himself staring up into Reese Chambers' sun-freckled face.

"Shut up," the man said without preamble. He looked tired and worried.

Before Michael could ask what the hell was going on, Talia climbed into the van looking nearly as tired as Reese did. As she slid the side door shut, he noticed the steeple of Chapel House looming over the row of bungalows they were parked in front of.

"Oh good, you're both awake now," the succubus said. "That makes my job easier. And frankly it was getting pretty tiring keeping you both dreaming. I'm good, but even I have my limits. Give her back her glasses," she said to Reese. It was then that Michael noticed Magda sitting on the floor next to him, looking slightly worse for the wear, hands bound behind her back, eyes covered in a thick blindfold.

"What the fuck's going on?" Michael exploded up from the floor, knocking Reese on his arse, and was surprised to find himself the victim of a well-executed leg sweep, landing him practically in Magda's lap. Before he could even blink, Reese had him in a chokehold, and he was seeing black spots, on the edge of passing out.

"I suggest you calm down and listen, before you make Talia angry," Reese said, barely breathing hard. "She can be rather foul-tempered when she's tired."

Michael tapped the floor as he'd seen wrestlers do to signify their submission. Reese loosened his grip, but just enough so that Michael wouldn't pass out, just enough to be sure that he would keep his word. "Where's Susan? What the hell's going on?"

"Susan's with the Guardian," Magda said, taking her glasses from Talia. She waited while the succubus slipped the knot on the blindfold, then she popped them on. "It appears we've been sabotaged," she nodded to Talia and shrugged. "Everything you've experienced up until now has only been a dream. Our resident succubus has been a busy little bee."

"Jesus! Do you have any idea what you've done?" Michael had to use all of his restraint to keep from throttling the succubus, though he figured if anything, she'd be more dangerous to tackle than even Reese was.

"We've given her a say in the matter," Talia said. "And if you two would have trusted her enough to do the same, you might have remembered, she's a fucking scribe."

"She's untrained," Magda added.

"Untrained, my arse. What the hell do you think she's been doing all these years, writing stories, getting paid for a craft she was born to. All she needed was to understand what was required of her, and you two were too full of yourselves to give her that chance. If anyone could come up with an alternative to your train wreck of a plan, it would be her."

"And your solution is to turn her over to the Guardian alone?" Michael shoved his way to his feet again. He had to get to her. He had to go to Susan. Maybe it wasn't too late.

This time it was Magda's hand on his arm that stayed him from opening the van door and heading straight for Chapel House. "She's not alone."

He froze.

"Alonso's with her," Talia said.

"Alonso?" He felt the burn of jealousy low in his belly. "Why?"

"Because the Guardian won't be expecting someone who's not… living," Reese said. "He won't detect Alonso's presence unless Alonso wants to be detected."

"And by the time Alonso reveals himself," Talia added, "it'll be too late."

"He should be announcing his presence any time now," Reese glanced down at his watch, then back up at Talia expectantly.

"That means we'll be needing your help." Talia nodded to Magda and Michael.

"Then perhaps you should tell us exactly what your plan is so we'll know what to do." Magda lifted her still bound arms slightly and winced. "I'm a captive audience."

"I swear, if any harm comes to Susan because of what you lot have pulled, I'll snap both your necks and stake the vampire."

Talia offered him a bland shrug. "You're welcome to try." She cut through Magda's bonds with an efficient upward slice of her

Swiss Army knife.

"No harm is coming to anyone," Reese said. "The plan's a good one." But Michael could see that Reese had his doubts too.

"Tell us, then."

While the succubus shared the plan, Reese filled Styrofoam cups with tea from a flask. Michael listened in horror as the details unfolded, unaware that he had crushed the cup in his fist until Reese knelt in front of him and mopped up the spilled tea with an old towel.

"I can't believe the goddamned vampire would drag her into something so insane. Magda, we can't let her do this. It's not too late. I know the Guardian will still be expecting me. We can still make this work. We're not letting her do this. We're not letting a vampire call the shots."

"It was her plan," Reese said between clenched teeth.

"Oh right, like I'm going to believe that she—"

"What?" Talia cut in. "That your little pet could actually think for herself? Did it ever occur to you that she turned to Alonso, to us, because you two shut her out, because you two wouldn't talk to her or listen to her?"

"Lest we forget that it was your fucking big mouth that got her into this mess in the first place. I trusted you. I fucking trusted you!"

"But you didn't fucking trust her, did you?"

"Shut up, both of you! All of you." This time it was Magda who spoke barely above a whisper, and the van was suddenly silent. She waited until all eyes were on her, then she turned her attention to

Talia. "Now, what do you need us to do?"

"Magda, you can't mean that," Michael said. "Dear God, you can't really mean that."

"The succubus is right, Michael. We should have trusted Susan. It's a good plan. Solid." She gave a lopsided shrug and shoved her glasses up tight against the bridge of her nose with her index finger. "It makes more sense than sacrificing you."

Before he could argue, she raised a hand, her gaze locked on him, and he felt the chill of it down his spine. "Michael, she'll need you more than ever once this is over, but if you can't see that, if you can't see this plan through, then we'll just leave you in the damn van." She nodded to the zip ties that had bound her. "You may be strong, but you're not that strong."

Just then Talia's phone buzzed an incoming text. She peeked at it, then stuffed the device back in her jacket pocket. "He's going in. We've got five minutes. Are you two in or out?"

Chapter Thirty-one

"What is this strange feeling?" the Guardian asked from wherever He was settled inside me, a place that, when I thought about it, felt like it might be just behind my breastbone. "I feel giddy, like your flesh has suddenly gotten heavier, and I can hardly keep my eyes open."

"I'm just tired," I said. "Having lots of sex does that to a mortal body and, though Michael doesn't need rest, or didn't when he was with you, it truly is one of the best parts of sex—that slide into the warm cottony afterglow of sleep after you're well sated."

"Then I must experience it," He said as I yawned mightily. "Oh, Susan, I must experience it all! I had no idea just how delightful female flesh could be to inhabit. My darling, you have opened up whole new vistas for me, for us. Perhaps I shall divide my time between inhabiting your flesh and my angel's, now that I know you are strong enough to house me. I think I should love to know what his cock feels like to you. I believe his substantial size would be a delightful pleasure thrusting up inside you."

I only nodded and yawned again. Though I would have much preferred to stay awake, I had to sleep if the plan were to work. Talia had assured me that I would find sleep with no problem when the time came. I wasn't sure what she had done to me, other than kiss me on the mouth and stroke me behind the ear, but it didn't matter as long as it worked.

"Then let us experience sleep together, my little scribe. When we awaken, I shall summon our angel, and perhaps we shall punish him together for keeping us waiting."

And we did. We slept, or at least I thought I slept. I thought I dreamed. I thought surely it must be Talia's doing. I drifted for a long time, aware of the foreign presence inside me, aware that it was only Magda's talisman that kept just enough of me safe and focused. Without it I would be easily taken over by that presence.

It was the champagne bubble effervescence coursing over my entire body that roused me from deep sleep to the place almost of waking, but not quite. The feel of a feather touch raised the fine hairs on my forearms, up my spine, on the back of my neck, goose fleshing the tops of my breasts and tightening my nipples to points.

"I'm here now, my darling girl. Don't be afraid. It will hurt but a little, and then you will feel nothing but pleasure."

I felt myself being lifted, cradled like a child in strong, hard arms. Then I inhaled the cold wild scent of the high fells and below it earth, solid and warmed by moss and fallen leaves, and I could have wept with relief, even as fear shot along all my nerve endings.

"Scribe, why is the vampire here with us?" The Guardian's voice was more curious than upset.

"We're dreaming," I mumbled. "A dream brought on by our self-pleasure, no doubt."

"How so?"

"Perhaps you don't crave the flesh of a vampire, but I assure you, we mortals do."

"Why?"

"Because vampires have what we don't—eternal life."

"But they are dead," He said.

"We mortals don't see them that way. To us they're

powerful, beautiful, because they symbolize lust and virility, and we fantasize about being taken by them."

There was a soft chuckle next to my ear and cool fingers against my bare nape, pushing my hair aside. "I did not know," the Guardian said. "It seems very real."

"Powerful dreams always do. Sometimes when we're in them, it's very difficult to tell if they're real or not."

"Then how do you know that this dream is not real?"

"A vampire would have no more use for you than you do for him," I replied. "And it was he who sent me here, remember?"

"Of course." The Guardian didn't question my logic further, for which I was grateful.

"We shall begin now, my darling girl," came the voice next to my ear. "You have only to let me take you, and when I am finished, when I have emptied you completely and hold your life force within me, then I shall give it back to you, only changed."

"Is this not the vampire from High View, scribe—the one who grovels before Magda Gardener?"

I felt a vibration against my neck that might have been a growl, might have been a purr. "It is, yes."

"And you find him attractive?"

"It's a dream," I said. "Go back to sleep."

"Careful, my darling girl, you'll hurt my feelings."

"I suppose he's comely enough," The Guardian observed. "A pity his flesh is not living. I might enjoy inhabiting such a fine, strong body."

"Good heavens, He is irritating, isn't He?" Alonso's voice

was soft against my ear and with a start, I realized the Guardian couldn't hear what Alonso said to me.

"He's dreaming, Susan. You, however, are not. You must tell me now if you do not wish me to continue, for once I have tasted you, especially in your lust and your vulnerability, there will be no turning back, and I do not wish for you to despise me for what I have done."

With an effort that seemed colossal, I slid my arm around his neck, amazed at how soft and dark his hair was. As I pulled him to me, he stayed my efforts, but only for a moment. He kissed my cheek then held my gaze, only for a second longer, and his eyes were darker than midnight. Then he lowered his mouth to my nape, to the vein pulsing like a driving drum beat. His lips were deliciously warm, and it came as a surprise when he ran the flat of his tongue along the length of the vein, pressing, lapping like a cat tasting milk, then pressing again with the tip as though he were probing for just the right spot.

The intake of his breath was like the sigh of a summer breeze. He kissed me once, on the spot where my pulse beat the strongest, and then again.

My hand in his hair tightened to a fist. I caught my breath and held it, waiting in his embrace. It was a sharp pain, precise and doubled—just two pinpoints of pain, like a surgeon's twin incision against the side of my throat. I had barely time to notice it before blinding pain took my breath away. The world flashed white hot around me and I panicked and began to struggle, but he held me tightly.

As the skin gave beneath his bite, as I felt my blood flooding to his lips, I heard his voice inside my head. "That is the worst of it done, my darling girl. Now you need only relax and let me take you."

"Ouch!" came the other voice in my head, reminding me I wasn't alone with Alonso and surprising me how badly I suddenly wanted to be. "That was not pleasant. Susan, are dreams usually so physical?"

"Talia, can you not silence him?" Alonso spoke inside my head again and, for the first time, I noticed the succubus sat at my feet, gently stroking my ankle.

She said nothing, but the Guardian gave a soft moan of contentment, or rather I did, but I knew it was His. And for the first time since He had deceived His way into my life, I was relieved that He was silent, that He couldn't touch me, even though I felt the fullness of Him pressing gently against the inside of my chest. I needed Him to sleep and to leave me alone for a little while longer. It was with that thought I realized I was clinging to Alonso's strong, well muscled frame and I wanted him like I had never wanted before. Christ! I wanted him to devour me, to take me completely into himself. I had never imagined it would be like this. Somehow I'd thought it would be more macabre, more solemn.

I would have writhed if I could have. I would have pulled him closer, but I was lost, drowning in the swift flowing river of my blood that he drew into his mouth in deep, thirsty gulps. That I couldn't move, that my body was completely held in thrall to the flow of my own blood into his mouth mattered less than the fact that he fed from me, an act so powerful, so incredibly intimate, that I felt shy, awkward.

"It is all right that you feel this way, my darling Susan, for so we all feel at our making." He spoke as though he'd read my thoughts, though in truth what I experienced was far too primal to actually be thoughts. "There is no act more intimate, no connection deeper than the taking and giving of blood. What I take now is meant to give me life, to give me your life, but only so I may give you back my own. In this act, we shall both find pleasure, and you will be more than my familiar. You will be the child of my own heart's blood."

There was a sudden thrashing behind my breastbone. Though I knew it wasn't physical, it was no less real.

"Susan, you have deceived me. I shall punish you very severely for this duplicity. Do you really think a dead creature can keep me from what is mine?"

The Guardian's voice was not raised, but in it was an edge of disquiet I'd not heard before. "For your impertinence, vampire, I shall take your succubus and use her long and hard, even if she does reek of your death."

"You can try." The voice that responded was different, and in my groggy, giddy state, a blurred apparition of Magda Gardener pushed aside the makeshift curtain that separated the mattress from the rest of the area. Even with her glasses still in place, her hair seemed to writhe and dance around her face, as though it lived and breathed anger and fury. "I won't hesitate to turn the scribe and the vampire if that's what it takes, and well you know this."

I felt as though my whole body jerked and struggled around the still point at which Alonso's mouth pressed against my vein, but in truth I had not physically moved. I was incapable of movement, completely enthralled by the ebb and flow of my blood and the kiss and bite of the vampire at my throat.

"That won't be necessary, Magda," Talia said, still caressing my ankle and my calf. "We've got this."

"You shall all suffer for this deception!" The words came from Talia's throat, but the Guardian spoke them from inside my body.

"Oh, I doubt it," the succubus managed in the next breath, her grip secure on my leg.

Then He spoke inside my head, only to me, and I knew that no one else could hear Him. "Susan, my darling little scribe, you can still set me free, just as you've done before. I can give you so much more than this vampire can. I can give you the mind of God. Release me, and I promise you there will be no punishment, no recriminations, but I shall embrace you as my own. What I have promised, I shall perform. I shall give you the mind of God."

"But you're not God. I know this now. As I released you, so I now return you to your captivity. Only this time, I hold the key in a place where you can never reach it." It was a thought, nothing more, but He heard me, and so did Alonso.

"Then I shall enthrall another to stake you and set me free," the Guardian said.

"I'm already dead," I replied. "If I become ash, I take you with me. All doors are closed to you. And now, you have your wish, a home in the flesh."

"Susan, no. Susan, please don't do this. There is so much I have to offer you, so much to tell you, to show you. Please don't do this." I heard His voice from a long way off, and for a moment I feared he was escaping, but the weight pressing on my chest became more desperate as the voice drifted farther and farther away. I must have moaned out loud. Perhaps I even thrashed.

But then Alonso's calming voice filled my whole body. "There is nothing to worry about, my darling girl. All is exactly as it should be. His efforts of desperation will end soon, for you are nearing your death, and then we will remake you. I promise you the Guardian cannot leave. As for you there is now no turning back, so is it for Him."

"Not long now," Talia said.

Suddenly my vision was filled with Michael, who stepped around Magda and pushed his way forward. My heart was filled with Michael no matter where the Guardian resided inside me, and I think I tried to smile. But even that was such an effort.

He settled on the mattress next to me and took my limp hand in his, pressing a kiss to my palm, then closing my fingers around it.

"Not long now," Talia said again.

This time, with my last effort, with my last coherent thought, I shouted in my mind, the only part of me that still worked, "I love you, Michael. Tell him I love him... Tell him... Please tell him..."

His fingers jerked against mine. A single tear slid down his cheek. He bent and kissed me tenderly on the mouth. It was the last thing I felt as I drew the breath of the living for the final time.

Chapter Thirty-two

Awareness returned slowly with an irritating *drip, drip, drip* of something between my parted lips. Even more irritating was the acid burn at the back of my throat as whatever it was trickled down. Whatever it was, I felt I should have known, but I couldn't for the life of me recall.

Drip, drip, drip! I coughed and choked, flailing to shove the hand away from my face that stroked my jaw, but my efforts were useless. I was weak as a kitten, and I had no context for my situation, a fact that frightened me, and I flailed harder.

Strong arms cradled me, cool fingers stroked my throat and someone spoke softly. "Swallow, my darling girl. You must swallow and take my strength."

Drip, drip, drip!

"She has to drink. You have to make her drink, or she'll die." There was another male voice, a voice full of worry. A familiar voice.

"She's already dead, Michael," a woman's voice commented.

"Shut up, Magda," came the reply, a reply which I barely noticed because my attention was on the fact that I was dead. I was supposed to be, wasn't I? Wasn't that the plan? And then something was supposed to happen after that. I just couldn't think for the irritating, burning, *drip, drip, drip* making my eyes water and my sinuses sting.

"Drink, my darling girl," the soft voice was still insisting in my ear. The cool fingers were still stroking my throat. "You must drink from me now, as I have drunk from you, and all shall be well."

I choked and gagged, then swallowed. The acid burn became warm and sweet and soothing down the back of my throat, bursting with richness and flavor, and suddenly I was starving for whatever it was that filled my mouth. The taste of it, the power of it was transformed to fire and heat and life, and I was freezing and shivering, and I couldn't get enough of its warmth.

"That's it, that's right, my darling; drink. Drink from me. The shivering will pass, and you will soon not notice the cold."

A large hand cradled my head and guided me toward the source of the liquid fire. My teeth punctured flesh and, for a moment, I thought I would be sick at the very thought. But then the *drip, drip, drip* became an even, steady flow that flooded my mouth and coursed down my throat into my belly. The world around me burst into sharp focus. Alonso held me against his bare chest and I fed from the vein just above his left nipple. I fed as though I was starving. I fed as though I would never get enough. Child of his heart's blood, he said I would be, and now I understood why.

"Welcome back." Magda Gardener smiled down at me.

I didn't respond. I had forgotten how to do anything but drink from Alonso, throwing my arms around him and pulling him closer to my lips, an act which caused him to sigh and moan softly. I couldn't tell if it was with pleasure or if I was hurting him and, to be honest, I don't think it would have mattered one way or another. I had little control over my need to feed at that point. It was far more instinct that drove me than it was any higher brain function and that, in itself, would have terrified me if I'd had the capacity to dwell on it.

Whether I was causing him pain or not, he made no effort to hinder me, and I fed aggressively. For me it was pleasure, but of the most primitive kind. It was the satisfying of hunger, urgent, demanding hunger, hunger that insisted I feed as though I might never feed again; hunger that had as little to do with filling my belly as a thunderstorm has to do with filling the ocean. And yet in spite of my raging need, I was keenly aware of everything around me. It was just that I could concentrate on nothing at the moment but taking more of the spiced wine heat of Alonso's blood into me. I had never tasted anything so sweet.

"It's best not to touch her just yet," Alonso said, when Michael reached out to stroke my cheek. "She is not herself. She is not yet safe."

"Of course she's not safe," Michael snapped. "She's a fucking vampire."

"She is not yet a fucking vampire," Alonso replied evenly. "She is not yet fully made. She must feed, then she must rest and then feed again. Until that has happened and, until we can help her control her urges, she is in danger, as are those around her."

"How long?" Michael ran a hand through his hair and paced the small space, shoving at the makeshift curtain. "How long before she's back to herself?"

"I do not know," Alonso said. "It is different with every person, and I have never sired before."

"Fucking hell! You mean you're making this up as you go along? Jesus!"

"Michael, sit down and shut up," Magda said. "Whether or

not Alonso has sired a million or none is irrelevant at this point. Susan made her choice, and Alonso will do what he must. It is also a fact that you must prepare yourself for that while Susan will still be herself at the core of her being, she will be changed in ways that may be… difficult."

"Christ!" Michael grumbled under his breath. "And the Guardian?" he asked, turning on Alonso, who growled a warning. Or at least I thought it was Alonso, but it was actually me. "Tell me at least that after what you've done to her that it worked."

"There's no sign of Him," Magda said. "But if he was in Susan's body when Alonso took her, he's still there."

"Oh, He's there all right," Talia said. "And not very happy about it, either. But I promise you, by the time He realized He wasn't just dreaming Alonso's presence, the process was too far along for him to escape."

"Can he hurt her?" Michael asked. "Can he use her as he did me?"

"He cannot use the dead," Alonso said.

Michael flinched as though he had been slapped.

But Alonso made no apologies for being blunt. In truth, he had other things on his mind. I knew because I could feel those things in the back of my own mind as though, by feeding from him, I also took from his thoughts. "She will sleep soon, when she is sated. Then we must get her, and myself, back to High View before dawn comes. This is not a safe place for either of us and, while I could manage in the crypt, I do not know what Susan's needs will be, and I can better anticipate them in my own home, which is designed with our kind in mind."

It happened so quickly that I almost missed it. The slackening of my mouth, the flickering of my tongue over my lips to make sure I'd not missed a single drop, and then I licked instinctually at the wound over Alonso's heart to seal it. I fell asleep before I finished. All the while Alonso spoke soft, calming words to me from the edge of the dream world.

That was my last memory until I woke in a huge bed in a deeply shadowed room with no windows. Alonso sat in an overstuffed chair that had been moved close to the bed. I was aware of Magda and Michael in the room, sitting in the shadows, but they didn't matter. For the moment, only Alonso mattered. I was in a black shirt that I knew was his, and nothing else, but then I had been naked with no actual memory of shedding my clothes when he had come to me at Chapel House. I could smell the high fells scent of him deep in the weave of the fabric, beyond the reach of the surface smell of laundry soap.

That was not, however, the scent that dragged me up from my sleep, but rather the scent of blood. A smell that filled my mouth with saliva and made my stomach clench and cramp in hunger. I was out of the bed and on Alonso's lap, clawing open his shirt, sending buttons flying so quickly that I barely had a sense of my own movement. Had I, it most certainly would have frightened me.

But when Alonso pushed me away and tried to ease me back in the bed, saying something about not being able to feed me, whatever I was becoming lashed out like a whip with strength and speed I neither knew I had, nor was I able to control. All I knew in that instant was unbearable hunger which I had to satisfy at all costs. The chair went over backward with me landing on top of Alonso, still trying to get to the source of nourishment.

A split second later, I was the one flat on my back on the floor, with Alonso straddling me, pinning my arms above my head and me yelling like a banshee, "Get off me! Get off me! Give it to me!"

I've heard that predators are often tunnel-visioned, unable to see anything but the prey in their sight once they begin to move in for the kill. Even as the thought horrified me, the fact that Michael and Magda now flanked Alonso and were yelling at me brought it home loud and clear that a predator was exactly what I had become. Even though I had known that would be the case when I had asked Alonso to take me, I was suddenly, painfully, aware of what that meant, even as none of the logic mattered, even as nothing in the whole world mattered but feeding.

"Listen to me, Susan," Alonso was all but yelling at me just to get my attention, and I wanted to rip his face off for it. Damn it, all I wanted to do was feed! "I cannot feed you, for both Talia and Reese have needed from me after our efforts at Chapel House. I am depleted, my darling girl. But Michael and Magda will feed you."

Michael had already shed his shirt and knelt next to me, pulling me to him as Alonso eased up his weight, and I lunged.

"Not from your heart, Michael," Alonso warned. "From your wrist, even your neck. But not from your heart, it's too dangerous."

"From my heart," came Michael's breathless reply. "Only

from my heart." He swallowed back a hiss of pain as I tore at the flesh above his left nipple in frustration, unable to access the vein as I had with Alonso.

He braced himself against my vicious tearing, crying out as I bit him again and again in desperation, only managing to bruise and lacerate and, while the surface bled, I could not get to the vein.

"Michael! Michael, there's a reason why you don't feed her from your heart's blood." It was Magda who spoke.

In that moment, Alonso wrestled me away from my efforts only long enough for Magda to slice a clean sharp incision with a knife, low on Michael's left pectoral. Before the first flow had fallen to his nipple, I lunged and Alonso released me. I threw my arms around Michael and pulled in the first delicious taste of his blood, so different from Alonso's, but no less heavenly, with the tang of summer fruit and woodland herbs, and he sighed with relief and cradled me to his chest.

"You romantic bastard," Magda said to Michael, settling back on her knees and catching her breath while she watched my efforts. "It has nothing to do with your emotions, idiot. The heart's blood must be opened by the giver, and that's why it's considered more intimate. It's a gift. It can't easily be taken by force."

Michael only nodded and moaned as I pulled him still closer. It was when he laid his head back against the bed and his eyes fluttered shut that I realized he could barely hear Magda. In fact, I doubted that he'd understood a single word she'd said. With one hand he gently kneaded and caressed my flank while the other stroked and fisted my hair.

In a moment of clarity, I felt the slow, deep shifting of his hips beneath me and became keenly aware that he was fully erect. My body responded in kind, nipples peaking, heat rising heavy and humid between my thighs and my own hips shifting. But instinct won out in the end. I would revisit the lust once the hunger eased. Somewhere in the back of my mind, I remembered Alonso saying that feeding and sex were both intimate acts best done together, and in private, whenever possible. Perhaps when I was finished feeding, I would fuck Michael. Perhaps when I was done drinking from the blood of his heart, I would reward him, reward both of us for his efforts.

I wanted him with every cell in my body. I had no idea I could hunger for him so deeply. So deeply that all I could think about, all I could imagine, was taking him into myself, taking all of him into myself, taking in his luscious dark ruby blood in large, thirsty gulps as though I would never get enough, and then mounting him and taking the essence of his life force in the same way, until we were both spent and exhausted from our efforts.

In truth, as we writhed on the floor, I felt as though the act of feeding would not be complete until we had coupled, but I needed strength before that could happen and Michael's strength, Michael's life's blood was exhilarating in a very different way from Alonso's.

From somewhere a long way off, I heard Magda and Alonso speaking in distressed tones, and I wished they'd leave us alone. I anticipated fucking Michael with each deep pull of his blood, and while I would have preferred not to have an audience, the need I felt was even beyond what the Guardian had roused in me. I was sure one act would not be, in and of itself completed without the other—certainly not when it was with Michael. Therefore, if they wouldn't leave, I would just ignore them and have him anyway.

But to my irritation, they had no intention of leaving, or even being quiet. They just kept getting louder, and Magda kept saying something over and over again. "Gederofim, gederofim, gederofim," it sounded like over the euphoric buzz in my ears. "Gederofim, geteroffim. Get! Her! Off! Him!"

With me fighting like a tiger, Alonso pulled me free. "Susan… Susan! You can't take any more from Michael. It's too much."

"Susan! You'll kill him," Magda shouted at me, just as she shoved her wrist in front of my open mouth. Only once I'd punctured flesh—damn near breaking bone in the process—and tasted the sharp, clean citrus of her blood, did I realize that Michael's eyes were closed and he was pale, so pale.

Alonso held the bed sheet tightly to the wound in Michael's chest and gently slapped his face until he roused with a gasp.

In that instant I felt shame, fear, horror. Yet I could no more stop feeding than I could have stopped the flow of time.

"He'll be all right," Alonso was saying. "He'll be fine. He'll be a little weak when he wakes up, but he'll be fine. He's an angel. He's stronger than an ordinary mortal."

And still I gorged. Even as I wept and sobbed at Magda's wrist, somewhere in the back of my mind, I realized that my tears were still salt and not blood. They were as bitter as they had been when I realized that Michael planned to sacrifice himself for me. I

had done all that I had done and still, he nearly died because of me—
most surely would have if Alonso and Magda hadn't intervened. I
wept bitterly between great gulps of Magda's blood. She held me in
strong arms, stroking my hair and speaking to me in some ancient
language I didn't understand, but being very careful not to withdraw
her wrist.

When I could manage a sane word, when I was sated enough
I was once again on the edge of sleep, I sealed the wound and pulled
Magda's face close to mine, careful not to jostle her glasses. "Keep
Michael away from me. Please. I don't want to hurt him and… I
don't want him to see me like this."

She tried to argue, but I grabbed her by the throat, and she
stilled as though she were one of her own creations made of stone.
"Promise me! I need you to promise me."

"All right," she said softly, and then I allowed myself to
tumble back into the sleep of the dead.

Chapter Thirty-three

I don't remember much of the next few days. Occasionally I would realize that Alonso or Magda were in the room with me, but mostly my focus was on whoever served as my meal.

The rest of the time I slept somewhere beyond the dream world, truly the sleep of the dead, I suppose. But I always woke ravenous, always beyond the grasp of my own rationality, always beyond the grasp of my own control.

Most of the time I wasn't familiar with whoever fed me, and as long as there was a source of blood, I didn't really care who they were. When my conscience did rear its seriously brow-beaten head, whoever was with me at the time would assure me that Michael was all right and that I had not killed or permanently maimed anyone.

On the third day, I came back to myself, my whole body tingling, especially my tongue and lips, which were pressed against the open vein at Talia's wrist. I gave a little shudder that could have possibly been an orgasm. After all, Talia was a succubus. As I eased myself away from her wrist with a quick lap of my tongue to seal the wound, the world righted itself and I was able to exert some control.

"Welcome back," she said, with a wicked smile. "We were beginning to think you would drain us all and all of Magda's household too before you were finally sated." She glanced down at the inside of her wrist. "If you can resist my blood, sweet little scribe, then I reckon you're well on your way to learning some control."

My stomach growled and she nodded down to it. "You'll have to learn to manage the hunger. It'll get easier with time and practice, but it never goes away, or so Alonso tells me. You were lucky to have his strength as well as Magda's and Michael's." She shrugged. "And yours truly of course, to keep you and everyone around you safe. You've been pretty much out of control for the last three days."

There was a soft knock on the door and Alonso pushed his way into the room, offering a huge smile when he saw me sitting up in the bed. "How do you feel, darling girl?"

"Different," was the only reply I could think of, and that was an answer no one would have understood better than Alonso Darlington.

"Of course you do. I would expect nothing else under the circumstances, but you also seem a little more yourself this evening."

"Well, she didn't try to rip my throat out when I pulled away from her," Talia said. When Alonso glared at her she only shrugged. "That's what she'd been doing, isn't it?"

"Your comments are not helpful, Talia."

She heaved a hard-put-upon sigh. "Sadly honesty is seldom seen as helpful, even when it's exactly what's needed." She kissed me lightly on the mouth, leaving a tingle in places far removed from my lips, then stood and left the room.

Before I could ask, Alonso answered my question. "Michael is fine, only frustrated and hurt that you won't see him."

The flood of relief was overshadowed by the gut wrench of knowing that I'd hurt him, that he didn't understand why I had to keep him away. I blinked back tears at the sudden tug of loss. "You know why I won't see him. I won't put him at risk again."

"He put himself at risk, darling girl, a thing which he would happily tell you if you would but allow it. Have you forgotten that he is an angel?"

"Of course I've not forgotten what he is. Nor have I forgotten that I nearly killed him."

"He could have pulled away from you at any time, Susan, but for his possessiveness. The foolish man wanted you to take only from him, a desire I can easily understand, being a rather possessive creature myself." I could tell by the inward turn of his smile that he was thinking of Reese. "I fear your angel is not pleased with the bond you now, of necessity, have with me."

"You mean he nearly let himself be killed because of a stupid testosterone pissing contest?"

Alonso laughed quietly. "We men are strange creatures, no matter if we are angels or demons. It is in our nature to view the world in terms of our territory and our possessions. It is in our nature to protect and provide for those we see as our own."

"Even if it kills you?"

"My darling girl, in our eyes, death is well-deserved if we are not man enough to take care of our own. If you are to understand your angel, you must learn this fact. And in all fairness, he should have been able to provide the nourishment you needed alone. He is strong enough, and as an angel he is quickly replenished of his life force and ready to meet your demands again. In truth, I would not have believed you could deplete him after I had fed you so well so recently. I have never known one so ravenous as you have been."

"I'm sorry. I... I couldn't control myself." I was suddenly unable to meet his gaze, the heat of shame scorching my face. "It's just that I'm always so hungry."

"Do not be sorry, darling one. Creatures such as ourselves are not known for their control. And let us be candid, your circumstances are extenuating to say the least. We do not know the effects of what you have taken upon yourself yet."

For the first time since Alonso made me, I had the presence of mind to remember why I had asked him to do such a thing, but I had no time to search inside myself to discover if the Guardian was there before Alonso continued. "I have brought you here in this safe place so that you may learn control, so that you may learn what is needed, so that you may learn to hunt properly when you must feed outside those who willingly serve as your source of nutrition, and so that you may give something back when you must do so. Sadly, I had no one to teach me in the beginning, and if it had not been for Magda Gardener, I do not know what might have become of me."

"So that's how she knows about feeding from the heart's blood."

He nodded. "I was little more than a revenant when she took me. When I came back to myself in my lucid moments, the horror of what I had done, the guilt, sent me scurrying back into my darkness. She took me into her home, isolated me in a cave she had prepared for my needs and fed me of her own blood alone until I was calm enough and rational enough to learn control, and to learn to live with what I had become. In that time with her, I discovered that there are many creatures such as I—and not all of them vampires by any means. We must all learn to live with our own darkness and find a way forward—not to make amends, for we can never right the wrongs we have done, no matter how many lifetimes our existence might be. But, instead, we must learn to live lives that are… of value in the present."

He held my gaze. "I have not killed for a very, very long time, my darling girl. But the memories of what I have done do not fade, just as I am sure Magda's do not. Nor will yours. My life lived well is my penance, and my joy, as yours will be, in time."

"Why?" I asked. "Why would Magda do that? Why didn't she just… you know, turn you to stone?"

This time his smile was edged with a bitter chuckle. "I believe I was very much hoping for a stake through the heart. I fear I would have single-handedly decimated a small village in the Yorkshire Dales if she hadn't hunted me down, brought me back to my beloved Lakeland and taken me under her wing. You see, the village elders sought her out for that purpose. Mortals are nothing if not a cunning lot, and surprisingly good at overcoming insurmountable odds. Indeed, Magda could have ended my miserable existence, and easily. In fact, I begged her to at least a thousand times during those dark days when she held me captive. I owe her much."

As though he anticipated my next question, he waved a dismissive hand. "Oh, it is always difficult to tell with Magda Gardener if her acts are done out of compassion or out of her own desires to add to the Consortium." Another chuckle. "That's what she calls those she has brought together when she's putting, how is it you say, the proper spin on it. But we all just call ourselves Magda's collection, of which both myself and the angel, and now you, my darling girl, are a part."

For a moment, we both sat in silence. Then he moved onto the bed next to me, unbuttoned his shirt, and with a quick flick of a fingernail, opened the vein above his heart, still holding my gaze. "In the days ahead of us, my little one, I will give you of myself but a sip here and there, to strengthen our bond and to make you stronger. While others will be the source of your nourishment, what I can offer of myself will help you in what you must learn, and it will comfort and calm you as well."

For the first time since my new life began, I didn't lunge; for the first time, I let him gently guide me to the flow, which I savored with light flicks of my tongue and pulls of my pursed lips.

He grunted softly. "You must be careful, my darling girl. The pleasure you receive from the taking is returned in kind, and while I am sure Reese would understand if I took you that way, living with a vampire and a succubus as he does, I am not sure I could forgive myself, and I am most certain your angel would not forgive me. In fact, I do believe he would seek out a stake for my heart."

I pulled away and sat up next to him. "I'm sorry. I—"

"Do not apologize, my darling. You must learn. I shall teach you. When you feed from your angel, you may take of his manhood, which will happily respond to your feeding, as you already know. In fact," he offered me a wicked smile, "you may feed him from your heart's blood," he made a negating sign with his hand. "Only but a little, for he will not be able to take more without becoming intoxicated. A little, however, will pleasure both of you in ways you will find startlingly delightful."

He re-buttoned his shirt and wiped a smudge of his blood from my lips with the pad of his thumb, licking it off with a quick flick of his tongue, which made my heart race. "And now, my dear girl, there is someone here who very much wants to see you."

There was a knock at the door. Magda stepped in with Annie at her side, looking startlingly well, if still quite thin.

"I have given her but a little of my own blood to help her heal," Alonso whispered next to my ear. Or at least I thought he had, but then I realized I had heard his voice inside my head. "Yes, my darling Susan, there are other connections besides blood that we now share." He nodded to Annie. "Go to her. You will not hurt her, of that I'm certain."

The thought was barely complete before Annie broke from Magda's solicitous hold on her arm and ran to the bed, throwing herself into my embrace. "You're all right! Oh, thank God you're all right," she sobbed against my shoulder.

I could see the hammering of her pulse in the vein of her throat. I could smell the sweet flowery scent of her blood within. But, inside my head, almost inside the centre of my chest, I could feel Alonso's reassuring nod. So, gently, carefully, I pulled her closer and found myself sobbing in empathy.

"You're a vampire now?" She pulled back, wiping her eyes and looking me over as though she expected me to flash my fangs. Fangs which I wasn't even sure I had, but surely I must, I had no problem getting to the source of blood offered from a wrist or a neck. And while Alonso had assured me that the vampire's lack of reflection is only an old wives' tale, I had not had the presence of mind to truly inspect myself for changes.

"I am, yes." I found myself blushing.

"And you did that for me?" A huge tear rolled down her thin but healthy-looking cheek. "Oh, Susan, I never meant for this to happen."

"I know." I pulled her back against my shoulder and let her cry. "It wasn't your fault, Annie. It wasn't your fault. If anyone is to blame it's me, and I'm so, so sorry."

"What has happened is no one's fault," Alonso said. "Blame will do no one any good in moving forward into a future that, while quite different from the one I'm sure we all anticipated, will be bright."

"Come, darling. We'd best leave our little scribe to get her rest." Magda shot first me, and then Alonso a glance from beneath her glasses as she motioned to Annie.

"Can't I stay just a little longer?" Annie protested. "Susan isn't going to hurt me. Susan would never hurt me."

"Best you don't just now," Alonso said, reaching to push her hair, which once again was a shiny golden blonde, away from her face. "Susan is just now coming back to herself, and she has much to learn about being what she now is if she is to remain safe and keep those around her safe."

On an impulse, Annie leaned in and landed a kiss on my cheek.

I was suddenly overwhelmed by the scent of her, the

powerful efforts of her blood to heal her, to restore her health, the fact that she lived and breathed and that her body held what I needed. I curled my fingers in her hair and pulled her close with more force than I intended. She gave a little yelp of surprise, but threw her arms around me in a bear hug. There was no fear in her in spite of what I had become, in spite of the fact that I wanted to taste her blood with a need that was so close to physical my chest ached and my stomach clenched.

With the preternatural senses I was still trying to get used to, I could not only see the tension tightening Magda and Alonso's bodies, but I could feel the change in their breathing, in their blood pressure, even a change in the very scent of them. They were nervous. They were afraid, both tensing to pull Annie away from me should things go tits-up, which I knew with the pounding of my own heart was a very real possibility.

I don't know exactly how it happened. It was all so fast, but I lowered my mouth just to kiss, just to touch that place where her heart beat in her throat with my lips, maybe with my tongue... Then there was a moan that sounded like someone in agony, and I was suddenly on the far side of the bed, up against the wall, trembling like a leaf in a Cumbrian storm.

Annie's eyes were huge and round as Magda all but jerked her to her side and stepped back beyond the threshold with no less preternatural speed. But just as Magda pulled her through the door, Annie grabbed the molding and stopped progress long enough to turn to me. "I'll see you soon, Susan. I think we're long overdue for a girls' night in, you know, a nice bottle of wine, a good chinwag?

She can drink wine, can't she?" she asked Alonso.

He offered his usual calming smile. "Do not worry, my dear Annie, our Susan will be able to drink wine, though she may no longer find its taste to her liking."

Annie gave a little hiccup of a laugh. "I can't imagine Susan Innes ever being dead enough not to revel in a good glass of Malbec." She blew me a kiss as Magda all but pulled her bodily through the door, and then I found myself sobbing in Alonso's arms, even as I smelled his confusion.

"My darling girl, whatever is the matter? Why are you weeping so? Do you not wish to enjoy a good chin-wagging with dear Annie?"

"Of course I do," I blubbered, "but you saw what just happened. You had to pull me off her. I'm not safe. I'm not safe!"

"Of course you're not safe, my dear scribe, and neither am I, but I promise you I did not pull you away from Annie. You backed away yourself, and a good thing the wall was stone or you would have gone right through it in your efforts to keep her safe."

Chapter Thirty-four

"Talia said there was no indication of the Guardian being present when Susan fed from her, and she should be able to sense Him if anyone could," Magda said. "Even Alonso hasn't been able to discover if He's there. Certainly no one else who's fed her felt anything unusual—aside from the obvious bloodletting, that is."

I stepped back around the corner at the sound of Magda and Michael's hushed conversation. I knew they were nervous about the fact that we'd had no clear evidence that the plan had worked, that the Guardian had been trapped inside me when I was changed. Since everyone had assured me that He couldn't be killed, then the only possibility was that He was trapped or that He'd escaped—a possibility that we all feared more and more as each day passed without any definite knowledge of his whereabouts. But then again, the truth was that none of us really knew what to expect.

I listened in silence as only the dead could, knowing that if it had been Alonso and Talia talking, or even Reese, they would have known I was eavesdropping. Sadly the connection with Michael through his mark seemed not to work any longer. I assumed that was due to my change. Though in all fairness I'd been avoiding him like the plague, and the fear of a repeat of what that link had allowed last time had prevented either of us from trying to connect, so I listened undetected.

"Is it possible He got away and is lying low until we least expect it?" Michael asked in a whisper I could have never heard when I was mortal.

"I don't see how He could have," Magda replied. "If

anything, Susan and Alonso's plan was much better than ours. I don't know why I didn't think of it."

Michael used some very colorful language in response to that. "Do you think that's why she won't see me, for fear the Guardian might still use the link between us?" Even in the quiet whisper, I heard the pain in his voice, pain I'd caused, pain that made me feel like my own heart had been ripped from my chest.

"She won't see you because you were a fool last time she did. She doesn't want to hurt you."

More cursing. "She won't! She won't hurt me, but between the damn vampire and his people and you and yours, I can't get close enough to tell her. I can't get close enough to apologize."

"Sorry, but that's what she wanted. Besides, you know there are way more variables involved now that she's a vampire, now that there's been no evidence of the Guardian in over a week. Everyone is playing it safe. You're at risk too, you know, after what He did to you through your link with her."

He gave a bitter laugh. "Maybe there is no link, not any more. Not now that she's..."

"Now that she's dead?"

I don't know if Michael flinched at Magda's choice of terminology, but I did. I still couldn't quite get used to the fact that while my heart most definitely beat, albeit much slower, I didn't need to breathe. Alonso was teaching me, however, that the living were not comfortable when one did not respire, as he put it. Superfluous respiration was essential in order for a vampire to blend in with the living, so I respired. Or at least when I remembered to, I respired.

Respiration was only one of a million things I had to learn, unlearn, or relearn. I had to learn to slow my every movement so that it didn't startle the living, so that I didn't crash into things, break things, frighten the hell out of people, or seriously injure someone. I had to learn to hold objects gently in order not to crush them. I had to learn to touch things tentatively. I had to learn to move much more awkwardly than I was now actually capable of in order to blend in and not frighten mortals. I had to learn to live in the night and protect myself from the sunlight. Most terrifying of all, I had to learn to manage the hunger so that I could feed without killing, even if I had to hunt to do it.

It was the learning to be gentle and handling things carefully that tripped me up in my attempt at eavesdropping. As I stepped back into the corner, further out of their sight, I accidentally knocked over a small ceramic figurine sitting on the edge of one of the many full bookshelves Alonso had liberally located around his home. In High View, one was never more than a few feet from a good selection of books.

My reactions had improved to the point that catching the figurine before it hit the floor was no problem. The problem was holding the delicate figure of a horse and rider without crushing it. This I was learning to do, but it didn't come automatically, and the thing shattered in my hand, emitting a loud crack overshadowed by my hissed "son of a bitch" as the shards bit into the flesh of my hand.

Both Michael and Magda were on me instantly, reminding

me with their own preternatural speed, that they were no more human than I was.

"Jesus! You're bleeding!" Michael said, taking my hand in his.

Try though I might, the fact that Michael was touching me, the fact that his touch was as wonderful as I had remembered, as I had ached for it to be again, I couldn't take my eyes off the racing of his pulse in the vein of his neck.

"Leave it." I jerked away. "It's nothing. I'm fine. I have to go."

Magda, who never missed anything, already had her mobile out, calling Alonso as I turned to flee. But as fast as I was, to my surprise, Michael was faster. He grabbed me by the arm in an effort to pull me back, ignoring Magda's command to let me go.

"You're not fine, Susan. It's a bad cut. It needs tending."

"I heal fast." Or at least I hoped I did. "Now let me go." Truth was, the sight of my own blood and Michael's attention to it both frightened me and aroused the hunger in me, a situation Alonso had warned me to be very careful in. And the crazy thing was, I wanted to fuck Michael senseless almost as badly as I wanted to drink his sweet rich angel blood down in thirsty gulps. Almost as badly as I wanted to open the vein above the swell of my breast and feed him from my blood, make him drunk from my blood, drunk with lust for me. My nipples hardened to agonizing points, pressing against the cotton of my blouse, and I wanted Michael with an ache that was physical.

I wondered if Alonso knew that women could be every bit as

possessive and protective of what belonged to us as men could. But we could be a hundred times more vicious if need be.

I shoved him away with such force that he landed with a hard *whump* up against the stone wall, and the oxygen left his lungs, along with more colorful language. Then I turned to run. I barely made it to the stairs before he was on me, grabbing my arm and pulling me back to him with surprising strength. "You're not going anywhere until we talk."

I could smell his blood, hot and earthy and summer berry sweet racing through his veins; I could smell my own blood, already drying from the wound on my hand, now healed, and hunger—both physical and sexual—nearly drove me to my knees.

I mumbled something about me not being safe as I elbowed him hard in the ribs, then turned and tore up the stairs with dangerous untested speed, Michael only a hair's breadth behind me.

Over our struggle I could hear Alonso on the phone, arguing with Magda. Fucking hell if the man didn't tell her to leave us alone, to let us sort it out! Dear God, was he out of his mind? How could he tell her that when he knew what it was like, when he'd been where I was and knew the worst?

At the top of the stairs, I shoved my way into the bedroom where I'd stayed before Alonso moved me underground for protection from the sunlight. It was a place I still liked to go after dark, to enjoy its exquisite view of the night sky. "Go away, Michael," I yelled, slamming the door behind me. "You don't know what I'm capable of. I nearly killed—"

My words died in my throat with a little yelp as I turned to find him already standing by the bed, hands fisted at his side, chest heaving, eyes blazing.

"And you don't know what *I'm* capable of," he replied, moving toward me so fast that even my preternatural vision couldn't register his motion. He had me in his arms before I could even blink. "You think you're the only one who struggles with power?" He pushed me against the wall and held me with one arm across my chest while he quite literally ripped his shirt off with the other hand. "I'm an angel, for fuck's sake! And, mortal or not, I'm still more than a match for any damn vampire. Didn't your maker tell you that? Or was he just wanting to keep you all to himself?"

"Don't you blame Alonso for this. The choice was mine to make. He didn't want to, and you know damn well I nearly killed you—would have killed you if…"

With a flick of his thumbnail, he opened the wound above his left nipple—with ease this time and, as the blood welled, I completely lost my train of thought as the ripe fruit scent of it overwhelmed my senses. I cried out and fumbled for the doorknob in a desperate attempt to get away, even as he held me firmly.

"You think I can't handle you? You think you're too much for me?" He curled his fingers in my hair and reeled me into a kiss that would have been fatal if I hadn't already been dead. Then he pulled away, breathing like he'd been running. "That's the trouble with you damn vampires, you're so fucking arrogant."

I shoved him with enough force to send him careening backwards over the bed and on to the floor behind. "Oh, and you goddamned angels are so full of humility!"

"I didn't say anything about humility." With terrifying strength, he grabbed the heavy wooden bedframe, an antique that must have weighed as much as a small lorry, and turned it upside down with a loud crash. "Did you ever hear me say anything about humility?"

When I made another run for the door, he tackled me, pinned me on my stomach with my arm up behind my back, me screaming and fighting and bucking until I unseated him just long enough to roll over and crabwalk back toward the door. Before I could gain my footing, he was on me again. He straddled me, wrapped his legs around mine and spread me into a Judo hold from which it was no trouble at all to feel his full erection.

If that didn't have my vampire heart racing, the blood running down his bare chest did. Just before he could get a solid hold on me, I bucked him off and shoved him back. His head hit the edge of the upturned bed hard enough to cause a hissed stream of expletives.

Quickly, I straddled him, with him cursing and roaring like an angry bear. The instincts of the predator took over, even as the scent of our lust nearly overpowered the scent of blood. I ran the flat of my tongue up from the waistband of his jeans, following the trail of fresh blood, careful not to miss a single drop as I lapped my way up to the wound. It was a shallow wound, enough to trickle freely without the danger of him bleeding out. Enough to make me work for my snack, and it was a surprise to discover that it was just a snack, albeit a very tasty snack. This was about play. This wasn't about life and death. Even predators played, didn't they? With a shock, I realized this was about sex, this was about possession. This was about the balance of power we had to find before we destroyed each other in ways that were far worse than the physical damage we could cause.

Chapter Thirty-five

Michael's groan was pure lust as I took the first deep taste of him. With the taste of his heart's blood, for a split second, it wasn't lust I felt. It was Michael's agony at my death, that he'd been helpless to prevent. It was his anguish at me shutting him out. It was all the pent-up feelings of more lifetimes than I could imagine, down through the ages when I only existed in his horrific knowledge of eternity in an instant, the agony of endless ages of waiting, only to be denied.

Alonso had warned me that there was so much more in the blood than just nourishment and lust, that the knowledge of the whole of a person's existence was contained in the blood, and even beyond, the history of their people. He told me that a vampire could access such information in that first ravenous sip, but I'd never had the presence of mind to do so before, though I'd quite possibly taken only from people who knew how to shield their own inner workings.

Alonso hadn't yet taught me how to preserve the privacy of the person upon whom I fed, and Michael was suddenly wide open, laid completely bare to me in a rush of information that was heartbreaking and terrifying and amazing all at once. There were glimpses of his relationship with the Guardian, there were flashes of him with Magda, there were images that made no sense in a context of anything that had ever been mortal.

Then, just as suddenly as it had flooded my consciousness, it was gone. It was as though a heavy curtain had descended, and what remained was the pleasure of nourishment and lust, twinned with the bond that I quickly realized had not been broken by my death after all.

I acted more on instinct than on any real knowledge of what I did, tearing open the front of my blouse and ripping the bra as easily as I would a sheet of rice paper until my breasts were exposed. I sat up, still straddling him, and opened my own heart's blood to him with a sharp flick of my nail, pulling him up to me to feed. To my delight, he took what I offered with a swirl of his tongue and an opening of his lips. He sucked hard and bit, just as he had when he had given me his mark.

With a sharp cry of surprise, he pulled away enough to meet my gaze, lips wet with the sheen of my blood. "It's still there. My mark."

"Stronger than ever," I said, nodding to the wound over his heart. "Because now you wear my mark as well." I pulled him back to me and felt the tight, delicious, almost painful pull of his lips and nip of his teeth, and it was as though he did the same between my legs. I felt it down there as surely as if his face were pressed between my thighs, as surely as if he fed upon my most intimate self.

Careful not to pull away just yet, I lifted my bottom and fumbled open the tight strain of his fly, feeling the hiss of his breath against my breast as I freed him, slid aside the crotch of my panties and guided him home with a deep duet of a groan. And he truly was home as I rode him and he rose up to meet me, kneading and cupping my breasts while he suckled. How could I ever not have realized that he was my heart and my only home?

"Not too much," I said, pulling away, him following me up with a groan of protest. "Too much will make you drunk and I don't want you drunk. I won't be done with you for a very long time yet."

He sealed the wound with a press of his tongue as he'd seen me do and offered an evil chuckle. "Then for your pleasure, I'll do my best to stay sober, Susan."

With that, he guided me back to him. Again, instinct took control with the first taste of him, and I sipped and licked and nipped until his whole pectoral muscle tensed and rose with each breath he took. Each breath which now came in heavy gasps and sharp little pants as though he battled for control. His nipple rose tight and dark pink beneath the brush of my chin, and I broke free from my feeding occasionally to give it a worrying lick or a sharp nip, just to hear him pant and moan, just to feel him surge inside of me before I returned to his vein.

His cock filled me so completely, and the glide and move of the two of us was so in sync, so deeply connected that time went away. Everything went away but Michael inside me—what I had craved and longed for for the length of my own eternity, which seemed desperately long before Michael filled it.

I arched over his body, and with a large hand curled in my tangled hair, he held me tight to the wound at his heart as I took from the nourishing flow of him, all the while undulating and shifting against the powerful rise and fall of him beneath me.

"I won't go away, Susan, so you best get used to it." He fisted my hair and pulled me away just enough that I was forced to look up into his deep ocean eyes. "You're mine. The vampire might be your maker, but I'm the one who waited an eternity for you. I'm the one who'll feed you. I'm the one who'll give you what you need.

I'm the one who loves you." He licked the taste of himself from my lips with a possessive tongue.

Then he rolled with me, pinning me beneath his massive body. For the first time I realized just how powerful he was, just how much control he had exerted in our lovemaking before I became a vampire to keep from hurting me, or even killing me.

As though that blood connection had somehow made him aware of my thoughts, he bent and nipped my own wound, licking it hard enough to make me squirm with transferred pleasure while he never lost the rhythm, the subtle increase of speed as we drew near our release. "You can't hurt me, Susan, I promise. At least not physically."

He lowered his mouth, and took my nipples in turn, cupping and caressing my fullness with both gentleness and strength. I held onto his arse, feeling the tensing and relaxing of fit, firm buttocks with each thrust. I couldn't help it. I was unable to resist biting his neck—just a little nip—taking just a sip, intuiting what my feeding on him did to him, as he pressed deeper inside me and the rhythm became frantic, wild with power, filled with a hunger that had nothing to do with physical nourishment. I dug my nails into his back and bit harder and he grunted with some mix of pain and lust.

"Oh dear God, Susan, I never want it to end, but I can't hold back much longer." His breath was warm and humid against my ear. "I want to know what it feels like to come while I feed you, to know that you possess me as completely as I possess you."

Words—sometimes words are as powerful as touch; sometimes words are the tipping point, and they were this time. They were enough to send us both over the edge, growling and grasping and trembling, as though we would shake each other apart or dissolve completely into each other. Perhaps we did both. As I drifted in and out of consciousness, I was completely unaware of where my body ended and Michael's began. He was still hard and I was still fully impaled and happy to remain that way.

He rolled to one side so that his weight wasn't completely on top of me and fumbled behind him for the duvet from the overturned bed. He offered me a wicked smile as he pulled it free. "Does this make me your familiar?"

"Don't know," I replied, hooking my leg around him, making sure he wasn't going anywhere. "I haven't had that lesson yet."

"Not sure how I could get much more familiar," he said, giving my breast an enthusiastic knead.

"Me neither, but why don't we give it our best try, just to be sure you're familiar enough."

He had just taken me in a kiss that promised to lead to far more serious things when there was a knock on the door. Michael barely got the duvet pulled over us before Talia shoved her way in, ignoring his curse and my little yelp.

"Oh good! You haven't killed him," she said with a sunny smile. "I brought food."

She sat a large covered tray on the one sailor's trunk that hadn't been turned over with the bed and gave the room, and then us, a knowing once over. "Alonso figured you'd need it, Michael, if your little scribe hadn't drained you completely dry. And he asks that I remind you not to linger too much longer before you head for the basement. Dawn will be coming soon." Then she left, chuckling under her breath.

"That woman's a pain in the arse," Michael said, taking the cover from the tray and biting the end off a freshly baked baguette.

"She's a good kisser, though. I'm just saying," I added, as he gave me the evil eye and shoved half the baguette into his mouth.

"So's Cook," he spoke around his efforts to chew. "But that doesn't mean I want you kissing him."

"You've kissed Cook?" I scooted closer and lifted the lid off a steaming bowl of lamb stew, taking note that even though I used to love lamb stew, it was now like thinking of eating cardboard soaked in water.

He shrugged. "We were both drunk at the time, and he had made a fabulous Beef Wellington for dinner that night. Worthy of at least a good kiss."

Once Michael had devoured everything on the tray, he ate me for dessert and then I returned the favor. At some point we'd managed to right the mattress, and tangle ourselves in the remaining bedding, but we didn't quite manage the rest of the bed before Michael took me from behind, me on my knees, hair fisted in his hand like I was the horse and he was reining me under control. It's quite possible that's exactly what he was trying to do. It didn't work. The control part, I mean.

"You kept your strength from me," I said, when at last we collapsed on the mattress and he pulled me into a spoon position.

"I had no reason to tell you," he replied. "I've kept my strength from everyone except Magda. I had to in order to interact safely with humans. You're all so fragile. Well, you were." He bit the side of my neck playfully. "Nice to be able to play rough, and even nicer not to have to wait for you to recover." He stood and offered me his hand. "Come on, let's get down to the basement and then we'll pick up where we left off." He gave his still erect penis a stroke with the other fist to demonstrate.

I gave him a tug and off-balanced him back onto the mattress. "I can't possibly leave without just one more little taste, and maybe one more little fuck. We have time. Besides, the shutters are drawn tight and we're down behind the bed frame. Alonso's just being a worrywart. We'll be fine."

Before he could protest, I straddled him and guided him up inside me. As he began to thrust and grind beneath me, I opened my vein for him to feed.

A long time later we fell against each other in an awkward twin orgasm that had us half off the mattress onto the stone floor before we collapsed.

"Okay," he mumbled in an intoxicated slur. "It's off to the basement for you, young lady." Then he was out cold, with me not far behind him.

Dreams of the fells sparkling in the summer sun roused me, drenched in sweat and half smothered beneath the body of a sleeping angel. My angel, I reminded myself, as the delicious memories of last night came rushing back to me, along with the mouthwatering scent of our lovemaking and our blood.

I stretched, then shoved my way out from under Michael, who mumbled something incomprehensible from his own dream world and gave my nearest breast an unconscious grope before I leaned in and kissed him. He aimed a half-conscious smacking of lips in my general direction.

"It's sweltering in here," I said, noting the sheen of perspiration on his brow. "No wonder I was dreaming of the fells in summer. We need some air."

"Susan? Susan, don't!"

"Oh, don't worry. I'm not going far," I called over my shoulder, as I threw open the shutter and flung the windows wide, taking in a breath of fresh fell air I didn't really need, lifting my face to the cool breeze.

As the sunlight struck me full on, a voice inside me all but erupted like the press of my heart against my chest, and something not unlike static electricity prickled over my skin. I gasped for breath, for strength, for context, as the voice filled every cell of my body.

"I may well be your prisoner, little scribe, but I will not be kept in darkness."

What happened next was over almost before it started. Michael exploded from the bed, roaring like a wounded lion. The next thing I knew, my world went dark, suffocatingly tight, and a heavy weight drove me to the floor with the force of a lorry.

Chapter Thirty-six

"What the hell are you doing?" We both yelled at the same time.

"Are you crazy? Get off me!"

To which he responded, "Are you out of your fucking mind?"

In spite of my efforts to buck him off, he held me tightly beneath his body, smothered head to toe in the duvet.

"What's going on? You two are supposed to be in the basement!" I heard the door crash against the back wall as it flew open and Reese burst in with Talia right on his heels, both talking at the same time.

Then I was airborne, hefted over Michael's shoulder like a sack of potatoes, with Talia shouting, "Get her out of here! Get her out of here! Get her down to the basement, goddamn it! What the hell were you thinking?"

"I woke up and she was opening the shutters, standing right there in the sunlight. I'm serious." Michael gave the door an angry kick shut that rattled my teeth.

"What the hell do you mean, she was standing in the sunlight?" Reese was saying. "She can't stand in the sunlight. She's a fucking vampire."

"Put me down, damn it! Michael, put me down." No matter how much I shouted and wriggled, they all ignored me.

"I swear it's the truth," Michael said.

"Put her down." There was sudden silence in response to Magda's voice that rose above the din. I found myself unceremoniously deposited on the hard stone floor, wriggling frantically to get out from under the duvet. When I popped my head out, remembering I was naked and quickly snatching the fabric to my breasts, I found myself in the heavy stone corridor, the only light being from the electric sconces on the walls. I was surrounded by Reese, Talia, Magda and a very naked Michael, who knelt next to me and grabbed my face in his hand, turning it from side to side before I slapped him away.

"What the hell?" I said in response to all eyes on me.

"You were standing in the sunlight," Michael responded. His voice trembled slightly and he swallowed hard. For the first time, I realized how frightened he was. Then it all came rushing back to me, and I felt faint.

"It was Him," I managed, my own voice none too steady. "It was the Guardian."

Suddenly everyone was silent and the air around me smelled of nervous adrenaline and more than a little bit of fear. "I was dreaming of sunlight, and when I woke up the room was hot. I didn't even think when I opened the shutters, not until he said that while he might be my prisoner, he refused to live in darkness."

No one was willing to take my word for my immunity to sunlight, so Talia brought our clothes out of the room for us— Michael not being willing to leave my side—and once we were dressed we all traipsed to the basement, where Alonso paced his study like a big cat in a cage. When he saw me, he pulled me into his arms, and both Michael and Reese bristled. Ignoring them completely, he stepped away just enough to take my face in his hand, turning it from side to side. "No damage?"

I shook my head, or at least tried to, but he held me firmly.

"You didn't feel anything at all? No burning, no rash, no unusual heat?"

"I only felt what I would have felt before you changed me—the warmth of the sun on my face. Honestly, I didn't even think about what I was doing until I heard the Guardian's voice in my head and felt Him move inside me as though He were trying to get comfortable."

"And you think this was his doing?" Alonso asked.

"Oh for fuck's sake, darling girl." The Guardian spoke inside my head, mocking Alonso. "Who else does he think it could possibly be? Are all vampires so dense?"

"It's Him. I'm certain," I said, gladly taking the chair that Magda pushed under my arse just in time.

"What did you do?" I asked the Guardian. "How did you protect me from the sun?"

Everyone leaned close, as though they expected a Regan moment straight from *The Exorcist.*

"First of all, you don't have to speak out loud for me to hear you. I'm inside you, remember? Secondly, I'm indestructible, as far as I know. Therefore, it only makes sense that my prison is protected by my presence." He chuckled softly. "Believe me, my dear little scribe, the irony of that is not lost on me."

"Is He talking to you? What the hell is He saying?" Michael said.

I opened my mouth to respond, and in my head, I heard—

almost felt—the clearing of the Guardian's throat. "If you'll allow it, little one, I can use your voice and save the tedious translation." Sensing of my reluctance, he gave a little huff of indignation. "I am your prisoner, Susan, not the other way around. I can do nothing without your permission other than protect you, for to protect you is to protect myself. You may banish me to the silent depths of your unconscious mind for all of eternity and there I would be forced to remain, for you control the vessel that is my prison. You may silence me or seek me out at your will, but I would advise seeking me often and silencing me seldom, for I promise you that with the plans that bitch of a Gorgon has in mind for you, you may well find my help most useful indeed."

With a feeling that I was somehow mentally laying a hand on the Guardian's shoulder just to silence him for a second, I spoke to those around me. "He'll use my voice, and He'll answer any questions you ask." The second part was a definite command, and I had a sense that, though He bristled slightly, the Guardian took me at my word.

"How do we know He's telling the truth?" Michael asked.

"Oh my darling angel, it cuts me to the quick that you could doubt my veracity when I have pleasured your body and seen your innermost workings."

Michael jumped back at the sound of my voice, only slightly changed, and yet unmistakably not mine. He nearly fell over Talia who, for once, wasn't seeing the humor in the situation as she placed a hand on his arm to steady him.

The Guardian smiled at the incident, a smile that no one but I could see, a smile that told me well he would make the best of his situation if I allowed it. When I gave him a silent warning, he offered the equivalent of a shrug, and then he continued, "I swear to you, I can tell no lies before my jailor. For you see, in truth I have at last achieved what I most longed for; flesh to house my intellect, my desires. A body to give me boundaries through which I may experience the world. Granted, I did not expect that when I found a worthy vessel it would belong to a vampire, but then one must be careful what one wishes for, mustn't one?"

"What do you want?" Alonso asked.

"What I want is to be free. But as far as prisons go, this one is far better than the last, and I think the scribe shall find me a model prisoner."

"Can you harm her in any way?" Michael asked, then quickly added, "Can you harm anyone?"

"I can do nothing of my own accord, and I assure you I am completely at the mercy of my jailor and the vessel in which I now reside. I can neither possess her nor use her in any way, though I am at her beck and call, and she may use me as she sees fit."

"So we're supposed to believe that you'll completely bend to Susan's will in every way?" Magda asked.

A chuckle escaped my lips, and I felt almost like I'd suddenly belched rudely in public, to have laughed at Magda Gardener. "My options are to do absolutely nothing, to basically not interact at all with my jailor and the outside world she commands through the body which she inhabits, or to do as she asks and play as much of an active role in her existence as she will allow. I would think that would please you greatly, Gorgon, knowing your plans for her."

"You don't know my plans for her," Magda answered calmly, as though they were chatting over coffee.

"I can refuse to aid her, it is true. I am her prisoner, not her slave. But it would benefit me little to sulk when I was beaten fair and square by minds far less capable than my own."

"Then the conditions of your imprisonment are mine to establish," I said.

Fuck! It was like talking to myself. "Of course," came the reply. "I would imagine we shall both take some getting used to, and you most certainly will be very preoccupied while your vampire teaches you how to exist as you now are."

"Why didn't we hear from you sooner? Why were you quiet?" Michael asked.

"I was, I suppose you could say, sulking. Also, I had neither been summoned, nor was there any need for me to interact until an explanation became necessary for our little vampire's astonishing tolerance for sunlight."

Just then Cook arrived, pushing a trolley laden with breakfast treats.

Without thinking, I tore into a fresh croissant and had it half devoured before I realized everyone was staring at me. My response was his, over a shower of crumbs. "Oh, of course she can eat food! She can eat it, and it will not harm her. She may even enjoy it if she chooses. How else shall she be able to interact believably with mortals? That is what you need, isn't it, Gorgon?" Magda bristled, but before she could respond, he continued, "However, the food she eats will not nourish her. Nourishment, she can only get from blood. But since I am here for the long term, I would prefer to enjoy the taste of something other than… body fluids."

"So she has the best of both worlds then?" Talia asked.

"She has the body of a vampire, with all that entails. She has the enhancements that one such as myself can give her—an attempt to decorate my cell, to make myself more comfortable, if you will. And, of course, she still retains her own creative powers as a scribe. Goodness me, our little Susan is very nearly the perfect being."

Both Michael and Alonso growled, and this time there was an internal clicking of the tongue. "They are a possessive pair, your men, are they not, scribe?"

That was for my ears only and I responded with an internal, "You have no idea!"

"I shall leave you all to your breakfast," He said, once again using my voice. "Susan has only to summon me."

"And will you be eavesdropping?" Michael asked.

"My dear angel, I am where I am. As I have said, we will all have to get used to each other. Before you growl at me, I would remind you that this was the scribe's choice, her plan, and in all things there are consequences. She knew that and willingly took the risk. That being said, may I also remind you that you live and breathe because of her choice?"

And just like that, He was gone. I had the feeling one has when one wakes up with a jerk in the middle of a dream of falling. For an instant everything went slightly out of focus. When it came back, all eyes were still on me, and both Michael and Alonso were kneeling in front of me.

"Is this what you were expecting to happen, Susan?" Alonso's voice was now inside my head.

"I don't know what I expected," I replied.

"Speak out loud so we can all hear, vampire, or shut the fuck up," Michael said. When Alonso looked at him with a raised eyebrow, he shrugged. "You're not the only one connected to her." He gently laid his hand above my left breast where, not only had he fed from me, but his mark thrummed stronger than ever against my heart, and I knew my mark on his chest did the same.

"I do apologize," Alonso said, coming to his feet and moving back to stand by Reese. "It is often my custom to communicate non-verbally with those who belong to me."

Michael growled at that remark and Alonso smiled an internal smile that only I could see. Then he added in his best conciliatory tone. "But you are right. Now is not the time for secrets. I only wish to ascertain if our scribe is unharmed."

Before the testosterone pissing could start again, I spoke up. "I'm fine. I'm just... well, it's a lot to take in, that's all."

Chapter Thirty-seven

"Talia said this is where you'd be." Michael sat next to me on a rock in the last of the afternoon sunlight. "She also said Alonso doesn't know you're here."

"I got tired of everyone watching me like I might explode or my head might start spinning in circles. I had to get out of there." I nodded to the cavern behind me. "Alonso's still worried about my tolerance of sunlight. That's why I'm here in the mouth of the cave. If I suddenly smell burning flesh, I'll make a dive for it. Where were you?" I asked, hoping I didn't sound as pouty as I felt. "You left in a hurry."

"I've been at home, making a few arrangements."

"I see," I said, but I didn't. I didn't see at all. I thought after last night we'd reconnected and made everything right, that we'd stopped pushing each other away, yet it felt like Michael couldn't get away from High View fast enough after the Guardian revealed himself. I suppose I couldn't really blame him. It was bad enough to watch your girlfriend become a vampire, but a vampire with a resident demon was surely a bridge too far—even for an angel.

"I had an important delivery," he said. "And I had workers coming to help install the blackout blinds. I didn't want to put it off any longer." Before I could do more than offer a surprised glance, he continued, "I was trying to make the house more vampire-friendly back when I didn't know you could tolerate sunlight." He shrugged and looked down at his hands folded in his lap. "I had to do something constructive or go crazy when you… when you wouldn't let me near you. Anyway, I suppose all that's irrelevant now, but the blinds had already been paid for and they seemed like a good idea—you know, just in case you do suddenly smell burning flesh."

He stood and offered me his hand, pulling me to my feet. "Come with me, Susan. Come back to my place with me. I want you to see what I've done, but mostly I just want you to myself. Oh, I know you've got to spend time with Alonso, and I'll make sure you're back first thing in the morning. It kills me that there are things the vampire can do for you that I can't, but at the end of the day when he's finished your lessons, I want you in my house. I want you in my bed, in my arms, and I don't want to wake up with half the vampire menagerie and a gorgon poking their noses in the door to see what we've got up to during the night."

"Alonso won't like it, and neither will Magda," I said.

"I don't care. Do you?"

I squared my shoulders and huffed out an exaggerated breath. "Nope! I'm sick of caring what everyone thinks is best for me. I'm not a child, and I'm tired of being treated like one. Let's go."

When I tugged him back toward the cave, he shook his head. "I know a shortcut to the Jeep. I parked it off the property so we could sneak away. They won't even miss us."

"Of course they'll miss us. We can't even sneeze without someone knowing."

"Well then, they'll surely appreciate a few less sneezes around High View."

It was just a walk across the meadow, then we were heading down Honister Pass, and I was away from High View for the first time since my new life had begun. We didn't talk much. There seemed less need to now that we bore each other's mark. That he wanted me to be with him, that he'd planned and prepared, even hoped, when things weren't looking very promising, that was enough for now.

At his house there had been several changes, but the most obvious was the Las Vegas-style blackout blinds in Michael's bedroom, just inside and above its lovely French doors. "I guarantee no sunlight will touch your alabaster skin through those monsters," he said, stroking my cheek with the back of his hand. "I know it's not an issue under the circumstances, but just in case. And the basement, well, I can have it made up any way you like if you'd feel safer there—you know, a study for you to write in, a library. I've even drawn up plans to have the basement loo turned into a nice bathroom with a spa tub. We can even move the bedroom down there if you want—just to be sure."

"Alonso's the worrywart, not me. I believe the Guardian won't let anything happen to Him, and therefore he won't let anything happen to me either."

"Yeah, well I didn't know that before this morning, did I? So that really didn't figure into my plan."

"Your plan." I sat on the edge of the mattress, feeling weak kneed all of a sudden. "Michael, are asking me to move in with you?"

He sat down next to me and folded my hand in his. "You can't go back to your old life, Susan. You've burned all the bridges in a major way."

"Writing and being a vampire aren't mutually exclusive. In

fact, under the circumstances, no one would know the difference even if I worked side by side with them—not unless I got hungry and decided to have a little sip from one of my colleagues."

I thought about my tiny closet of a flat in Brixton that took the lion's share—and then some—of my income, just so I could live alone, and—technically—live in London. The truth was, I didn't want to go back. The truth was, I couldn't help feeling excited about the life ahead of me now, even as the thought terrified me.

"That's not the point." He gave my hand a squeeze. "You belong to the Consortium now, and Magda will want to keep an eye on you. I reckon she's already making arrangements to have your flat lease terminated. She'll want you to stay with the vampire until he teaches you the ropes, though what that means is up for question now that you've become prison warden for the Guardian."

"That doesn't answer my question. Are you asking me to move in with you?"

"Oh, Magda will find you a fantastic place, I have no doubt. She always does, and I know the vampire would keep you there as long as he could, but—"

"Michael, I'm not a charity case. I can bargain and negotiate for myself. I want to hear it from you. Do you want me here, or do you feel obligated because… well, because Magda sent you to steal me." I made quote marks around the word 'steal'. "If you're doing this out of—"

Michael stopped my words with a kiss that felt as hungry and voracious as I felt when I fed, pulling me tightly to his chest, to the pounding of his heart, quite literally pulling me onto his lap. For a moment, I forgot what the question had been. I forgot what planet we were on as his hands skimmed my back and then moved up to cup my head, stroke my hair and hold me close.

When he pulled away, breathless, he shook me slightly, as though he were trying to wake me up. "How can you even ask such a question, when having you with me is the one thing I've wanted for more lifetimes than you can imagine? Of course I want you here! I want you in my arms when I fall asleep; I want you in my arms when I wake up; I want you like the air I breathe, all the time, Susan! All the bloody time! If you don't want to live here, if you want a place in which you've had a little more input in the choice and the decoration, that's fine. Anywhere you like. Just say the word. I just want you, that's all. I just want you."

I stopped any further conversation with a single word of my own, a word which I breathed into his mouth and pressed deep onto his hard palette with my tongue. "Yes! Yes," I repeated again and then again, as I pushed him back onto the bed and straddled him. After that it was a long time, a very long time, before either of us spoke again.

Long toward midnight we dozed in each other's arms, and I dreamed. I dreamed of following a trail of blood, sparkling like a path of rubies on the snow. I followed the *drip, drip, drip*, like a trail of breadcrumbs through a darkened alley in a place I didn't recognize, and into the entrance of a cave that was no cave at all, but concrete and brick. I followed it deep underground, to a candlelit chamber where shadows danced like phantasms against the stone. There it ended in a stain on the chamber floor that looked inky black beneath the pale body of a man curled on his side, face toward the wall. Before I could see who he was and if he still lived, there was a groan deeper in the passage, beyond the play of candle flame. When my eyes adjusted to the gloom, I saw another man chained to the wall—arms spread wide, shoulders slumped, bare back sheened in sweat. It wasn't until then that I saw the third man, only a silhouette that, try though I might, my dream vision could not resolve.

"I've been waiting for you, scribe," he said softly, and his voice crawled over my skin like I'd walked through a heavy spider's web.

I woke with a jerk to find Michael raised up on one elbow, watching with concern. "Bad dreams?"

"Strange dreams." I moved to lay my head on his chest and told him in as much detail as I could remember, unable to shake the feel of spider webs over my skin.

When I finished, he kissed the top of my ear and let out a slow, even breath. "Do you think it was because of Him—the Guardian?"

"I don't know. Possibly. I mean, there was a man chained in a deep cave, but nothing was very obvious, if it was about the Guardian. And why would there be three men?" I shrugged. "It probably should have been a nightmare, but even though I was in it, I watched it all from a distance. It didn't feel like a nightmare. I don't know what it felt like. Yes I do. It felt… almost prophetic. But then again, it was just a dream," I added quickly, embarrassed at such a ludicrous idea.

"Have you talked to the Guardian since your first surprise

visit?" he asked, his hand moving down to stroke my back.

"No, but I will. I mean, I have to. He lives inside me, and that's a real head job—even though I was prepared for it, or as prepared as I could possibly be. He's right; the situation will take some getting used to for both of us. I can't help but feel there are things He could tell me, things He could teach me. Whether He will or not, I don't know, but the one thing I do know is that He's intrigued by our situation. Very intrigued." I decided not to add that I was too.

Michael lifted my chin so that our eyes met in the darkness. "Susan, it's dangerous to trust Him. You know that."

"He's with me twenty-four-seven now, Michael. I can't ignore Him. There are things I need to know. I would feel better about our situation if I could discuss a few ground rules and ask a few questions. I just can't believe that if I say nothing, ignore Him, as he's said I could, for the next however many years I have ahead of me, that He'll be blissfully quiet. Clearly He doesn't trust Magda. Not that He would have any reason to. I get that." I gave a dismissive shrug. "But if I now belong to her, as it appears I do, if she wants me to do some nebulous work for her that has something to do with my abilities as a scribe—whatever the hell that means, well, I can't think it'll be a waltz in the park. I have… options—way more options than I had when I first came to Manchester to see Annie. And because of the Guardian, I have even more options than I would if I were just a vampire. I also have a whole new life—a double life—that I haven't begun to understand yet, and like it or not, the Guardian is a permanent part of it."

He pulled me on top of him and hugged me until I groaned. "All right, whatever it takes, whatever you feel you have to do, I'll be here. You gave me back my life, Susan. You gave me the chance to share it with you, a chance I thought I'd lost forever. I'll take that on whatever conditions I have to—vampire, demon and all. All I ask is that you don't try to bear it all alone—what's ahead of you, what the future holds. I know Magda, and I can help you deal with her. I know the Guardian probably better than anyone. Certainly I'm the only one who's lived to tell the tale—except for Annie, of course, who was just his pawn. And I know Alonso and his familiars. Everyone is quirky. Everyone has an agenda of some kind. I'm no different. But I know that all of us, everyone associated with the Consortium, we all want what's best for you." He curled a finger under my chin. "But I'm the one who loves you, Susan. I've loved you forever, and that'll never change, no matter your choices. I want to be a part of your life. I want to be there to help you deal with whatever comes next. But mostly I hope that I can be there just because you want me by your side."

I pulled him close and buried my face in his shoulder, next to the thudding of his pulse, resisting the urge to lick him there possessively. "Of course I want you by my side, or I wouldn't be here in your bed right now. Maybe I haven't loved you forever, but I promise you, I got around to it as soon as I possibly could under some pretty trying circumstances, and like you, I'm not planning on going away. Will that do?"

He kissed me fervently and offered a smile that warmed me to the core, which always felt slightly chilled now that I was a vampire. "That'll do, Susan. That'll do just fine."

He slid up into a sitting position, bare back pressed against the headboard. With what had become a rather expert flick of his nail, he opened the flow of his heart's blood to me and pulled me close.

As I fed next to the steady *beat, beat, beat*, even knowing how uncertain the future was, I felt happier than I could ever remember feeling. If Michael was with me, if we were together, then it would be all right. Deep in my chest, in some nebulous place, I sensed the Guardian waiting, waiting to see what His future would be. Our uneasy truce, our sudden change of circumstances, reminded me again that my uncertain future might be a lot of things, but it would most definitely not be boring.

Epilogue

"Is everything all right, Alonso?" Magda knew that it wasn't. She'd heard the little altercation between the vampire and his lover, and even had she not eavesdropped, she would have known what it was about. Everyone at High View knew what it was about. It didn't take a great deal of intuition to figure it out.

"Fine. Everything is fine." He made no effort to sound convincing. He knew she would know it wasn't, and the look on his face told her he was resigned to her poking her nose in where he wished she wouldn't.

"You'll have to send her away, you know that, and the sooner the better. If you love Reese."

"*If* I love Reese?" He spun around to face her with such speed that one with human vision might have thought it magic. However, one would have to be blind not to see the anguish on his face. "Dear God, Magda, you know how much I love Reese. There is no 'if.' Besides, against my wishes, Susan is with the angel tonight." The word angel was tinged with bitterness, the bitterness of jealousy. Then he added with a forced smile, "There, you see, the fledgling has left the nest of her own accord. Does that please you?"

"Michael's place is just down the road. Do you think that's far enough to keep you away from the child of your heart's blood?"

He ran a hand through his hair and paced in front of the open French doors that looked out onto the night garden below, which Reese had built for him, to which the man had fled in his anger only minutes before. "Of course it won't be enough. There's no place in Cumbria, not likely any place in Britain, where she'd be far enough away from me that I wouldn't go to her. She's like my own soul. I never would have imagined it could be thus, since my maker didn't take the time to bond with me or aid me in any way. I didn't know."

He turned to face Magda, the desperation etched deeply on his beautiful face. "I didn't know."

"Even if you had known, the bloody demon left us with little choice. We all did what we had to, and you and Susan bore the brunt of the horrific choices we had to make. And now, now that we know He'll be taking an active role in protecting and watching over her, I'm not sure if I feel better or worse. It behooves Him to take care of her, to cherish her, and I know He can't escape her, and yet still it makes me nervous. There are so many variables."

"That's what I have told Reese ad nauseum; that's why I can't send Susan away, not until she's ready." He nodded out to the garden again, to the place where Reese paced on the slate pavement. "He wants me to bring him over, and I keep telling him that I will as soon as Susan is able to fend for herself and do no harm. I can't make him understand that I am not capable of giving two fledglings what they would need of me. There are times when I'm not sure I can even care for one as I ought. That is pretty evident, I suppose. But I can't make Reese understand, in fact I fear that even his desire for me to bring him over is only because he fears losing me to Susan. How could I bear it if I brought him over and it was not truly what he wanted? We must think this choice through carefully. It can't be made in a jealous heat, in an act of desperation. He sees it as though I am choosing her over him, and the damned angel's jealousy only makes matters worse."

She dropped the bomb, figuring now was as good a time as any, and Alonso would take it better than Michael would, of that she was certain. "I've decided to take matters out of your hands. I'm sending her to New York City."

"What!" He was at her side in what would have seemed like an instant to anyone with human eyes, but Magda's eyes had been far from human for more centuries than she cared to count. Before he could reach for her, before he could lay distressed hands on her, she stepped aside, and he caught himself with all the dignity, all the grace for which vampires are known, straightened his jacket and took a deep breath she knew he didn't need. "You can't take her from me. She's not ready."

"I can, and I will. In case you've forgotten, Alonso, she's mine to do with as I see fit. She belongs to the Consortium now. She came at a very high price, and there's no overestimating her value, especially now that she's a vampire who can walk in daylight, now with the Guardian inside her. You may be her maker, but that doesn't mean you know what's best for her, and neither does Michael."

"She's not ready," he repeated fervently.

"I know she's not ready, and I'd never send her out into the world unprepared. You know that. But here is not the place for her training, not under the circumstances. I've been in touch with Desiree. She owes me, and she's agreed to complete Susan's training in all that pertains to vampires living amongst humans."

He made a derisive sound in his throat at the mention of Desiree. "For what price?"

She shrugged. "Everything has a price, and it was one I was happy to pay, one that will benefit Susan in the end. I've heard rumors of a siren living in New York City." She waved a dismissive hand. "Oh, I know that the chances of such a glorious creature still existing are very slim at best, but the rumors have been consistent and… well, let's just say I feel that they should be checked out. It won't be a difficult assignment for Susan, but it will be intriguing and satisfying—that along with what Desiree has in mind for her, should ease her into her new role with the Consortium while she gets her feet under her as a vampire—so to speak. Here, she's disruptive, at least at the moment."

She nodded to Reese in the garden. "In New York, she'll be a benefit to both me and to Desiree, and she'll learn what she needs to without the twin distractions of you and Michael. She wants you as badly as you want her, Alonso, and you know you're both just a breath away from doing something you'll both regret, something from which there'll be no turning back. She may want you, but she loves Michael, just as you love Reese. She needs to be away from both of you, from all of you for a little while. The feelings you have for each other are a normal part of the sire and fledgling relationship, but that's assuming that neither is in a previous relationship or are not monogamous. Between you and Michael and Reese, there's enough jealous testosterone in this house to make me dizzy. I can't have that for Susan. I need her focused if she's to realize her potential, and she'll never be focused here, at least not without a little space away from both you and Michael. You know this, Alonso. You know it well. It's only for a couple of months, just long enough for her to come to terms with what she is and what she's capable of doing. Then she can come back without needing you or Michael. She can come back on equal footing."

"She has never needed us. She has always stood quite well on her own. If anything, we've needed her."

"And yet here you and Michael are, behaving like two stags in rut."

For a long time they stood next to each other in silence. A light breeze lifted the curtains on the French doors, and Reese now knelt next to one of the stone benches tending to some little detail in the garden—perhaps a stray patch of weed, perhaps a slate chip in the wrong place.

At last Alonso spoke. "Have you told them?"

"Not yet. I will in the morning when they return to High View."

"Does this have anything to do with the Guardian's use of the angel's mark on Susan? Are you afraid He might try to take over his body again?"

"It's a precaution, nothing more," she said, careful to keep her voice neutral. No one had any idea just how neurotic she was for her people, and what had happened between Michael and the Guardian had thoroughly unnerved her, even more so when she feared she'd have no choice but to take the life of her beloved angel.

Everyone else within the Consortium was allowed their neuroses and foibles and public displays of bad behavior—what could one expect from a loose affiliation of monsters, mutants, and renegade gods? It took one to know one, she thought. But they didn't have to know that, did they? They only had to trust that she had their best interests at heart. And her own, of course.

"When will you take her?" It was the deep sadness in Alonso's voice that brought her attention back to the present.

"I've been on the phone with Desiree, and my pilot is making arrangements. He'll fly from Manchester on Wednesday. Desiree will meet her at JFK."

"That's only three days." Alonso made no effort to hide the disappointment in his voice. "They won't be happy."

"They'll get over it. The truth is that it's three days too many. Every day she lingers in this volatile, complicated situation, the risk rises of something going terribly wrong. Emotions are running high in a group of very dangerous predators. I will not have the bear kill the lion, nor the tiger kill the eagle. I'll tell them in the morning and then I'll be keeping a very close eye on her, on all of you, until she's safely on board the plane."

There was another stretch of silence.

Reese now sat on the bench looking out over the beck below, unaware that he was being watched by monsters, though Magda figured he'd grown dangerously used to that by now.

At last she pulled in a long breath and stretched her aching back. "Go to Reese. Make it right. He's waiting for you. Surely you can see that. I've never minded members of the Consortium having relationships, and even I'm enough of a romantic to know that when it's right, it's worth preserving. Trust me, in three months, when Susan returns, you and Michael will both see more clearly; Michael will hold her more dearly and you will hold her more loosely, as it should be. In three months all that's passed between you and him, all the strife between you and Reese, will be seen from the proper perspective that time lends to all things."

Alonso said no more, nor did he gesture his leave-taking. He simply turned and moved through the French doors. Halfway down the path, his pace slowed to a more human pace, a pace that would not startle Reese. When Reese made no response to his approach, Alonso came to stand behind him and rested his hands on the man's shoulders before bending to speak in his ear. Whatever it was Alonso said, it had Reese reaching over his shoulder to pull the vampire into a kiss.

Magda realized she was smiling. God, would she never outgrow the romantic streak that softened her heart ever so slightly? But then it was good to see such devotion, good to cultivate it in others whenever she could. She had long known that was as close to the high walls around her heart as love would ever get. None of them had any idea how tenuous the thread that tethered her to humanity was at times, and a little romance in the Consortium helped her strengthen that bond.

They all feared her, as well they should. But she knew as none of them would ever know, that she was by far the most dangerous of all of them, the most dead, in many ways, and what she had built, what she had created, her Consortium of wayward monsters, had been the family she'd never had. They did what she wanted. She was the tyrant who ruled them, and yet their happiness was not something she could be jealous of when it was one of the few things that touched her heart. She would have Reese and Alonso happy. And in time, Alonso would bring Reese over, but not because Reese felt threatened by Alonso's attention to another.

In time, Michael and Susan would be together. Oh, not in Michael's little house. She had other plans for them, plans that demanded they be together. Her plans were always way more wide-reaching and far-viewing than any of them knew. That was how she had kept herself safe all of these centuries. That was how she made sure no one could take what belonged to her. But, where Michael and Susan were concerned, well she hardly had to force the love of eternity, did she? All she had to do was cultivate the right circumstances, the right conditions. That's all she ever had to do, actually. And it had never been that difficult with her intuition and the fact that she was the scariest bitch any of her monsters had ever dealt with.

In the meantime, there might just possibly be a siren seducing the Big Apple with magical songs. Now that would definitely keep Susan occupied for a couple of months. She turned to the credenza and poured herself a glass of Glen Morangie, which Alonso kept on hand especially for her. She drank it back and poured another.

Soon Susan would learn, as they all had, that—for good or ill—time was irrelevant in the gaping jaws of eternity, and it was the monsters with which one surrounded oneself that staved off the emptiness and made that dark endless throat of time a little more bearable.

"To the Consortium." She raised her glass in salute, watching Alonso and Reese, side by side on the bench, heads together, no doubt talking quietly which, knowing them as she did, was foreplay for a night of passion. "To the Consortium," she said again, then she drank back the whisky and turned to go home.

The End?

Susan and Michael's story continues in
Blind-Sided: Book 2 of the Medusa Chronicles

Blurb:

In New York City away from those she loves, living with the enigmatic vampire, Desiree Fielding, Susan Innes struggles to come to terms with life as a vampire whose body serves as the prison for a powerful demon. When prophetic dreams of blood in the snow and three men in a deep cavern become harrowing nightmares, Susan begins to question her sanity until Reese Chambers arrives from England, desperate for her help. Alonso Darlington, his lover and her maker, has been taken captive and Reese has been warned to tell no one but Susan. Before the two can make a plan, Susan receives her own message from a man calling himself just Cyrus. He not only holds her maker prisoner, but also her lover, the angel Michael, and if she wishes to see either of them alive, she'll come to him and not tell Magda Gardener, the woman they all work for and fear. With no help coming from Magda or her Consortium, Susan and Reese must turn to the Guardian – the terrifying demon now imprisoned in her body. He alone can help them, but how can she possibly trust Him after all he's done?

Chapter One: Sirens, Demons, and Scarier Stuff

Three Months Ago

> *So what do you think? Is she a siren?*

Susan viewed Michael's text under the edge of the table where she sat wedged in between a woman who smelled like a flower shop had thrown up on her, and a bodybuilder the size of New Jersey. She was damn lucky to get a place at all. Seats were at a premium. There was a buzz of anticipation all around the room. She texted back.

> *The crowd's excited. People are actually flicking their Bic lighters, like they're at some big rock concert. But then the duo does call itself Flame.*

The Dark Side Lounge felt a bit like the Tardis—bigger on the inside than on the out, though that wasn't saying much for the tiny converted brownstone. The dozen or so miniscule tables were all but on top of each other, hemmed in by too many rickety chairs that looked like they'd been pulled at random from neighboring brownstones. There was a tiny wooden stage built in one corner on which a piano was crammed up against one wall to make room for whatever instruments and kit were needed by the night's performers. The previous set—a small upbeat jazz band, had just taken their bows, and though the audience had been appreciative, it was clear everyone was anxiously awaiting Flame while a small group of volunteers from the two front tables maneuvered the piano into the center of the stage and adjusted the lighting.

There were just two people that Susan could identify as actually working at the Dark Side. The place was attended by a barrel-shaped bartender who could have come straight from a 1950s gin joint. A skinny-assed waitress moved in and out of the crowded space like a wisp of smoke, never bumping a table, never spilling a drink, never losing the look on her face that said she was at the very threshold of Nirvana and she wasn't going to let this lot fuck up her inner peace.

Just before each act, the bartender stepped from behind the bar, wiped his hands on his white apron and announced the performers into the microphone of a sound system that seemed far too sophisticated for the unpretentious place. Yet the acts were always stunning—each one of them. The cover charge had been minimal, and the house was full clear onto the tiny little patio fenced in wrought iron. Flower lady told Susan that a lot of great acts had been discovered here. She named several Susan had never heard of, then she added quickly that the locals took bets on who would get their next big break from performing at the Dark Side. Smart money was on Flame at the moment, the bodybuilder added enthusiastically.

They're the last act, Susan texted. Then she added. *Place is bursting at the seams. Don't think they could fit one other person in here if they tried.*

But she was wrong. They did fit someone else in. She felt his entrance with the shifting in the atmosphere of the room, a slight discomfort just beneath the human threshold of recognition. With her heightened senses, she felt it like a palm pressing hard against her breastbone, and she could smell it among the audience, though they were completely unaware of the change. The man's presence was just enough to raise the blood pressure and elevate the heart rate the tiniest bit, but then that could have simply passed as excitement, anticipation of Flame's imminent performance.

She felt the change, though. She felt it with the certainty that she would have if an icy blast of wind had suddenly blown through the open door. She felt the exact shape of the man as he entered the room, felt the way he took in everything around him as though he were a predator looking for the most succulent, most vulnerable prey. New York City was full of predators. Hell, she was one of them now, and Desiree had taught her to recognize others like her and others who were… different. This man was very different. The shape of him, the shape that he presented to the small audience of the Dark Side, was not his true form, not his true nature, and his true nature made her skin crawl.

It was the subtlety with which he presented himself that she found most disturbing. He was a wolf somehow perfectly disguised among lambs, and she was the only one who knew it. With the shuffling about and the changing of the stage, suddenly the bodybuilder got up and left for no reason Susan could see. No one was giving up seats just before the featured performance. There was another shifting of the air closer to her and Susan's skin prickled as the scent of flower lady was subsumed in something that was no scent at all—not really, and yet it grated on her hyper-sensitive nerve endings in a way that was far more physical than simple scent, and far more unsettling.

Just then the bartender announced Flame, and the crowd rose to their feet and applauded as two women took the stage. One wore a blood red dress that bared her shoulders and the tops of perfect breasts. Her waves of blond hair fell like light around her shoulders. She left the audience gasping at her sheer beauty even before she opened her mouth and sang the first few bars of *Someone To Watch Over Me* a capella. And her voice truly was exquisite. Everyone was totally captivated with her beauty, her full-bodied contralto, her presence.

But it was only when the other woman, the unobtrusive one in a black tux and bowtie, the one who wore her dark hair slicked back in a tight chignon settled into the first chords at the piano that the music became multi-dimensional, vibrant, as though her touch on the keys infused every note with breath, with life, with a heartbeat of its own all the while keeping the attention completely focused on the beautiful singer, all the while making certain no one noticed that it was the pianist who infused the music and the performance with power, with magic that held the audience in thrall far more than the singer's voice or beauty. It was the pianist making certain that Flame was good enough to get gigs and make money, but drew only the attention necessary and no more.

With trembling fingers, Susan texted. *Magda was right. It's the piano player. She's the one. Of course she's not going to sing. It would be too dangerous.*

She'd barely got the message sent when she realized that she wasn't the only one who was aware of the predator that had just settled lightly into the bodybuilder's seat. The scent of the siren was one of hyper-awareness, one of a person who was used to compartmentalizing, used to keeping herself hidden, used to expecting that at any moment her identity might be uncovered. Her heart rate didn't elevate, but for a moment, the moment when prey recognizes predator, it became strangely arrhythmic, and then it actually slowed to an even *thud, thud, thud*, slowed to the beat of the song in such perfect rhythm that no one might have noticed. In fact anyone who was looking at more than just what was happening on stage, anyone who was seeking prey might have been fooled into not seeing her at all.

As Susan remembered the stories from Greek mythology of the sirens luring the sailors onto the rocks to their deaths, she wondered what else the woman was capable of. She was just about to text Magda Gardener when another presence got Susan's full attention, a presence she had not heard from since it had first taken up residence inside her and made it known that while this demon might be captive inside the body of a fledgling vampire, he would not live in darkness. And He was no more subtle now than He had been that morning a month ago at High View Manor in Cumbria. His essence all but exploded behind her ribcage with such power that she nearly dropped her phone. "Susan, we need to leave now."

Before the shock could wear off enough for her to respond, another voice spoke next to her ear, so softly that it disturbed no one but her, and it disturbed her deeply. "A vampire with something extra, if I'm not mistaken." A cool hand came to rest on her shoulder and gave it a gentle knead.

"Susan, we need to leave now," came the voice inside her, and the urgency of the pressure in her chest made her feel like she just might be about to have an *Alien* moment.

Ignoring the voice of the demon hammering on the inside of

her chest, she turned to find herself face to face with a dark-haired man who had the chiseled airbrushed look of a hero from a cheap billionaire novel or a prince from a fairytale. While the man might well have been wealthy, he was no prince. She was certain from the way his touch made her skin crawl and the way the demon in her felt like He was taking a sledgehammer to her sternum, that he was no man either.

"A great deal of something extra, it would seem," he said, a purr of a chuckle raising the hairs on the back of her neck. "A vampire and a scribe. Such an intriguing combination. I had no idea such a thing existed in all the world, but then the world is a very big place, isn't it, my darling?"

"Susan! Now! I mean it!" The demon's voice was loud enough to drown out the gorgeous sound of Flame still wafting from the stage, where the siren kept herself well and truly disguised behind the piano.

But even the Guardian's voice couldn't drown out the soft whisper of Prince Scary-ass, all but making love to her ear. "Tonight I'm here for the entertainment, scouting new acts," he nodded to the stage. "Sadly business before pleasure, but there'll be another time." He folded a card in her hand, his fingers lingering longer than necessary. And suddenly she was no longer certain if he meant there would be another time to listen to Flame or another time to talk to her.

Before she could contemplate further, before she could think what to do, she found herself jerked from the chair, stumbling and twitching toward the door like a marionette with a drunken puppeteer.

"What are you doing? What the hell are you doing?" It might have begun as a silent conversation, but it became quite vocal as panic exploded inside her when she recalled the last time the demon had used her this way. She elicited several glares from the audience members closest to her, and the bartender gave her the evil eye. "What the bloody hell are you doing?" She spoke between gritted teeth. "You told me you couldn't control me. You told me that you were mine to command. Stop it! You're drawing attention to us."

"You're the one drawing attention to us, Susan," the voice inside her spoke again. "Just do as I tell you and all will be made clear once we're safe."

That got her full attention. "Now then, that's better. Listen to me, walk back to the subway and get on the train. Then get off at the next stop."

As she calmed enough to relax the tiniest bit, she found herself once again in control of her arms and legs, and the Guardian spoke again. "Now then, that man in there, the one who sat down next to you—Darian Fox, I believe his card says."

"That's right," she said, forgetting that she didn't need to speak out loud. It didn't matter, though. This was New York City. No one really paid too much attention when someone talked to themselves. People just assumed they either had a Bluetooth or they were a little loopy, and that was all right too as long as they kept their loopiness to themselves. "Do you know who he is?" This time she spoke only in her head.

"I know he means us no good, and I fear he would mean our

little siren even less good, if he knew of her existence. Fortunately his main interest, as with most of the males of your species, is for the beautiful one who sings and what she can do for his cock. As long as he looks to serve his libido, and our little siren continues to keep a low profile, she should be all right. You, however, or should I say us. He was more than a little intrigued by us. We don't need that kind of attention, Susan. He could hurt us. He could hurt the people we love."

What's going on? What the hell's going on? Susan? Are you all right? Talk to me.

Are you all right? What about Samantha Black? Is she the siren?

My darling girl, I felt your distress. What has happened?

The three texts were repeated, with minor variations multiple times by Michael, Magda-bloody-Gardener, who as always, was all business, and by Alonso Darlington. Alonso was the vampire who had made her. His deep connection to her had caused strife between him and his mortal lover, Reese Chambers, and between him and Michael.

Magda would suffer no such tension among members of her Consortium, so she sent Susan to New York City where she could learn to be a grown-up vampire under the testosterone-free tutelage of Desiree Fielding. Desiree, a vampire who was much older than Alonso, owed Magda a favor. Didn't everybody? Christ, Susan owed Magda a debt she could never repay, and now she was busy doing detective work for both Magda and Desiree. Up until tonight, her assignment had been easy and the experience of living in New York and being trained by a scary-powerful vampire had not been difficult. But up until now, the Guardian, the demon who was imprisoned in some nebulous place inside Susan, had kept His word to not make His presence known unless she called Him, and she hadn't. She hadn't! And the fact that He'd exerted enough control over her that He had for all practical purposes possessed her was more than disturbing.

"Oh, for fuck's sake, Susan," came his voice from inside her once she had followed his instructions and was safely on the Q line with no destination in mind. "Did I not tell you that I would always keep myself safe, even when that means keeping my prison safe? Surely you could tell that man was neither human, nor did he mean to do you good."

"I'm a fucking vampire," she blurted out, "I think I can take care of myself." The only other two people in their carriage, an elderly African American couple, gave her what she referred to affectionately as the NYC eye-slide. It was a way New Yorkers could glance at a total nutter while appearing not to notice.

Inside her chest, the Guardian was giving her the disembodied version of an exasperated sigh. "Surely you are not yet so full of your tutor's arrogance as to believe that your undead state renders you invulnerable. Do you really think I would have bothered if this... monster was no threat to us? Really, my darling scribe, if you are entertaining the idea that I did what I did out of jealousy, well then I must counter that you can hardly expect me to be jealous when our intimacy is so complete and so permanent. Neither your angel nor your maker can boast such closeness."

She gave the Guardian the mental version of the finger, and He might have chuckled. That in all the time He'd been in residence He'd not once exerted his power until tonight made her more than a little nervous. Still, she had nightmares about what had happened in Manchester at Chapel House, what He had done to her friend, Annie, what He would have done to her and what it had nearly cost Michael. Surely He was a fine one to talk about who was dangerous. The one thing she knew from experience about the Guardian was that he couldn't be trusted. She cut him off mid-chuckle. "If you ever pull a stunt like that again, I will personally stake us both—"

"A vampire can't stake herself," he interjected.

"Shut up! Just shut up! The last time you pulled a stunt like that I thought you were going to rape me. Shut up!" she said again when she felt him about to argue the semantics of his thwarted 'seduction.' "I don't care what you call it, I know what it was, and let's not forget you deceived me into damn near sentencing my best friend to death. I suppose that wasn't rape either, what you did to her. No! No, I almost forgot, that was attempted murder."

"The only one who committed murder, my dear scribe, was you when you convinced your vampire to do what he did. You are not the only one who has suffered. I have suffered double, I have suffered treble with the loss of three that I love."

His words felt like a gut punch. Surely He didn't mourn His losses other than the unpleasant fact that He was now a prisoner and could not continue His fun and games. But she found herself trembling and too close to tears to carry the conversation farther. "I need you to be quiet now." She felt the weight of His loss as though it were her own and, with an ache sharp as a knife wound, she realized that it was her own loss she felt.

Unintentional or otherwise, he had deftly brought it to her attention, and she wished he hadn't. Being who she was, being what she was, had separated her from Michael and from Alonso, had separated her from the life she had known, from her best friend, from her home. At the same time, it had bonded her in a strange way she still didn't understand to Magda Gardener, who terrified her far more than this Darian Fox person, even as she found herself admiring the woman.

It was a brave new world, and while she put on the British stiff upper lip most of the time, the occasional reminder of her lost life made her feel like she had just jumped off into a bottomless abyss and was plummeting toward the bottom with no idea of what would happen next.

The Guardian kept silent after that. She answered her texts and found, to her surprise, when she got off the subway, both Magda and Desiree were waiting for her. She didn't even know Magda was in New York.

To her surprise, the woman took her into her arms, and she felt the Guardian flinch inside her. He didn't like Magda at all, and Magda sure as hell didn't like Him. He had nearly cost her the life of her angel—twice.

While Susan didn't flinch, when Magda pulled away and held her face in her hands as though she were examining her for damage, she had the slight feeling of vertigo she always had when Magda Gardener looked at her. Even through the dark designer glasses the woman was forced to wear, her gaze was unsettling and her touch was always somewhere between a minor electrical shock and a buzz of pleasure. Uncomfortable didn't begin to describe how a person felt when she was the center of Magda Gardener's attention. Susan wondered if she'd ever get used to it.

"Are you all right, my darling?" Magda asked. "You had me scared half to death." Susan had not seen that look of genuine fear and concern on the woman's face since she feared she'd lose Michael to the Guardian. "Darian Fox is not to be trifled with, and his is attention you don't want."

"You know him then?" Susan asked.

"I know of him. My people in Las Vegas have been keeping an eye on him, trying to figure out just exactly what he's up to. What they do know for certain is that he's very dangerous, and you are to stay completely away from him in the future. I'm glad you had the common sense to realize that he was something other than human and to get out as quickly as you could." She shot a quick glance in Desiree's direction and even the older vampire flinched, but then, Susan reminded herself, no matter how old Desiree was, she was nowhere nearly as old as Magda. "Sometimes your kind can be arrogant and overconfident in their powers—especially when they're only newly made as you are. You can't afford arrogance, Susan, nor overconfidence, even with our demon in residence sworn to protect you."

Susan told no one about the Guardian's intervention in her unexpected, and rather ungraceful, exit from the Dark Side. She wasn't sure why she'd kept silent. Perhaps it *was* her vampire arrogance that she didn't want anyone to know how easily the Guardian had overpowered her and forced the issue. She didn't want to know herself, but now she would be forced to engage with that fact and figure out how much control he actually could assert on her.

Three weeks later, Flame left New York City for Las Vegas to perform at Illusions, Darian Fox's club. It was no small gig. The club was a big deal. It didn't take much for Susan to learn that it was the glorious blonde who had forced the issue. Samantha Black, the piano player, had not wanted to go. But then the blonde was only human. She couldn't see that Fox was a predator. She couldn't see past the stars in her eyes—that and Fox was fucking her. To her surprise, Magda didn't send Susan to Las Vegas to continue observing the siren. She said Susan had done her job and she wasn't willing to risk her prize scribe to Fox. She was adamant, so Susan was left to complete her training with Desiree and to do her bidding. After that it was a long time before she spoke with the Guardian again.

About the Author

Voted ETO Best Erotic Author of 2014, and a proud member of The Brit Babes, K D Grace believes Freud was right. In the end, it really IS all about sex, well sex and love. And nobody's happier about that than she is, otherwise, what would she write about?

When she's not writing, K D is veg gardening. When she's not gardening, she's walking. She walks her stories, and she's serious about it. She and her husband have walked Coast to Coast across England, along with several other long-distance routes. For her, inspiration is directly proportionate to how quickly she wears out a pair of walking boots. She also enjoys martial arts, reading, watching the birds and anything that gets her outdoors.

K D has erotica published with SourceBooks, Xcite Books, Harper Collins Mischief Books, Mammoth, Cleis Press, Black Lace, Sweetmeats Press and others.

K D's critically acclaimed erotic romance novels include, *The Initiation of Ms Holly, Fulfilling the Contract, To Rome with Lust*, and *The Pet Shop*. Her paranormal erotic novel, *Body Temperature and Rising*, the first book of her *Lakeland Witches* trilogy, was listed as honorable mention on Violet Blue's Top 12 Sex Books for 2011. Books two and three, *Riding the Ether*, and *Elemental Fire*, are now also available.

K D Grace also writes hot romance as Grace Marshall. *An Executive Decision, Identity Crisis, The Exhibition, Interviewing Wade* are all available.

Find K D Here:

Websites: http://kdgrace.co.uk/

http://www.thebritbabes.co.uk

Facebook: http://www.facebook.com/KDGraceAuthor

Twitter: https://twitter.com/KD_Grace

Pinterest: http://www.pinterest.com/kdgraceauthor/

If You Enjoyed *In the Flesh*

If you enjoyed *In the Flesh*, you may also enjoy the following titles, which are available at all good book retailers. Find more information at K D's website:

Lakeland Witches Book 1: Body Temperature and Rising

American transplant to the Lake District, MARIE WARREN, didn't know she could unleash demons and enflesh ghosts until a voyeuristic encounter on the fells ends in sex with the charming ghost, ANDERSON, and night visits from a demon. To help her cope with her embarrassing and dangerous new abilities, Anderson brings her to the ELEMENTALS, a coven of witches who practice rare sex magic that temporarily allows needy ghosts access to the pleasures of the flesh.

DEACON, the demon Marie has unleashed, holds an ancient grudge against TARA STONE, coven high priestess, and will stop at nothing to destroy all she holds dear. Marie and her landlord, the reluctant young farmer, TIM MERIWETHER, are at the top of his list. Marie and Tim must learn to wield coven magic and the numinous power of their lust to stop Deacon's bloody rampage before the coven is torn apart and more innocent people die.

Lakeland Witches Book 2: Riding the Ether

Cassandra Larkin keeps her ravenous and dangerous sexual appetite secret until she seduces Anderson in the mysterious void of the Ether. Anderson is the sexy, insatiable ghost who can give her exactly what she needs.

But sex is dangerous in a place like the Ether…

When the treacherous demon, Deacon, discovers the truth about the origin of Cassandra's powerful lust, he plots to use her sex magic for revenge on Tara Stone and the Elemental Coven, who practice their own brand of sex magic.

Cassandra must embrace the lust and sexuality she fears and learn to use its power. Will she stand with Anderson, Tara, and the Elemental Coven against Deacon's wrath or suffer the loss of friendship, magic and love?

Lakeland Witches Book 3: Elemental Fire

Obsessed with revenge, KENNET LUCIAN makes a deal with a demon, a deal he comes to regret when he meets TARA STONE, head of the Elemental Coven, and a powerful witch with a desire for revenge at least as great as his. Even though the attraction between the two is magnetic and the lust combustive, Kennet must betray her to accomplish his goal, which is ultimately her goal as well; to put a final end to the demon, Deacon's, reign of terror. But can Tara trust the man who has wormed his way into her heart and the heart of the Elemental Coven? Can she trust LUCIA, the demon with whom Kennet is allied, a demon with her own agenda. The path to Deacon's destruction is far from clear, and the price that must be paid to be free of him forever may be too high, even for Tara Stone.

Demon Interrupted: A Lakeland Witches Serial

What secrets does a man have that would cause him to

chooses to live under a spell that magically erased his past? When that spell is broken Ferris Ryder must choose to remember all that he was, all that he has done and all that drove him to willingly forget. If he chooses not to remember, the consequences will be dire for himself and the Elemental Coven, who are now his family.

Is the mysterious Elaine, who both fears and desires Ferris, a ghost with a past all her own, or merely a figment of his fevered dreams as he struggles against time to remember the past he fears or destroy the very people for whom he chose to forget.

Brit Boys: With Toys

From coast to coast and city to country Brit boys enjoy playing with each other and their toys. Not any old toys, though; guitars, rope, plugs and Moleskine journals all prove to be enormous fun. Throw in a shop that's wall to wall with kinky ideas, a journalist on the lookout for the next big thing, and Dominants who insist on obedience and there's sure to be something to cater for everyone's taste.

Whether it's a quickie or a slow indulgence, Brit boys know how to hit the spot and they aim to please every time. So take a ride, fly high, come enjoy these sexy boys and their toys.

Brit Boys: With Toys is an anthology of M/M stories written by British authors, featuring British characters in British locations. If this steamy set of stories has whet your appetite for more don't miss Brit Boys: On Boys.

CPSIA information can be obtained
at www.ICGtesting.com
Printed in the USA
BVHW041936051118
532233BV00013B/69/P